THE LAST
DREAM
BEFORE
DAWN

THE LAST DREAM BEFORE DAWN

D.V. BERNARD

STREBOR BOOKS

NEW YORK LONDON TORONTO SYDNEY

SBI

Strebor Books
P.O. Box 6505
Largo, MD 20792
http://www.streborbooks.com

© 2003 by D. V. Bernard

ISBN 978-1-59309-140-8
ISBN 978-1-4516-7898-7 (e-book)
LCCN 2002100263

First Strebor Books trade paperback edition July 2003

Cover design: www.mariondesigns.com
Cover photograph: © Keith Saunders/Marion Designs

10 9 8 7 6 5 4 3 2 1

Manufactured in the United States of America

For information regarding special discounts for bulk purchases,
please contact Simon & Schuster Special Sales at 1-866-506-1949
or business@simonandschuster.com

The Simon & Schuster Speakers Bureau can bring authors to your
live event. For more information or to book an event, contact the
Simon & Schuster Speakers Bureau at 1-866-248-3049 or visit our
website at www.simonspeakers.com.

For my sisters, Petra, Antonia, and Corinthia

Petra, I'm always amazed by your generosity; I've come to see that your intentions are always in the right place.

Antonia, if you taught me one thing, it's the importance of dreaming big—no matter the consequences.

Corinthia, I can still remember you reading to me as a child and giving me my first reading lessons. You didn't even seem to mind reading my first horrible stories. I'm eternally grateful that you're my sister.

...Every one (of us is) a drum major leading a parade of hurts, marching with our bitterness. And some day—the armies of bitterness will all be going the same way. And they'll all walk together, and there'll be a dead terror from it.

—JOHN STEINBECK, *The Grapes of Wrath*

PROLOGUE

LOUISIANA, THE LATE 1970s

Roland Micheaux's dreams were still those of a little boy. While he slept, he saw images of a girl from his class; but in the dream, she was more beautiful than she had ever been in reality. Her hair was someone else's hair; her clothes were other people's clothes. In fact, her body was a compilation of countless women he had seen in movies and magazines. In the dream world, she was everything he thought he was supposed to want. Entire nights had passed with him staring at his creation—but in the mornings, he would always awaken with the uneasy sense that his dreams were stupid, and that they would never bring him happiness.

Now, as he opened his eyes to the world, his dream girl was already receding into the nothingness. The usual uneasy feelings were there for a moment, but then something made a shiver go up his spine. Instinctively, he turned to the bedroom window. The morning sun was rising above the tenements; and on first glance, it seemed like the beginning of any other hot, muggy New

Orleans summer day. Yet, something was not right. He sat up in bed, frowning. When he put his hand on the nightstand to get out of bed, he noticed it was shaking. As he moved toward the window, his feet hardly seemed to touch the ground. He was like a ghost, drifting through the air. Then, he was at the window, staring at a world that suddenly made no sense.

He had been seeing these streets for all thirteen years of his life. He knew how they hardened you inside, and distorted even the simplest perceptions—but today, he felt something he had never felt before. It wasn't a new-found feeling of revulsion at the sight of the crumbling and burnt-out buildings of his neighborhood; it wasn't the sight of an old man pissing against the side of one of the graffiti-covered tenements; nor was it the stench from the toppled, dog-ravaged garbage cans just below his second-story window. On the contrary, those were the only things about the place that he recognized. He took a tentative step closer to the window now, his eyes moving warily about the landscape. It was only when they came to rest on the pale morning sun that his eyes stopped, and his frown deepened.

Somehow, the sun seemed dead—as if God had sucked the life out of it while he was asleep. When he looked around, the bricks and concrete all seemed fake—like dull shapes painted against a canvas. Even the sounds in the air—a honking horn from down the block; a blaring television from a neighbor's apartment—sounded hollow and "canned," like a bad recording. He stood there confusedly, wondering what all this could mean, until the sudden realization of what day it was, made him shudder and back away from the window....

Eight hours later, Roland once again emerged from his thoughts; but this time, instead of the ghetto streets, he saw a lonely stretch of Louisiana highway. He glanced to his left then—to the driver's seat. A state trooper was sitting there, his face grim as he stared ahead in silence. They were driving west, and the pale, lifeless sun of that morning was before them. Roland felt lost and dazed; but in the distance, he could clearly see their destination: the prison....

Everything was coming full circle now: all the things he had ever wanted to know would be realized when he reached that place; all the things he had known, but forgotten, were coming back to him; all the things he had suspected, but been unable to prove...it was all there before him, in the huge, ugly prison complex in the distance.

They had been driving for two hours now; yet, even with the prison in sight, Roland felt as though he had been caught in a side channel in time. The state trooper had a country music station on. The crooning voices were barely intelligible through the static of the AM station—not to mention the droning of the car's engine and the howl of the wind as it blew past the open windows. Across the highway, for as far as the eye could see, there was marshland, with towering grass waving gracefully in the wind. The peaceful ebb and flow made Roland think of the evening tide; but after a few moments, he began to feel seasick.

He looked straight ahead now—through the windscreen—and took a deep breath to calm himself. With the flatness of the landscape, he had been staring at the approaching prison for fifteen minutes now. At first, it had been a jagged speck on the horizon; now, it stood off to his right, only fifty meters beyond the chain-linked fence. It was huge and dark, and its gothic architecture made him think of a vampire's castle at sundown. Within a matter of minutes, Roland was going to be entering that place. The realization made his guts clench. For a moment, he thought about flinging himself from the car and fleeing into the tall grass—but he knew the car was going too fast for that. He was about to beg the trooper to take him home, but as he watched the white man's grim, sunburnt face, he kept his silence.

The change in the pitch of the car's engine told him they were slowing down; but as he looked ahead, and saw what lay before him, his breath got caught in his throat. He tried to get his bearings, but he was utterly lost now. Somehow, he had been staring at the prison so intently that he hadn't noticed the chaotic scene unfolding at the front gate. It didn't seem possible, but there were hundreds of people and scores of vehicles ahead. He could make out the state police and prison guards, who were already clad in full riot gear. The crowd seemed like a huge churning mass—like a cresting wave, about to engulf him. And yet, even here, there were contradictions. Some of the people were holding signs and yelling chants of protest; some were having cookouts and laughing, as if it were a tailgate party at a football game. The dozen or so camera crews added energy and motion to all of the contradictions. Their news vans and satellite dishes formed a phalanx along the fence, like some kind of battalion. Even the network anchormen were here—this thing had become that huge!

Reporters were already posing in front of cameras; cameras were already rolling; the various factions were already being interviewed. The scene reminded him that this was all a media circus. He remembered how he had had to stay inside for days, because reporters and camera crews had camped outside his door; he remembered having to fight his way through them, and *run* from them. In his mind, he heard their high-pitched, indecipherable voices... And it had been surreal to see himself on television. He had watched himself in shame a few times, thinking that he looked like a madman. On the television, he was always running in terror; people were always asking him what he was thinking...if he was sorry...if he wanted to give a statement to the press! Like a soldier who had barely survived the last battle, he was terrified of being returned to the front lines—but now that he was here, he closed his eyes and bowed his head, knowing that there was no turning back.

The state trooper made a right-hand turn when they

got to the front entrance, then started driving up the crowded prison driveway. The sea was spreading slowly before the car, engulfing them. The car's windows were open, and Roland could hear them: the *roar* of them. Many of the people were yelling incoherently; some were singing softly, but their words were just as indecipherable. Then, all of a sudden, a scrawny white man with a bushy beard ran up to the passenger side of the car with a sign that read: "Abolish death row! Kill them all now!" The man was yelling gibberish; but for some reason, Roland stared at him, trying to understand. He tried to read the man's lips, but all he could see was a glob of spittle on the man's beard, where his lips were supposed to be—

The state trooper slammed on the brakes and began honking the horn. Looking though the windshield, Roland saw that an old white woman was standing in front of the car. The strange thing was how peaceful she looked as she swayed rhythmically to the song she was singing. As she swayed, she held a candle in one hand and a rosary in the other; and standing there like that, in a long, white flowing dress, she looked like one of those statues of Saints from the church. It was all so strange...and a steady stream of curses now flowed from the trooper's lips as the woman swayed peacefully and sang her song.

The trooper was now banging on the horn as if it were a surrogate for the old woman's head. Roland watched the man warily, half-expecting his head to explode, like a cartoon character's. However, other state troopers were coming about now. In a millisecond, the woman was quickly and gruffly pushed to the side by one of the riot-gear-clad troopers. And then, as the woman fell to the ground, one segment of the crowd let out whoops of approval; while amongst the other, there were shouts of anger and outrage. A man from the latter camp stepped up and kicked the offending trooper in the chest. A baton came out; more troopers flooded into the area; and instantaneously, everywhere, people were yelling and fighting and running. The cameramen and sound crews were soon mixed in the fray, seeming just as insane as their subjects as they clambered for the best vantage points. There were jeers and shouts of agony—and, in the midst of it all, an inscrutable kind of laughter, which rose in the air like the wailing of cicadas.

Roland stared ahead blankly, overcome by the fears and uncertainties that had had a hold of him all that day—all his *life*, it seemed. Just then, he realized the trooper was yelling something; startled, he read the man's lips as he screamed, "Close the fucking window!" His hands trembling, Roland did as told. Yet, as he glanced outside, he saw a man running past the car, screaming, his face bloodied and gashed open....

Roland closed his eyes, yearning for the illusion of peace and solitude he had had in his mother's home. That place seemed so far away now... He thought back to earlier that day: he had sat on the edge of his bed, waiting for the trooper to arrive. The window had been to his back, showing another muggy New Orleans summer day; and with his back turned to the world, Roland had seemed to be shunning it all. Down on the street, he had heard the neighborhood children playing. Their laughter had been unbearable, wafting up through the air like the stench from open sewers. Like the Louisiana heat, there had been no way to escape it, so he had endured it all as he waited for the trooper to arrive.

In the next room, he had heard his mother clanging pots and moving around the furniture in her quest to find hidden dirt. She had been trying to preoccupy herself with tasks that didn't have to be done, but there had been no peace for either of them. All that day, the thing had been in their eyes: it had bent their frames and brought inevitable frowns to their faces. For the last *eight years* of their lives, in fact, death had stalked them. It had been nibbling away at their souls all this time; but today, it would take the last bite, and carry one of them off into the nothingness.

In this sense, they had spent the last eight years trying to fight the inevitable. Roland only felt the full weight of it as he looked past the chaos of the riot—and up at the grim walls of the prison. He nodded his head now: his father was somewhere in that huge, ugly complex; and in a matter of hours, the state's executioners were going to put him to death—

Someone threw something—a *brick!*—against the windshield of the state trooper's car. In the closed vehicle, the noise was like an explosion. All at once, a mass of concentric circles and snaking lines appeared on the windshield. With the riot going strong, people were now bumping into, and being thrown against, the car. Roland was beginning to feel seasick again. As for the trooper, the man seemed like some trapped beast. He had gotten out his gun, and his eyes darted about wildly, as if looking for something to shoot. Roland scrounged down in the seat; but as he looked up at the trooper's sunburnt, peeling face, he remembered that the man had had to bring him here, because his mother, and everyone else but him, had refused to see his father. His coming here had been his first true act of defiance against his mother. It seemed as if he had sacrificed everything for this last chance to...he didn't even know what. He had driven across three parishes and borne the silent disapproval and disappointment of his mother, just for the chance to eat a final meal with the man he hadn't seen since he was five years old.

Yet, to say that he had never known his father belied the fact that the man was now a national celebrity. His father's picture was all over the news now—especially since the Supreme Court had denied his final appeal. There would be justice at last, or so the pundits were saying. This week alone, there had been at least four network specials done on the implications of his father's execution. Conservatives were touting the curative effects that the execution was going to have on a nation that had "lost its moral compass." Liberals were lamenting what they called the misguided bestiality of capital punishment, and working hard for a last-minute pardon. However, the governor, whose reelection campaign always seemed to be in full swing, was lobbying to be the one to pull the switch!

As for Roland, his father's crime had been the defining element of his life. Supposedly, they had found his father's semen inside of that hacked-up white woman. Her blood had been splattered all over his clothes when they found him stumbling down the block in that drug-induced daze. His scratched skin had been underneath her fingernails; his bloody fingerprints had been all over her rummaged apartment; finally, not only had several people seen him exiting from the woman's apartment, but her wallet had been in his pocket when the policemen picked him up. The crime had been brazen and stupid. It inflamed passions and drove people over the edge—like a kind of madness. Beyond the state trooper's car, the battle lines had been clearly drawn. Some viewed the "evidence" and concluded that his father should be handed over to mob justice. Others, confronted with the same "evidence," were convinced that it was all a frame-up by those desperate to get a conviction and mollify the white community. Among this latter group, there were even those who saw the "open and shut" nature of the case as proof that he couldn't have done it.

As for Roland, however, he had never really asked himself if his father was guilty. He had said the words to himself of course, but he had never *felt* them. Thousands of times over the years, he had found himself wondering about his father's innocence the way that he wondered about the existence of God and Eternal Life. For both, he had come to the conclusion that it would be great if it were so, but that it just seemed, in the face of everything, either unlikely or irrelevant. Maybe irrelevant described his mindset better. It wasn't that he didn't care, but that he wasn't yet at the stage where he *could* care. All of this was like the Louisiana heat: it was out of his hands, so the only thing to do was accept his fate.

The riot was still going strong. To Roland's left, a man was lying prone on the ground—either unconscious or dead. A short distance away, a reporter was pointing at the body frantically—not to get the man help, but to get his cameraman to record it. Something perverse had poisoned their souls. Like oil speculators who had found a few barrels of oil near the surface, they sank dozens of wells down into the depths of the earth, hoping insanely for more. Roland now saw it in the eyes of the people fighting beyond the state trooper's car—and the cameramen who rushed to cover it. The world was mad; but worse than that, it seemed to need that madness to keep on functioning. It was like the stock market: millions of people driven by greed and hope and fear and uncertainty and rumor and a thousand other neuroses that Adam Smith had attributed to the invisible hand of God....

The riot outside the car was finally dying down. As shots were fired in the air, and reinforcements were called in, the more violent of the offenders scrambled away—back toward the highway. Looking up in a daze, Roland saw that a column of troopers was now outside the car. A trooper was knocking on Roland's window, trying to get his attention. With all of the man's protective gear, he at first stuck Roland as Darth Vader—as some fictionalized character impinging upon the real world. Roland sat there in a daze, staring at the man until the latter's tapping turned into annoyed banging. Coming to his senses, Roland unlocked the door. He was trembling so much that he almost collapsed when he tried to step out of the car. His legs didn't feel like his own. The trooper that had driven him here was somehow beside him now. The man held Roland by the shoulders, then the others formed protective flanks on either side of them. Once they were ready, they began walking toward the entrance. The huge metal door was about twenty meters away; but as Roland stared ahead, it seemed to stretch off into infinity.

There was a pall in the air. The crowd, beaten back, stood their distance and watched the troopers like cornered animals looking for a chance to strike. Most of them had fled back toward the highway. However, when the reporters saw Roland, they began running toward him. The reporters were trying to yell over one another now. Cameras and microphones were being inserted between the phalanx of troopers; a couple of the reporters were gruffly pushed away, but seemed undaunted. The crowd had seemed subdued just seconds ago, but now it became raucous once more. The people were again organizing themselves into their camps. They yelled their slogans over the sirens that continued to wail in the air; but as Roland stumbled along, the rhythmic chanting reminded him of the neighborhood children taunting him with:

Roland's papa killed a cracker
Roland's papa booty scratcher

He hated them all at that moment—all the reporters, the protesters, the troopers...even those flipping by these images on their television screens! It made no difference to him what their stances were. Those claiming to sympathize with and speak in favor of his father were no different from those who, in their hatred, wanted to rip the man apart. They were all killers—parasites feasting on death. Just then, Roland looked to his right, where a white woman and her camera crew were trying to get his attention. All those bastards were chasing after him as if trying to *reap* his shame... *Why wouldn't they just leave him alone*! The hatred surged within him then, like vomit threatening to choke him. He despised *everything* at the moment. Like a suicide bomber, he wished he could step into the midst of them now, release his murderous hate, and watch the world being engulfed in fire. He was hopelessly lost in this fantasy now, seeing all the filth purged. He was about to laugh out insanely when the trooper tightened his grip on his shoulder, pulling him back into reality...

Somehow, he was inside of the prison now. The contrast with the outside world was so stark that Roland looked around confusedly, unable to grasp the dark vastness of the place. Instead of chanting crowds, there was now an eerie silence. He could still hear the chants if he concentrated, but they seemed like distant whispers—like insane voices in the recesses of his mind. He shook his head to chase them away; and as he looked around, he realized most of the troopers had disappeared. It was only the three of them now: Roland, the trooper that had driven him here, and a prison guard. The trooper's grip was still firm, but the man was leading Roland deeper into the prison now; and with each step, he felt himself unraveling.

His eyes were open, yet he could barely see. The lighting seemed at once dim and blinding—maybe it was the contrast with just having been outside.... Now, they were taking him through labyrinthine cement passages, which had locked steel doors about every thirty meters. The guard had to yell out to a remote station for the electronically locked doors to be opened and closed. The stench of industrial floor polish was nauseating. The floor was so shiny that they reflected the overhead fluorescent lights. The feeling of loneliness overwhelmed him again. The silence, in contrast to the din of the mobs, was still eating away at him. The silence left him time to think about his father, and he couldn't stand that. The thought that he would be seeing the man in a matter of minutes almost made him collapse. The added fact that the man would be put to death that night was too... *unreal.*

Yet, what could death possibly mean to him? Death on the ghetto streets was a colorful spectacle, with flashing emergency lights and sirens. It was a chance to stand around and watch the show, giggling at the half-naked, swooning mothers who ran out into the streets to find their murdered sons. It was all a joke: a spectacle made unreal by the frequency....

In the next corridor, there was a prison cleaning detail. Two old black men—both well over sixty-five—were mopping the floor. They stopped and looked up when Roland and his guides entered. The two men had probably been in prison for most of their lives, because they had the aura of an animal that had been broken and *knew* it. Their frames were bent and frail, as if from a lifetime of heavy labor. Now too old for that labor, they were good for nothing but these few menial tasks. Roland suddenly found himself wondering if his father was like that now. The resurgent anarchist side of him, fed by his newfound hatred, hoped not. It hoped to find his father a defiant bastard who would curse the world with his dying breath: who would remain, even when strapped into the death chair, fearsome and fearless. Yes: better for his father to be a despised *nigger* than a lap dog. He suddenly needed to find the man strong and unbroken—as unrepentantly evil as everyone was saying. For some unaccountable reason, *his* manhood, or whatever passed for it, depended on his father's strength.

They entered a small cafeteria that could seat no more than forty men. By its size—and its emptiness—Roland guessed that it probably wasn't for the general population of inmates, but was perhaps only for the guards. From an adjacent chamber came the aroma and sounds of something spicy being cooked. However, in the face of all that had passed that day—and all that *would* pass—the prospect of food was suddenly nauseating. The trooper was saying something: Roland's father had been summoned and would arrive in a matter of minutes. The words and their meaning probably didn't register in Roland's mind until minutes later, by which time the trooper and the guard had wandered over to the other side of the cafeteria by themselves, leaving Roland sitting alone.

A rhythmic chinking sound brought Roland to his senses. He looked about confusedly before realizing that it was coming from down the corridor. At first, it terrified him simply by its echoing loudness; but then, as he realized that the clinking was from chains—*from his father's manacles*—he began to panic inside. He looked over his shoulder, but the trooper and the guard were still talking on the other side of the room. As always, he was alone. He got up nervously, then sat back down as the trembling proved too much for him. And the chinking was getting closer—

Two guards came in with the man—*with his father*! The man's eyes were bright, almost *beaming*, as he saw his boy sitting there. Roland couldn't move. The man before him seemed fatter and softer than he remembered. The man was older and more...*benevolent* than the man in the mug shot they were always showing on television. Looking up, Roland realized that the man's hair was now in one of those James Brown perms. In the parlance of the streets, the hair made him look like "an old faggot"— or, at least, that was what popped into Roland's mind. Then, while the guards unlocked his father's manacles, the man smiled and stared at Roland so intently that he felt uneasy and shy.

The last meal was being brought out of the kitchen now. Two cooks were bringing it out in huge metal cartons and placing it on a table deeper into the room. From the scent, Roland knew that it was gumbo and the kind of spicy Cajun food that his grandmother cooked down on the bayou. His father had been unrestrained. *He was coming over now*!

Roland didn't know what to do! Somehow, he managed to stand. His father was putting out his hands! The man was hugging him now! Roland let the man hold him. The reality of the man's body next to his was unnerving. The warmth of it—the *fullness* of it—again made him panic inside. This man was going to be dead in a few hours! Roland hadn't seen him in eight years, and all that would be left were these purloined moments. *Who was this man?* Was there even time to know him? Forgotten were all the moments of shame and resentful hatred. Forgotten were · all those broken childhood promises—some of which had been due to drunken forgetfulness, but most to blatant lying and indifference. This man, holding him tightly, was his father; and maybe he didn't love the man—*could not* love the man, in fact— but he could, like countless others, love the thought of loving his father, and of *being* loved. The fantasy was there, making the tears well up in his eyes. He was coughing on his tears now. An entire lifetime had come down to this. What did his father's death mean to him? What could it possibly mean, in the face of all that had happened...?

His father was detaching from him now, holding him at arm's length so that he could take him in. "You've gotten big, praise the Lord!" the man boomed. Roland didn't know what to say, so he nodded. He looked up into the man's bright, searching eyes, still not knowing what to think. But then, Roland suddenly noticed a big silver cross around his father's neck; and as the man saw his son's glance, another smile came to his face.

"We all gotta have the Lord in our lives, son," his father started in a gleeful tone. "The Lord's with me now. He's holding my hand now!" he said with more urgency. And then: "He's *forgiven* me, son!" he shouted with a strange, boundless kind of joy. "He's been so good." Roland stared up at his father, a frown slowly building on his face. *Pray* with me, son!" the man cried suddenly. "Only the Lord can save you! You, me...we *all* sinners, son! Only in *Him* is there life!" he rejoiced. Then he grabbed Roland's hand, holding it so tightly that Roland let out an inadvertent yelp at the pain. "*Pray* with me son!" the man demanded again, raising Roland's throbbing hand above his head like the evangelists did. "Oh *God!*" the man suddenly broke down, "I couldn't help the madness, son—sin coming down on me, *burning* in me like hell, itself...driving me to evil. Satan had a hold on me, son! You can't resist the Devil on your own—you need God's help for that! Surrender to God, son! You're *useless* on your own...!"

The man began praying then, screaming out his subservience and gratitude to God, while Roland stared on in bewilderment. For those first few moments, Roland was only aware of his squeezed hand—of the *pain!* He was lost...*confused*, but then he looked up at his father, seeing the man's tears—his *fear*—seeing, for the first time, what a defeated bastard the man was. Roland had wanted to see defiance, not this! All that he saw was some scared nigger feigning redemption because he was afraid of burning in hell. The realization made new tears well up in his eyes; and then, when he could stand it no more, he wrenched his hand from his father's vise grip

and pushed the man to the ground. In two steps, he
was at the door, darting wildly down the corridor; but
in the maddening recesses of his mind, the voices were
screaming,

Roland's papa killed a cracker
Roland's papa booty scratcher

BOOK
ONE

WORLD ON THE VERGE OF A NERVOUS BREAKDOWN

NEW YORK CITY, THE LATE 1990s

Months later, Roland would think of this night as the beginning of the end; but while he was in the moment, he was in paradise. His woman straddled him in the spacious luxury of his Mercedes-Benz's back seat, taking pains not to damage the fragile material of her two-thousand-dollar evening gown. The gown had been a gift from Roland. They were in an underground parking garage, supposedly on their way to the Mayor's banquet. Needless to say, they had gotten somewhat sidetracked.

The woman, Candice Parker, was on top of him now. She put her head back and moaned as he caressed her body; looking up at her in the darkness, he smiled. Now, he was burying his face in her ample cleavage, deftly unzipping the back of the gown...and he was free. He was beyond the world for those few moments: beyond its problems and the expectations his social success increasingly demanded of him. In a matter of days, he was to give his opening statement in a huge class-action suit worth *millions*. He was a rising star in a society that loved rising stars. He was young and handsome and wealthy. His dating choices had somehow become the fodder of celebrity gossip magazines; and after being named one of the ten most eligible bachelors in the city, women had begun to approach him on the street, and offer up their bodies in not-so-subtle ways. The world had created an entire mythology around some movie-star-like romantic entity and put Roland's face on it. The more successful he became, the *easier* success became. What began as myth, was becoming reality—yet, it all seemed like a preposterous dream.

What made it all seem so unreal was that only three years ago, he had been an overworked, underpaid attorney with the Public Defender's Office. If his present life was a fantasy, then the five years he had spent as a New York City Public Defender had been a nightmare. He had dealt with every conceivable form and byproduct of scum: from those who seemed to have demons in them, to those who seemed to lack genuine evil—but were either in the wrong place at the wrong time, or victims of that invisible current that sucked black and minority men into the prison industrial complex.

Roland felt as though he had escaped from that night-mare—even, at times, that he had sold out in order to feast and grow fat at the trough of corporate law…. The fact of the matter was that he had gone into law with that naïve, "I want to save the world" mentality; but being around so many wasted lives—lives that he had in time come to realize that he had no chance of ameliorating—had hardened him inside. In a sense, the more disheartening the things he had seen, the less he had absorbed into himself. He had gone about his cases with the same uncompromising drive as before, but with a mental and spiritual detachment that had been his only shield against the fatally flawed judicial system.

Yet, all of that was years behind him in time, and seemed like a whole other reality—like someone else's life. Indeed, the feeling of peace seized him as he held his woman in the solemn darkness of the parking garage: she drove away all the restless spirits; in a strange sense, she allowed him to be alone with himself. Nothing was a match for the touch of a good woman. Being with Candice was like nirvana, cancelling out all the problems of the world. He breathed in the delicate fragrance of her perfume then, feeling somehow that he was pulling her into him—that he wasn't simply breathing in her scent, but her essence.

As he continued to unzip the back of her dress, it wasn't simply that he was disrobing her, but himself and the concerns of the world. And it was so wonderful that they were the only ones there: there were no media or courtroom expectations to be met, no cultural mores to defer to...nothing but the smooth softness of her body. He unconsciously smiled to himself at that moment; however, it was then that Candice laughed out suddenly, startling him as she breathed heavily into his ear:

"You're a *killer*, Roland Micheaux!"

"—*What*?"

"You have a murderous heart, Roland Micheaux," she whispered in her sultry Caribbean accent. Roland looked up at her like a dazed child roused from a good dream; she giggled and continued, "Sex, Roland...women can lie with it—can do one thing and have their minds on something else, or on nothing at all; but with men"—she kissed him on the tip of his nose and he recoiled slightly—"it's their only moment of honesty. If they're in love with you, you can tell it in their sex; if they're tired of you, you can tell that as well. You, Roland Micheaux, are a *killer*."

"...What the hell are you talking about?" Roland said in bewilderment. However, he was momentarily distracted by her exposed nipple; and as he looked at it, she giggled and slipped off of him, moving to the far side of the back seat. She then zipped herself up with the agility of a contortionist and sat there, amused by his confusion. He looked at her for a moment, totally baffled; then, watching her smile of sexual triumph, he sat back and chuckled to himself. Young, beautiful women were like gas station attendants who knew their gas station was the only one for hundreds of kilometers. Due to the forces of economics, those gas stations always had the worst service.

With the magic of their session broken, Roland's strange nirvana departed, like the contours of a dream after the day had begun. Still chuckling to himself, he started buttoning up his shirt—

"You don't like my philosophical musings anymore?" she said with a smirk, crossing her legs seductively. "I thought my philosophizing was the only reason you've been with me so long."

"Right you are," he teased her in the playful manner that he always fell into when he was with her, "—my goal in life is to figure out the mysteries of the universe."

"Is that what you were looking for under my dress?"

He looked across at her and smiled.

"What has it been?" she went on in the same playful tone,"—a month now since you met me at that party? Me: a poor Grenadian girl with an expired student visa; and you: the great Roland Micheaux, lawyer extraordinaire, rated one of the ten most eligible bachelors in the city...I amuse you, that's why you keep coming back for more."

He stared at her for a good three seconds before he shook his head and smiled. Their strange way of talking to one another—as though they were characters in a 1930s melodrama—was a kind of foreplay. It turned him on not only sexually, but on a level that approached spirituality. In a sense, it was her singularity that made her real to him. She wasn't like all the other women he had met, who looked the same, dressed the same, talked the same, and even *smelled* the same. She was an individual, in a world where people—particularly the young—seemed to get their personalities out of the latest fashion magazines and music videos. For some reason, it felt good to be around her; he felt for her something visceral— something *tangible*—that wasn't as mundane as love or as shallow as desire. When he was with her, he felt as though he would figure out something vital about himself. Of course, he wasn't entirely conscious of all this, and it mostly manifested itself as a feeling of comfort.

Whatever the case, he again smiled to himself; remembering the banquet, he held up his watch to the fluorescent light outside and looked at it fixedly. It was approaching nine-thirty: they were already fashionably late, verging on being boorishly late. Resolved to leave for the banquet at once, he began putting on his bowtie. However, when he looked up at Candice, he realized that she was still smirking at him.

"Oh-oh," he said with a laugh, "what are you plotting in that head of yours?"

"Just thinking about you."

"You seem to spend an inordinate amount of time doing that," he joked, still putting on his bowtie.

"Well, you're an interesting subject."

"*Subject*?" he returned, laughing at her phrasing, "—and what is your prognosis, professor?"

"Some minor neuroses, but nothing that a few years of intensive therapy won't cure."

"I see," he said, chuckling. "And what is your proposed method of treatment?"

"First, we have to uncover the roots of your murderous heart."

"My *what*?"

"Like I said before, you're a *killer*, Roland Micheaux."

"Are we on this again?" he said, groaning playfully.

"Yup," she said, moving closer to him and lowering her voice to a sexy whisper, "—so tell me, when is the last time you thought about killing someone—"

"What are you talking about?" he said, instinctively putting up his hand to keep her at bay.

"Don't try to tell me you've *never* thought about it," she said, smiling at him oddly; then, in a nonchalant manner: "I think about it all the time."

"*Killing* someone?"

"Yes."

He looked at her calm, seemingly affected expression and burst out laughing. Shaking his head, and ready to put the entire thing out of his mind, he checked the breast pocket of his tuxedo to make sure he still had the invitations. Yet, when he glanced up from this task, he realized she had been staring at him fixedly all that time, as though coming to some conclusion—or waiting for the right moment. When their eyes locked, she spoke up in the same nonchalant manner, saying, "I've *killed* someone, you know."

"...What?"

"I've *killed* someone—you're the first person I've ever told." Then, with a strange smile, she continued, "I guess

you're one of those men that women want to unburden
themselves to."

"...What the *hell* are you talking about?"

"I'm a killer as well," she said, serenely.

He stared at her for a while, as she sat there with a
smirk on her face; and then, dubiously: "Who'd *you* kill?"

"My first lover."

For some reason, he burst out laughing.

"He wasn't a real lover," she protested.

"Of course," he said with a chuckle.

"...He was about sixty—a big, fat, sweaty man." Roland
looked up sharply, his smile replaced by an expression
of uncertainty. "He lived right next to us—back in
Grenada—up on a mountain. He started with me when
I was twelve." Roland sat up straighter, his frown deep-
ening. "It was off and on—probably about three times
in all. Months would go by, and I would convince myself
that nothing had happened. It was like a dream: the
longer you're awake, the less real it seems; and after a
while, it seemed so unreal that I couldn't believe it had
happened. He would come and visit my parents, joking
with us all...and I would think to myself: *Nah, I must
have imagined it.*

"But that day...I came home from school and saw him
walking up the lane with my little sister, to his house. I
followed them up there; and when I saw for myself, I
knew, right then and there, that I had to kill him. It
wasn't a murderous rage or anything: it was calm—a

logical conclusion. His car was in the driveway; and as my father was a mechanic, I had picked up some things. It was all so perfect, as if God had mandated that I do it, because a toolbox had been lying right there. I cut the brake cable on his car. Grenada has a lot of mountains, see. The lane from his house led right down into a deep ravine; and without brakes to make the turn...well, that would be that.

"When my sister came home, I saw it all in her eyes: the same shock that I had felt that first time... But everything was going to be fine. I went to bed and bided my time; and that night, while I was lying there, looking out of the window at the moon, I finally heard the crash and loud explosion as his car dropped into that ravine. With the fire, there wasn't enough of him left to fill a shoebox.... Justifiable homicide, Roland?"

"*What*?" he whispered when she said his name and broke the spell that had held him. Her voice had had a strangely hypnotic quality: he shook his head to be free of it.

"You think they'd convict me?" she asked him earnestly.

"You're *serious*?"

"Of course. Was it justified or not?"

"...I don't know what your laws are," he said evasively.

"Screw the laws—what do *you* say?"

"I say you're a dangerous woman," he said, trying to smile.

"Isn't that what men want?" she said, smiling, "—a

little hint of danger in their women to spice up their sex lives?"

"Only the self-destructive ones want that," he joked. He laughed, but it was nervous laughter. Indeed, he was so desperate to be free of this strange discomfort that the laughter soon consumed him. Now that he thought about it, her story of childhood murder had to be a joke—another of her woman tricks to get into his head. Yet, she was scrutinizing him with a look that he couldn't quite gauge; and regardless of whether or not he thought she was a murderer, he had the unsettling feeling that she was seeing through him, reading his thoughts—

"What do you want from me, Roland Micheaux?" she asked abruptly.

He hated it when she used both of his names: it reminded him of his mother, who was now dead—and therefore doubly sacred. When he looked at Candice, he saw that there was again a smirk on her face; and something about it, and the way she was sitting there, made him laugh.

"What makes you assume I want anything?"

"Men always want something," she purred, "—it's in their nature."

"What about women, don't they want anything?"

"Women don't have wants, they have *prerogatives*."

"Thanks for clarifying that!" he said, laughing. "Anyway, why bother asking me anything? According to you, a woman can tell anything she wants to know by *screwing* a man—"

"That's not what I said!" she protested.

"Didn't you just say that a man is only honest when he's screwing," he teased her, "—and that I'm a killer? Since I'm a killer and you're a killer, we can have a little death orgy: put one another out of our misery."

"...Maybe," she mused oddly.

He frowned imperceptibly, having detected something unsettling in her voice. He went to ask her if she was all right, but instinctively retreated; and besides, he was suddenly weary of their exchange. It was a war of sorts: a battle royal between the sexes. At the moment, they both seemed to be taking unacceptable losses. Again looking at his watch, he sighed and shook his head at nothing in particular. "Let's just get going," he said then. Yet, as he glanced at her in the darkness, he was suddenly disturbed by the smirk that had been on her face for most of that evening. He quickly opened the door and went to exit, when,

"What are you running from, Roland Micheaux?"

He sat there, with the door open and one foot outside; then, slowly and deliberately, he turned around and looked at her. She was still smirking. His voice was low but emphatic: "Stop it, okay. Just *stop* it." He took a deep breath, inwardly angry with himself for having allowed her to get under his skin: she had won that battle. "—Look," he went on quickly, "let's just go and have a good time. We've got invitations to spend the evening at a banquet with the Mayor of New York City—"

"And all the other social elite."

"...Candice," he began, his tone more contentious, "if you don't want to go, I can get you a cab back home."

"Stop being such a grouch," she said, giggling and caressing his shoulder.

He watched her for a while, then groaned again as he exited the car and walked around to her door. "I don't want to talk about murder anymore," he warned her as he opened the door for her. "And I've heard enough of your 'philosophical musings' to last a lifetime." But by then, she was standing before him. She was tall and statuesque, and her beauty and poise made his annoyance and misgivings ebb away. She was a weird woman—perhaps even a *disturbed* one—still, he couldn't help thinking that there was something magical about her. *Beauty is a horrible thing in a crazy woman*, he thought with a smile. How many fools, over the eons, had died for it—had felt compelled to give up their lives in defense of it? How many otherwise intelligent men had made stupid decisions for the sake of it? She stood there posing for him with one hand placed seductively on her hip, and he almost laughed out loud at the entire game: the farce that was the mating ritual. There she was, playing the role of the classic vixen: a carefully contrived combination of sexual aggressiveness, mystery/nuttiness, and, to win over that macho streak in all men, a tinge of defenselessness. For the first time, it occurred to him that her seeming originality might just be an act. Or, maybe it was only that her story of childhood murder was still percolating in his mind, setting off alarm bells. She seemed somehow different to him now; and, as was so often the case when a once-perfect lover was shown to have a blemish, the relationship was thrown into crisis—not by the flaw, itself, but by the debilitating blow that came with the loss of the illusion of perfection. His vessel of nirvana was somehow lost to him, so that he wasn't merely losing his woman, but his religion.

Now that he thought about their one-month relationship, he allowed himself to acknowledge that he had always been somewhat wary of her. At first, he had thought that that wariness was what women referred to as "a fear of commitment." But he now realized that what he feared wasn't belonging to her, but losing himself within her. Nirvana could only be wonderful in passing—as a respite from the world. But continuous nirvana was death; and every time he was with Candice, he came away with the feeling that there was an abyss within her: a vast void of nothingness, waiting to suck him in. Even when having a simple conversation with her, he would find himself tumbling into her depths, falling deeper and deeper into her nothingness. With her story of childhood murder percolating in his mind, his sense of inner panic couldn't be denied. He looked at her uneasily then, and nodded to himself, knowing that his time with her was drawing to a close.

It was perhaps to shelter himself from the specter of

a nettlesome breakup that his thoughts gravitated toward the imminent pleasure—indeed, the social triumph—of attending the Mayor's banquet. Strangely enough, he and the Mayor were locked in a titanic struggle—a gentleman's fight to the death. It was all the result of a case that Roland had won three years ago. It had been his last case with the Public Defender's Office; and with his mental detachment almost complete, he had cared less about whom he was defending. The defendant had been a middle-aged white supremacist who burst into City Hall one day, ran up to Mayor Randolph—a Republican who had the quirky distinction of being a black man—and declared that the Mayor was "a dirty, no-good nigger." After the man was arrested, the case had of course been seized upon by the media. Suddenly tossed into the spotlight, Roland had seemed perfect for television: poised, handsome, giving impassioned homilies about freedom of speech and "The American Way." When he won the case, the Mayor had invited him to a diplomatic banquet—and had been inviting him to dinners and social events ever since. It had seemed like a friendly gesture, but Roland rightly saw it as a declaration of war. *We'll see who breaks first!* the Mayor had seemed to be saying. However, Roland's career had taken off after that. With all the media attention from the trial, the young, dynamic firm of Rosencrantz and Associates had quickly retained his services; and after being on a legal team that won a fifty-million-dollar settlement against a negligent automaker, his reputation and future had been guaranteed.

For whatever reason, Roland again smiled to himself and felt at ease. Despite the uneasiness Candice's story had inspired in him, he now took her by the hand and led her away. A confrontation with her was imminent, but he didn't want it to be tonight. Right now, the only thing he wanted was peace from his thoughts. And there was something almost magical about the dark, eerie emptiness of the parking garage, where their steps echoed in the darkness and left him with the feeling that they were the last two people on earth. He liked the solemnity: the sense of peace and well being that came when one was with someone and there was nothing to be said. They walked along like that for a few moments, until Candice looked up abruptly and said:

"Do you ever think about the world ending, Roland?"

"What?" he said, at once alarmed and irritated that she had broken the spell of peace.

"—Ever think that all the craziness in the world might be a sign from *God*?"

"...Not particularly," he said, giving her an odd look.

"I mean, *think* about it," she went on. "You turn on the television and all you see is death: kids going to their schools and gunning down dozens of people. People starving and desperate in every corner of the world... People *butchering* one another in wars... *AIDS*... And in New York, we even have our own kind of craziness:

trigger-happy cops sticking plungers up people's asses... mothers leaving newborn babies in garbage cans...and then there's that crazy Hair Jacker, or whatever he's called, running loose for the last two years, shaving people's heads. The world's mad, Roland. Something's wrong somewhere—something's *sick!*"

Roland's sense of inner panic began to surge within him again. Her words struck a sensitive cord in him—*disturbed* him, in fact. His previous compulsion to get away from her, seized him again. But she had stopped and was staring up at him imploringly; and as he looked into her eyes, he had the sense that all her defenses were down, and that he was seeing the *real* her. He didn't quite know what to make of it, but he felt something inside of him melting. Like a fool, he found himself thinking, *She has big, puppy dog eyes.* She seemed young and naïve to him just now, and Roland was overcome by the self-destructive male urge to protect and comfort her. He took her in his arms then, holding her tenderly. Unfortunately, just as the spell began to envelop him again, she blurted out:

"I knew one of his victims, you know."

He groaned and released her. "What?"

"One of my friends got her head shaved by that Hair Jacker guy," she went on. "She had this long hair weave, and he snuck up behind her one night and shaved it all off. Why do you figure he does it?"

"Who *cares*," he said, annoyed with her again. He started to walk away on his own; but oblivious to his snub, she came up to his side and looped her arm though his.

"They say it might be more than one man," she went on, "—a whole cult of them. Almost three hundred people have had their heads shaved in the last two years—that's a hell of a lot for one man—"

Roland was about to lose his cool and tell her to shut the hell up, when a wretched-looking black man suddenly stepped out of the shadows—actually, from behind one of the concrete columns. The man said nothing: the gun that he brought from his pocket did all the talking. The man was shorter and slighter than both Roland and Candice, but a gun elevates even the lowest weakling to mystical proportions. Roland abruptly stopped and raised his hands. Candice merely stopped by Roland's side and looked at the man with her strange nonchalance.

"Empty your pockets!" the wretched-looking man demanded. He looked like a starved stray dog. His clothes were all *caked* with dirt—as though he had fallen asleep somewhere and been buried alive when he was mistaken for a corpse. The man even smelled like death.

Taking all this in, Roland took out the cash from his wallet, handed the wad of bills over to the man, then went to put the wallet back in his pocket.

"Gimmie your wallet!" the man demanded.

"My credit cards will be canceled in fifteen minutes—"

"Not if I blow your fucking brains out!" the man pointed out.

Roland couldn't deny the man's logic. He extended his suddenly trembling hand to give the man his wallet.

However, the man held the gun in his right hand, and when he stretched out his left hand to receive the wallet, he let his right hand, and the gun, drop somewhat. Instinctively, something was triggered in Roland; and before he even knew what was going on, he knocked the gun out of the man's hand! For a second, they both stood there in shock. But it was Roland who let that vicious left cross fly, breaking the man's nose and knocking him back into the concrete column. A brutal left-right combination followed, and the man was on the ground.

Roland was kicking the man now, stomping his head mercilessly with the hard soles of his dress shoes. The man wasn't moving anymore. In truth, he had been knocked senseless by the initial blow, and the subsequent fifteen seconds of vicious blows were all superfluous. It was Candice who stopped Roland—who brought him back to his senses. She came up and tapped him on the shoulder; and when he looked over at her, he was both startled and confused: first, to see her standing by his side; and then, to see the bloody, unmoving form lying at his feet.

"*See*," Candice said then, her smirk widening to a grin, "I *told* you you're a killer...."

The night was cold for mid May. Roland was shivering—or maybe it was only the dawning realization of what had just happened. Candice was leading him across

Park Avenue, to the banquet hall. He was suddenly frail and dazed...*lost*.

Candice wrenched him back, just as an angry cabby zoomed past, honking his horn. He and Candice were in the middle of the wide avenue, and he was suddenly terrified. He felt like a deer startled by headlights. Zooming cars seemed to be everywhere, their headlights blinding.

Candice tugged on his arm again and they finished running across the avenue. Roland was panting when they reached the pavement. He looked back in horror, toward the parking garage:

"You think he's *dead*?" he whispered.

"Probably," she answered, still with that godforsaken smirk. He instinctively drew away from her, but she looped her arm through his and steered him toward the other end of the block, where the banquet hall was located.

"Nothing to worry about," she purred to him again. "It was simple self-defense: you were *justified*. *See*," she said with a laugh, "I don't need to know what your laws are to make my decision. There is a natural law—fighting for survival: defending yourself against those who threaten you. I'm right, aren't I?"

"God," he said anxiously, glancing back again, "why the hell did we run—we should have called the police!"

"First of all," she corrected him, "we didn't 'run' from anything. Second, why should we take our time to call anyone about that fool? Why waste more time on him and let him ruin our evening? I mean, *really*: think about it. If you step in shit, do you call someone to report it? No, you wipe your shoe off as best you can and go about your business."

"I guess," he said, distractedly. Then, looking back warily, "You think anyone *saw*?"

"Of course not—there was no one else down there: that's why he was there. And besides," she said with a laugh, "You're Roland Micheaux: the golden boy—*everyone* loves you. In fact," she said with a chuckle, caressing his chest, "I bet you could get away with *murder*—"

He cringed at her laughter, stopping abruptly. *What's wrong with this woman!* But she only laughed louder when she saw his expression.

"God, you're wound up tight!" she said, shaking her head. "Get a hold of yourself, man," she went on, taking his hand once again. "It was self-defense, Roland. It's as simple as that. In a while, someone's going to come upon the body. They'll see some scrawny black bum with a gun. If he's dead, they'll check his fingerprints... probably find out he has a record as long as my arm. And so another black criminal will be found dead... quickly forgotten. There's not even anything to link you to him. I wiped the gun down, didn't I?—just in case you got any fingerprints on it—and we took your money back. People won't know what to make of it. We took care of everything, didn't we?"

"Yeah," he said, his voice strangely hoarse; and then, "I was forgetting that you've done this before."

She burst out laughing; and, for the life of him, he was startled to find the ends of his lips rising and a kind of chortling laughter escaping from his chest. Yet, there was something about laughter that drained one's strength and will; and instead of feeling relieved, he felt more dazed and disillusioned.... They continued walking. His legs felt wobbly, but Candice was there, helping him along. Candice was there, both supporting him and draining his strength....

"We'll just stay here for an hour or so," she began. "We'll go in and act naturally: you can flirt with as many old white women as you want," she joked again. "By then, somebody would have found the body and there won't be anything for you to worry about...."

They were nearing the building. About half a dozen police officers were in front of the door; and when Roland saw them, his guts seemed to knot themselves. A crowd of about fifty eager celebrity-seekers was waiting eagerly; and behind a barricade, a flock of paparazzi had their cameras at the ready, in expectation of the next celebrity. When Roland and Candice were about twenty meters from the entrance, a limousine stopped before the awning, and a celebrity couple—whose names escaped Roland at the moment—emerged from it. The couple waved to the crowd and walked ceremoniously up the red carpet; and as they did so, the cameras of the paparazzi went off like machine-guns. Roland froze!

"*Cameras*!" he gasped, gaping at Candice. "You think that garage had surveillance cameras!"

"Don't worry about it," she assured him again. "Even if they do, that'll only prove that it was self-defense. You're Roland Micheaux—"

"You have *no* idea what can happen to us!" he yelled. "Footage of me knocking some guy's head in would *ruin* me! I may have just *killed* a man—doesn't that mean anything to you! I'm a goddamn lawyer...and I fled from the scene of a crime! We wiped the gun clean and ran away!"

"What are you talking about? You're famous, nothing—"

"America *hates* celebrities!" he raged, his mind instinctively going to the never-ending stream of celebrity scandals. "Look at them!" he ranted, pointing to the people standing before the entrance. "You really think they give a shit about me? They're freaking *vultures*!"

"Calm down, Roland!" she said, seeming concerned—and *sane*—for the first time. Some of the people in the crowd were looking in their direction, but it was dark; and despite his tuxedo, Roland looked too harried to be a celebrity of any importance, so they turned away.

"Relax," Candice cooed to him once again, to which Roland nodded nervously. "Come on," she said, coaxing him toward the entrance when he seemed to have collected himself. "You have those invitations?"

"Yeah," he said, getting them out. His mind was blank, which was odd, since it was racing on at a feverish pace. Everything was passing him by. It was Candice who took the invitations and showed them to the police officer when they got to the entrance. It was Candice who waved and smiled at the crowd, positioning Roland so that they could pose for the paparazzi. The attention and applause was all proof that he was a rising star, but he was too preoccupied to care. For the first time in a while, he was thinking about his father. Candice had been wrong about the parking garage: at first, he had merely defended himself, but then something had taken over. Some horrible instinct had possessed him, and it had felt good. There was a taunting, ever-present voice of vengeance in his soul, and that voice was his father's. He knew the thought was totally irrational, but he had never been able to get over the sense that his father was still with him, *haunting* him. Somewhere out there, the man was plotting his revenge—both against the world that had killed him, and the son who had deserted him in his moment of need—

Get a hold of yourself, Roland...! But he felt like a hapless fool who had gone too far down a treacherous road: there was no turning back. A man was lying back at the parking garage—and that man could be dead! There was still a chance to save the man by calling an ambulance, and yet he knew he did not have the courage. He felt suddenly filthy—and *lost*. He had made a wrong turn somewhere, and was now falling helplessly into the gutter....

Candice and he were beyond the entrance now, passing through a grand anteroom. In the main hall, about five hundred elegantly dressed people were milling about. Their laughter and conversations seemed to be an extension of the music that the live jazz quartet was playing. Roland stared at the scene uneasily—as if the people within it were creatures from another world. The Mayor was about ten meters from the entrance, surrounded by about fifty people. Mayor Randolph said something then, and the people around him laughed uproariously at his punch line—

Something exploded in the air, and everyone jumped. After a moment of confusion, they all realized it was coming from outside. Roland and Candice abruptly whirled around; even those laughing at the Mayor's story stopped and turned in that direction. Candice instinctively went to see what was happening; Roland followed her unconsciously, the way an insecure child followed his mother.

When they got there, they saw that dozens—perhaps *hundreds*—of black people were now on the sidewalk. Roland couldn't even begin to explain it. It was as though time had gone haywire again. The people were everywhere, stopping traffic and displacing all the celebrity-seekers. The people were chanting, "No justice, no peace!" Yet, they were chanting with such vehemence that it was as though their voices would bring the world crashing down. It was yet another thing for Roland's overburdened mind to account for. It was as if they had appeared out of the nothingness: been *beamed* there, straight from some netherworld.

While the people chanted, the cameras of the paparazzi went off with the same machine-gun-like explosiveness. Somehow, network camera crews were now on the scene, joining in the fray; and while all this went on, the six police officers stood before the door, desperately calling for backup. The chaos all reminded Roland of going to see his father that day; and placed in that light, the body in the parking garage suddenly seemed like an omen of coming madness. He had killed, just as his father had killed; and like his father, he had looked at the work of his hands and fled like a scared nigger—

"No justice, no peace!" the people screamed into the night. Roland's mind was still sputtering along, but he suddenly connected the protest with a brutal killing that took place two days ago. Four undercover officers on a drug sweep had shot an unarmed black youth twenty-seven times—some inconceivable number like that. Somehow, they had mistaken his cell phone for a gun. It was a case made for television—especially after people found out the kid was an honor student. One couldn't turn on the television without hearing comments from the police commissioner or the Mayor or the victim's crying mother—

"No justice, no peace!"

While the protesters chanted in front of the banquet hall, Roland felt as though his head were being pried open and jammed with filth. He was drifting further away from reality now. None of it seemed real anymore— not the corpse in the garage, not the chanting crowd...

It was like he was trapped in someone else's dream. He shook his head, bewildered. He was about to retreat into the banquet hall when he detected footsteps at his back; and when he looked over his shoulder, he saw the Mayor followed by dozens of people! For some reason, he rushed to the side, as though he feared being trampled.

Several bodyguards were trying to restrain the Mayor now, yelling that it wasn't safe, but Randolph scoffed at this, especially when he looked into the night and saw that the protest was being led by Charles Marenga. The latter was a tuxedo-clad, rotund black man about fifty-five, whose history of flamboyant protest had made him a kind of laughingstock—particularly to the mainstream. In fact, Randolph instinctively smiled when he saw the man.

As for Roland, he felt sick. He kept seeing the body lying in the parking garage; and once, when he glanced out on the crowd, he *swore* he saw his father's grinning face. The world seemed to be swirling before his eyes now. He felt like he was only moments away from passing out. He braced himself against the wall, but when he looked up, Mayor Randolph was walking past. The man winked at him—which was the way they usually greeted one another. Roland barely managed to nod....

Mayor Alexander Randolph was a tall forty-eight-year-old, who had been a star athlete in his youth; and as the man stopped in the doorway, looking out boldly, he seemed so heroic that cameramen scrambled to get a shot of him. Outraged, Charles Marenga stepped up as far as the police officers would allow him. He was a microcosm of black rage; and at the sight of Randolph, the protesters' chants intensified. It was again as though their words would bring the world tumbling down—make buildings crumble at their foundations...cause streets to rip open and buckle, as if from underground fault lines. Marenga was waving his hand wildly in the air now—all the protesters were. On top of all that, Marenga's gangly sidekick, Botswana Glade, was at his side, urging the people on to even more hatred and outrage and madness.

Yet, despite all of that, Randolph seemed perfectly at ease as he surveyed the situation and inquired in a booming voice: "What's the problem?"

Strangely enough, the chants stopped. Some people—particularly those from the banquet—naturally relaxed and smiled, because that was Randolph's catch phrase: the slogan that had swept him into City Hall four years ago, and which was constantly being repeated in his reelection commercials.

In the sudden silence, Marenga screamed back: "You and this racist system are the problem, Randolph!"

"Yeah!" Botswana Glade and the rest of the protesters screamed in unison.

Roland's head was swirling!

"A young, unarmed black man has been shot by the police!" Marenga screamed. "—*Murdered!* Ruthlessly gunned down by twenty-seven bullets! And you have the *nerve* to be holding a banquet!"

"Yeah!" the protesters yelled once again.

The tension in the air seemed palpable; some cosmic explosion seemed imminent—at least to Roland. Nevertheless, Randolph merely looked on with pursed lips, then smiled as he said: "Do you want to come in, Marenga?"

"...What?"

"I see you came in your tuxedo," he said. There was laughter from the people at Randolph's heels, while Marenga and his protesters looked on confusedly. It was while Marenga was standing there, somewhat disarmed by Randolph's question, that Randolph walked down, past the six officers, and gripped the much shorter Marenga by the shoulders, saying: "Come in, come in..."

There was something compelling about Randolph's manner; and he was so decisive that he brought Marenga though the entrance in a matter of seconds, leaving the rest of the protesters standing there ineptly. As easily as that, the protest was over. Botswana Glade and the rest of Marenga's cronies looked like puppies watching their master go. There was something sorrowful and pathetic about them now.

"We'll talk later," Roland heard Randolph say to Marenga as they walked past him. "Man can't live on politics and conflict alone," Randolph said in a louder voice, laughing; then, poking Marenga in his pendulous gut, he teased, "—see how bloated it's gotten you!" Everyone again laughed as Marenga was whisked away, scowling. Yet, despite the scowl, his face betrayed an inner hopelessness, as he asked himself how in the *hell* Randolph had managed to do it to him!

Roland looked at it all, and was acutely aware that the world was mad.

All the guests were returning to the main hall now, most of them talking excitedly amongst themselves— like children after a Saturday matinee. Even while aftershocks from the parking garage continued to eat away at him, Roland was relieved beyond reason that the protest seemed to be over. A side of him really had believed their words would bring the world crashing down. As the other guests returned to the banquet hall, Roland just wanted to stand there by himself and recover his composure. The dark images of the parking garage were now taking on supernatural dimensions. It was not even criminal prosecution or his own conscience that he feared anymore, but something more amorphous and dire. He had to find a way to reconcile those dark realities—to *purge* his soul of them—before they drove him mad. Unfortunately, it was then that Candice again looped her arm through his and pulled him along. He had totally forgotten about her. He took a few unsteady steps toward the main chamber when, all at once, a voice boomed:

"Micheaux!"

Looking up in alarm, Roland saw one of the partners from his firm: Dallas Phelps! In his mind, the man represented everything he had spent the last twenty years building—and everything that he stood to lose! He felt himself being pushed toward the edge again. His mind lurched off wildly, conjuring more horrors as it went.

Phelps was a white man in his forties, with premature gray—almost *white*—hair. The man came up to Roland, giving him a hearty handshake and patting him on the shoulder. Feeling himself drawing closer and closer to the edge, Roland had to bite his lip to keep from screaming. Alarm bells were going off inside of him. He looked at Phelps' smiling face and knew that self-preservation meant getting away: *fleeing*... But common sense told him that was impossible for now. Pooling all his will, he forced himself to smile: to effect the intonations and expressions of those around him. He felt as if his face were going to crack—his smile, or whatever passed for it, felt that phony. He didn't know how much longer he could keep it going. However, just then, as though offering him a reprieve, Phelps looked at Candice and asked,

"Who is this *beautiful* young woman?" It was annoyingly cliché, but Candice smiled.

Roland distractedly introduced Candice to Phelps; she quickly took the lead and introduced herself.

"I like your accent," Phelps declared, smiling down at her.

"Oh, you like talking, do you?" she joked in her usual fashion. "You must be one of those new sensitive men."

"I ain't too sensitive," Phelps drawled, "but I've been known to bruise easy!"

While they laughed, Roland found them both insufferable. He felt the urge to leap at them and strangle them both—

Control yourself, Roland!

"Hey, Dallas," Roland interrupted their flirtatious laughter, "why don't you take her to get a drink? I have to use the bathroom."

"It would be my honor," Phelps said quickly, offering her his arm; and without further ado, they walked away together, into the hall. Phelps, Roland just then remembered, was married to one of those blond, Barbie Doll wives. As Roland watched Phelps sauntering away with Candice, he suddenly doubted that the wife, Cindy, was here. But he also didn't care. To hell with them all....

He needed to rest—to get away and clear his head. He began scanning the hall, looking for the bathroom—but now that he was alone, another of the aftershocks from the parking garage drained more of his strength and will. He was looking around desperately now—for the bathroom. Just five or ten minutes alone in a bathroom stall should be enough for him to compose himself. The jazz quartet was playing on a dais on the far side of the room. There was an archway beside the dais, and he finally noticed that the icons for the bathrooms were underneath the archway. He took a step in that direction when, all of a sudden, a skinny black man stepped before him. The man was middle-aged, with a bushy afro that was way out of style.

"Ah, Mr. Micheaux," the man said in a deep baritone that was out of proportion with his gaunt frame, "—I knew you would be here!" The man then patted Roland on the shoulder and looked up at him as though they were old friends.

Roland again bit his lip to keep from screaming! It was as if something had exploded in his head! He couldn't take it anymore! He had a sudden impulse to bash the man's head in; and as he realized the nature of his thoughts, more of his precious strength was drained away! *Relax, Roland!* But he felt hopelessly lost now.

The man was still staring at him knowingly; marshaling his strength. Roland blurted out, "I'm sorry, do I *know* you?" Yet, even as he said it, he avoided eye contact with the man, anxiously looking in the direction of the bathroom.

"You've been trying to know me all your life," the man responded matter-of-factly.

What...? Roland felt as though the room were swirling! The feeling of hysteria again welled up inside of him, so that he felt himself even closer to screaming and ranting. Desperate to get away, he made a curt nodding gesture with his head and went to leave, but the man again stepped into his path.

"What the *hell* do you want!" Roland cursed, no longer even pretending to remain calm. He stood there panting like a beast, while the man laughed and shook his head in a self-deprecating manner.

"I'm sorry," he said with a laugh, seemingly oblivious of Roland's outburst—of the murderous rage in his eyes. The man again patted Roland on the shoulder, going on: "I got so excited that I forgot to introduce myself. My name is Jasper Kain, Mr. Micheaux. I am a statistician for the Mayor." Kain stretched out his hand then, and Roland shook it confusedly.

"A pollster?" Roland said, fighting to understand—and to *focus*.

"Yes. I do calculations and give probabilities."

There was something weird about that response, but Roland did not have the strength to unravel it. "—You said you were expecting me?" he went on quickly. He was taking deep breaths to calm himself—and it seemed to be working.

"Yes: you are part of a survey I've been doing."

"*Me?*"

"Yes."

"I...I don't understand." And he didn't. He was so far gone that he didn't know if that lack of understanding was a result of his mind being unable to decipher Kain's words, or because Kain's words were indecipherable. A side of him suspected that his mind was skipping over entire sentences, discarding huge chunks of vital information—

"Everything will be made clear tonight!" Kain suddenly exulted—or so it seemed to Roland. "Ever since you won that big freedom of speech case," the man continued, "I've been keeping an eye on you, Mr. Micheaux. You're the inevitable byproduct of these times. Since back then, I knew that we were all going to be here on this night— all the big players: you, Marenga, Randolph, Botswana Glade... Probabilities are becoming certainties, Mr. Micheaux!" the man said, smiling triumphantly.

"What are you talking about?" Roland said from the depths of his frustration. And just then, he abruptly looked in the direction of the quartet—the music seemed strangely cacophonous just now; the surrounding laughter all at once seemed disconnected and unsettling. It was all a warning for him to get away. He felt as if the ground were falling away beneath him; and as another of the aftershocks from the parking garage hit him, he shuddered, as though a jolt of electricity had gone through him. Images of the corpse lying in the darkness, and Phelps' good cheer, and Marenga's shouting match with Randolph, and all the other random events, were swirling in his mind. He definitely couldn't take much more. The world seemed to be going out of focus; and for a moment, he found himself wondering if Kain, with his bushy afro and his disconcertingly deep voice, was even real. Maybe the man was some delusion cooked up by a mind that had long cracked. He shook his head to drive away those thoughts, but everything seemed useless now. He was losing his grip, disappearing into the darkness within himself—

"You've been thinking about the end of the world," Kain said—again seemingly out of nowhere.

Roland stared at him for a long while: it took him that long to focus himself—to *re-imbed* himself in reality. "...*What*?"—and then, remembering his conversation with Candice—"Did Candice send you over?"

"No one *sent* me, Mr. Micheaux. I'm here because of your madness: I was *drawn* to you."

Roland stared on confusedly, his face creasing as he tried to make sense of it. "...What is this, some joke?" he said at last. It had to be a joke: that was the only thing that made sense. Grasping at straws, it occurred to him that maybe Candice—or some playful colleague at work— had put the man up to this; maybe all of it, including Candice's annoying weirdness and the beating in the parking garage, was some prank that was spiraling out of control; and suddenly desperate for the great punch line that would release him, he eked out a twitching grin and blurted out: "It's a *joke*, right?"

Kain only shook his head solemnly. "Why is it that people only ask that question when it is clear to them that nothing funny has been said? I am here because of *madness*, Mr.—"

"*Stop* it!" Roland demanded. "Look, I don't know who put you up to this, but it's not funny anymore."

"I'm not here to amuse you, Mr. Micheaux."

"I don't give a shit why you're here!"

"—Of course you do," Kain said calmly. "Thanks to your father, you've been trying to understand madness all your life—"

"*Stop* it!" Roland screamed hysterically; several people in nearby groups looked up at him sharply. "Shut up!" Roland repeated. However, Kain only laughed softly, seeming satisfied. There was something murderous in Roland's eyes—he could have easily snapped the man's neck; but after a second or so, he found himself snickering nervously. *It had to be a joke*! He looked around expectantly for Candice—or even Phelps—still waiting for them to come out and yell, "Gotcha!" He needed to laugh—but he was suddenly out of breath ...*Had Kain really mentioned his father*? Of course not...nobody knew about his father. Nevertheless, he realized he was sweating profusely. It was all collapsing around him, and he didn't know how much longer he could keep himself together. He once again looked around for Candice—this time in desperation—but she was nowhere in sight.

Roland was getting ready to storm past Kain and flee to the bathroom, when the man smiled and said, "I thought you said your goal in life was to figure out the mysteries of the universe, Mr. Micheaux?"

Roland looked up sharply! As Kain looked at him coyly, a cold, creepy feeling went down Roland's spine. That's what he had said to Candice back in the parking garage! How the hell could the man know about that! A hundred irrational thoughts went through his mind in the blink of an eye, all of them draining a little more of his strength.

However, Kain laughed calmly then, going on: "No need to be distraught, Mr. Micheaux: I'm not a mind reader."

But how else could the man know what he was thinking! Roland had taken another one of those blind steps into the nothingness, and now everything seemed to be turned on its head. On top of everything, Kain's continued ease eroded something vital in him. The man seemed to know him—there was no denying that. Roland felt like he was on the threshold of something horrible. His nightmare thoughts—about his father's demon residue walking free—made his legs feel wobbly.

That was when Kain laughed softly again, saying, "The fact of the matter is, Mr. Micheaux, that I followed you tonight—"

"*What!*"

"I know everything that happened in the parking garage—quite inadvertently, of course." Roland's jaw dropped! "I'm not normally a snoop, Mr. Micheaux—but as I said, I've been keeping an extensive survey, and you're a part of it. I had already parked in the parking garage and was walking out to the banquet, when I saw you driving past with your girlfriend. *Candice*, right?" he said, frowning, while Roland stood before him like a frail old man. "Like I said, I didn't mean to spy," he went on with a chuckle, "even though the evidence does make it seem so. See, I had intended to walk down and introduce myself to you right then, but when I got there, you and your lady friend were too preoccupied." Roland twitched. "I must admit that I was rather like a snoop when I crouched by the door and listened to your conversation; and then, when you were getting ready to leave, I snuck behind one of the columns. Thank goodness Candice asked you what you were running from: that gave me time to make my escape. I didn't want us to be introduced on those terms, with you thinking I was a garden-variety peeping tom. I stayed in the shadows...and I saw it all; and now, I'm even more convinced that you're just the man I need, Mr. Micheaux."

Roland exhaled forcefully! He had unconsciously been holding his breath all that time. "What do you want from me!" he managed to whisper, looking pale and distraught. "—You want money!" he said with a suddenly hoarse voice.

However, Kain only laughed out then, again with his usual calmness. "First of all, I wanted to point out a simple fact to you, Mr. Micheaux: people are all too willing to believe in the supernatural when facts dictate a more mundane answer. I profess no powers other than those of quiet observation and attention to detail. Those skills will serve you well as I tell you about the facts of the world, Mr. Micheaux."

Roland could only stare; his mind kept repeating, *He*

knows! For a moment, he was again overcome by the urge to bash the man's head in, but he shook his head to chase away those thoughts. He had to figure out what to do! Of course, with his mind a wreck, nothing came to him; and to bide his time, and keep Kain occupied until he could figure something out, he instinctively blurted out, "*What* facts?"

"Like I said before: the facts you've been trying to understand all your life."

Sensing where Kain was going, Roland shook his head, like a fool begging his attacker for mercy. "Look," he pleaded then, "I can't really talk right now." As he said it, he looked around nervously for Candice and Phelps, but Kain shushed him as if he were a disagreeable baby.

"I know you, Mr. Micheaux," Kain continued, "because I know myself—and I understand madness."

"—I'm not crazy!" Roland blurted out. The sweat was streaming down his face now, and he was a mess. Still, Kain's only reaction to Roland's outburst was to again laugh calmly—the way someone laughed at a child's foolishness.

"Don't misunderstand me, Mr. Micheaux," Kain started with his usual way. "When I talk about madness, I am not talking of that sensationalized drivel you see in tabloid news broadcasts. One shouldn't confuse chaos and madness. You turn on the news today, and all you see is chaos: murder, rape, self-destruction... On the other hand," Kain continued, as Roland looked on in utter disarray, "the madness you have inside of you—*true* madness—is subtle. Unlike chaos, it doesn't have to bare its wares garishly, like an old whore on a street corner. It sneaks up on you, so that you don't know it's there. You become *comfortable* with it; it becomes your reason, and you start using it to make decisions." Roland was trembling. "It takes over everything, Mr. Micheaux, and you never realize it. In fact, when men like yourself, Randolph and Marenga—and God only knows how many others—become endowed with enough of this madness, the world of chaos and self-destruction is bound to come crashing down—"

"Look, I'll pay whatever you want!" Roland cried in desperation, but Kain only looked up in surprise, then pity.

"You think this is about money?"

"Look, I'm ready to talk reasonably—I'm sure we can arrange something."

"You think I'm trying to *blackmail* you for a couple bucks?" Kain said, laughing in genuine disbelief.

"Then what do you want from me?"

"I want your *soul*, Mr. Micheaux."

"My *what*?" And, for some reason, he snickered. "Who are you supposed to be, the Devil?"

"Of course," he said, matter-of-factly. At first, Roland laughed, but when the man didn't smile, an eerie shiver went up Roland's spine, and he retreated to another level of numbness—

"You know what's wrong with the world?" Kain went on after a sigh. "Everyone prefers mystery and romanticism to facts." Roland went to shake his head. "That's what's wrong with the fucking world," Kain cursed now, seeming to grow annoyed for the first time. "Everybody's like cigarette smokers. They smoke the goddamn things for forty years, knowing full well how filthy they are, and then when they get cancer, they sue the tobacco companies, saying that they were duped. That's the great loophole of stupidity, Micheaux: seeing your problems as the result of someone else's scheming."

"Look," Roland tried to plead with him—

"No, *you*, look!" Kain raged. "I've been patient with you, Micheaux, but I have some things to say to you, so shut the hell up!" Roland cringed like a scared puppy. "And stop that goddamn shivering!"

Roland, for the life of him, nodded compliantly, wiping away a stream of sweat from his forehead.

"Okay," Kain resumed, trying to refocus himself. "Let's get to the heart of the matter, Mr. Micheaux. It felt good to kill that man, didn't it?"

"*What*!" he squeaked, feeling yet another wave of alarm going over him.

"It felt good to beat that man with your bare hands! Don't lie to me now!" he warned when Roland began looking around nervously, as though trying to hedge. "You got off on it, didn't you? *Well*!"

"—Yeah, I guess," he blurted out, responding more to the insistence in the man's voice than anything else.

"You *guess*?" the man said with a mocking laugh. "You've never felt such freedom before. Even now, what worries you, is not the act, itself, or the consequences, but that you enjoyed it so much: that you were able to slip into it so easily and *totally*."

"No—I'm not like that!" he cried defensively.

"Come off it, Micheaux!" Kain mocked him. "That was the single greatest moment of your life!" Roland shook his head feebly. "You've done something that most people only dream about! For a few seconds, you seized the power of the gods, and are now ready to take your rightful place in society." Roland again shook his head: it was the only thing he could manage. "You're a killer, Micheaux," Kain continued, "just like Candice said. *See*," Kain said now, laughing, "even she could sense the greatness in you. That's right," Kain continued, fully in the throes of his rant, "all the self-destruction you see out there on the streets is a sign that we're on the path to greatness—"

"What are you talking about?" Roland mumbled, looking dazed and wretched.

"I'm answering all your questions, Micheaux: equipping you with the tools to complete your mission. In fact, self-destruction is the most successful product that our society has ever produced, Micheaux. Every time you see a thirteen-year-old gunning down his classmates, you see a successful business transaction. That child has bought a product he's seen advertised all his life! But not only has he bought the product, he

becomes the product—and we in turn become the consumers! We don't tune in to the news merely to be
informed—but to be *entertained*! You said it yourself
when you saw those people waiting outside the banquet:
They're *vultures*, waiting around for scandal and death!
That's how fucked up we've become as a society: we're
reassured when somebody else's life is more fucked up
than ours! But that's the beauty of capitalism, Micheaux:
everything can be commoditized—even death and suffering!"

"What are you talking about!" Roland cried weakly—

"And take note," Kain's voice rose above his, "I'm not
talking about people being brainwashed by TV or being
desensitized to violence—none of that insipid shit! I am
saying that they *need* it, like we've come to think we
need a BMW. In fact, we are no more brainwashed than
one is brainwashed into buying a pair of Nikes!"

Roland blinked slowly—as though doing so required
effort—

"And while there have always been murders and rapes
and all of that, with TV, we have added a new, perverse
element, Mr. Micheaux: an *audience*—a vital consumer
base!" Roland nibbled his lower lip nervously, wondering how the hell he was going to get away. "In fact,"
Kain continued, "if death were on the stock market, its
stockholders would be rich beyond reason! People are
talking about the Internet Revolution: we're in the midst
of the *Death* Revolution!"

"*What are you talking about?*" Roland said in frustration.

"Why do you think the lead story of the evening news is almost always the most violent story, Micheaux? That pulls in viewers—*consumers*! In fact, all the crime and violence and self-destruction you see on TV are no different from McDonald's hamburgers and Diet Coke! They are products, and everyone's buying!"

"*Damnit!*" Roland screamed, unable to take it anymore. "I have *no* idea what you're talking about!" he cried, looking as though he were on the verge of tears. "Nothing you're saying...none of it makes sense! What do you want from me?"

"I'm telling you the facts of life, Micheaux! I'm talking about shit and piss and all the mess you got inside of you! I'm talking about a society that's buying its own destruction: consuming its own filth, and yet can't understand that it's poisoning itself!"

"*So what!*" Roland raged. "What does that have to do with anything—or with *me!*" People in nearby groups were still looking at them oddly; Roland lowered his voice and leaned into Kain. "Look, if you're going to blackmail me, then blackmail me already!"

"Okay," Kain said, laughing maliciously. "You want to be blackmailed? Shut the hell up or I'll tell everyone what you've done!" Roland's face went blank and he seemed to shrink away. "How is that for blackmail, Mr. Micheaux? Close your fucking mouth and listen to what I have to say or I'll ruin your goddamn life! How is that? Do you understand me now?"

Roland stared at the man hopelessly for a moment, then nodded. A stream of sweat went down his temple again, but he didn't even bother to wipe it away.

"Okay, Mr. Micheaux," Kain went on after a sigh, "you asked what this has to do with you. Obviously you haven't been listening to me, but I'll tell you one more time. This society loves raising people up, and loves tearing them down—look at all the celebrity scandals. It's like a kid with those building blocks: building becomes part of the process of destruction—and of *pleasure*. This is our new national pastime—which is where you come in. You're like Michael Jordan, Mr. Micheaux: you can do no wrong—the perfect media object. The only thing is that nobody suspects the madness you have inside." Roland went to shake his head, but was suddenly too weak to do even this. "You've always been at odds with the world, Mr. Micheaux," Kain continued, "—even before they killed your father—but you're going to be the seed that brings all the chaos crashing down. You're a new paradigm, Mr. Micheaux—a new *product*: a kind of Trojan Horse, ready to deliver our blessed madness to a society that is already devouring you whole. You, Marenga, Botswana Glade, Randolph—even Charlotte McPrice, Randolph's opponent in the upcoming election...all of you are part of it...and all those fools out there are going to gobble you up before they even realize what you are—"

Somehow, miraculously, Roland was laughing again.

He put his head back and laughed helplessly. At first, he laughed simply because it occurred to him that Kain was mad. But then, he became lost in the laughter— *trapped* within it. It sounded and looked horrible: it was more like the baying of a wild animal, than human laughter. It shook his entire body, seeming as though it were rending his insides. He had gone too far; and now, he was being consumed by the laughter, the way a lunatic was consumed by his delusions. He now had no idea what was going on around him—and no way of making sense of it.

As expected, Kain stood there calmly, smiling as he watched Roland being consumed by the madness. When Roland realized that he had lost control—and that he had absolutely no idea why he was laughing—he stopped abruptly. When he looked up, the nearby people were frowning at him. Roland had to get away—to flee while he still realized that he should flee! In a last-ditch effort to save himself, he tried to walk off—

"You're not going anywhere!" Kain said, laughing mordantly and gripping Roland's arm. "You've wanted to talk about this all your life—"

"Shut up!" Roland begged. But Kain held him there, seemingly with little effort.

"—Just a little bit more," the man explained, "then you can go." Roland shook his head feebly, like a toddler trying to exert its will. "I'm about to go and do something now, Mr. Micheaux," Kain went on, still holding Roland's arm, "and you need to know why—"

Roland shook his head—

"*Listen* to me, Mr. Micheaux!" Kain demanded. "There's no reason to fear what's coming. In fact, this is a joyous time," Kain continued. "The foundation has already been set; now, all I have to do is play my part and hook them in. I'm going to talk to them like your father talked to them." Roland recoiled. "I'm going to inject myself into the intravenous tube that's filling their veins with the self-destruction and scandal they crave. And being a student of this society, I know that a guaranteed way to get people's attention and hold onto it for at least a few weeks, is to *kill.*" Roland shuddered. "Yes, slaughter as many people as I can—just like those thirteen-year-olds! That's guaranteed to get people's attention, Mr. Micheaux—guaranteed to attract *consumers*!

"I'm going to be the ultimate product, Mr. Micheaux," Kain went on, his face horrible, "—and I'm going to do it through the very violence they're addicted to. And when they gather around to consume me, I'll rip their goddamn heads off. I'll set off the explosion that will clear the way for you and all the others to finish off the job! I'll be everything they want—let them gorge their filthy bellies on me… But I'll be too pure for them," he said with a laugh, "—like heroin right out of the vat. They'll overdose on what I've got: puke out their goddamn guts and burst their veins with what I got!"

And then Roland shuddered as the man began to laugh. It was as though Roland had been hit by a cold breeze that reached some inner place that he had never even known existed. Still, Kain only smiled when he saw that Roland understood on some level. It was then that the man released Roland's arm. Looking suddenly peaceful, Kain smiled and walked away from Roland. Now, the man was navigating his way through the banquet. Roland looked on numbly as he followed Kain with his eyes; then, he shuddered when the man looked back to make sure that he was still watching—

At that moment, the music stopped. The Mayor stepped up on the dais and waved his hands to get everyone's attention. Something churned in Roland's gut when he realized Kain was walking straight for the Mayor! Roland started off in that direction himself, rudely pushing past old ladies as he looked nervously from Kain to the Mayor. The Mayor was talking on the microphone, telling a mocking story about Charlotte McPrice, his Democratic opponent in the election that fall—

"Roland?" It was Candice. She and Phelps were standing in his path, looking at him oddly. However, he pushed past them and continued on his way. His eyes were on Kain, who had reached the dais; and just as Randolph was about to give his punch line, Kain leapt onto the dais. Randolph looked over at Kain confusedly; the bodyguards at the foot of the dais, who were used to seeing Kain around the Mayor, also didn't know how to react. Then, when Roland was no more than fifteen meters from the dais, Kain gripped the stunned Mayor around the neck with one hand. With the other hand, he took a shiny metal object from his jacket pocket and put it to Randolph's head. Kain had had to wrench Randolph's head down, because of the man's height. Some people, like the jazz quartet, instantly realized what was happening and darted for cover; others, perhaps succumbing to the morbid streak Kain had raved about, craned their necks for a better view. Several screams pierced the air now. Roland gasped, unable to move from the spot. *Kain was actually doing it...!* The bodyguards went to attack, but:

"Stand back or I'll do it!" Kain yelled over the microphone. He then giggled as they all backed away grimly. Everyone stared up at him in the sudden silence, unable to quite believe what was happening. Roland was beyond numb. *This is it!* he kept thinking. This was the coup de grace of his descent into madness. Kain made eye contact with him at that moment, as if to confirm this. Kain was about to blow the Mayor's brains out, but it was nothing but Roland's final rite of initiation. This entire night—Roland's entire life, in fact—had been nothing but a prelude to this. He had the feeling that he was floating in an ocean—drifting on the current—and that there was nothing around him for hundreds of miles.

Kain was about to kill the Mayor of New York City— yet, only seconds earlier, the man had been standing with Roland—*touching* him. Kain still gripped the mayor's neck; his grin was still wide and triumphant—

But just when Roland thought he had figured it all out, someone near the front looked up at Kain and whispered, "What the hell is that in his hand?" In response to this, everyone looked up at the implement in Kain's hand, frowning. They had all thought that it was a gun, but—

"It's *him*!" someone whispered in frightened awe.

"Who?" several more people whispered in confusion.

"It's the Hair Jacker," an old man squeaked, just as Kain flipped a switch and started up his clippers. The man laughed out triumphantly then, sounding like a cartoon villain; and then, in two deft swoops, the quickness of which no one could believe, Kain shaved the Mayor's head, leaving only a stubby, misshapen Mohawk.

Jasper Kain is the Hair Jacker...? Roland tried to understand it, but it was all happening too quickly for him. The accumulated bizarreness of the night was too much for his system. Indeed, they all seemed caught in that place, unable to move or make a sound—

Yet, presently, not far from where Roland stood in his dumbfounded daze, there came a booming fit of laughter. Everyone looked to see Marenga squealing with delight. Indeed, the man seemed barely able to remain on his feet. While the Mayor's two burly bodyguards tackled the grinning Kain and dragged him off—and Randolph stood ineptly on the dais, feeling his butchered head— Marenga watched it all, squealing in delight. The man was holding his pendulous gut as though it were going to burst. Tears now rolled down his cheeks as he pointed at Randolph's horrified expression. All Randolph could do was stand there, looking like a naked man who didn't know how to get away from a crowd of onlookers. It all proved to be too much for Marenga when a conscientious old lady tossed Randolph her flowery church hat; and making do, Randolph pulled it low over his head and made a hasty—but utterly unglamorous—exit by way of the ballroom.

Marenga practically doubled over at the sight of it; and by now, dozens of others were forcing back laughter themselves. Unfortunately for Marenga, just before the incident, he had taken a mouthful of hors d'oeuvres (which had been tumbling from his mouth as he laughed). As expected, some of them inevitably went down the wrong way, and he promptly began to choke. A doctor standing nearby recognized all the signs and ran over to help, but Marenga's gut was too big for him to perform the Heimlich Maneuver; and panicking, and weak from lack of air, Marenga fell to the ground, where he lay choking. Seeing him in that position, the doctor decided to improvise, and promptly did a kind of professional wrestling high dive onto Marenga's gut. There was a disconcerting squishing sound, the sound of Marenga hacking, and then the sight of the well-meaning doctor getting up with his face and tuxedo splattered with lumpy green paste.

On that ignominious note, the banquet was concluded.

Roland didn't know how he had gotten outside. Like a sleepwalker, he merely became conscious that he was outside—and that an unspecified amount of time had passed. He was standing against the outer wall of the banquet hall. In the air, there were wailing sirens from police cars and ambulances; flashing emergency lights seemed to be everywhere, forcing him to squint. The sidewalk was packed with hundreds—if not *thousands*— of people. The ones in tuxedos and evening gowns were obviously from the banquet, and Marenga's protesters still had their signs and their strange aura of menace, but hundreds of others seemed to have appeared out of nowhere. Just then, a police van took off from the curb, sandwiched by two police cruisers; and as Roland watched the awe-stricken crowd, he was vaguely aware that Kain was in that van. From the haze of his memories, he recalled how the police had put Kain in there: how everyone had come out to look, standing on the sidewalk as though mesmerized.

As Kain disappeared down the block, Roland wondered what it all meant. Kain had babbled on about the end of the world—and Roland's role as the vessel of madness—and then the man had gone and shaved the Mayor's head. Roland tried to piece together the man's logic, but it was useless. Kain had clearly been insane, and yet, the man had *known* him. Kain had seen him so clearly that Roland wondered if that meant he was insane as well. He remembered how he had tried to laugh at

Kain in the banquet hall, but other people's madness could only be reassuring when one thought one's self totally insulated from it. No, there was some deeper connection between them. Meeting Kain had been like déjà vu. He didn't believe in destiny or second sight or any of that, but there was something about Kain that troubled him, simply because it seemed so *familiar*.

The huge crowd continued to linger outside, even in Kain's absence. As he looked at them, Roland realized Kain had triumphed tonight. Soon, millions would be swept up in the scandal and spectacle of the famous Hair Jacker's capture. Kain had worked his magic, and they were all trapped in his spell. Camera crews were now zipping around, interviewing people and trying to understand what had happened. Yet, all at once, it occurred to Roland that what he needed was not understanding, but oblivion. Kain, the events of the parking garage, Candice—indeed, *everything*—was systematically draining his strength and will. His was the kind of exhaustion that could only be counteracted by total inactivity. He needed to *forget* everything that had happened. He didn't want to think anymore; he was tired of trying to make sense of and reconcile events that seemed as though they had sprung up from hell to confound him—

"There you are!" someone cried; and startled, Roland looked up to see Candice and Phelps approaching. There was a tinge of excitement in Candice's eyes—as there seemed to be in everyone's eyes. "We've been looking everywhere for you," she went on. "Can you believe what just happened!" she said with a little laugh. "And remember how we were just talking about that Hair Jacker, too—how's that for a coincidence... You all right, Roland?" she said at last, scrutinizing his forlorn expression.

"Just tired," he replied. Yet, as he watched them, he knew that he couldn't be around them right now. "...Dallas," he started in a new voice, "you live in Brooklyn, don't you?"

"Sure."

"Can you drop off Candice for me—since you're both going in the same direction?"

"Of course!" Phelps said with his usual good cheer. "My limousine is waiting around the corner."

"You sure you're all right?" Candice went on. "Didn't I see that Hair Jacker guy talking to you?"

"Yeah."

"What'd he say?"

Roland's guts clenched. "Just a bunch of nonsense," he said, avoiding eye contact. At the same time, he looked at the chaotic scene outside the banquet hall, and considered the possibility that Kain really had started something horrible tonight. The man had seemed confident when they talked; Roland remembered Kain's grin as the officers dragged him away. Indeed, as Roland stood there, it was as though he could hear Kain laughing in his head—

"Hey," Candice continued as something occurred to her, "I'm sure the TV guys would *love* to hear what he said to you—"

"*No!*" Roland said with too much force. When the other two looked at him oddly, he quickly went on, "I just want to go home and get some sleep." And then, to Phelps: "You're sure dropping off Candice won't put you out?"

"Of course not."

"You don't mind, do you, Candice?" Roland asked.

"Roland," Candice started again, still looking unsure, "since Dallas has his limousine ready, maybe we should drop you off or something. You can pick up your car tomorrow."

He shook his head. "I'll be fine." He was so desperate to get away from them that he didn't realize what Candice was saying about the parking garage. "I'll be fine," he said again, as if trying to convince himself as well. "I'm just going to go home and get some sleep ... Rosencrantz has been a slave-driver lately," he tried to joke. When nobody laughed, he simply nodded abruptly and walked off. Candice and Phelps stared after him, but he did not look back....

There were so many emergency vehicles and news vans parked in the street—not to mention curious on-lookers—that traffic was hopelessly snarled. At the curb, sitting in the back of an ambulance, Marenga received treatment. Camera crews and photographers captured the entire thing, while reporters yelled questions that

Marenga did not even acknowledge. The man's eyes seemed glazed, and his body seemed deflated. Roland nodded his head as he watched the scene: one way or another, Kain had touched them all tonight.

With the traffic jam, Roland was easily able to make his way across the street. He needed to get away. He was running at last, jogging down the block. A kind of numbness came over him, and he was happy for it. It wasn't until he was in the parking garage, riding down the empty elevator to his sub level, that something vital occurred to him: *What if the body's still there!*

When the elevator doors opened up, he froze. Perhaps a good five seconds passed as he stood there, staring out into the dark, cavernous chamber.

The body wasn't there! At least, it wasn't where they had left it. They had left it right by that column over there, but it was gone. A side of him, suddenly unable to believe in anything without concrete proof, began wondering if the incident had even happened; now that Kain was gone, the man's existence seemed questionable as well.

Roland stood in the elevator so long that the doors began to close. He threw out his arm to trigger the sensors, then he stepped outside. Unfortunately, when the elevator closed behind him, he felt trapped—and alone. The body was gone, but the eeriness of the place remained. His car was parked on the far side of the chamber—next to the ramp and the stairs that led upstairs. Seeing that he would have to walk all the way across the dark, cavernous chamber by himself, he hesitated for a moment. Yet, even when he began walking, his steps echoed horribly in the dark, empty expanse of the place. He kept looking around anxiously, as if expecting a monster to leap out of the shadows. It all reminded him of when he was a kid, visiting his grandmother on the Louisiana bayou. As a city boy visiting the swamp, every bush and vine would either seem like a monster—or a potential hiding place for one.

Now, as he made his way across the parking garage, he realized his heart was thumping in his chest—and that his old childhood fears were coming over him. He kept looking between the cars, as if expecting a monster to leap out—

Get a hold of yourself! he cursed himself for the hundredth time that night. He took a deep breath as he neared his car, but that was when he heard a moan. He jumped; then, looking fixedly at the dimly lit staircase, he realized that a man—*the* man—had collapsed in front of it! Roland froze. In a sense, it was like a nonbeliever seeing the face of God: all doubts fell away, and there was only fear and trembling. He wanted to run away, but something held him there—just like Kain had held him. For the first time, he wished Candice had come along. He didn't want to be alone; but at that moment, a loud moan from the man made it clear that he wasn't. The moan had the strange effect of stifling his panic; and before Roland could think about what he was doing, he walked over to the staircase. The man was lying prone on the ground, dying like an animal. Regardless of what the man had done, Roland knew that he couldn't just leave him there. This, it suddenly occurred to him, was his last chance to redeem himself—to prove that he wasn't some frightened lunatic in the making. This was his chance to fight off Kain and Candice and the ever-present specter of his father, and be a man.

Looking up, he noticed an emergency call box by the stairs. He walked over and picked it up. When a man on the other end of the line answered, Roland calmly stated his name, his location, and the nature of the emergency. When that was concluded, he nodded to himself and replaced the receiver on the phone.

Inside the police van, the siren had a hollow, unreal quality. Kain was chained into his seat, sitting erectly and proudly. Every time the speeding vehicle hit a pot-hole, or swung around a corner, he was jostled and wrenched in the cold metal seat. The manacles were tight, cutting into the soft flesh at his wrists and ankles. Yet, he liked the realness of the sensation—especially after all that had happened.

This was it: the final step in his two-year plan. In fact, the media circus had already begun. The image of Kain holding his clippers to the Mayor's trembling head had been captured by a stationary camera from the banquet hall's balcony. The story was quickly becoming national news. Reporters were still broadcasting from the site of Kain's triumph, getting eyewitness reports. Considering the scope of what Kain had done—and to *whom*, in the end, he had done it—they would no doubt throw the proverbial book at him. Nevertheless, as he sat in the back of the speeding vehicle, Kain began to laugh. If anything, he felt a sense of peace at the thought that there would be no more hiding—no more *running*.

Indeed, soon there would be no more running for any of them. It was only a matter of time before all those self-deceiving fools were shocked back into consciousness. All of society's invisible strings were finally going to be shown for what they were. Even now, their devil-gods were beginning to show their faces; and as their faces became clear, their lies began to crumble under their own weight.

To enter the devil-god's paradise, you needed the latest cars and houses and high-tech gadgets—so that happiness not only had a price, but a corporate logo. And this strange religion told them that there was always something else to be attained and consumed—so that attaining happiness meant that one was never *content*. And getting the latest tantalizing products required power for factories, mines and vast tracts of land for raw materials. Oil needed to be pumped out of the ground; workers needed to be paid or coerced or manipulated into producing the vessels of our happiness. And in their drive to attain this strange happiness, people had developed party affiliations and television shows and commercials to tell them that they were doing all right, or that they could do better. And something was good if it made money, because that meant that someone was being made happy. And the proof of the devil-god's existence was in a gaudy billboard, flashing, "Buy me!" And those who didn't approve, were heretics; and those who realized that they were unhappy, were sinners; and those who set out to find happiness beyond the arbitrary dictates of the economy were un-American, unwise, unrealistic dreamers who had no idea what kept the world running. And those who rebelled against all the invisible strings of society, were either mad or in jail or looked upon pityingly by the rest of society as fools who didn't *deserve* to be happy. All this, Jasper Kain saw, and all this he saw coming to a crashing end—either by his own hand, or through the logical dictates of the cosmos....

The police van swerved around a final corner, then came to an abrupt stop. After the jolt of pain to his wrists and ankles, Kain waited patiently in the darkness. The siren continued for a few seconds, before being cut off. In the relative silence, Kain could hear his own breathing; his heart, while not racing, was beating loudly and steadily. He waited; and then, suddenly, the doors at the back were hauled open. The chaos of the outside world was like an explosion. Kain squinted at the lights; he instinctively ducked down at the sound of dozens of people screaming at him at once. However, after his initial reaction, he smiled. The news had already gotten out that he was going to be there. The voices of the reporters—and of the hundred or so people in the crowd beyond them—rose in the air. The noise was more like the clanging of pots and pans than human voices; nevertheless, the din was like music to Kain's ears; the sight of them filled him with joy—and was yet another sign that his plan was on track.

Presently, two policemen came in and unstrapped him from the seat; then, pulling him up gruffly, they hauled him out into the world. The dark, ugly police station was to his right as he exited. However, the spring breeze was nice and cool on his skin. He smiled at the sensation, seeming like a drunkard as he stumbled along in the manacles. Finally in the light, his beaten, bruised face could be seen. The hematomas beneath his black skin, from when the bodyguards tackled and restrained him, made him seem even blacker—even more threatening. His afro was now a disheveled mess; and as the bystanders looked at the rest of him, they saw that the Hair Jacker wasn't as big and muscular as some of his victims, in their post-traumatic ranting, had claimed. He was actually of average height, and below average weight. Yet, as he had ascended to the status of media star, there was some unaccountable power about him.

The dozens of cameramen were maneuvering for the best vantage points now, seeming like snakes wrangling with one another in a pit. A few of them, in their eagerness, tripped and fell to the ground, almost becoming trampled by their onrushing colleagues. Kain walked proudly before them—the way a general walked before his troops. True, they were still possessed by chaos, but it was only a matter of time before they became co-opted by his madness. These were the ones who would go out into the world and spread the seeds of his religion....

The reporters were now yelling an endless stream of questions at him. Their questions passed him in a meaningless blur—as did their faces; but then: "Will you plead insanity?" a reporter yelled, finally managing to crack the barrier of Kain's consciousness. Still stumbling along, Kain thought about it for a while, then laughed to himself—laughed *insanely*, they would report the next day.

He was still smiling when they finally marched him into the building, and beyond the reach and sound of the crowd. He was satisfied. He had done everything he could; now, all that he could hope, was that it would be enough, and that his missionaries would be true ambassadors of his faith. He was like an arsonist who wanted to burn down an entire forest with one match: the placement of the spark was tantamount—and there were still random factors, like the wind and rain...and Roland Micheaux.

He was being marched through the building now. There were curious police officers standing in the corridors, looking on with the same awe as everyone else. They came out of their offices to get a look at him. There was a strange silence about the place—even other criminals looked at him in awe.

In time, he was brought to an interrogation room. Two middle-aged white cops were there. They were both overweight and stood with their shirt sleeves rolled up to their elbows, and cups of coffee in their hands. They were scrutinizing Kain closely, as though trying to come to some conclusion about him. Kain's escorts made him sit down in a seat before the two cops, then they left. The two cops were still observing Kain closely; after a while, they looked at one another and shrugged their shoulders: obviously he wasn't what they had been expecting—

"Lieutenants Franklin and Parks!" Kain said, smiling again. The men again looked at one another confusedly, wondering how Kain knew them. "You're the leaders of the famous squad set up to capture me. Congratulations are in order, gentlemen!"

On the wall across from Kain, there was a huge mirror, no doubt masking an observation room on the other side, and Kain looked at his reflection. His smile was so strange and unsettling, that one of the officers spoke up to break the uneasy silence:

"You've been apprised of your rights, sir?"

"I have—everything was aboveboard and legal."

The two men again exchanged an odd look as Kain sat there smiling at them.

"Can you state your name for the record?"

"My name is Jasper Kain."

"Are you really the Hair Jacker?" one demanded, jumping to the chase.

"Of course I am."

The two men's faces brightened.

"Did you have any accomplices?"

"Of course," Kain declared matter-of-factly. "My lawyer will tell you all about it."

The two men suddenly seemed crestfallen.

"Your lawyer? Things might go more smoothly for you if we did this without a lawyer."

Here, Kain only chuckled to himself, before declaring: "I have no interest in making things go smoothly. I want things to be as messy as possible."

The two men again looked at one another confusedly.

"Okay," one said at last, "who's your lawyer?"

"Roland Micheaux, of course."

Mayor Randolph sat in the back of the SUV in a daze. When the driver pulled up to the official mayoral mansion, Randolph opened the door and walked into the building by himself. There were officers at the front entrance; he usually joked with them, but today he ignored them and walked in. What had just happened to him was *inconceivable*! He headed for the luxurious dining room, where he would fix himself a drink. The TV was on in the room. At first, he assumed one of the servants was watching it. He was about to ask the offender to leave, when he looked in and saw his wife sitting there. She was an English professor, and had left a week ago for some symposium or another. It was as though he had forgotten she existed.

She was still in her business suit—as though she had just arrived. She was a good-looking woman, but this sparked no reaction from him; even her presence sparked nothing in him but surprise.

"The symposium ended early," she said, staring at him intently.

He nodded; and as he looked over at the TV, he saw that the episode with Jasper Kain was already airing! When he shook his head, he realized that his wife was still looking at his head intently—and that he still had that old lady's flowery hat on. When his wife saw that he realized this, she started snickering.

"You think this is a joke?"

"Even you have to admit it's a *little* funny."

He grunted noncommittally.

She got off the couch and walked over to him: "Let me see your head."

At first, he tried to keep her away—but with a deft grab, the hat was off. Instantaneously, she burst out laughing. He watched her sullenly for a while, as she stood there squealing with the same delight as Marenga,

then he walked over to the couch and sat down dejectedly before the television.

"Come on," she said when her laughter subsided,
"you're overreacting."

"Am I?" he said in annoyance. "Kain was my *head*
pollster! When that gets out...! I can see the headlines
now: Randolph's Policies Steered by Nut Case."

She stared at him for a few seconds, then shrugged
her shoulders, seeing the logic behind his words. Taking
one last sly glance at his head, she sat down beside her
husband and watched the TV as well. "By the way," she
went on, "Lester just called."

"And what does our wonderful son want? More money
to blow on frat parties? Isn't school over yet?"

"Yes—he's going to Mexico with some friends for the
summer. Anyway, that's not why he called. He saw the
Hair Jacker thing on TV—"

"In *California*?"

"Yeah, it's showing on CNN."

"Goddamn!"

"Alex...look, the story will go away eventually. It's
only because they've been chasing that guy for two
years now. He's become a kind of folk hero all over the
country."

"It's on *CNN* already," he said in disbelief. "Images of
me getting my head shaved by a man who was not only
a lunatic but a trusted aide, are being shown all over the
goddamn country."

"It could be worse."

"How could it *possibly* be worse!" he exploded. "Why in the hell do people say stupid shit like that. 'It could be worse,'" he mocked her.

"I'm just trying to be helpful, okay."

"Well, you're not helping!" he said, getting up and going over to mix himself a drink.

"Well..."—she searched for something hurtful to say—"the world doesn't revolve around you, Alex!" she screamed at last, getting up and marching out of the room. Looking at her go, it suddenly occurred to him he had never loved her. It wasn't that he hated her, but that he didn't have any intimate feelings for her. Twenty-five years ago, he had married her because she was the type of woman a man should marry: beautiful, intelligent...but he had never really loved her. He had married her for the same reason someone bought a Volvo station wagon: more out of considerations of security, than passion. They had acted toward one another the way married people were supposed to act; but in the end, it had all been an act. Coming on the heels of all that had happened that night, the realization was harsh. For a moment, he wondered if this entire Hair Jacker thing had pushed him over the edge in some way, but he knew that it wasn't so. On some level, the reality of his marriage had always been clear to him. Now, for the first time, perhaps in his entire life, he was overcome by a feeling of loneliness—and *fear*. All at once, the glib, confident politician with the readymade answers and sparking smile fell away. Like a newborn baby, he looked out on the world with fresh senses and new appetites. Even though political necessity demanded that he get out and have a press conference as soon as possible—to put a political spin on the events of the night—all he wanted to do was stay here and have a few drinks in private. For the first time in decades, he looked at the world not as a politician looking for votes, but as a man in search of his soul. It was this sudden change that put him on the path to ruin.

Roland got up from the ground when he heard the sirens coming down the ramp. He had been sitting on the ground—in his new tuxedo—staring at the shabbily dressed man. At first, the man had breathed shallowly, and Roland had watched his ribs expanding with each breath, but Roland was not sure the man was still breathing anymore. He could have checked the man's pulse, or tried to rouse him, but he had suddenly been terrified of touching the man.

The ambulance came down first, followed by a police cruiser. Roland glanced at his watch: it was a little after eleven o'clock. As the paramedics rushed out, and the two police officers strolled up to survey the situation, Roland instinctively stepped away from the body.

"Do you know the victim?" a paramedic asked as he rushed to examine the body.

"No—he was lying there when I got here."

Looking at his tuxedo, one of the officers asked: "Hey, you just come from the thing across the street?"

As Roland nodded, the man's partner said, "It's a *madhouse* out there! It took us fifteen minutes just to get down this block alone."

Working frantically—but with a precision that came with practice—the paramedics turned the mugger over and placed him on a stretcher.

"Goddamn!" one of the cops yelled. "Somebody really fucked this guy up!"

"—Hey," the other cop interrupted, scrutinizing Roland, "ain't you somebody famous?"

The first cop looked at Roland as well, his face brightening: "Yeah, he's that lawyer guy: Roland something or another—"

"*Micheaux*," his partner corrected him. Roland nodded distractedly while the officers smiled at their accomplishment. It was as though they had just won at charades. In the meanwhile, the two paramedics were still working frantically—

"We found a wallet," one of the paramedics declared.

"Give it here," said an officer, "—I'll run a check on him." The officer took the wallet and was about to go back to the cruiser to do a check, when—

"He's got a gun, too!" announced the same paramedic. Roland only then remembered that Candice had put it in the man's pocket after she wiped it down—

The officers were suddenly sober. The officer with

the wallet had started to walk back to the cruiser, but stopped abruptly, and came back.

Roland felt like he was going to faint—

"Any gunshot wounds?" an officer asked the paramedics.

"Not that we can see—but he's really messed up. His pulse is weak."

And then, turning to Roland, an officer asked: "You see anybody else when you got down here?"

A wave of alarm went over Roland! He concentrated on keeping his voice steady: "No, only him."

"He say anything to you?"

"No, he was just moaning—that's the only reason I noticed him."

"Well, lucky for him that you came along. He looks like—"

The paramedics had ripped the man's shirt open; the officer's partner had been frowning at the man's bony chest, on which there was a tattoo.

Suddenly, his eyes grew wide: "Hey, Vinnie! I think I know who that guy is!" He pulled an ID out of the wallet in his hand, his eyes growing even wider. "It's Lamar Smith!"

"*The* Lamar Smith?" asked his partner, "—you *sure*?"

"Yeah! Look, that's his chest," he said, pointing at the tattoo of a 1970s pimp with a fuzzy, wide-brimmed hat and bell-bottoms. "And I got his wallet—his *driver's license*."

"*Jesus*!" the man said, realizing it himself.

"What...?" Roland said, confusedly.

"This guy is about the biggest drug dealer on the east coast," one of the officers explained.

"*Him*?" Roland said, dubious.

Just then, the paramedics rushed Smith and the stretcher to the ambulance, leaving the other men standing about.

One of the cops went on: "Yeah, we busted his entire operation last week, but he managed to escape somehow. We froze all his assets, arrested about fifty of his gang members, and have been keeping tags on everyone he knows. He's been wandering about, trying to hide and survive...*robbing* people."

"I guess he wasn't a real good mugger!" his partner said, laughing.

"I guess not! This is a damn good night: first that Hair Jacker weirdo, and now this guy!"

While the men laughed, Roland nodded his head, exhausted beyond reason.

When the paramedics secured Smith in the back of the ambulance, and slammed the door, the police officers headed for their cruiser. One of them turned back then:

"Hey, you have a card or something—in case we need to get in touch with you for testimony?"

Roland numbly got a business card out of his wallet.

"Thanks a lot!" the officer yelled, before rushing to the cruiser to follow the ambulance.

Roland was left standing there by himself. But he didn't want to be alone again—especially down here. He quickly went to his car and pulled out after the police cruiser. *Was it over*? he wondered. Probably not... there were so many complications. A *world* of maddening complications... And what if they called him to testify at Smith's trial...! He was still somewhat proud of himself that he had called the ambulance—even though he had lied to the policemen. Yet, the complications set off alarm bells in his mind. If there was any consolation, it was that Candice had been right about the police reaction to Smith. Once the men saw that criminal record, nothing else had mattered....

At the front entrance of the garage, the nervous-looking attendant waved the ambulance and police cruiser through. Roland drove up to the man slowly and stopped to pay his bill.

"Nothing like this ever happened before!" the attendant felt compelled to inform him. It was a pimple-faced white kid, probably just out of high school. "We're a pretty safe garage."

Instinctively, Roland found himself saying, "Don't you have surveillance cameras or anything?"

"Nah," the kid said absentmindedly, "—too much space to cover, I guess."

Roland nodded his head equivocally. "...How much do I owe you?" he said, handing over the ticket.

"It's on the house," the kid replied, distractedly looking in the direction of the street. "What a crazy night. The street's still blocked from that Hair Jacker thing."

Roland nodded again, then moved on.

Like the kid had said, the street was totally blocked. He couldn't believe it: thousands of other people had joined those already there, so that the entire block seemed to be a solid mass of traffic and people. After honking his horn for about five minutes and getting absolutely nowhere, he looked up to see the two cops from the parking garage coming through the crowd! He froze, like a fugitive seeing his captors closing in. His first thought was that Smith had come out of his stupor and told the police everything. However, as the men neared his vehicle, Roland saw that they were smiling. One waved at him; dazed, Roland waved back.

"Thank goodness we caught you! On the other hand," the officer continued, gesturing over his shoulder, "you weren't going anywhere anyhow."

All Roland could do was stare.

"The call just came over the police radio," the other officer continued.

"What?" Roland managed to mumble.

"You're wanted at the precinct."

Roland felt *sick!* So this was it!

"Yeah, something to do with the Hair Jacker."

"*Kain...!*" Roland whispered. Had Kain told them what Roland had done in the parking garage!

"Sorry about this," one of the officers continued with

an apologetic laugh. "Just follow us out—we have the cruiser waiting—we'll give you an escort."

"What about Lamar Smith?" Roland managed to ask.

"Oh, *him*," one of the officers said in an offhand manner, "he's dead."

"*What!*"

"Yeah, like I said before, somebody *really* fucked him up—but no bother."

"Just follow us," his partner continued, "—we'll get you out of here."

Roland nodded.

Smith was dead. Roland had *murdered* a man! It was too unreal to be true. He had killed a man, and now the police were taking him to see Kain! He felt sick to his stomach; his hands were trembling so much that he could barely hold onto the steering wheel. The two cops were directly in front of his car, waving people out of the way, and Roland had a sudden impulse to stomp on the accelerator and run them both over. He shook his head to chase away the thought, but he felt *trapped.*

People were everywhere. He felt suddenly claustrophobic. *And he had killed a man*! The realization ripped through him again, making him want to retch. All the hysteria of the banquet hall was coming over him again. There were too many things to deal with at once—too many *complications!* It only seemed to be a matter of time before everything came crashing down around him....

The police had led Roland out to their cruiser, and

now he followed their car as they inched their way through the crowd. He felt like he was following his jailer to the scaffold. What the hell did they want him for! What had Kain *said* to them! Kain was manipulating him like a puppet—even from behind prison walls. Roland banged the steering wheel in frustration, but there was nothing to do but follow the police cruiser....

They were free of the crowd at last. Roland didn't know whether to be relieved by the freedom or disconcerted by the fact that that freedom only meant they would reach Kain quicker. He had an impulse to make a turn at the next corner and zoom away from the police. Desperate, he realized he would do *anything* to keep Kain from touching him again. Yet, he couldn't help thinking that Kain's mark was already on him. Like Cain of the Bible, Roland seemed marked by the inescapable will of God. An hour or so ago, when he left the banquet, he hadn't thought he could feel any more drained and disillusioned, but he was falling into a bottomless pit of horrors....

Roland flinched when he saw the huge crowd waiting outside the police precinct. It was as though they were all waiting around to see a rock concert. There were even vendors along the sidewalk, selling ice cream and t-shirts and all sorts of incomprehensible things! He realized, all at once, that these people had come to hear Kain's words—just as the man had said they would. The man was a *celebrity* now. Most of the people would probably be happy if they simply caught a *glimpse* of him! It was all happening like Kain had said; and now, right on cue, Roland was being summoned to play his part.

They parked in front of the building; and just like in his childhood memories, Roland was given an armed escort up to the entrance. The crowd was *huge*; camera crews were everywhere. They came up to Roland, yelling questions, but the officers pushed them away—and Roland was too dazed to decipher what they were saying. He stumbled along, seeing the excitement—indeed, the *madness*—that Kain had already inspired in these people; and he knew, all at once, that somehow or another, he had to stop Kain from speaking to them. He had to *silence* Kain, and somehow keep the madness from escaping. The thought set off more hysteria and alarm bells in him, and he groaned, shaking his head.

It was now a quarter past twelve, and the night had no end in sight. He was finally marched through the entrance. Officers were standing there in full riot gear... Roland walked through the police precinct in a daze. The two officers finally brought him to the observation room—which looked out, through the one-way mirror, on the interrogation room that held Kain. The sight of the man made Roland's stomach churn. There was a camera set up in the observation room, taking in Kain's every motion. There were also about five men sitting around in the dim lighting, watching Kain in awe. Kain was the only one in the other room, smiling contentedly as he stared into the mirror. It was as if there were no partition, and the man could see them all clearly. Roland glanced at the man, then looked away nervously.

"Roland Micheaux?" one of the men in the room asked. All of the men were getting to their feet now, as if awakening from a trance.

"Yes," Roland replied, swallowing deeply.

"Do you know why we called you?"

"No..." His voice was horribly hoarse.

"Do you know Jasper Kain?"

He again swallowed deeply: "No...not really..." He groaned nervously, realizing that he had no poise. Still, he went on: "He came up to me at the banquet tonight—that's the first time I met him."

"So you aren't his *lawyer*?" one of the men said with a hopeful smile.

Roland paused for a second; but seeing the lieutenant's smile, he instinctively smiled as well. "*Me*?"

The men in the room were laughing now. "—Just what we figured, Mr. Micheaux."

Roland nodded equivocally; but then, one of the officers asked, "What did Mr. Kain talk to you about?"

Roland's stomach convulsed; he felt slightly faint, but he forced himself to remain calm. He took a deep breath of air, releasing it slowly. "He said that I was all part of some plan," he began when he had scrounged together enough composure, "—and that he had been keeping an eye on me for two years... And then he went and shaved the Mayor's head."

The men in the room suddenly looked at one another

and began to chuckle amongst themselves. Roland again looked on confusedly, until one revealed: "Kain seems to be under the impression that you were one of his accomplices—"

"*Me?*" Roland said again; and as the other men continued to laugh, he suddenly found himself joining in. Like back at the banquet, he needed to laugh. His mind worked feverishly, telling him that he could use this. The more insane Roland made Kain seem, the less they would believe him if he told them about what Roland had done to Smith. He felt so very filthy then: he had killed a man, and now he was lying to protect himself. Still, there was no other way to get out of this. He was still laughing with the officers. It was the way he had laughed after Candice told him that she was a murderer: he was pulled in by the thing, and *trapped.*

When the laughter began to die down, and the other men began talking amongst themselves, Roland walked up to the glass and stood watching Kain—who was still smiling confidently. *What the hell are you planning, Kain!* Roland's old fears came over him again. There was some incomprehensible power about the man. Roland couldn't deny that. One only needed to look at the man to see it. Kain was like a restless, insane spirit. He couldn't think of Kain as a man anymore. Kain wasn't flesh and blood: he was a vapor—an aroma—rekindling memories of far-away places and distant, long-forgotten dreams. All at once, Roland's father flashed in his head—

"Don't let him speak," Roland blurted out then.

The men at his back looked up confusedly from their conversation.

Roland turned to them: "Don't let Kain speak," he repeated. "He's only doing it for the attention—that's one of the things he told me. All he wants is the publicity...he's *nuts*." And then, when the cops smiled to themselves: "I think he was stalking me or something," he went on quickly.

"Yeah, exactly what we figured!" Then, with a smile, "No need to worry: that guy will be spending a couple of decades in a nut house for sure. We just called for a psychological evaluation."

Another of the men made a joke then, and the offers began to laugh again. Yet, Roland couldn't be intoxicated by their laughter anymore. The best he could manage was to nod his head gravely.

"Thanks for coming to see us so promptly," a detective started in a tone that said the interview was over.

"Actually, I got a police escort," Roland said, trying to smile.

"Well, we spare no expense around here. Have a good night, sir."

Roland was getting ready to leave, when he was called back: "Hey, you have a card or something—some way we can reach you if we have any questions, or need you to testify?"

A wave of numbness came over him. "Sure," he said,

getting out his business cards for the second time that night. When that was done, the detectives again gave their thanks. Yet, as he was walking out of the room, he glanced back at Kain, who was still sitting there patiently, smiling. *What the hell are you so confident about!*

At least they were going to lock Kain up. Something about the idea of Kain locked away somewhere, unable to wander the streets, calmed him somewhat. Nevertheless, while he walked down the corridors of the precinct, a hysterical internal voice asked him if a restless spirit could be confined by walls.

A flashback of all the night's events drained even more of his strength. He was acutely aware that he wasn't the same man he had been just six hours ago. He had killed a man; and even now, as he walked through the police precinct, he realized he feared Kain not as a *man*, but as the reincarnation of his father....

The crowd outside was still boisterous—and it seemed to be growing. A few reporters, seeing Roland coming out of the precinct, rushed up to him, but he had nothing to say. He was exhausted beyond reason. He drove off aimlessly, his mind in the obligatory daze of the night. It wasn't until he was halfway across the Brooklyn Bridge that he realized he was going to see Candice. He didn't want to be alone tonight, and Candice was the only one he could call.

Unfortunately, that was when something unsettling popped into his mind. About a week into his relationship with Candice, they had been making love. It had been their second time in all, and the entire act had still been heightened by the excitement of nuance. She had been on top of him, riding him with wild abandon, when she cried out, "You want a slut, don't you—a real cheap whore!" Before he had been able to say anything, she had purred, "Well, I'm the bitch for you: no strings, a real good fuck...so you can get your rocks off!" She had said all of this while she galloped on top of him; but when her words finally reached him through the shroud of sex, he had instinctively pushed her away.

"What's wrong, baby," she had purred again, "I'm only being what you want."

"That's not what I want," he'd said, gruffly.

"Oh?" she'd said, smirking....

The entire sequence of events probably passed through his mind ten times as he drove down the Brooklyn streets. And, as thoughts of pathological sex swirled in his mind, he suddenly found himself remembering how he had lost his virginity. A loud, obnoxious girl from his neighborhood had seemed to do it out of spite, groping him in the fetid basement of their tenement. It had been early fall, a few months after his father's execution. That same afternoon, right after they were finished having sex, she had gone out of her way to tease him before all the neighborhood children. Then, looking at him pointedly, she had laughed at the very notion that a woman would ever see him as a sexual prospect. While

the neighborhood children laughed, and her triumphant, vindictive eyes bore into him, it had occurred to
him that it was not even that their moment together—
their supposed intimacy—meant nothing, but that she
had allowed it just to point out this very nothingness.
All those years ago, when he slumped back to his room
to escape their laughter, it had occurred to him that
receiving emptied the soul more thoroughly than taking; because in receiving, you were inevitably forced to
let down your defénses and open up your soul.

What it all meant, however, Roland had no idea. The
only thing he knew for sure, was that he didn't want to
be alone tonight. On this strange night of murder and
madness, he had been reduced to the level of a child,
afraid of the emptiness of his bed, and the ghost-like
images that kept flaring up in his imagination. In fact,
he was so desperate to drown his thoughts that he
turned on the radio, putting up the volume so high that
he could feel the music vibrating in the steering
wheel....

His mind was relatively blank when he entered
Candice's block. It was about one-thirty in the morning
now. He turned down the radio and was looking for a
parking space, when he looked up and saw a figure step
out onto Candice's stoop. Suddenly numb, Roland
drove past to make sure, but there was no doubt. *It was
Phelps!* The man's limousine was double parked in front
of the building; and for a moment, the man stood on the

stoop with his tuxedo jacket held in his hand in an impromptu fashion, and his unbuttoned shirt hanging out of his pants sloppily. From the way the man's hair glistened in the light, Roland realized that he had just taken a shower—no doubt to wash off the scent of sex before he went home to his wife. Roland saw all this in a matter of seconds, and sped up the car to make the yellow light at the intersection.

RANDOM ACTS OF VIOLENCE

Two months later, it was now New York City's hottest summer on record; and with much of July and all of August still to go, it only seemed that things would get worse. Every day now for over a month, there had been reports of people dying from heat strokes and acute respiratory attacks. People were more short-tempered and on-edge. Passing incidents, which would have resulted in a shouting match a few weeks ago, now regularly ended in deaths and trips to the emergency room.

Scientists of all sorts emerged to offer theories about the heat. They warned of exhaust from car-jammed city streets, and drifting pollution from distant states. They demonstrated how the summer sun was cooking up all the airborne filth, producing chemical reactions that should have been left to test tubes. They designed elaborate computer models, showing how heat was being trapped near the surface by the noxious clouds. Yet, the longer the heat wave lasted, the more people began to suspect that it was not the work of science alone. They stared up at the smoggy skies with a kind of pagan awe;

they whispered when talking of the heat, as if terrified of the works of their god.

Even when nighttime came, and the sun and the smoggy skies faded into the darkness, the heat and uneasiness remained. With all the pollution, the night sky was a reddish brown, which grew darker and more menacing as the night went on. Scientists offered theories about this as well, talking about longer summer days and the illumination of the smog banks by the moon— but the people had lost their faith in science by then.

The odor of the small Brooklyn apartment was a nauseating combination of stale sweat, stale perfume, stale semen and whatever was rotting in the dark, unkempt recesses. Everything from candy wrappers to used condoms lay trapped in the dust piles on the floor. The place was *filthy*—yet people came here to live out their fantasies.

Six months ago, when Nikolai Andropov finally gave in to the urge to take a woman, he had told himself that he only came to this whorehouse to remember his wife. That was a lie. His wife of twenty-five years was back in Russia—along with their four children; and after a year in New York, away from them, he knew he could not care less if he ever saw them again.

He had been a university student in Moscow when he met his wife. She had been a frail fourteen-year-old when he saw her loitering around a local market. He had introduced himself with a joke that had made her smile. After talking to her for a few minutes, he had bought a bottle of vodka from the market and taken her to a third-rate movie. They had gotten drunk, groped one another in the fetid darkness of the theater, then stumbled off to a smelly alley to do their business. Two minutes into their impromptu courtship, they had been set upon by the police; and in the police station, Andropov had discovered that his new girlfriend's father was a high official in the politburo, who demanded that Andropov make "an honorable woman" out of his daughter. So that, as they say, had been that.

Whether it was his party connections, or his scientific prowess, Andropov had eventually become a respected chemist. He had accepted his comfortable life without thought, and allowed himself to believe he was happy. Unfortunately, when the Soviet Union tore itself apart, people like him had become refugees of history. When his government-funded research lab had shut down for lack of funding, he had found himself jobless and without prospects; indeed, his entire life had unraveled so quickly and easily that it had been as if none of it had really happened.

Still, Nikolai Andropov had always been a dreamer. For most of his life, his great dream had been America, itself. His conceptualization of America had been like a thirteen-year-old boy's idea of the women in *Playboy* magazine. The promises of America had been like the smiling models spreading their legs within those glossy pages. Everything had seemed easy—and *accessible*—in America. Thus, it had perhaps been those masturbatory fantasies that drove him to make a deal with the Russian mob a year ago. They had smuggled him across the Atlantic in the cargo hold of a rusting ship. At least a thousand others had made the journey; at least five of them had died en route, and had been thrown overboard when their corpses were discovered.

Yet, even in those cramped, filthy quarters, Andropov had had his dreams. He had kept thinking of all that he would do when he reached New York. He had kept telling himself that he would quickly be granted citizenship, given his university background. While other passengers had lain prone beside him, retching from tubercular attacks, he had imagined the entire world rising to applaud his scientific discoveries.

But those fantasies were dead. Now, as he groped the whore in the darkness, the layer of sweat between them seemed like sticky muck. Every few seconds, like clockwork, she let out a dutiful, "Oh yes," in a thick Belorussian accent. Those two words of English were perhaps the only ones she knew—and the only ones that she would ever need to know. She had the plump face of a babushka-wearing peasant. There was a gap in the curtains, and light from the streetlamp outside highlighted her face. He guessed she was about twenty at most, but her face was a dead mask. Even while he rattled the bed with his exertions, he knew she was dead inside. The mob had preyed on all their fantasies, and now they were slaves. With his knowledge of chemistry, Andropov now spent his time "cooking" various illicit drugs for the syndicate. The woman beneath him, who had nothing to offer but her body, was also required to repay the syndicate that had brought her to the land of her fantasies.

Just then, the woman feigned pleasure by writhing beneath him and uttering another dutiful, "Oh yes." However, as Andropov watched her, she seemed like some tortured spirit caught between life and death. He had a sudden impulse to put her out of her misery—to choke her and throw her out of the third-story window. The thought made him nervous; he pumped his penis into her more savagely now, hoping to trigger the pleasure or forgetfulness—or whatever this act was supposed to cause. The bed was rattling horribly now. That din rose above the sickening sound of his sweaty body slapping against hers. Her droning cries of, "Oh yes," which were supposed to spur him on to the fulfillment of pleasure, only mocked him.

With all this going on, he did not initially notice when the pimp started banging on the door and yelling at him in Russian. Maybe an entire minute passed before he acknowledged the voice and cursed: "I'm almost done!" But what was he supposed to be *doing?* Looking down, he saw that the whore was now staring into the corner blankly. The farce had gone on so long that she did not even feel the need to *pretend* to moan in pleasure. It was obvious that neither of them was feeling anything.

Yet, the banging on the door, and her continued indifference, made the panicky feeling grow within him. He had a sudden impulse to strike out; the thought of putting her out of her misery—of putting them *both* out of their misery—gripped him again. He was pumping into her viciously now, and she accepted him the way a broken horse accepted its rider's urgings to go faster. The bed was creaking horribly; outside the door, the pimp was cursing loudly...but it was all without meaning—*senseless*. Andropov was now sweating so profusely that his entire body was slipping against the whore—

"That's enough in there!" the pimp screamed. Andropov swore viciously and gnashed his teeth in a final, all-out attempt to derive some fleeting pleasure out of the whore's body; but a few seconds later, when he saw his goal was nowhere in sight, he let out a final curse and rose from between the woman's legs. Finally free of him, she turned over and pulled a filthy sheet over her numb body.

The pimp was still banging. Out of breath, and slightly light-headed from having breathed the putrescence of the room for an extended period, Andropov almost passed out as he stood up and groped in the darkness for his things. The pimp's curses grew louder—

"I'm coming!" Andropov screamed in anger, then grunted at the annoying irony of the words. He needed to be away from the whore—away from this room and everything it represented. In a few seconds, he had on his pants and shoes; he was just buttoning up his shirt when he opened the door and looked out.

The lighting in the hallway was dim—*shady*; the paint was peeling from crumbling plaster walls, creating a heightened impression of desuetude. The first face he saw was the pimp's. The man was an emaciated, middle-aged man about average height who had the pallid complexion and scheming eyes of a Gestapo agent. To be an enslaver, one either had to be without conscience, or hate those whom one had to enslave; sometimes, one attempted the latter to achieve the former. Whatever the case, the pimp glowered at Andropov before walking away. Now stepping up were two men whose presence made Andropov's stomach twinge. The men had achieved the consonance of both looking like stupid gangsters and actually being that. They had everything from the black suits—notwithstanding the heat—to the slicked-back hair.

"What the hell do you two want?" Andropov demanded, closing the door behind him and stepping farther into the hallway. He glanced at the cheap digital watch he had bought in Chinatown, seeing that it was just past nine o'clock.

"We need someone to make a delivery," started one,

producing a package that Andropov knew contained drugs.

"*Me?*" he protested. As the feeling of outrage grew in him, he blurted out: "I was a university professor!"

"—But now you're a delivery boy," joked the other goon, at which time both thugs laughed. Andropov glared at them with a snarled lip.

"Don't be angry, pops," jibed one of them. "We brought you a little present." At that, he produced a smaller package. All of a sudden, Andropov's expression became more contrite. He first took the bigger package; then, with a guilty quickness, he took the other.

The two men watched him slyly, then smiled. One of the goons then proffered a handgun from his pocket. At first, Andropov shook his head, but then he accepted it begrudgingly. Looking up at the two grinning men, he had an impulse to put a bullet hole in each of their smug faces....

He walked out to the car—a huge, 1977, gas-guzzling *tank* of a Dodge. *How the hell had he come to this?* No: he couldn't think about that now. He had to keep on going: keep rushing on, as if fleeing from thought, itself... The red, menacing night sky made him uneasy for some reason, so that he grimaced and walked faster.

However, plastered to the dumpster by the curb, were campaign posters for Charlotte McPrice—the woman who was to face Mayor Randolph in the upcoming mayoral election. As he always did, Andropov stopped and looked down at the poster, somehow captivated by the comely woman on it. "We're Americans, damn it!" declared the inscription above her smiling picture. That rallying cry had swept her to a landslide victory in the Democratic primary; but now, as Andropov looked down at the poster, her self-assured smile only seemed to mock him. He moved on.

As soon as he had settled himself in the car, he retrieved the smaller package and took a pinch of the white powder—just a little to tide him over and bring the amnesia back. Outside, the night was sweltering, but nowhere near the hell of the apartment. The stench of the whore was still on him... When he sat back in the seat, the gun dug into his back. He took it out and looked at it oddly, hefting it in his hand....

When he started up the engine and drove down the block, he again felt the stirrings of something horrible in his soul. He couldn't even begin to fathom what impulse had brought him to the whorehouse, but he sensed it was something dark and self-destructive. His mind hovered on the threshold of that darkness, before faltering. Besides, the white powder was beginning to work its magic.

Presently, he was driving through the Coney Island section of Brooklyn, where many Russian immigrants had settled. As the drug flowed through him, the streets all blurred together; after a while, he saw only flashes of multi-hued light, streaked against a backdrop of incomprehensible darkness. He smiled for no good reason then, and sat back in the seat, enjoying the sensation of vapidity.

In time, he found himself driving through the slums, watching the blacks and Latinos as they congregated on the streets. With the heat wave going strong, those without air conditioners were almost compelled to stay outside—where the air at least had the illusion of circulating. To his right, some kids were playing in an open fire hydrant, dancing with glee in the heavy spray that flew into his window and wet his pants. Andropov looked at them intently, startled to realize that there was a strange kind of joy about them. He looked at their dilapidated tenements doubtfully, suddenly convinced that their joy had to be a sign of stupidity. When a soul became dark and troubled, other people's joy was always jarring. There was a gross injustice somewhere: the ignorant, worthless people of these slums were rightful Americans, while someone of his intellectual stature was a criminal, hiding in the shadows. The injustice made the hate surge in him.

That was when a laughing kid ran out into the street, chasing a ball. Andropov's car was a good half a block away from him, so the boy chasing the ball wasn't totally reckless. However, Andropov's mind was blank as he watched the kid's smile—and as he watched that smile die. In that strange moment, the only clue that the car was speeding up, was the higher pitch of its engine.

The world again became a place of blurred, streaking lights. There was a low thud, as the car mowed down the kid—then a louder crash as the body flew over the hood, splintering the windshield. The body flew over the car then, and disappeared into the darkness. After that, there was only the whining pitch of the engine as Andropov sped into the night. The red light at the intersection of course meant nothing to him by now; and so, still locked away, he crashed into the car that had the right of way. The sound was like an explosion; the steel and glass around him seemed to blow apart in every direction, leaving him toppling through a void. Even with his seat belt on, he banged his head against the steering wheel. The explosion of pain in his head was like the explosion all around him.... And then, for a long moment afterwards, it seemed as if there were only silence—*nothingness*. It seemed so peaceful—and *sudden*—that he hoped that it would last forever. Unfortunately, the driver of the other car came around and started cursing him through the open window. It was a young black man, and his brand new BMW was now a pile of twisted metal. It took Andropov a long time to acknowledge the man; but when he did, he got out of the car with a calmness that the black man must have taken for shock—or contrition.

When Andropov had shot the man in the face, he didn't exactly know. He was aware only of the echoes of the shots—and the sight of the bloody corpse, which he looked down at, still feeling nothing. This horrible numbness—the same feeling he had felt as he pumped his penis into that whore—was all about him now. For a moment, he thought he would be trapped in it forever, but the angry mob was coming up the street now.

The people of the slums were descending upon Andropov now, with hate and madness in their eyes. With cold efficiency, Andropov rose the nozzle of his gun and fired into the mob—into those worthless scum who had the nerve to be Americans! Some fell to the ground and others scattered in horror; but still others continued to charge, gripped by the injustice of it all. Against the backdrop of the red, menacing sky, the images were unreal. However, the gun was soon empty; and as the most incensed of the mob continued to charge, it was only a matter of time before they were upon him. Whatever it was that Andropov felt then, he did not exactly know. Maybe it was terror—maybe even regret at the realization that he had just killed several people and a child. Whatever it was, he was soon smiling as he felt the first blows of the mob and thought, *Yes, my friends, help me to forget it all!*

Little did Roland Micheaux know that the seeds of his destruction were being sown in the Brooklyn streets. While the people of the slums were spilling out into the streets to take their revenge, Roland was in Manhattan, sitting in the back of a cab. Even though the cab's air conditioner was broken, and the heat was unbearable, he rested his head against the back seat and smiled. He had had a good day; and as his smile widened to a grin, the Pakistani cab driver watched him suspiciously via the rear view mirror. Roland's designer suit had initially put the cabby at ease, but one always had to watch one's fares for the slightest sign of insanity.

It was just after 9:30 when the cab darted somewhat recklessly down Broadway, toward Greenwich Village. Yet, driving in New York City required a certain amount of recklessness. Drivers who only drove on peaceful country roads had no business driving in New York. Navigating the big city required a certain amount of viciousness. In fact, the cabby had almost crashed three times: twice into jaywalking pedestrians, and a third time into another cab—which had swerved across the road to pick up a passenger. Roland's cabby had had to stomp on the brakes; but even then, something about it had made Roland laugh out loud, as if he were drunk.

Just this afternoon—just *hours* ago—Roland had settled a huge, multimillion-dollar class-action suit! He had just left the press conference, where he had undoubtedly been the star. A nationwide hamburger chain had sold hamburgers tainted with E. coli bacteria, and twenty people, most of whom were kids, had died. The company had settled out of court for one hundred million dollars, catapulting Roland into a new legal clique.

Now was the time for celebration, and that was why he was headed toward the little cabaret in Greenwich Village—where the men of his firm always congregated after a court victory.

On top of everything, Roland was going to be appearing on network television tomorrow morning. He was feeling good—*invincible*. Jasper Kain, and all that had happened in the spring, was out of his system now. Kain was locked away in a nut house, and Lamar Smith had long been forgotten by anyone who matters. Indeed, with all of Roland's startling success, the events of that spring night seemed like ghosts from a passing dream. Even as the cabby zoomed through an intersection where the traffic light had changed from yellow to red a second before, Roland smiled to himself. That smile was still on his face when the cabby came to a screeching halt in front of the cabaret.

Yet, when Roland exited the car, the oppressive heat seemed to collapse on him like a building. His frame literally bent with the weight of it. When he glanced up at the red, menacing sky, he frowned for the first time, probably only then noticing it. It was one of those weird signs, which people either ignored or heeded as omens; but as this was the time for celebration, Roland put it all aside and walked up to the cabaret.

From outside, the place looked like a fine restaurant—with an awning and a plush red carpet leading up to the door—but Roland smiled to himself, knowing that it was all a façade.

While in the Brooklyn slums, terrified parents ran out into the streets, desperately looking for their children, Roland entered the establishment. The bouncer, a black man of gargantuan proportions, recognized him immediately and smiled. Roland shook the man's hand and walked on. However, on the threshold of the huge chamber, he stopped for a moment, just taking it all in. The most discordant thing was the strobe lights: everything seemed to be moving in slow motion. The place was as crowded as usual, with about five hundred people, and Roland always felt somewhat claustrophobic upon entering it. There were several stages scattered haphazardly about the place, with women in varying stages of undress capering about as if in the throes of demonic possession. In addition to that, scantily clad women were everywhere, either gyrating in the men's laps or serving drinks. The music, a cacophonous techno mix, was ear-splitting. The clientele either sat there in a daze, stupefied by drink, or screamed out and leapt about, as if they were having seizures. There was a kind of panicky laughter everywhere, and something about it made Roland's skin crawl. Those professing to be religious would call it a pit of sin; but from where Roland stood, it seemed worse than that. It was a pit of forgetfulness—of make-believe—where women pretended to be something that they were not, and men pretended to want something that in their heart of hearts, they knew was not real.

With the strobe lights, it was difficult to make out

faces; but eventually, Roland's eyes came to rest on Dallas Phelps. When they did, he felt an uncomfortable twinge in his stomach. He had been feeling that twinge for weeks now. On the surface, it seemed to be nothing but jealousy and resentment—things that were supposedly beyond a man of success—but it was more than that. Phelps had been a kind of mentor to him. Roland had gone to firm galas at Phelps' million-dollar brownstone in Brooklyn Heights, feeling genuine awe—even *envy*—at the opulence. Once upon a time, even Phelps' home life had seemed, for lack of a better word, "perfect." The man had a young, beautiful wife called Cindy, and a sickeningly sweet, three-year-old daughter called Mindy. In fact, Cindy and Mindy dropped by the office to "see Daddy" so often that Mindy had gotten into the habit of calling Roland, *Uncle* Roland! With all that, Roland used to find himself thinking, *Phelps has everything a man can want.* ...But it was all lies.

It no longer bothered him that Candice had slept with Phelps—especially since he was no longer seeing her. However, the thing that troubled him was that he now suspected she was Phelps' full-time mistress!

After he stopped returning her calls, Roland had assumed that would be the end of it; but about a month ago, at the office water cooler of all places, Phelps had come up to him and announced that Candice was now his daughter's live-in nanny! Roland had spilled an entire cup of water on himself!

As for the coupling of Phelps and Candice—and their new living arrangements—that was just sick. In fact, it seemed too unreal to be true. He kept thinking that maybe he had gotten everything wrong: that there was nothing sexual between Phelps and Candice. He tried coming up with scenarios to explain why a freshly show-ered Phelps would be coming out of her apartment. Maybe Candice ("a poor Grenadian girl here on an expired student visa," as she had described herself) was just working for Phelps—and nothing more. He was almost desperate for it to be true. He didn't love Candice—and he didn't want her back—but he cared enough for her to know that he didn't want her to end up as some middle-aged married man's slut.

Roland sighed. He wished he could forget about it—the way he was forgetting about Kain and Smith; but every time he looked at Phelps, he felt the discomfort of someone who knew things he didn't want to know.

While in the Brooklyn slums, the rioters inadver-tently began to turn on their own kind, Roland began to make his way toward Phelps. The man was sitting by himself, at a small table right in front of one of the stages, dancing in his seat with a bottle of beer in one hand and a wad of bills in the other. Once upon a time, that image would have been somewhat comical—if not shocking—but not anymore.

Roland's face was grim as he neared the man; how-ever, when he finally got there, something occurred to

him, and he looked around in confusion. No one else
from the firm seemed to be there. When Phelps noticed
Roland standing there, he smiled vapidly and went back
to ogling the woman. Roland's frown deepened:

"Where is everyone else?" he said (he had to yell with
all the noise).

Phelps only gestured with his head for Roland to sit
down next to him, in the seat that the man had obviously
been saving. Then, after Roland had complied, Phelps
leaned over to him, but kept his eyes on the naked
woman as he announced: "I wanted you *all* to myself,
Micheaux."

The man's breath reeked of beer and his eyes were
glossy and dilated from all the drinking he had already
done.

Roland's face unconsciously soured. "What?" he said,
fighting to understand.

"I sent everyone else away, Micheaux," Phelps replied,
still ogling the woman.

While in the Brooklyn slums, one of those searching
mothers was knocked senseless by a youth who, staring
at her intently, finally recognized his own mother,
Roland sat there confusedly. He definitely didn't want
to be alone with the man—especially in this drunken
state. That was when something else registered in
Roland's mind: what had Phelps meant by, "I wanted
you *all* to myself, Micheaux"?

Phelps now had a simpering grin on his face as he stared

at the stripper. Following the man's gaze, Roland watched the gyrations of the huge-breasted, bleached blonde woman. After a few seconds, he realized he was more amused than aroused by her nakedness. As for the strippers, they all seemed fake. Their bodies were all so similar that it was as if they had come out of the same mold—or at least the same plastic surgeon's office. Eighty percent of them had breasts that were so obviously fake that it was, upon reflection, revolting to think that women were willing to have their breasts cut open and propped up with sacks of gel, just to get the dollar bills that these fools stuffed down their panties—

"Yes, indeed!" Phelps said out of nowhere, turning to look at Roland's startled face, "—the patron saint of our firm!"

"Huh?"

"Don't be bashful," the man said with a slurred laugh, "you doing us good, Micheaux."

Roland smiled in response, but mostly at the fact that Phelps' drunkenness had allowed his southern accent to slip out: usually, the man sounded as if he had been born and bred in Cambridge, Boston.

"Lawyers," Phelps started again, slurring his words slightly, "...nobody has faith in us: they're just waiting for us to fuck up. Well, you know what I say?"—he leaned in closer, staring intently at Roland with his glossy eyes—"I say *fuck 'em, too!*" At that, he howled with laughter. Phelps was apparently one of those good-natured drunks. Some men got morose when drunk; some, like Phelps, became congenial and talkative. The man patted Roland on the shoulder then, going on, "But you're not like other lawyers, Micheaux! I've been keeping an eye on you. Yes, sir, you been moving up—both in and out of the firm. And you gonna be on TV in the morning, too, right!"

Roland had been looking on in bewilderment, wondering how he was going to get away; but at Phelps' prompting, he responded: "Yes, sir, that's right."

"Well, see now," Phelps said with a glowing smile, "that's just what we need: lawyers like you, doing pro bono work and such, helping out the community."

"I suppose."

"Don't be bashful, Micheaux!" Phelps said, patting him on the shoulder again; Roland winced at the repeated touch. "Now, if it's one thing I can't stand," Phelps went on, "it's bashfulness—especially in someone who has no need to be. You been hanging with these northern boys too long. You and me, we're just two southern boys here with these Yankees. They're bigger and faster, but they ain't smarter, are they!" He said with a drunken laugh. "They don't know about the ways of the world, like us southern boys. These northern boys got all the tools," he howled, suggestively, "but don't know how to use 'em, do they!"

"I suppose not, sir," Roland responded flatly.

"Now what you looking so troubled for!" Phelps said,

sizing him up. "This is supposed to be a *celebration*, ain't it!" he bellowed, patting Roland on the shoulder once again, this time with a lingering squeeze. He called over a scantily clad waitress then, belting some slurred orders at her. When he was done, he looked at the stage again. Apparently the stripper had done something he liked, because he screamed out suddenly and flung a one hundred dollar bill at her. The woman snatched up the bill, flashed him a suggestive stripper smile, and began gyrating with even more enthusiasm.

Roland was just beginning to think he had been given a reprieve, when Phelps again turned to him and said: "You ever read Edgar Alan Poe, Micheaux?"

"...Some," Roland said, unable to keep from smiling at the strangeness of the question in a strip joint. Roland wanted to say, *Is that who you think about when you look at naked women?* but he checked himself.

"Brilliant writer," Phelps began, staring dreamily at the stripper again, "...wrote about perverseness—about folks doing precisely what they shouldn't do...almost about people going out of their way to fuck up their lives. A *brilliant* writer...would have a field day with our times. *Perverseness*—the desire to go out and do something you *know* is wrong. It's the ultimate thrill ride in modern times," he said, turning to Roland again. "It's like when you talk to some of the faggots today and ask them why in the hell they keep fucking one another up the ass"—Roland grimaced at the image—"...some will say some bullshit about they were born that way; but then, there are others who will be honest and admit it: who will say: 'Because getting pussy's too goddamn easy!' Too *easy!*" he said, laughing. "It's all a thrill ride, Micheaux: playing chicken with fate."

While in the Brooklyn slums, the rage threatened to reduce the world to ashes, Roland fidgeted in his seat. Luckily, that was when the waitress came up with two drinks on her tray. Phelps salivated at the sight of the woman; and when she put the drinks on the table, he caught her and whispered something in her ear, so that she giggled. Phelps then felt her buttocks with one hand; and with the other, he reached into his pocket and brought out another hundred-dollar bill. Roland watched as Phelps folded the bill with his free hand—Roland was actually quite amazed by Phelps' dexterity!—and inserted the bill in the crotch of her panties. At that, she caressed his face and walked off. Phelps stared at her retreating buttocks; Roland did as well, and not without appreciation—

"Come back here with me, Micheaux," Phelps said suddenly, getting up.

"*Sir?*"

"There are back rooms here—*you* know...more private."

Roland got up feebly, the consternation registering on his face.

"Don't forget your drink," Phelps called over his shoulder.

Suddenly numb, Roland picked up the bottle of beer and followed his superior. There was a curtain in the far corner of the room, which was manned by a guard. The guard nodded knowingly at Phelps as they passed. Beyond the corridor, there was a dimly lit corridor, lined with about eight doors. Phelps walked to the second door on his right. He was about to open it when the door across the corridor opened. Roland, who was standing at Phelps' heels, turned with Phelps when the door opened; and there, standing in the doorway, was a tall black man in an elegant suit. Time seemed to stand still; Roland's jaw dropped!

It was Mayor Randolph!

Roland froze; Phelps took in the scene with a nonchalant shrug of his shoulders, and chuckled. "How's it hanging, Alex!" he joked; and then, while Randolph twitched in shock and embarrassment, a young bleach blond woman (they all seemed to be blond in this place) came out of the room. She was so petite that she easily passed by the rather tall Randolph. In fact, she was perfectly at ease as she winked at Phelps and Roland; then, within seconds, she brushed past them and walked back into the main chamber of the strip joint. They all turned and watched her.

When she was gone, Roland and Phelps looked at Randolph again; but as if fearful of their eyes, the Mayor fled in the opposite direction from the woman—out the secret door hidden at the far end of the corridor. There was a brief glimpse of the alley as Randolph made his hasty retreat.

Phelps chuckled then, declaring: "Now I know why I voted for him!"

"That was the Mayor...!" Roland said in disbelief.

"Of course it was—and why shouldn't he be here!" Phelps said, as if outraged. "If President Clinton can get blow jobs in the Oval Office, why shouldn't our own venerable Mayor be able to get one in a strip joint!"

"...The Mayor," Roland said again, still numb. And then, as the reality of it filtered through his mind, "That's probably why his wife's leaving him."

"*Fuck* his wife!" Phelps cursed as he opened the door with a practiced ease and walked into the small chamber. "Man wasn't meant to screw one woman all his life!" he went on.

As he was still in shock, Roland wasn't really listening; accordingly, his mind was elsewhere as he followed the man into the room. The room's illumination came from a red light—no doubt to give it that perfect ambiance. However, as it reminded Roland of the night sky, it only deepened his uneasiness. Something about the light was mesmerizing—or maybe it was only the residual effects of seeing the Mayor of New York City coming out of a room with a hooker. Whatever the case, it was only after Phelps closed the door behind them that the voice of panic reawakened within him.

He looked at Phelps warily as the man walked calmly

over to the couch against the wall—the small room's only piece of furniture—and sat down in a calm, leisurely manner. Still standing by the door, Roland felt like he was trapped in a bizarre nightmare. Now that he was within the cramped room, its effluvium almost made him pass out. The stench of stale beer and cigar smoke commingled, nauseatingly, with cheap perfume and vomit. He felt light-headed and sick—

"Did I ever thank you for introducing me to Candice?" Phelps said from the couch.

Roland was seeing spots before his eyes now, squinting in the strange lighting to keep a wary eye on Phelps. "...No," Roland said at last, distractedly.

"She's been a *godsend*!" Phelps said with a strange gleam in his eyes.

Roland wondered if this was Phelps' way of boasting that he was screwing her. The man was smiling at him, and his ease and confidence disturbed Roland. It reminded him of the smirk that Candice had had on her face all those weeks ago, and he didn't want to think about that night. He had to get the hell away from this place! He needed some fresh air—and *space*! And as the strangeness of the last ten minutes re-exerted its force, he again remembered what Phelps had said in the beginning, about wanting him alone. His mind tried to go to it, but he had neither the strength nor the patience. He had the sudden sense that if he didn't get out of here soon, he would be done for! It was the same eerie feeling he had felt when Kain gripped him that spring night. *Just get the hell out of here*! a voice screamed within him; he was about to take a step toward the door, when Phelps broke in:

"You ever had a *white* woman, Micheaux?" At that, Phelps crossed his legs in a professorial manner and looked up at Roland earnestly. Yet, the question was so abrupt—so strangely unsettling—that Roland was left dumbfounded. Phelps laughed at the expression on his face, saying: "Getting a white woman ain't nothing, Micheaux—not like in your daddy's day!"—*Roland* winced; Phelps went on—"In your daddy's day, a black man taking a white woman...now, that was perverse—in *Poe's* language, I mean. You ever think about that, Micheaux: taking a woman like your daddy done—"

"*What*...!" Roland blurted out.

"Don't be so squeamish there, Micheaux," Phelps said with a laugh—

But just then, two women—one of whom had been the waitress that Phelps groped—came in. The room was so small that when they entered, Roland was forced to move over to the other side of the room, where Phelps and the couch were; nonplused, he sat down beside the man, unconsciously cringing as he stared at the grinning women.

Phelps let out a drunken laugh then, declaring: "Yes, indeed, it's time to *celebrate*! All hail Edgar Alan Poe and perverseness!" With that, he giggled and nodded to the women, who started slobbering over one another and grabbing one another's breasts.

A resurgent wave of panic and revulsion went over Roland, leaving him numb for those first few moments. While Phelps watched the women intently, Roland stared ahead blankly, feeling himself falling deeper and deeper into the abyss. It again occurred to him that he hadn't felt this way since that spring night—

"Here, it is for us, Micheaux," Phelps spoke up then, "—a perfect laboratory before our eyes. Now, why you figure they're feeling up one another like that?" he said, feigning confusion. "Lust?" he queried, before shaking his head. "Don't make me laugh...that's a human ploy: ascribing everything we don't want to understand—all *perverseness*—"

"Stop this, Dallas," Roland said in a voice so low and menacing that he barely recognized it as his own. Phelps stopped and looked at him oddly; Roland gestured to the two women, who continued to grope one another, oblivious. "What are you trying to prove with all this?" he went on, "—that all people have their price?" His voice became gruffer then, "You trying to *blackmail* me with some bullshit about my father?"

"*Blackmail?*" Phelps stared at him, incredulous, then laughed in genuine amusement. "—About some shit your daddy done twenty-five years ago!" His laughter was so hearty that Roland felt foolish. "You been watching too many bad television mysteries, Micheaux!" Phelps went on, laughing so hard that there were tears in his eyes now. "Nah, Micheaux," Phelps said with a strange zest, "this is about *science*: about the scientific method and experimentation. It's about that age-old question"— he leaned in closer to Roland, still reeking of beer as his hand moved up Roland's thigh—"why do people do the sick shit they do!"

Something horrible stirred in Roland! Phelps was just about to burst out laughing when Roland leapt up and hit him in the jaw. Phelps went flying to the ground. The commotion finally freed the women of their strange lust, because they cried out and cringed against the wall.

Phelps' mouth was bloody and hanging loose; he tried to get up, but couldn't. He lay moaning on the floor while Roland stood above him, trembling with rage. And that was the same beast that was rising to ascension in the Brooklyn slums. Upon seeing it, the terrified women gripped one another in terror. Roland was in a realm of pure rage now, where there were no consequences. The vengeful voice of the beast cried out for more blood. It yearned to leap at Phelps—to *obliterate* the man. The beast in him wanted to say fuck it all! Fuck his career, his life—all of that nonsense, and *kill*. However, at that moment, the women cried out; and upon seeing their terrified faces, some emergency brake was triggered in his mind. He looked about confusedly for a while, utterly lost, until he saw Phelps collapsed on the ground.

He had just knocked out a partner in his firm! Something in him died away as the full extent of it hit him; and with that death, he was finally able to see the precipice before him. It was Lamar Smith all over again! Smith and Kain and his father were reincarnating themselves everywhere. Roland looked down at Phelps in horror, glanced at the cringing women—who screamed out again, as though fearful that he had intentions of coming near them—then he fled.

The rest of the strip joint passed him in a blur; actually, he escaped through the same hidden exit that Randolph had used, perhaps feeling all the horror that Randolph had felt; and then, he was out on the street, first walking, then running at full speed. *I'm running away again*! he thought, about two blocks later. He stopped then, leaning against a lamppost to support his suddenly frail body. He was panting and sweating profusely, trembling as the reality of what had just happened passed through his mind. However, Charlotte McPrice's self-assured, smiling face was looking up at him from the poster on the lamp post, declaring that they were Americans, damn it! And seized by a resurgent wave of dismay, he moved on.

They pummeled Andropov's unmoving body, even as the police sirens sounded in the background. That pummeling seemed to be the only way to exorcise the demons—both within Andropov, and themselves. While both parties survived, there could be no sanity. Destruction was their only salvation. There was something otherworldly in the air: screams that didn't sound as though they could possibly come from human beings. The people ran out into the streets and saw their loved-ones' unmoving bodies reduced to the level of gutter trash. Those sights pushed them over the edge: What had started with the hit-and-run killing of a young boy, was escalating wildly out of control. They were setting cars on fire now. They attacked anything that was standing—anything that seemed to represent stability and "the system."

A garbage can was thrown through the window of an all-night diner across the street; and then, some of the people rushed in and began raiding the cash register. The police found them in this state; the ambulances and fire engines arrived, but feared entering into that chaos. Some of the people became incensed, because the paramedics were just standing there, refusing to help their loved-ones. As their rage grew, they attacked the paramedics as well. The police, seeing this, pulled out their guns. Unfortunately, that didn't mean anything to the people anymore. Even Andropov didn't mean anything to them now. They left his bloody, unmoving body and ran off wildly, in search of more destruction. One man, who had just lost his son, was shot in the face when he ran up to a policeman with a baseball bat in his hand.

Nothing could stop them now—except death. The more they destroyed, the more they felt the need to destroy....

The white neighborhood was a few blocks over: they were going there now, to show those people what it meant to lose everything. The police were beginning to see that firing their guns into the air had no effect. Terrified by what they saw before them, they lowered their guns, pointed them at the charging mob, and fired... just like Andropov.

Mayor Randolph stumbled down the city streets in a daze. On some level, he felt everything that the city felt: all the pain, terror and madness of the Brooklyn slums. Either he was going mad, or he was becoming sane so quickly that the shock was too much for his system. His mind was a chaotic jumble; a mocking voice was blaring in his head, telling him that it was all over.... Earlier that evening, when he snuck away from his bodyguards at that mid-town charity benefit and made his way down to the strip joint, it had been as if a demon had possessed him. He had run out into the night, transfixed on the idea of filth. He had wanted a *filthy* woman, as though desperate to hasten the end that was the inevitable consequence of the last few weeks. He had met the hooker at the strip joint through an escort service a week ago; and tonight, he had run to her, not merely driven by lust, but madness. He had called her on his cellular phone, and she had told him to meet her in the alley behind the strip joint. They had groped one another for a while behind a huge dumpster. It was incredible how much the insanity of it had turned him on. There had been people walking out in the street just a few meters away, and rats crawling about in the garbage.... It had been the woman who protested: who had told him to come into the strip joint, where there were private, air-conditioned rooms. They had entered through the secret door....

Randolph felt sick! Of all the men to run into: Roland Micheaux and Dallas Phelps! *Wait until the media hears about this!* he kept thinking. In this scandal-obsessed country, it was only a matter of time before they brought him down. He felt like one of those deformed movie monsters, fleeing from the village peasants.

While in the Brooklyn slums, police cruisers were being set on fire by the mob, Randolph wrenched off his jacket, as if feeling the heat. He kept trying to figure out when he had lost it all; and every time he searched his soul, Jasper Kain sprang out from the emptiness within. In fact, ever since Jasper Kain shaved his head and made him a laughingstock, everything had come tumbling down. It was inconceivable how far he had fallen...! The image of him standing on the dais in shock as he felt his shaved scalp, had been an *international* joke. For weeks after the fact, late-night talk show comedians had done entire acts on him. Foreign dignitaries visiting City Hall had eyed his head—which, in the initial aftermath, he had shaved completely bald—with a knowing slyness. In the first two days alone, he had dropped twenty points in the polls to Charlotte McPrice! That tiny pebble had torn a gaping hole in reality, setting off a chain reaction; and now, boulders were rumbling down the mountain. All of a sudden, everything had seemed to go wrong: his career, his marriage...the very values that had given him the drive and foundation to reach the top of the mountain.

Still, he had tried to fight Kain's madness at first. Even when he saw everything he had worked for slipping through his fingers, he had laughed at those initial urges, telling himself that he would never act on them. He had laughed at himself the first time he called that phone sex line—and when, a few days later, he called up that massage service. But the more he laughed and shook his head, the more his self-indulgent mid-life crisis had gripped him. And initially, that was all it had seemed to be: a mid-life crisis, triggered by the fact that he was now a laughingstock. As strange as it seemed, he had been reassured by the thought that he was only joining the ranks of other self-absorbed, foolish men, who had achieved some measure of success and stability in their lives, but were now eager to risk it all for something base and transient.

...How that prostitute's underwear ended up in his jacket pocket, he couldn't remember. His wife had found it, and confronted him, and he had had no excuses ready—no words at all. Yet, before then, he had explored filth so carelessly that it had been like playing Russian roulette. A few days ago, he had called up that ten-dollar-a-minute phone sex line, and heard himself asking the panting woman on the other end what kind of panties she was wearing. Yet, he had known, while she breathed heavily into the phone, describing their laciness—and their sudden dampness—not only how ridiculous it all was, but that he was addicted to that very ridiculousness. Even after his wife left him, and set a scandal in motion by filing divorce papers, he had been unable to stop. His only thought had been to fling himself headlong into the filth, in some desperate kamikaze act to either save himself from Kain's madness, or succumb to it totally and know the nullifying peace that lay within its depths.

He no longer even tried to pretend he was sane—he had gone too far for that. Every few seconds, he saw the stunned faces of Micheaux and Phelps, knowing there was no going back.... He groaned in the darkness and stumbled down the sidewalk.... A bum sleeping in the mouth of the upcoming alleyway ended Randolph's reverie. As Randolph was about to pass by the alley, the man gave a resounding snort, then woke up, screaming: "Eureka!" It was a grizzled white man, who looked like some old prospector who had been up in the hills sifting gold for the last twenty years. The man looked around wildly, leapt to his feet, then ran up to Randolph, demanding: "I need a dollar, mister."

"...What?" Randolph said, distractedly.

"I need a dollar!"

Randolph looked him over, saw nothing but an old bum probably thirsting for a bottle of cheap wine, and went to walk off.

"I know you got money, mister!" the old prospector shouted, stepping into Randolph's path. "Guys like you always got money!" He started patting Randolph's pants pockets—

"Get the hell off of me!" Randolph cursed, finally coming to his senses.

"Give me a dollar!" the old man demanded again. "I *know* you got it!"

He then went for Randolph's pockets again. There was something wily about him. Randolph was bigger and stronger, but the old man was as nimble as a fox. Randolph tried to grab him and fling him away, but the man kept darting out of the way and reaching for Randolph's pockets.

Finally having had enough, Randolph lurched at the man and tackled him to the ground. But even then, the man leapt to his feet, leaving Randolph on the ground. Just as Randolph got back on his feet, the old prospector took out a rusty knife. The prospect of a street fight suddenly reminded Randolph of being a kid in the ghetto again: of being the kid who could take on anything—the star athlete, the magnet for the young girls—

The old man slashed at him with the knife! Randolph

barely managed to leap out of the way, but the tip of the blade sliced him across his chest. He backed away, staring down at the cut in disbelief. It was a flesh wound, but as he was sweating profusely, it stung.

"You should have given me that dollar, mister!" the old man warned, coming at him again.

"A dollar!" Randolph screamed hysterically. "You want to kill me for a goddamn dollar!"

"We could have done this the easy way, mister, but you had to be all stingy!"

"What are you, a crackhead!" he cried in bewilderment, still backing away.

"Hell no!" the man said, as though outraged by the allegation, "I need it to buy a lotto ticket!"

"*What*!"

"See, I was dreaming just now," he explained, "and my Great Aunt Emelda, she gave me those numbers. Twenty-five million dollar jackpot this Saturday! Emelda, she was always *real* good to me... So I got to get me a dollar to buy that ticket!"

Randolph looked on in disbelief. "Here!" he said at last, hurriedly taking out his wallet from his jacket (which he still carried in his hand) and grabbing the first bill he saw. "Here's twenty dollars; buy *twenty* tickets!"

The old man grabbed the bill greedily, then a huge, hideous, toothless grin came to his face as he held it before him. Satisfied, he disappeared down the alley, whistling merrily. Randolph watched him disappear, then leaned against the wall in shock. He had almost been killed because an old nut wanted to buy a lotto ticket...! Maybe tomorrow—or whenever he was sane again—he would laugh at it; but in his state of mind, it simply seemed like more of Kain's doing. Another devotee of Kain's madness had accosted him, and they had merely exchanged salutations.

Yet, as bizarre as his thoughts were, he had a sudden suspicion that he was not the only one thinking them. There had to be others like him out there—others at the vanguard of Kain's madness. Out there, there had to be a chosen few—soul mates of a sort—wandering about aimlessly, trying to discover the route back to their sanity....

His chest was still bleeding, but to hell with it. He stumbled down the street, still unable to believe how far he had fallen. Was he the Mayor of New York City? It seemed too farfetched to be real. He was a man of the gutter now: a man who needed darkness and filth to survive. He saw a clean-cut young white couple coming down the sidewalk, and crossed the street to avoid being seen. At the curb, a homeless man was collecting alumi-num cans and bottles from the garbage can.... Randolph moved on with haste.

While in the Brooklyn slums, SWAT teams arrived to combat the spiraling violence, Randolph suddenly realized he didn't have a home to return to. His wife had moved back into the townhouse, and Gracie Mansion (the Mayor of New York City's official residence) was too big and empty to be of any solace. However, City Hall was about seven blocks away; and now that he thought about it, that was the only place he had to go. He set off down the block, but his mind was in a daze, and his pace was languid—

His cellular phone had already rung four times before he noticed it was ringing. He had forgotten that he was even carrying it. In fact, the only people who had ever called him on it were his wife and his little brother; and with divorce proceedings in effect, it had probably been about a month since it had even rung! With everything that had happened that night, he was so desperate for even the illusion of the love he had had with his wife, that he convinced himself she was the only one who could be calling. Maybe she wanted to reconcile! He was like the Prodigal Son in the Bible now: after exploring filth, he was suddenly desperate to go back home to everything he had turned his back on. When he answered the phone, his voice was breathless and eager:

"*Hello?*"

"Hello," said a woman.

The voice was too high and young to be his wife's, and his spirits crumpled. "Who is this?"

"Don't you recognize my voice?" the woman said with a laugh.

After a frown, Randolph shuddered: *it was the stripper*! He recalled that he had given her the number after he met her through the escort service! It seemed hopelessly stupid to him now, but during those weeks of filth...!

"What do you want?" he managed to whisper.

"Is that any way to talk to me?" she said with an inscrutable laugh, "—especially after the beautiful night we shared?"

"...Why are you calling?" he said. He stopped on the dark street, looking around nervously, as though fearful someone might have overheard.

Again she laughed, and went on in a confident, menacing voice, "I'm calling because I like the sound of your voice, Mayor. I like talking to you."

He paused for a moment, more uneasy than ever. "What do you want to talk about?"

"I want to talk about my needs."

"Your *needs*?" he said in a faint, monotone voice.

"You know," she explained, "—the usual: a nice place to live, a little something in the bank for a rainy day...."

For some reason, Randolph chuckled. It was the laugh of a man at the end of his limits. "And if I don't?" he asked, a side of him genuinely curious.

"Well," she went on casually, "you'll be surprised to hear that there are cameras in all those little rooms in the strip joint. That's why I made you come inside—to get some security. See, now it isn't simply your word against mine. I have *evidence*—"

The phone had slipped from Randolph's hand, but he didn't realize it at first. He stood there, with his empty hand against his ear, looking pale and distraught. He saw, in that instant, that he was totally at her mercy. The blow was so severe that it was like having an "out-of-body" experience. Everything seemed to be going in slow motion—indeed, he was able to look down in time to see the phone smashing against the pavement. He looked down in awe, seeing it shattering into half a dozen pieces—

So this is it! he thought at last. Indeed, he couldn't think of anything else. A side of him was probably relieved that the proverbial die had been cast, and that he wouldn't have to be afraid of ghosts anymore. However, he still felt gutted, knowing there would still be a long, painful ride to the bottom. He left the shattered phone where it was and walked on with a stiff, feeble gait.

While in the Brooklyn slums, all the inadvertent devotees of Kain's madness rose up to destroy the world, Randolph stumbled across Broadway, finally entering City Hall Park. *How the hell had it come to this*! he wondered, like Andropov had wondered just an hour before. He was so numb that it was now as though time had stopped. The outside world was like the blurry background of a dream. He heard nothing, saw nothing... was aware only that he was moving, and that his life was over—

"Hey!" a gruff voice screamed. Randolph had just climbed over the barricade, which, for anti-terrorist purposes, now surrounded City Hall. Two officers were now running up, their guns drawn. Randolph stepped numbly beyond the barricade, as though he hadn't heard them. "*Freeze!*" the men screamed. Yet, at that moment, an insane voice blared in Randolph's mind, telling him to run—or move his hands aggressively—so that they would gun him down and put him out of his misery.

"*Don't move!*" the officers yelled again; finally stopping, Randolph watched them disinterestedly. They came up to him, their guns pointed at his head. Randolph continued to look up at them with a bizarre nonchalance as they told him to keep his hands where they could see them; but just then, in turning his head, his face was at last illuminated by a street lamp—

"*Sir*...! We didn't know...!" The two men stood there trembling, making excuses that Randolph neither heard nor cared to hear. He waved his hand in a distracted manner and walked into the building. Other guards, hearing the disturbance, came running; but when they saw Randolph walking by with his shirt bloodied by the cut, they only stared confusedly.

Maria Santos sat on the edge of the news van's passenger side seat, watching her cameraman anxiously as he sped down the Brooklyn streets. She wasn't anxious because she thought he was going too fast, but because she was sure he wasn't going fast enough! They had heard the story over the police radio about thirty minutes ago:

there was a full-blown race riot in progress! As she sat on the edge of her seat, she let out a squeal of excitement that was almost orgasmic.

The way they were rushing, it was as though they were paramedics speeding to an accident scene. Yet, she found herself hoping that the ambulances hadn't arrived yet: that she would get there in time to see the dead and dying lying on the ground. She found herself hoping that the police hadn't quelled the strife yet, and that the gleam of mob violence would still be in the people's eyes. It was like finding a treasure map and hoping someone else hadn't already dug up the treasure. Yet, after twelve years as a roving reporter on New York's streets, Maria Santos knew all the tricks of treasure hunting. As she repeatedly reminded herself, she was not only a woman in a man's world, but a swarthy minority woman who was approaching middle age, in a youth-obsessed society that had an anorexic swimsuit model as its ideal. So what if she had to "put out a little ass" every once in a while to get a story or placate her boss? What if she had had to have a couple of plastic surgeries—not to mention liposuction and a tummy tuck? This was the way of the world. You either had to put out or get out. It wasn't that she didn't have jour-nalistic integrity, but that she was honest about what it was that she did. She was a *slut*, and her johns were viewers who couldn't get enough of her hard-hitting investigative series on the disastrous mistakes of penile enlargement surgery. That one had been a masterpiece, producing her most memorable line: "Choose your doctor carefully, lest you end up with the short end of the stick...."

Her exposés on suburban housewives turned street-walkers, and the sex cult operating out of a city council-man's basement, had catapulted her to nationwide acclaim. Some said she went too far, but Santos' worry was never of crossing some mythical line, but of not going far enough! Besides, if she didn't do it, then someone else—someone younger and prettier and less constrained by social guilt—would.

As her sense of excitement grew, she looked over at the cameraman and barked at him to drive faster—to run red lights if necessary! All her life, she had had to content herself with other people's scraps. A story like this would make her career. If she managed to be the first on the scene, the entire smorgasbord would be hers for the taking. A quivering smile came to her lips now, as she thought of all that was to come. Unfortunately, when the cameraman turned the corner and entered the blocks of the rampage, about five ambulances and fif-teen police cars were on that one block alone. About three fire trucks were there as well, extinguishing a burning building. The dizzying array of flashing lights made Santos squint as she looked gloomily down the block. The police presence was *massive*: they had defi-nitely learned from the L.A. riots. They had hit the people hard and fast, with overwhelming force, so that they wouldn't be emboldened by the freedom of rioting.

Dozens of people were lining up to be put in police vans. In the air, over the sirens, there were intermittent gun shots; and a few blocks down, it seemed like everything was engulfed in flames: cars, houses... Against the backdrop of the red, menacing sky, it would have all been perfect, if not for the fact that several other television crews were already on the scene. She saw them darting around, interviewing the stunned populace. When she looked up, she saw two news helicopters hovering overhead, giving a bird's-eye view of all the chaos. Then, as she sat there staring, another news van zoomed past.

"*Shit!*" Santos cursed out loud as she came to her senses and gestured for the cameraman to move in fast. *Scraps again*!

For the first few minutes, Roland was in shock. He walked down the city streets as if he had just seen the Devil. He was walking up Broadway, toward his midtown condominium, but he felt *lost*. With the heat, he had wrenched off his jacket. He now carried it balled up in his hand, like a rag. His shirt was soaked with sweat. When he instinctively took a deep breath to calm himself, he coughed: the city air was thick and foul, leaving an aftertaste in his mouth. Worse, his mind kept replaying the scenes from the strip joint. None of it seemed possible! Had he really been on the verge of *killing* Phelps? Had he really left the man bloody and unconscious on the floor? Had all that really happened? Roland looked down at his right fist as he walked: his hand was still sore. He flexed it nervously, and noticed it was trembling.

While on television, helicopters gave bird's-eye views of bands of looters breaking into cars and any open businesses, Roland stumbled up Broadway. Somehow, something quintessentially sacred had been desecrated in him. He looked at smiling couples walking hand in hand, and wondered about their secret perversions. His faith in the world had been shaken; and now, he could only see the evil in people. Like Phelps, they were all filthy inside; and now that he thought about it, Phelps had *deserved* his brutality. By any stretch of common decency, Roland had been *justified*...but what was going to happen once Phelps regained consciousness? What if the man reported him to the police? What if the man went to them, crying with his black eye and bloody mouth? Who would they believe—him or Roland? Roland bit his lower lip anxiously. What was there to do now? For the slightest instant, the beast reappeared, and told him to go back and finish the man off—to leave no evidence behind—but he shook his head, because those were the thoughts of a madman.

What was there to do...? Phelps wasn't like Lamar Smith. At worst, men like Smith could *kill* him, but men like Phelps destroyed their enemies *totally*—stripped them of their dignity, their means of earning a living... *everything*—so that in the end, their lives weren't *worth* living. That was power; and in a battle between Roland and Phelps, it was all too clear who the eventual winner would be. Phelps would *ruin* him now—Roland was certain of it! If the man's depravity had no limits, then what could ruining Roland's life possibly mean to him?

Presently, Roland stumbled on the curb, as if rocked by the weight of the realization. What was there to do...? Halfheartedly, he thought about suing the firm and taking them for *millions* of dollars! For entire minutes, he thought about taking Phelps and all those other bastards to court—and *ruining* them, the way they wanted to ruin him, but he was too good a lawyer to believe any of that would work. Given Phelps' stature, Roland's story would sound *insane*. It would be his word against Phelps'. The eyewitnesses—the two women in the strip club—would most likely be bought off, or threatened into silence...and Roland would flounder in the courtroom, and become a laughingstock.

He shook his head decisively. He had no idea what he would do, but no matter what happened, he knew he had to keep his dignity. He would fight Phelps as a *man*; and if the day ever came when he could no longer be a man, then he would surrender to the beast. The thought was horrible, but it was there nonetheless. It did not reassure him about the future, but it laid out his options so succinctly that everything suddenly seemed clear to him.

He nodded his head and walked on. About a block later, the heat began to feel so oppressive that he began thinking about hailing a cab home. He was about to scan the street when he was distracted by the gaudy neon sign above the upcoming building. The sign announced that jewelry and electronic equipment could be pawned there for "Big $$$." While Roland was watching it, a white girl suddenly emerged from the pawnshop's doorway. She was no older than fourteen years old, and wore a black miniskirt that clung tenaciously to her boyish figure. When he looked, her face seemed as though it had been *painted* with makeup, not simply that makeup had been applied. Now, as she stepped before Roland, a sordid imitation of sexiness flashed in her eyes. She was chewing a huge wad of gum, and something about it made Roland think of a cow chewing its cud.

"You want a date, baby?" she drawled.

"What...?" he said, taken aback.

"Looking for some fun?"

Roland frowned, and stood staring at her. "You're a *prostitute*?"

"No, no...nothing like that," she said defensively; but something about Roland's bewildered expression seemed to disarm her, and her eyes dropped. "...I'm just trying to get something to eat," she said at last.

He looked at her bony figure and her anemic eyes

then, shaking his head. She was probably some run-away, either chasing big dreams or running away from irreconcilable nightmares. He took out his wallet then, and handed her a hundred dollar bill.

"Where you want to go?" she said, smiling again.

"I don't want to go anywhere—"

"I wasn't begging, you know," she said, as though hurt.

"I know you weren't," he said solemnly. "You were just hungry. Go get something to eat," he went on. "... Go home if you can." Then, in a lower voice, "Hunger's a dangerous thing to have in this city...leads you to do things you might regret later." At that, he nodded vaguely and went to leave—but it was then that a car pulled up on the curb, startling them. Roland whirled around, then froze as he saw two police officers step out of a cruiser!

"Don't move!" the pudgy one shouted, resting his hand on his gun as he rushed out. Roland's first thought was that Phelps had called the police on him! All his old fears came flooding back! He was trembling now, raising his hands in response to the officer's demand. His mind was so chaotic that everything seemed to be passing him in a blur—

"What's going on here?" the other cop, a lean, stern-looking white man, demanded. "You trying to buy some fun tonight? We *seen* you exchange money!"

Roland's lips were trembling: "No...*no*!" he said as if just realizing what the words meant. "It wasn't like that.

She said she was hungry. *Ask* her," he said, turning to the equally fidgety girl. "I was just helping her out—I didn't even want to go anywhere with her." He was babbling on, sounding like one of those fools that he used to defend when he worked for the Public Defender's Office.

The lean one turned to the girl: "You a runaway?"

"...Yes," she whispered, bowing her head.

"*He* telling the truth?" he went on, gesturing to Roland.

"Yeah," she said, "he was real nice to me—gave me a hundred dollars to get something to eat."

The pudgy cop had been squinting at Roland, as if trying to place his face: "Ain't you that lawyer guy?"

Roland's stomach convulsed. He felt terribly ashamed for some reason—as though he actually *had* tried to pick the girl up; but seeing no use in denying his identity, he nodded.

"What you doing out here?" the lean one inquired.

"I was just walking home," Roland pleaded again, sounding pathetic.

"Well," the lean one started in a conciliatory air, "you better get on home—especially with this heat. There's a riot going on in Brooklyn as we speak. Heat drives people mad, you know." Roland nodded contritely. "They get like rats in a cage...start striking out at the closest thing to them...don't care who or what it is."

"You better get on home," the pudgy one said now, while he gestured for the girl to come with them.

Roland nodded to the officers, glanced uneasily at the girl, then walked away briskly. However, once around the corner, he began to run at full speed.

The city was composed of millions of different universes. Even as violence spread through the Brooklyn slums, most of the city was still oblivious to it. Councilwoman Charlotte McPrice, the mayoral challenger, stepped out of the banquet hall and smiled. She walked with the confident stride that had become her trademark; and in her wake, there were scores of clapping well-wishers. Photographers were there as well, as if she were a model on a catwalk.

A reporter asked her something. She did not really hear, but she stopped and smiled at him, and he smiled back, forgetting that he had ever asked a question. Her long mane of red hair fell gracefully to her shoulders, and seemed to glow supernaturally in the posh lighting beneath the awning. Even while others faltered in the heat, she stood there as though even the forces of nature were no match for her. Behind her, the people were still gathering in an attempt to get a final glimpse of her. It had been her most successful fund-raiser yet— four thousand people at five thousand dollars a plate. Her keynote address—a boisterous speech on why Randolph was no match for her—had garnered ten minutes of standing ovation. It had taken her an hour just to reach the door: everyone had wanted to shake her hand—to touch her essence, as if the thing could be rubbed off. They had followed her out here: middle-aged women in glittery evening gowns and corporate CEO types who stared at her, transfixed, succumbing to the same spell that had bewitched the young West Virginia rednecks.

The limousine was waiting on the curb; but seeing it, she suddenly remembered something. She turned around, looking for someone; and seeing her inquisitive expression, her campaign manager—a short, perpetually harried-looking old man named Ned Wisinski—rushed to her side.

"Have you seen my husband, Ned?" she asked, having to bend down to talk to him.

Wisinski shook his head, seeming heartbroken that he hadn't been able to answer her question and put her mind at ease. This desperation to please had always amused her, so that she smiled now, if only to console him.

"He probably left early," she said nonchalantly, again waving to her cheering supporters before heading for the limousine. That was the ease that they all knew and loved....

She had grown up in the mountains of West Virginia—a coal miner's daughter, just like the country song. It had been some backwater town, replete with the mandatory trailer parks: a virtual wasteland, where the cultural center had been a tavern on the interstate highway, where all the long distance truckers stopped to eat. It was a world where the men had been drunkards whose ultimate wish was to own a pick-up truck with a gun rack, and the women had either been brazen hussies who liked the abuse of their men, or saints who hated it, but endured it for the sake of the children.

It had been a world of clichés—a maudlin country song brought to life. Instead of living, they seemed to carrying out badly written tragic roles to their inevitable conclusions. Growing up in those surroundings, the youngest of seven children, she had gotten a good view of it all; and by age five, she had known that she wanted no part of it. Her mother had loved God, but had seemed to hate everything else—including her "uppity" daughter. Her father had managed to freeze to death while stumbling back home from the interstate tavern, but her mother's love of God had only grown after that—as if her husband's death had been the answer to her prayers.

Since she was a little girl, McPrice had planned her escape. She had had to be a clandestine warrior, fighting against everything and everyone she had ever known. With the men, it had only been their laughable, teenage lust that she had to outwit; but with the women, it had been the more complex—more *driven*—force of jealousy. She had had to figure out when to be strong, when to be soft, when to seem indifferent—and when, finally, to risk it all and stand up for what she really cared about. Needless to say, with those early dealings behind her, the most vital lessons of politics had been learned: make yourself seem accessible, but from a distance; make them want you, but keep out of their reach, so that they can't soil you.

After graduating first in her law class at Yale, she had moved to New York City and joined one of those liberal, civil liberties/civil rights organizations. On that record, she had been elected to the City Council four years ago. And now, on to bigger and better things....

Upon reaching the limousine, and the chauffeur who was holding the door open for her, McPrice waved to her supporters one last time. There was genuine love in her for those people. At the same time, she couldn't help thinking that there was something exasperating about them, which reminded her of a dog's too-eager, too-animated welcoming of its master.

When she entered the vehicle, she saw a figure slumped over in the darkness. After the initial surprise, she saw it was her husband. At first she thought he was sleeping, but then she discerned, from his glossy eyes— and the stench of whisky—that he was drunk.

"I want a divorce!" he belted as soon as she sat down beside him.

She groaned noncommittally while he glared at her. She had met him at Yale: a rich kid from good South Hampton stock, now an insufferable bore, bored with his daddy's immense fortune.

"I could ruin you, you frigid bitch!" he went on. "All

your beloved fans would hate you...if they only knew what a *cunt* you are!"

She sat there staring at him with a bemused expression on her face; the silence unnerved him, so that he felt compelled to go on: "There are things that I could say! They'd give me six figures for a book on you!"

However, she only laughed. Her voice was still calm as she said: "I'm only a New York City Councilwoman. Don't you think that you could blackmail me better *after* I became Mayor?"

His eyes opened wide: "Yeah...that's right!" he said in amazement, as if he had never given it thought before.

"Of course I'm right," she cooed to him, resting his head tenderly on her breasts. "Rest now," she whispered as the car started off, "you'll be able to ruin me soon enough."

While the chaos spread through the streets of New York City, Charles Marenga was thousands of kilometers away, in Ghana. He had left New York soon after the Kain debacle, and was now in the third week of a five-month tour of Africa. Outwardly, he cursed Randolph and America as vehemently as ever; but inwardly, he was sick of all the political posturing. In truth, something had changed in him—and had perhaps been changing for some time now. Whatever the case, he emerged from the doorway of the beach cabin and stared out dreamily at the pre-dawn sea. He yawned at that moment, then smiled vapidly as he began to walk toward the ocean. His expression soured when he saw that his gut drooped down over his swim trunks, but there was no one to see him here. He liked the solitude of this place. Without other people's demands weighing him down, he felt like he was finally getting healthy.

The sand tickled his toes as he moseyed toward the ocean. He again smiled contentedly to himself as he looked down the Ghanaian coastline and saw the thin band of dawn. At the moment, the morning sky was one of those dreamy mauves: it was dark and mysterious now; but as the sun rose, it would become bright and spectacular. He was getting a knack for such things now— an ease of spirit that allowed him to see things that only weeks ago would have been beyond his comprehension. Some of the stars were still visible: he stopped on the edge of the ocean and smiled at them as well.

He had spent most of his trip camping out in distant parts of Africa: there would be no five-star hotels and tourist resorts for him. It was the night sky that had given him his first dose of sanity after he decided to take a few months away from America. The stars had glittered so brilliantly that they had seemed like sparkling diamonds, hanging from the heavens. During his first night in the Moroccan desert, he remembered thinking that no one could be troubled when staring up at such a sky. His African guides openly laughed at him—the funny black American who acted as though he had never seen stars and plains and valleys—but Marenga didn't care.

Marenga let out a peaceful sigh, and stepped into the ocean. The water chilled him at first, so that an inadvertent squeal escaped from him; but after plunging himself headlong into it, he found it warm and soothing. He waddled out farther then, enjoying the sensation of near weightlessness. When the water was to his neck, he began to swim, going out farther. He laughed for no good reason, then took a mouthful of the brine and spit it out playfully, like he had seen dolphins do off the coast of Mauritania. All at once, he had the feeling that here, for these few moments, the world was his and he could do whatever he wanted. It occurred to him that he could swim naked if he wanted; and as the thought passed through his mind, he wrenched off his trunks and threw them toward the shore. Giggling to himself, he swam out farther, giddy with the sudden, carefree joy. *This is what it means to be alive!* he thought to himself. No more New York, filled with psychotic weirdoes like Jasper Kain; no more rallies; no more Mayor Randolph...no more protests to lead—no more senseless strife that was doomed to be forgotten after the initial media frenzy …

Marenga swam deeper into the ocean; and as the waves washed over him, he felt as though layers of his life were being washed off—like dead, ugly skin. The feeling of peace and well-being again seized him, and he laughed out for no good reason. However, as he hadn't exercised in decades, he was soon exhausted from his efforts. He used to be a vigorous sprinter in his youth, but now he was a flabby man on the verge of old age. He floated on his back for a while, panting for air and staring up at the dreamy sky. *Just enjoy the moment*! he thought to himself. He was about to smile when he realized something strange was happening.

He had stopped swimming, but he was still going out to sea. Looking over his shoulder, he saw that the shore was about one hundred and fifty meters away—and that he was still being drawn out at an alarming rate! He was caught in a rip tide! *Don't panic*! he said to himself, trying to recall everything he had ever heard about rip tides. Yes: he should let it take him out, and not fight it. His mind went over everything, and the realization that he was reasoning it out filled him with excitement. Indeed, while the ocean pulled him deeper into itself, he laughed almost insanely at his triumph over it. It was trying to thwart his peace—to steal him away from Africa—but he would outwit it. He was still smiling when he began swimming parallel to the shore—just like he had read in books. That was the way to outsmart the ocean. However, he was so gripped by the game that he didn't realize how spent he was. When he finally freed himself from the pull of the ocean and looked back toward the shore, he saw that he was about four hundred meters out!

The first pang of worry hit him: it wasn't a game

anymore. He began swimming back—way too quickly. His weak heart began to protest and ache; his lungs felt as though they were already filled with water; and as for his limbs, as he hadn't exercised in years, they felt like lead bricks. The panic began to build in him. He had been paddling for two exhausting minutes, and yet the shore still seemed as far away as before. It occurred to him that maybe he was still in the rip tide—and was still being pulled out to sea! He began to swim harder: to expend energy that he didn't have. He was practically thrashing in the water now! All that he could manage was an ungainly doggie paddle. He misjudged a paddle stroke and went under, gulping down a mouthful of seawater. He wanted to look up and see how far he was from the shore, but he couldn't bear the thought that he was still being drawn out. *Oh, God*, to die like this...after all that he had been through—all the protest marches... He had marched with Martin Luther King for God's sake, getting clubbed over the head by southern sheriffs during the 60s; he'd been shot at by rednecks, and attacked by dogs; and after all that, he would die like this—something as mundane as a drowning! A *drowning*, due to the fact that he was a fat slob.

That was when he remembered he was naked. They would find his naked, bloated body washed up on the beach, there to repulse the first hapless fool to come upon it. God, to die like this—like an animal: *senselessly*...! By now, his heart felt as though it were being squeezed in a vise. He wanted to scream out at the sensation, but every time he opened his mouth, another gulp of the sickening brine went down into his belly.

The prospect of death sent his mind off wildly. As he remembered all the dreams of his youth, his life suddenly seemed like a waste. What had he really accomplished? He had been at the vanguard of a direction-less procession. He had allied himself with people like the self-avowed Black Racist, Botswana Glade, and taken as his constituents those whom one might be tempted to call the rabble: the poor and marginalized residents of the slums. But all of that ostensible rabblerousing had been a farce; his education at Princeton and Oxford, where he had been a Rhodes Scholar, had been a farce. As a youth, he had set out to fight racism and inequality, but he had lost his way. When had it all stopped making sense? When had the fight for justice been co-opted by dollar signs? When had police brutality cases begun to *excite* him, like some kind of vile, scatological pornography? Somewhere along the line, he had lost his soul... but it was all coming to an end now.

Marenga's exhausted limbs thrashed the water feebly now. His weak heart seemed to pump not blood, but rhythmic pulses of pain. His stomach was full of seawater by now; and with all the water that he had already inhaled, his nasal passages and throat burned. He glanced up, about to look at the shore one last time, when he miraculously saw that it was no more than thirty meters away!

How was it possible! New life filled him from nowhere;

his limbs felt stronger; his paddle strokes were actually moving him through the water now. The shore was ahead! He could hardly believe it! He was paddling violently now. *Sand*! There was land beneath him: he touched it first with his flailing, unbelieving hands! He tried to stand up, but he was too exhausted for that, so he stumbled along, hunched over like some deformed beast, before collapsing onto the beach. He retched suddenly and violently then, vomiting up the brine that he had swallowed; but then, all of a sudden, he was laughing: giggling between gasps for air. He laughed at the pain in his chest, at his lightheadedness—at *everything*! Somehow, he had survived. *How*, he didn't know and didn't care. All that he knew was that he was alive, and that these moments were his. He lay there naked and carefree, dreamily watching the sunrise.

News of the riot hadn't reached the Mayor yet; and about everything, there was that proverbial calm before the storm. Randolph ambled down the luxurious corridors, toward his office. However, now that he was safely within City Hall, even hiding didn't make too much sense anymore. All that he could think about was that new thing: the stripper and her demands. As odd as it seemed, he wasn't really horrified anymore. He had made his bed, and now he would sleep in it. In fact, he was so exhausted by the night that a side of him couldn't really be bothered. All about him, there was that sense of peace that came when one knew everything was out of one's hands. Also, for the first time in a long while, he felt *sane*. He knew there would be horrors ahead, but he no longer felt encumbered by the need for filth.

The door of his office was open, and the light was on. He walked in, still in a daze. He would sleep on the couch in the corner. He went to the attached bathroom and washed out his cut. As he did so, it occurred to him he would probably need a tetanus shot. Eventually, he got a clean shirt from the adjoining closet—which was stocked with several shirts and suits—then he walked back into his office, buttoning up his shirt.

He was at the window, staring out dreamily, when a man walked into the room. Randolph only became aware of the man's presence because he was whistling. When the Mayor turned around, he saw a short, fat Latino of middle age whom, by his uniform, and his cart of cleaning utensils, seemed to be the janitor. When he noticed Randolph standing by the window, he stopped abruptly.

"Sorry, I didn't know you were here."

"No problem," Randolph said in an offhand manner, "finish your work." At that, he turned back to the window, and was soon lost in his thoughts again. However, within a matter of seconds, a young aide ran into the room, colliding with the janitor's cart. Randolph jumped and swung around at the commotion. It looked as if the aide had just woken up: his shirt was hanging out of his pants and his tie was crooked; he came running up, panting and wide-eyed:

"Sir! Thank goodness you're here! They said I'd find you in here!"

"What is it, Radix?" Randolph said, a note of alarm already sounding in his voice. The janitor had stopped sweeping and was staring anxiously as well.

"It's *crazy*—there's a race riot going on in Brooklyn, sir! People have been killed—*dozens* wounded!"

"A riot?" Randolph whispered strangely, wondering why he wasn't surprised. Somehow, he had sensed it, and he frowned—

"*Crazy*," Radix repeated. "...First, this white man runs over a young Puerto Rican kid with his car, then speeds through a red light, hitting another car. Then, after the accident, the man gets out of the car and shoots the other driver; and then, as the mob runs up to him, he shoots several others before he finally runs out of bullets and they attack him.... After beating him unconscious, the crowd began to riot. The police shot about *ten* of them, sir!"

The janitor gasped!

"*God*," the young aide went on, nervously combing his fingers through his hair, "we're lucky Marenga's out of the country! And heaven only knows what Charlotte McPrice is going to say when she finds out!"

Randolph was a little annoyed by the mention of those

two; and to get the aide's mind back to the matter at hand, he demanded, "When did this begin?"

"About an hour ago, sir. The police are still containing the violence."

"But it *is* under control, right?"

"It's hard to know, sir. There are still some trouble spots, but the police have broken up the larger groups... and then there are all the fires to put out."

"Is the shooter still alive?"

"We don't know, sir—the police haven't been able to get to him yet!"

Randolph groaned equivocally to himself; then, shaking his head, he signed loudly and said: "Okay, get me the police commissioner on the phone and gather everyone else together. As soon as the riot is under control, set up the usual press conference at the hospital where they take the worst victims." When Randolph nodded his head to show he was finished, the aide ran out of the room, leaving Randolph alone with the janitor.

Randolph went over to his desk to fetch something; the janitor's concerned eyes followed him.

"It's pretty bad," the man ventured.

Randolph looked up in surprise, having forgotten that the man was there. After a pause, he replied: "Not any worse than usual." He seemed distracted, but not in a standoffish manner. There was a side of him that watched his own actions and was surprised and relieved to find himself acting like the Mayor again. He felt *real*

again; and having reacquainted himself with the sensations of a man of respect and power, he was desperate
to forget about the madness of the preceding weeks. He
looked at the janitor, suddenly assured by the expression of respect and faith in the man's eyes. Buoyed by
that faith, Randolph went on: "We have to act quickly,
before it spreads." He was silent for a while; then he
added, in a thoughtful voice: "New York—all the big
cities, in fact—they're just accidents waiting to happen.
A few incidents like this, back-to-back..." He shook his
head ominously and left it at that.

But that was all that needed to be said. They stood
there, in the sudden silence, thinking it over. A short
moment later, the young aide again ran into the room
and broke the spell. The janitor unconsciously stepped
aside when the man entered; and then, while plans were
made and the screechy, defensive voice of the police
commissioner came over the speakerphone, the janitor
nodded his head and stepped outside.

Roland ran the remaining blocks and into his building. He startled the old doorman—Sam—as he darted
past. He was panting when he locked his front door
behind him—even though he had taken the elevator
and his door was practically right across from the elevator. He felt as though his insides were turning to mush!
The realization that he had babbled to those policemen
like...like *a scared nigger*—ate away at his soul. And what

would have happened if that runaway had said that he tried to pick her up! He would have been ruined—if not legally, then definitely in the public eye. He could have easily ended up as one of those fools that appeared on the local news every night, going through that daily nigger dance: paraded before a media gauntlet while trying to hide their faces from the cameras—

The phone rang, and Roland jumped! It was a cordless phone, and he had left it on the couch. After the panicky feeling subsided somewhat, he walked over to the couch and picked up the phone.

"Hello?"

"Roland!" shouted a woman.

"Yes?" he said, still trying to place the voice.

"It's me," the woman said, "*Candice*!"

"Candice," he whispered, suddenly numb.

"Dallas went crazy!" she shouted.

He paused for a few seconds. "What?"

"He came home drunk with his face all beat up, and kicked me and Mindy out!"

"*What*!"

"I'm out on the street!" She started crying. "I couldn't think of anyone else to call. He's *nuts* when he's drunk!"

"He threw out his three-year-old daughter?"

"He came home with a big bottle of champagne, saying something about this was the time for celebration." Roland shuddered. "He told me to grab Mindy and 'get the hell out!'"

"Maybe you should call the police," he said uneasily.

"The police?" she cried. "Can't we just come over," she pleaded, "...spend the night—until he cools off?"

Roland had forgotten that she was an illegal alien—she didn't want anything to do with the police. He still felt sick to his stomach—and alarm bells were raging in his mind; nevertheless, he sighed, seeing no other way.

"...Yeah, I guess you can come over," he said at last. "Can you get a cab?"

"Yeah," she said, seeming relieved, "I'll be right over."

He stared into the darkness after she had put the phone down; he stood there listening to the dial tone, not quite able to believe that it had really happened. He felt *sick*! He put the phone down—tossed it back to the couch—and collapsed on top of it. Lying there, he wondered, like Andropov and Randolph and Marenga had wondered before him, how the hell he had come to this place. He felt like he was on a yo-yo, spinning wildly between courage and craven despair—or maybe from one paranoid delusion to another. With all that had happened tonight, he was sure that he was going mad.

Suddenly needing to drown his thoughts, Roland grabbed the remote control from the coffee table and switched on the television. He began flipping through the channels. After about thirty seconds, something caught his attention:

"...At least a dozen people shot—six now confirmed dead," Maria Santos said breathlessly, "...dozens of others wounded by mob violence...and then there is the seven-year-old boy that this beast ran down with his car...!" The chaotic scene at her back was mesmerizing, with the flashing lights of emergency vehicles—and the darting urgency of police officers, firemen and medical technicians. As he watched those scenes, he found himself thinking about his father again. He offered up no defense to those thoughts this time: they were something that he could no longer profess to fight. Indeed, every day, some little thing happened to remind him of his father. A few months ago, he had been watching television when the station announced that the FBI had finally captured some ax-wielding serial killer. Roland had sat there frozen as they prepared to show the captured man. The reporters had been talking about how brutal the man's murders had been—and about how many lives had been lost and ruined; and yet, Roland had been aware of an inexplicable sense of relief when he saw the killer was white....

Roland emerged from his reverie and looked over at the television once again. After Maria Santos described the killer as a middle-aged white man, Roland sat back, lowered the volume and closed his eyes....

Andropov didn't really have a body anymore: he was just a conglomeration of throbbing nerve endings. His momentary emergence back into consciousness was more alarming than the devastating extent of his injuries. He suddenly realized a paramedic was over him, yelling some gibberish that he had no time to decipher. Or, maybe the man wasn't yelling at all. Maybe it was only the echoing in his head. A bone was sticking out of his chest, which, upon reflection, he realized was a rib. The siren was drilling into his head, as though a jackhammer were opening his skull. Whispers reverberated in his ears; swallowing was like eating fire; breathing was like having a trunk falling on his chest. All of his front teeth had been knocked out, and his eyelids were swollen to the point of almost closing. Everything looked red and blurry to him; and as he rode in the ambulance, he was only vaguely aware of what had just passed.... In reality, the police had had to fight to get to him; the people, incensed, had almost rioted again when the paramedics tried to take him away before a boy with a broken leg—

But the stultifying darkness was coming over him again; everything was fading away—all light, all sensations...all thoughts and awareness. Therein lay bliss.

Botswana Glade was getting dressed in the darkness of his bedroom. He could have turned on the light, but he preferred the darkness somehow. He dressed himself in a dapper suit, and tied his bow tie with what seemed to be the practiced ease of a blind man. When that was finished, he brushed his long, straightened hair before the mirror—even though, in the darkness, all that could be made out were the whites of his bulging eyes. His wife tossed in bed, but was sound asleep. Less than an hour ago, the phone had awakened them both. After picking up the phone and listening to the young aide's high-pitched ramblings about how the police had shot into the crowd, Botswana Glade had only said a single word into the receiver: "Yes." As he often got calls in the middle night, his wife of twenty years had thought nothing of it; but as he completed the finishing touches to his coiffure, Botswana Glade was possessed by the same tingly feeling he had had while the aide talked about death and destruction....

Once he was confident of his preparations, he walked quietly toward the bedroom door. When he opened it and stepped into the light, a young, dreadlocked aide— actually, the one that had called from Marenga's head-quarters—stood at something resembling attention. Botswana Glade stepped out into the hall and closed the door behind him. Now that he was in the light, the equine face could be seen. He had a hideous overbite— which he was known to bare when enraged. These features were a godsend to political cartoonists, who exaggerated his appearance into a ghoulish caricature.

The aide was dressed in a colorful dashiki, while Botswana Glade was in a dark suit that fitted elegantly over his slim figure. He walked down the hallway with the erect posture of a classical dancer. The aide stared after him for a while, then, coming to his senses, he caught up with him just as he reached the front door. After the youth ceremoniously opened the door, Botswana Glade stepped out onto the stoop, looking like a dictator greeting his subjects from the balcony above the square. However, this was Harlem; and across the street, were cheap tenements. Instead of subjects, there were half a dozen people—camera crews and a handful of photographers and reporters. Botswana Glade looked out at them—generally, avoiding eye contact. Indeed, contempt flashed in his eyes as a quivering grimace came over his face. They excitedly trained their cameras and lights on that face; their first indecipherable onslaught of questions littered the air, but Botswana Glade gestured for them to be quiet:

"Here we go again!" he screamed, his horse teeth finally bared to the world. "Look at what the filthy bastards have done...!"

Roland burst upright and looked around confusedly. What his dream had been about, he had no idea: he only knew that he was terrified. He looked around warily, trying to get his bearings—and to make sure there wasn't some monster hiding in the shadows. The television was still on. The same woman was on the air, screaming about death and madness. Roland grabbed the remote control and switched off the television.

When he remembered Candice's call, he wondered

how long he had been sleeping. He looked at his watch, which said that it was a little after one in the morning; yet, as he couldn't remember when he had come in, that information was useless to him. He now found himself thinking that perhaps Candice's call had been nothing but a dream; perhaps all that had happened with Phelps, and his confrontation with the police and that runaway, had been nothing but a dream within that dream. It was all so bizarre—so farfetched.

He sat on the edge of the couch and took another deep breath, wondering when it would end. He suddenly remembered his court victory, and his booking at the network morning show, but in his exhausted mind, those things all seemed farfetched as well.

He got up and walked over to the French doors. Beyond the French doors, the city twenty stories below him suddenly seemed magical. Even the red, menacing sky didn't trouble him anymore. The skyscrapers in the distance were like towers of light and magic; and he stood there, with his face pressed against the glass as if he were a child staring into a candy store.

The sight of the city always triggered a sense of excitement in him—especially when he looked at it from a distance. He wanted to be out there, proving himself. Remembering his booking on the TV program, he suddenly wished that it were dawn already—so that he could go out and prove himself on the airwaves. Revived by his strange yearning for the world, he slid

open the French doors to go out on the terrace. However, as soon as the doors were open a crack, a blast of
the stiflingly hot city air made him shut them and
retreat back into the air-conditioned room. He took
another step back before he realized that he was shivering. *What the hell is wrong with you*! he cursed himself.
The heat wave was driving him crazy, too: putting him
on edge like everyone else—

He whirled around in a panic as something blared in
the air; after a moment of confusion, he realized the
phone was ringing. It was still on the couch, where he
had tossed it. He stared at it in disbelief, having to
somehow convince himself that it was only a phone. He
took a deep breath to calm his racing heart, then walked
over and picked up the phone:

"Hello?"

"Sir, it's Sam."

The doorman? Roland thought to himself, frowning.
"Yes?"

"That woman you used to date is down here." Then,
somewhat more ominously, "she's got a kid..."

"Candice," Roland whispered, seeming suddenly frail.
He sat down heavily on the couch, staring blankly into
the darkness. Candice reminded him of Phelps and
everything that had happened that night. He felt *trapped*.
He wanted to hide—to *flee*—but he knew it was pointless. Phelps was probably still drunk somewhere, or
sleeping it off; but imagine what would happen tomor-

row, when the man fully realized that Roland was his enemy. Slowly, as Roland sat there, he came to the conclusion that he would probably have to *destroy* Phelps in order to save himself. Men like Phelps didn't take half-measures—and Roland would have to fight the man the same way, if he was going to have any hope of survival. Just the scope of it left Roland in a daze, trembling slightly from the ruthless demands of the beast within him. He stared helplessly into the darkness, bewildered by the extremes of his mind; but then, as the doorman asked if he was still there, he whispered: "Send her up, Sam."

He sat there for about twenty seconds after he had put down the phone, his mind numb. He had felt charged with energy just moments ago, but now he was drained. He was sick of this strange yo-yoing.

It was not only Candice's connection with Phelps that was weighing him down, but the queasy feeling he always had at the prospect of seeing old lovers. Candice was a beautiful woman, but like all the other women he had ever been with, she had never really touched his soul—or been able to dwell there for long. Without that spiritual connection, all that there had ever been between them was the soulless act he had shared with countless others. Also, with Candice, there was that strange fear he had always had—that she was able to see into his soul. Viewed in this light, all his past sex suddenly seemed joyless and meaningless.

The doorbell rang. He bolted to his feet, then walked over to the door warily, as if a killer were waiting on the other side. An internal voice kept reminding him that Phelps was his enemy, and that he had to get more evidence against the man—evidence that Candice, as the nanny, could provide. When he opened the door, Candice was standing there, looking haggard; Mindy was sleeping in her arms—

"I didn't know where else to go!" Candice cried. She looked like a pathetic welfare mother now. Roland wondered where the glamorous woman of his fantasies had gone—the one who had intrigued and mesmerized him. Either Phelps was bringing them all down, or that woman had never really existed....

"Come in," Roland said, gesturing for her to enter. He hastily turned on the light as they entered—only then realizing that they were in darkness—and led Candice deeper into the room.

"He came home like a *madman*!" Candice went on. "He just burst into my bedroom and told me to take Mindy and leave—I guess so that he could have sex with Cindy."

"—*Cindy*!" he said anxiously, only then remembering her, "—you think he might do something to her?"

She shook her head, as though the idea were ludicrous. Then, "Even if he does, it's their way, if you understand me. They do *weird* shit," she said, lowering her voice. "You know how crazy rich white people are. Sometimes I hear them screaming out in the middle of the night!"

Roland stared at her uneasily; but, despite himself—despite the fact that a man forcing his three-year-old daughter and her nanny out into the streets in the middle of the night was beyond the pale—he smiled. Or, maybe it was just the expression of amused bewilderment in Candice's eyes that made him laugh— or maybe it was only that he was tired of thoughts of Phelps just now, and wanted to rest.

Just then, Mindy stirred from sleep, probably roused by their voices.

"Uncle Roland!" she screamed upon seeing him.

Roland caressed her cheek and smiled. There was something wondrous about the excitement of little children; as Roland saw it, all his thoughts of hate and madness fell away. For now, all he could think about was caring for the little girl, and protecting her innocence for as long as he could.

He turned to Candice then, saying, "Take Mindy to the guest bedroom. You can sleep in my bedroom: I wasn't going to sleep anyway."

At that, Candice smiled in gratitude and walked out of the room; Mindy waved back at him as she and her nanny disappeared into the darkness; but when Roland was alone, he stood there wondering what the hell he had gotten himself into.

On the city streets, the unrest was ostensibly winding down. The fire and police departments seemed to have everything contained. Unfortunately, it was just as the last of the wounded were taken away in ambulances that the violence really began to flare up. Miraculously, just before Maria Santos and the rest of the media had gotten there, a bystander had videotaped Andropov's rampage from his bedroom window. Those dark, grainy images were being sent out to all the news organizations now. The bystander had gotten the footage of Andropov emerging from his car just after the hit-and-run murder, and the accident at the intersection. The bystander had zoomed in on Andropov's pasty, inhuman face as he began firing at the charging mob.

In time, the footage would be playing as far away as Bangladesh. The bystander captured the mob mauling the man, and the first appearance of the police on the scene; he had captured the first people being shot down by police bullets...and the last corpse being carried away. It was all on videotape: irrefutable proof of madness. The video was like a vision from God—like an icon before which the faithful could genuflect and sing their praises to the heavens. Moralists and hand-wringers were already posing with those images as a backdrop, asking how it could have happened in America; and somewhere in Hollywood, a producer was trembling with excitement at the prospect of a movie. The video made the real unreal; it turned fact into fiction and fiction into fact, but that was the alchemy that kept the world kept running.

Just before dawn, while Roland lay on the couch, sleeping soundly, Candice came up to him. She awoke him by caressing his face. He was surprised—first, that he had fallen asleep, and then that she was naked. She kissed him before he could say anything. She kissed him sloppily, shoving her extraordinarily long tongue down his throat, so that he almost retched.

"Candice," he said the first chance he got, but she put her index finger to his lips.

"No strings," she said. Not waiting for a response, she bent over him once again, and kissed him; he stared up at the ceiling in bewilderment, numb again. He was in a pair of shorts and a T-shirt. She took off the T-shirt, practically flinging his arms over his head, so that she could wrench it off. And then, with equal alacrity, his shorts were off, and she was stroking his penis. His erection was due more to the pre-dawn accumulation of urine in his bladder than sexual arousal, but the sight of it made her smile, nonetheless. He stared at her, wondering what the hell was happening; and while he was still trying to make sense of it all, she straddled him— was on top of him, moaning sonorously, while he lay there in a daze.

She was holding his hands above his head—he hadn't moved them since she flung them there to take off his shirt; her breasts, firm as there were, were nonetheless hitting him in the face as she rocked back and forth on him. In the early morning light, her face had a strange,

demonic expression, which he assumed was pleasure. A
few shrill cries escaped from her, making Roland
cringe. She was one of those screamers, Roland remembered. He winced every time she screamed—and every
time her tits hit him in the face. She must have taken his
wincing for pleasure as well, because she giggled suddenly as she began to ride him with more urgency. He
hated being held down like this—being hemmed in by
her thighs and hands. He had a sudden impulse to push
her off: to fling her from him and cover her mouth with
a cushion so that she would shut up. As she screamed in
his ears and ground herself against him, he suddenly
remembered Mindy, who was sleeping in the other
room. The thought of the little girl coming out and
seeing them there was sickening.... *Was this the way
Candice was with Phelps?* Roland thought suddenly. Was
this why she was such a "godsend," as Phelps had called
her? The thought of being up in something that Phelps
had...he shuddered! It occurred to him, suddenly and
strangely, that Candice had been wrong: that women
couldn't read men's minds during sex after all—since
the only thing he felt was disgust.

   She was still holding him down; and as she galloped
her way to orgasm, she dug her fingernails into his arms.
Roland was grinding his teeth to keep from screaming;
having had enough, he tried to push her off, but gripped
by the throes of ecstasy, her strength was twice that of
his. He couldn't take it anymore! Like a horse fright-

ened by something in its path, he reared up and threw his master. They both fell to the plush carpet then. In his desperation to be free of her, he was ready to fight her—to *strike* her if necessary—but she was laughing now: giggling with that strange post-orgasmic joy that she always seemed to get.

"You're still great!" she purred as she sloppily kissed his neck and panted in his ear. The end of her screams had curtailed his madness, but now he felt suddenly inept—*bereft*. While he was lying there in confusion, she rolled him over, so that she was again on top; and before he could do or say anything, she kissed him, got up and ambled off to the bathroom.

Roland got up like an old man—like someone drained of life. His erection was still there, mocking him. He walked over to the French doors then, wrenched them open, and stumbled out. The stifling heat blasted against his body, but he didn't care. He stumbled to the edge of the balcony like a drunkard, looking at the pale sun rising on the horizon. He felt suddenly dizzy—and nauseous—so he stumbled back against the wall, already covered with sweat as he panted for oxygen in the filthy air. Crumbling into a patio chair, he sat there with his head resting heavily in his hands, wishing, for the slightest instant, that he were dead.

THE DEVIL'S LAUGHTER

Just before dawn, there was a soft glow in the heavens; and for those few moments, the smoggy skies were lit up in hues that were so spectacular that it proved, once again, that beauty could be found in anything, including filth.

It was about half past five now. Mayor Randolph sat wearily in the back seat of the limousine as he and his chief aides sped toward the hospital news conference. There was a strange, anxious feeling in him. After all, there had been a riot. People were dead—many from police bullets. Madness, itself had infected the streets; and if not for the massive, uncompromisingly brutal response of the police, it could have been much worse. Yet, even at this quiet time—this lull in the madness— Randolph sensed something horrible.

He had just toured the blocks of the rampage, looking at burned-out husks of buildings, smoldering wrecks of cars and garbage-strewn streets. The police presence along the blocks of the rampage was still massive. The rage that had swept through those communities was the type that could flare up at any time. The authorities had

managed to put out most of the blaze, but the rage continued to smolder beneath the surface. People were still
standing on street corners, waiting for something to
come and make them whole again. There were reports
of them attacking the police when asked to disperse. It
was Randolph's job to pacify them—but their neighbors
and relatives were dead and maimed now, and those
things were difficult to forget and reconcile.

In fact, the maniac who plowed over that kid was still
alive. Despite his injuries, the man was holding tena-
ciously to life in the hospital Randolph was to visit.
However, blood demanded blood, so the people of the
streets swore they would not rest until he was dead. A
kind of death vigil was already going on in front of the
hospital. Those who had lost—and *could* lose—loved
ones were there now, mourning their losses. However,
the vast majority were simply there to hear that the
maniac was dead. Some of them were literally praying
for his death, calling on gods and demons to right the
wrongs that had been done to them. Some of them,
gripped by their new religion, seemed ready to storm
the hospital and make everything right, themselves.

Later that morning, Botswana Glade was planning to
hold a protest rally in front of the very same hospital
that Randolph was to visit. The man was already appearing on TV, blaming the police for causing the riot and
escalating the violence with their brutal response. He
was saying that the police were no different from the

maniac. Thousands of his supporters were on their way to the hospital now—in order to demand their version of justice.

Everything was becoming myth now. Randolph had stayed up all night, planning and coordinating things that he could now barely remember. As Mayor, he was supposed to make sense of it all, but he felt like he was using a sieve to move water from one bucket to another. Everything seemed pointless. Moreover, with the shadow of the stripper's threat hanging over anything, he was too numb to act proactively. At this point, he was barely holding on.

Presently, as he neared the hospital, he looked over at his three aides. They were talking excitedly amongst themselves, trying to formulate strategies to save the city and resurrect Randolph's political fortunes. Randolph stared at them for a while, trying to follow their arguments, but it all seemed pointless to him now. His chief of staff, Abraham Levin, was a balding, middle-aged man with a perpetually unhealthy appearance. For some reason, Levin always reminded him of a vegetable. Today, it was a potato that had been left in the bag too long. Chet Radix, the aide who had found him in his office last night, was a baby-faced man just out of college. Radix was like some demented acolyte to him, whose fragile innocence and faith were in his hands. Last, his speechwriter, Bill Dalton, was a pencil-thin "stuffed suit," whose only redeeming quality was that his prattling speeches seemed to mirror the views of the voting public. Randolph looked at the men with an intensity that they must have taken for gravity and consideration, but he was far away from them now. In his heart of hearts, he knew that what had happened in the Brooklyn slums was beyond whatever statements and proclamations he could ever make. Alexander Randolph, the glib politician, who had risen like a star in this world because he had been able to convince people that he cared, now essentially didn't give a shit. And it wasn't that he was preoccupied with his own ruined life: he suddenly didn't give a shit about that either. He felt like his soul was being rewritten—that he was metamorphosing as he sat there, and that the new being that arose would either be a god, or a devil....

They were now about seven blocks from the hospital, driving through nondescript neighborhoods that were lined with the usual apartment buildings and store-fronts. It was only half past five in the morning, but the great multitudes were already beginning to come out on the streets. The city that had never really been asleep was shrugging off the night. People were headed to their jobs; parents were taking their children to daycare. Yet, like last night, when Randolph looked at them, the only thing he wanted to do was flee....

He definitely wasn't ready for this news conference. He tried to conjure his old self, and rekindle his political instincts, but it all seemed so very hopeless to him now. He needed time to rest and get himself right—but when he looked out of the window, he realized they had reached the hospital. There were hundreds of agitated blacks and Latinos outside. For these protesters, there were at least a thousand policemen—and dozens of camera crews and reporters. If there had been some kind escape clause—some way to turn his back on it all and flee back to his sanity—Randolph would have exercised it. However, he was trapped. For the first time in his life, the prospect of a media frenzy revolted him— seemed *evil*. Something about the scene reminded him of devil worshipers. They had sold their souls to something that offered them only pain and suffering. The more they worshiped their devil, the more pain they felt. Many of the people were chanting; but as Randolph listened, all he could hear was the devil's laughter—

He took another deep breath, trying to regain his focus. However, it was then that the car door opened. His aides seemed to push him out into the stifling heat of the world. The din of the crowd was like a declaration of war and madness. As his aides steered him toward the press conference, he felt like a student who had forgotten everything he had spent the night cramming.

The massive crowd surged on either side of him, held back only by the vigilance of the police. The reporters were the first to come, all waving their microphones in his face; and then, beyond them, were the protesters. Some of them were chanting for justice/revenge, while others professed to be chanting for peace. He looked at everything—the media, the chanting crowds, his agitated aides...feeling panic and revulsion welling up in him like vomit in his throat.

It was at that moment that Maria Santos stepped boldly into Randolph's path. Somehow, she had managed to circumvent the police barrier and the rest of the reporter corps. Randolph instinctively recoiled as she stepped up with her cameraman and shoved a microphone in his face:

"A stripper in Greenwich Village claims that you *raped* her last night!"

A moment of silence seemed to grip the world. At first, Randolph didn't really hear: he was only able to make sense of the words after they echoed in his mind a few times. And then, as he stared at Santos in horror, he found himself thinking, *So this is it!* Everyone looked at him oddly. Santos stood before him with a smug smile on her face, reveling in his reaction. Yet, for some incomprehensible reason, Randolph soon found himself laughing. *It's all over!* he thought; but, for the life of him, he laughed even louder. It was all so strange that Santos' smug smile turned into a frown.

Randolph was far away from her now—far away from *everything*. Like the chanting protesters, he had sold himself to a devil as well. Now, the devil had come to collect, and Randolph knew it was pointless to fight. At first, Levin had been reassured by Randolph's laughter—but the longer it went on, the more horrible it sounded. There was no joy in it; and as a creepy feeling went up Levin's spine, he grabbed Randolph's arm and hauled him away.

Little did Roland Micheaux know that the seeds of his destruction were being sown in the events currently taking place in the city. Yet, the life cycle of seeds can be anywhere from a few minutes, to decades—even centuries—

A pealing noise brought him out of his stupor. He was still on the balcony, drenched in sweat as he stared up at the clouds of smog. He had been staring at the airborne filth as if they held some secret to his soul. When something began ringing inside the condominium, images of Candice flashed in his mind. He shuddered….

The phone was still ringing. He stood up and went to the threshold of the French doors, looking in uneasily—as though expecting some monster to attack him. Shaking his head, he entered the room. Since he was drenched in sweat—and *naked*—the air-conditioned room chilled him, but he moved quickly now, to reach the phone. It was on the coffee table; when he picked it up, his hand was trembling slightly—

"Sir, it's Sam."

"Sam…" he said—but more to remind himself that the man was his doorman. His mind was dazed, and he hardly recognized his own voice.

"You have visitors, sir."

"Who?" He instinctively looked at the wall clock, which said that it was twenty minutes to six.

"A couple," Sam went on. And then, holding the phone away from his mouth, he asked the people to repeat their names. "...Dallas and Cindy Phelps, sir."

Roland almost dropped the phone! He almost *collapsed!* He was trembling all over now, as though he were standing out in the middle of the arctic, freezing to death. Candice came out of the bedroom then. When she saw the distraught expression on his face, she stopped in the doorway with a mixture of curiosity and concern.

"Sir?" Sam said again." Are you there?"

"Yeah," Roland said in an uneven voice; he cleared his throat nervously. "...What do they want?"

"They came for their daughter."

Roland made an equivocal grunting sound—

"Should I send them up, sir?"

Roland was nibbling at his lower lip.

"Sir?"

"Yeah," Roland blurted out, responding more to the insistence in the man's voice than anything else. It was only after Sam put the phone down—and Roland found himself listening to the dial tone—that the full extent of it hit him. *Phelps and his wife are on their way up here!* He suddenly realized he was naked. He tossed the phone on the couch and dashed for the bedroom. Candice was still looking at him oddly—

"Phelps!" he explained, rushing past her to get a robe. He had to prepare—but he was running out of time.

Candice was still looking at him oddly when he tied the robe around himself. And then:

"I wonder how they knew you and Mindy were here?" he mused.

"Dallas called me this morning," she answered in an offhand manner. "I have a cell phone," she said, taking it out of the pocket of her robe and holding it up so he could see. Then, frowning again: "You all right, Roland?"

Her nonchalant tone—and a flashback of what had happened an hour earlier—only unnerved him further. It reminded him of the night of the banquet, and he definitely couldn't deal with that now. Phelps was coming... *God*, he didn't feel well at all! On top of everything, he suddenly remembered he had that TV appearance this morning! He had to be in the studio in an hour! He grimaced.

"You all right, Roland?" Candice asked again.

"Yeah," he said tersely. She took a step toward him, but he couldn't be around her now. Like before, when she came to him on the couch, he had the urge to push her away: to *strangle* her! "I'm fine...I'm *fine*," he said as she continued to come to him. He was on the verge of screaming it for a third time, but the doorbell rang. Roland flinched. Candice, seeing his reaction, was again about to ask him if everything was all right. In order to get the hell away from her, he pushed past her and walked out of the bedroom.

How am I going to play this! he wondered as he walked to the door. He had no idea! The night before, the reality that Phelps was his enemy had given him clarity of purpose, but Phelps' coming here now was a grand outflanking maneuver that even Sun Tzu would have envied. The war was beginning and he had been caught without even his drawers on!

He glanced over his shoulder nervously when he reached the door. Candice was still standing in the bedroom doorway with a combination of curiosity and concern on her face. He looked away from her uneasily, taking a deep breath as he grasped the doorknob.

He opened the door the way people did in horror movies: brusquely, like he was expecting a monster to leap out at him. However, when the door opened, Phelps' beautiful wife was smiling back at him. In fact, when Roland looked around, he saw she was the only one there. "Cindy?" he said confusedly. "Where's Dallas?"

"Oh, he's just getting something from the car," she said, giggling suddenly. "We didn't wake you up, did we?"

Roland watched her smiling face, nonplused. She was wearing a white, frilly blouse and a kind of tennis skirt: something that seemed indelibly connected with the ease of well-to-do country clubs. Her long blond hair was arranged in a sophisticated manner around her shoulders. There was a youthful healthiness about her; and yet, Roland found himself thinking that she either had no clue her husband was a monster, was in denial about it, or was too stupid to realize it—

"Thanks for keeping Mindy and Candice for us last

night," she went on in her usual giggly, schoolgirl tone. "I hope we didn't put you out."

He had been staring at her confusedly, his mind anxiously going over what Phelps could possibly be planning for him; but seeing her imploring smile, and remembering that she had asked him a question—and that he had kept her standing out in the hall—he quickly brought her in, saying, "No problem at all."

Cindy and Candice waved to one another in greeting, both smiling.

Roland unconsciously shook his head to keep from thinking about the bizarre sex triangle. Candice was leaning against the bedroom door now, still with her godforsaken calmness.

"Can I get you anything?" Roland said abruptly. He had needed to say something.

"Just Mindy," she said. "It's all Dallas' fault," she went on in her giggly way. "He's desperate to get out to our house in the Hamptons for the weekend. He's always acting on the spur of the moment. And with all that rioting stuff in the news, I can't really blame him. You know," she went on breathlessly, "Dallas was *mugged* last night!"

"Oh?" Roland said.

"Yeah, he came home with his face all bruised. But you know Dallas: nothing can really get him down. Even with the mugging, he came home with a bottle of champagne...such a romantic, that man."

"*Romantic?*" Roland said, unable to believe what he was hearing.

"Yeah," she said, snickering coyly, "that's why he made Candice and Mindy spend the night with you.... And sorry again to wake you up so early," Cindy went on, apologetically, "but Dallas wanted to get out of town right away."

"Yeah, I know the feeling," Roland added under his breath; she frowned at him, then smiled vapidly.

It was then that the doorbell rang again. Roland had left the door slightly ajar, and Phelps walked in before Roland could move. The left side of Phelps' face was swollen and discolored horribly. Roland grimaced at the sight of it, and then a shudder went down his spine when he realized the man was actually in his home—

"I know," Cindy responded to Roland's reaction, going up to her husband and caressing his shoulder, "that mugger really got him good."

"He sure did," Phelps said, laughing enigmatically. There was a gleam in the man's eyes that made Roland cringe. And just then, as if Roland were not confused enough, Phelps handed him the small, glossy bag in his hand.

"What's this?"

"It's your present. I almost forgot it in the car. Congratulations on winning that case!"

Roland looked at the package uneasily; part of him thinking that maybe there was a bomb in it. "What is it?"

"Open it and see!" the man said, smiling.

Candice came over then, and they all stood around eagerly as Roland looked in the bag and pulled out a small case. "It's a Rolex," Roland said in disbelief.

"Yes," Phelps said with a laugh. "All our new partners get one."

"*Partner?*" He looked down at the watch uneasily. Was it all a trick to disarm him? Phelps was his enemy, he reminded himself; but instead of the necessary hatred, all that came was confusion and uneasiness. Worse, he realized Phelps was still at ease. All about the man, there was the confident aura of someone who never lost. Even the man's wife didn't suspect anything. If Phelps could do all that, then think about what he could do to Roland! The others were cheering now; Roland tried to smile and act graciously, but his mind was sputtering along. He opened his mouth, looking for something to say—

"Mommy and Daddy!" Mindy screamed joyously. When they looked, they saw her rushing from the guest bedroom. When she was close enough, the little girl leaped at her parents. Phelps caught her and held her up, so that the three of them stood there hugging and kissing. Everyone was laughing now; but as Roland looked at them, a wave of revulsion washed over him.

It was all fake: Phelps' love for Cindy and his daughter...Phelps: a depraved man playing family man; Cindy, a good-natured, but essentially clueless woman playing the perfect wife and mother. The only real one was Mindy—but only because she was too young to see the lies. As for Candice, he had no patience for her either. She stood there cheering at the scene, as if last night had never happened. He just wanted them all gone: out of his home, out of his *life*... !

"Candice," Phelps began, interrupting their saccharine love fest, "get dressed and we'll all head off."

Candice dutifully went to the bedroom.

"Daddy!" Mindy exclaimed, "what happened to your face!"

"Just a little accident."

"Do you want me to kiss it and make it better?"

"Of course!"—Mindy kissed him with a loud smack— "...Ah," he said in relief, "*all* better."

Roland felt like he was going to throw up! Phelps glanced at him then; and seeing Roland's expression, his tone changed immediately.

"Sweetheart," Phelps addressed his wife then, "take Mindy to the car: I want to talk to Roland for a moment."

Roland's stomach churned at the words; he felt the blood draining from his face! This was it: the battle was about to begin!

"Bye, Uncle Roland!" Mindy called, while Cindy giggled again and whisked the little girl out of the door. Roland stared at their retreating forms, panicking inside. Now that the others were gone, Roland knew the real Phelps would come out; the smiling family man would disappear, and the demon from last night would take his place. Roland prepared himself for battle; unconsciously, he balled his hands into fists.

At first, neither of them spoke. When Roland glanced at Phelps, he was surprised to see the fear in the man's eyes. Phelps wasn't meeting his eyes, and the prospect of Phelps' weakness reassured him somehow. Yet, even then, he wondered if that weakness might just be an act.

Roland forced himself to speak up. "What was last night about?" he said, finally broaching the subject. He was still holding the watch in his hand: "What is this?" he added, holding up the Rolex, "—an attempt to buy me off?"

"Look," Phelps pleaded, looking sorrowful, "I was drunk...I don't know what came over me."

Roland was feeling better all the time! "Is that it?" he said with a bemused frown, "—the *insanity* defense?"

"Nobody has to know about this, right?" he said, uneasily.

Roland stared at him for a while; then, smiling, he shook his head. "Look, I don't want anyone knowing about last night, any more than you do. I guess on that count, we can come to a truce. What you do with your life is your own business: I only ask that I not be involved in it."

Phelps nodded nervously.

Candice came out of the bedroom then, dressed in the clothes of the previous night. When she reached

them, she smiled and caressed Roland's shoulder, and
he had to summon all his will not to shudder at her
touch—not to go into a rage and strangle them both.
Somehow, he managed to keep his head. Then, after
Phelps nodded contritely to him one last time, Roland
found himself standing there alone.

He stared at the closed door in disbelief. Either it was
over, or it was just beginning; either Phelps was a
pathetic fool, or the man was some maniacal genius, in
whose web Roland was trapped. Roland felt even more
depleted than ever; and just then, remembering the TV
appearance, he groaned and rushed to the bedroom to
get ready.

Somewhere in the building, a man was screaming
hysterically. Dr. Joel Fishman led his twelve students—
and two burly orderlies—down the wide corridors of
the New York Institute for the Criminally Insane. They
all walked with a kind of dignified silence—as though
they were true believers on a religious pilgrimage. The
outside world, with its polluted skies, oppressive heat and
impending chaos, seemed like another universe. In here,
the air conditioner was on full blast, and everything
seemed almost preternaturally clean. Indeed, everything
was white: their lab coats, the wide, empty corridors,
the orderlies' uniforms, the fluorescent lights above... It
was like the Arctic—a huge wall of whiteness, in which

one could lose one's sight and sense of proportion. Someone was still screaming; but in this strange place, it seemed almost melodious—proving, once again, that beauty could be found in anything, including madness.

Dr. Fishman was a slender man of moderate height and middle age. There was a certain smugness and self-satisfaction about his movements, which reminded one of a celebrated maestro about to conduct a masterpiece. Ready to begin the first movement, he stopped before one of the locked metal doors, then nodded to the two orderlies, who came to the front and opened the door.

It was a small room—about twelve meters by seven meters. The orderlies and Fishman's students entered first. A skinny black man was lying supine on a cot, staring at the ceiling. There were no windows in the room—just blank white plaster walls. Following their training, the two orderlies positioned themselves by the man's bed—one at the head and the other at the foot. In the meanwhile, the students formed a semicircle around the supine man's cot. When that was completed, Fishman ceremoniously entered the cramped room and stepped into the semicircle. He paused then, and looked around the room dramatically, before declaring: "Here, ladies and gentleman, is the famous Jasper Kain…."

Two months had passed since Kain's capture, but they had never let him speak. They hadn't even given him a proper trial. They had only hidden him away, as they were hiding him away now. Even Roland Micheaux had deserted him—running away like a scared child; so that now, Kain's years of work were all for nothing. Kain had lain there for weeks now—at first, waiting for the destined madness, and then wondering where he had failed. Throughout those internal deliberations, he had been like a Buddhist monk entering a trance, unaware of what was going on around him. Orderlies had come around, forcing him to eat and change his clothes and take his medicine. Psychiatrists had come to him, trying to talk to him. None of those things had really registered in his mind; but now, when Fishman walked into the room and pronounced his name, Kain looked across for the first time.

There was something about the sound of Fishman's voice that wrenched him from his apocalyptic daydreams. Confused by his emergence back into the world of men, the pink, eager faces of those gathered around him made him recoil. However, his eyes soon came to rest on Fishman: in the cramped room, the man was no more than a meter from him. Frowning, he finally recognized the man.

Fishman had been the "psychological expert" at his court hearing. The man had come to Kain the morning after his capture, asking him pointless questions about his mother and childhood. Spouting his Freudian drivel, the man had then reappeared as the featured witness at the farce that found him "mentally unfit to stand trial." Kain's lawyer had been a sweaty thirty-five-year-old who, in his five years as a public defender, had only managed to win two cases! It turned out that both the public defender and the district attorney had wanted to get Kain declared incompetent; and so, the entire thing had all been a farce.

With the strangeness of time over the last few weeks, it was as though those events had happened years ago. Kain instinctively found himself looking at Fishman the way one looked at someone whom one hadn't seen in ages. He looked to see if the man had more wrinkles now, or had gotten fatter. The fact that there was no change at all, added to Kain's belief that Fishman was somehow immutable—some inert substance floating through the universe.

It was then that Fishman turned halfway to his students and began, in his precise monotone: "In Jasper Kain, we have the prototype of a new kind of mental illness—a uniquely *modern* illness." He paused dramatically then, as though allowing his students to soak in the poetry of his words. "Jasper Kain is not merely a man misled by his delusions of grandeur—and his own dissatisfaction with his life—he sees himself as some kind of vengeful angel. And it is in this mindset which we see the truth behind not only his actions, but his psychological makeup. He is another in the long line of criminals who have been gripped by the sexual allure of violence."

Kain had been listening intently, but seeing where Fishman was going, he lay back on the cot, staring at the ceiling again. Fishman went on:

"Ironically, when we look at Kain's actions, we see

that while he was pulled by the allure of being *known* for violence, he went out of his way to avoid *being* violent. This is the telling thing about him. He wanted the reputation of a Jack the Ripper, who brutalized women— who sliced them up and *killed* them. He wanted the sexual release—and, indeed, the *notoriety* that dismembering an innocent person entailed in his mind; and yet, he chose something that when severed, would cause no pain—and cause no blood to be spilt. He chose *hair*!"

While in Brooklyn, the forces of self-destruction gathered to hear Botswana Glade's words, Kain smiled to himself. Fishman continued:

"But the mere cutting of hair never satisfied him. Of course, how *could* it! He wanted to be violent, but his violence was never, so to speak, *consummated*. He remained unfulfilled—*impotent*, if you will." Kain snickered to himself. "As it was," Fishman said with a frown, annoyed by Kain's interruption, "Kain eventually became a laughingstock. He wished to inspire terror in his victims; but over time, it turned into gales of laughter. The hair grew back, leaving a strange kind of celebrity status for his supposed victims. They appeared on television by the dozens, somehow ascendant and jolly, despite his attempt at desecration and dismemberment. Indeed, toward the end, people even began to fake attacks upon themselves by giving themselves hackneyed haircuts, so that that they, too, could become celebrities. This further thwarted and marginalized Kain, who was now a secondary character in his own supposed reign of terror. He was never gratified by the act that was supposed to spur him to ecstasy.

"This," he added with a flourish of his hand, "explains the comical conclusion to this entire affair. It is obvious that Kain wanted to get caught. He wanted to once again become the focus of his own fiasco; and so, in an orgasmic, climactic farce, he effected the means by which he could be captured—and captured in the *spotlight*. He attacked the Mayor of New York City, in what amounts to broad daylight, knowing what it would mean. He made sure that it was an event where the cameras would be rolling. He didn't even *try* to escape! He just stood there, grinning. He wanted his great moment of martyrdom to have a grand cinematic appeal. That had been the moment of no return: the moment when he could have been violent—taken the plunge, so to speak—and slaughtered not only the Mayor, but socialites from the banquet. But even then," Fishman went on, raising his hand theatrically, "he remained a laughingstock. Instead of taking action, he remained impotent. It was then that people—even those who rushed to get a glimpse of him and afford him ephemeral celebrity status—saw him for what he was: a small man who needs help. And," he concluded compassionately, "he will be helped, my young colleagues, through therapy and medication. Like I said before, he is *thoroughly* harmless. Once he is freed of his delusions—and acknowledges whatever sexual failings he has suffered through his entire life (I bet he is even a *virgin*!)—he will once again be a productive member of society."

Fishman had paused dramatically, ready for the reverent sighs and nods which were the psychiatric equivalent of a shower of applause, but all that there was, was Kain's sudden, howling laughter. Fishman first looked at him in surprise, then annoyance. After listening to Fishman, Kain was suddenly reassured that everything was on track. He laughed out triumphantly then, looking as though he was going into a seizure on the cot—

"Orderlies," Fishman said with a groan, gesturing for the men to restrain Kain. However, when the two goons tried to hold him down, Kain laughed louder—as if they were tickling him. His voice was now supplanting that of the lunatic screaming down the corridor. Fishman had been around madness for thirty years now, but something about Kain's laughter took even him aback. This discomfort was rare for him, and he didn't like it. He found himself fleeing from the room, bumping into a few of the students as he made his retreat. Yet, even when the orderlies locked Kain back in his room, the man's laughter still echoed down the halls.

Randolph was inside the hospital now. The protesters and Maria Santos were behind him for the moment, but peace was nowhere in sight. Everything was falling apart! He kept seeing the smug, vengeful expression on Santos' face. The woman had been out for *blood!* In an hour, all the major news services would be carrying the story. This was the calm before the storm, but even the calm was chaotic and churning....

He was walking down a corridor now, surrounded by an entourage that now included about twenty people. Most were reporters and camera crews, who had been handpicked to show Randolph visiting the wounded. It was all staged. Seven video cameras now faced him; the cameramen were walking backwards, like crabs. In a few moments, when the frenzy of his scandal seized them, they would rip him apart...a photographer kept snapping his picture, and each time the flash went off, it was like an explosion in his brain.

Was his life really over? After his disgrace, he would be thrown out of office—probably *impeached*—and then he would be as good as dead. How the hell had it come to this...? But what was the use anymore?

He suddenly became aware that the police commissioner was walking by his side. The latter was a fat, ruddy-faced man who had a perpetually sorrowful expression on his face. The commissioner's placement had also been planned in advance, to show that the Mayor supported him. However, as Randolph walked along, he began wondering what good these machinations could do. The thousands of people gathering outside didn't give a shit who walked by Randolph's side...!

They finally reached the first victim's room. A teen-age Latino was lying comatose in a bed with myriad tubes and bandages and pieces of equipment attached to him. He had been the first one that the maniac shot down; afterwards, the boy had been trampled by the mob. Two women were by the side of the bed, crying and consoling one another. Randolph, the commis-sioner, and the rest of the entourage, took in the scene with reverent silence. Yet, even as Randolph stared at the scene, he felt himself drifting away from them all. In fact, even before Levin pulled him away from Santos, Randolph had felt himself withdrawing from the world. He saw everything that was happening around him, but he saw it all as though from a great distance. His mind wandered, and he found himself yearning for his youth.

Indeed, thirty-odd years ago, he had been like a god—a tall, muscular god, with blazing speed and the courage to take on anything. The image of Randolph winning the national championship for his college football team was indelibly burned into the myth of America. The footage of Randolph first fighting off two tackles, faking out two others, then throwing that perfect pass to his on-running receiver, seemed to be the embodiment not only of what Randolph was—but of what America could be. He had always been a man of motion—a *star*—running confidently toward what he knew to be his destiny. Even as a boy, growing up in Harlem, he had *known* he was going to be great; and as a sense of confidence with one's own life tended to make one appear more attractive to others, Randolph had always been popular. Somehow, everyone had assumed he could see and do things that no one else could; and as the lost and confused were likely to put all of their trust in those who seemed to know where they were going, he had been a born leader.

As for women, in those carefree days, he had been able to take his pick. Even before he reached puberty, the young girls had tried to get a piece of him: to *brand* him with their love. Even the young girls had seemed to have nothing but love to give. Like their mothers before them, the less hope they had, the greater they had loved—and the more desperately they had tried to *prove* their love to him. For those quickly blossoming girls, he had been their imagination, their hope, their will, and their purpose in life. He had been their fearless god— but they had all been fools, mistaking his blindness and stupidity for courage.

His athletic scholarship had been to one of those midwestern universities in a town whose population dropped by eighty percent when school wasn't in session. That had been his first glimpse of life beyond New York City. There had been farms all around the campus—so much open space! At first, the peacefulness of it had taken him aback.

There had been so much freedom to roam and breathe that he had felt small for the first time. He had walked around that rustic town like a country bumpkin gawking on his first visit to "the big city." And then, everything had happened so quickly... There had been the frantic rush to register for classes, and the first few grueling practices for the fall football season. Even then, Randolph had been at ease. He had shrugged off the strange antagonism of some of his white teammates and classmates, and gone confidently about his business.... And then, a month later, everything had been further heightened when he was thrust into the starting quarterbacking role—a position usually reserved for whites. He had become a national figure overnight—especially after leading the team to two straight victories against national powerhouses. Still, even as sixty thousand fans cheered for him, and his teammates carried him off the field on their shoulders, it had been just another natural happenstance to him—not some great milestone, as everyone was saying.

Whatever the case, the national press had hovered around him, constantly asking for interviews as he led his team to victory after victory. On campus, he had been a kind of god, insulated from everything by his athleticism on the field. Things had been so busy that he didn't go back home until the next summer.... So much had changed in a year—or maybe it was only that the gulf of time had allowed him to see things clearly. He had stepped from his sheltered, fairytale existence, into reality. At first, he had had to readjust himself to the unsettling density of the slums—and the constant noise. For a moment, walking down Lexington Avenue with his suitcase in one hand, he had wondered how it was that people managed to live stacked on top of one another, like animals. Everything had seemed new and suspect. When he finally got home, he had hardly recognized his little family—which he had always idealized as being some pillar of strength and rectitude. He had found his mother sitting on the couch in a sleazy-looking feathery robe, watching a soap opera. Everything had seemed...*warped*, as if these were strangers that he was meeting. He had come home to find out not only that his younger brother was a junkie, doing a five-year stretch in jail for armed robbery, and that his fourteen-year-old sister was seven months pregnant, but that their mother seemed to care less. He had seen the filth of his home for the first time: the overflowing sink, the dusty corners, the peeling plaster...the reality of his family—their emptiness and *neediness*—had repulsed him.

Indeed, for the first time, he had been ashamed—not only of his family, but of his people and their needs. Finding out that he was back in town, everyone had come around, clumsily trying to ingratiate him—or herself with him. The young women had again renewed their assaults with their love; obscure childhood playmates had seemed desperate to convince him they had been the best of friends. It had all repulsed him—just as his mother's request for a little cash to buy some beer had repulsed him. For the first time, he had looked out of his window and seen a horrible, crumbling place. When he turned on the television, everything had been there: reports of the Vietnam War, protests about the war, protests about racism and inequality, about *everything*, it seemed. Bewildered, he had gone for a walk, finding out that one of his closest childhood friends was now dead—and that many others were either in jail or hooked on drugs...or had been shipped off to Vietnam. Suddenly, his childhood—with all of its imagined peace—had seemed like a farce; and for the first time, all that he had wanted to do, was flee. Like a man whose house was burning wildly out of control, he had had to choose between escaping with his life and trying to save those within. And maybe he had chosen the path that his people had always seemed to take. Black people—*his* people—who had run from the south to the north, foolishly thinking that they could escape racism. They had run from the supposed bigotry of the white man, yet they seemed even more terrified of the desperate black man whose needs they could never satisfy...*black* people, who, in trying to escape the horrors of slavery, had found it impossible to escape the entanglements of freedom...he had been just like them when he fled.

After two days in the city, he had fled back to Iowa without saying goodbye to a single person. As it was summer, the campus and the town had been practically deserted. He had been in the student union, watching the news. Apparently, in some city, there had been a race riot, set off by frustrations and fears and outrage that had been out of proportion with everything he had ever felt before. He had watched it in a daze, and come to the conclusion that that was what happened when people became victims of their needs.

Just then, a flirtatious white woman had come up—one of those liberal types who was desperate to show how open-minded she was. He couldn't recount the details of how it had happened, but a few minutes later, they had been in his room, having sex. There had been no real propositioning—no coquettish questions about one another's dating status. It had all been instinctual: *animalistic* maybe. Even attraction had hardly seemed to apply. They had both been attractive in the classical sense, but they had been far beyond that: beyond words, beyond definitions and categorization. It had happened in a whirlwind: he had found himself sucked under, unable to breathe and terrified of drowning. It had hardly even seemed like sex at all. Caught in the terror of the whirlwind, he had groped her body, and yet he had hardly seemed to be seeking pleasure. In fact, they had hardly seemed like partners at all, any more than two victims of an avalanche could call themselves partners. They had been whisked away, as powerless to stop the outcome as they were to stop gravity.... An hour later, whatever had gripped them and dragged them away, relinquished its grasp. It had all been so strange to him. He had stared into her blue eyes as she lay there panting. He had had sex with her, yet it had not seemed to be about her, as much as it had been a grand struggle against his past. Somehow or another, he had been annealing himself with her shrieks of ecstasy. He had been, in a sense, losing his virginity—exchanging his cosmic blindness for the hardened shell he knew he would need to survive....

Back in the present, Randolph nodded thoughtfully to himself. After all these years, the hardened shell had cracked. He and the entourage were once again walking down the corridor, going to see another of the wounded. His aides watched him anxiously as they walked, suspecting that something horrible was growing within him—but nobody said anything.

The next room was The Maniac's. That was what everyone was calling the shooter—since even the FBI couldn't figure out his identity. Given the fact that so many people were calling for the man's head, four policemen were posted at his door. When Randolph reached the room, the reporters and camera crews were of course excluded—since images of the man would probably only incite further violence.

Randolph, the police commissioner, and a doctor entered the room; and after they entered, the door was quickly closed behind them. The maniac seemed to be covered in bandages from head to foot. His left leg and right arm were in casts; his neck was in a brace, and his face was bandaged, leaving only openings for his eyes and mouth. Randolph stood there staring. The window was open slightly, and he could hear the mob gathered outside. The sound was like thunder rumbling in the distance. The people outside were desperate to rip the man apart; but now that Randolph's sex scandal was imminent, he felt strangely connected to the man. Indeed, as these thoughts passed through his mind, he walked up to the side of the maniac's bed and looked down at the man's bandaged face—

Suddenly, the man's eyes opened! Randolph recoiled, the way one would recoil at the sight of a corpse coming to life. Yet, when he realized the man's lips were moving, he instinctively bent down, putting his ear to the man's lips. When the doctor saw the man was conscious, he came up—and was about to ask Randolph to step to the side—when the Mayor jumped back.

"—Kill me!" The Maniac was repeating, over and over again.

"What's he saying?" the doctor and the police commissioner asked in unison, but Randolph was too numb to hear. He felt dizzy and sick as he fled the room. "Kill me!" the man had said; and for a strange moment, Randolph had found himself considering it—both for the man and himself. He had felt himself being soothed by the thought, drawn into it the way one was drawn into quicksand. He fled from the room, but reporters assaulted him with questions as he burst into the corridor. At the sound, he cringed against the wall, seeing that he was trapped.

Roland was staring at his new Rolex watch when the cab stopped in front of the studio. It was a quarter to seven. His mind kept drifting back to what had happened at his condo. Part of him wanted to celebrate his apparent victory over Phelps, but he couldn't get over the feeling that it had all been a trick....

He had rushed to get here on time; but after getting out of the cab, he stopped and looked around confusedly. There was a chaotic scene in front of the warehouse-looking building, with hundreds of agitated, shouting people marching up and down the sidewalk. With the heat wave, they seemed like tortured spirits, roasting in hell. As he listened, he realized they were chanting, "No justice, no peace!" Roland instinctively looked up at the bulletin board then, and nodded his head when he saw the show's lineup. The protesters were there to support the man who seemed to be the featured guest of the morning show: Botswana Glade.

The bulletin board read:

TODAY:

Activist, Botswana Glade

Supermodels, Alana and Trudy

Attorney, Roland Micheaux

Bestselling Author, Armand Deville

While in Brooklyn, the forces of self-destruction gathered to hear Botswana Glade's words, Roland shook his head at it all. When would it end...?

His cellular phone was ringing. He took it out of his jacket pocket and looked at it oddly. "Yes?" he answered the phone.

"Micheaux, this is Mr. Rosencrantz!" his boss announced in a gruff voice.

"Mr. Rosencrantz..." Roland repeated. For some reason, he was uneasy. "Is anything wrong, sir?"

"Report to my office this morning," the man said in a stern voice that was out of character for him.

"I'm about to appear on TV."

"I'm aware of that!" he said in annoyance. "Report to me after that's done. I'll expect you at ten o'clock."

"Is anything wrong?" Roland said again.

"Something very *serious* has just been brought to our attention," Rosencrantz said in the same uncharacteristic tone. And then, Roland was listening to the dial tone. He stood there for at least ten seconds, still holding the phone to his ear. *This had to be Phelps' doing*! What to do now...!

He was looking around desperately now, as if the answer might be lying right in front of him. Happening to glance down the sidewalk, to his left, he noticed a side entrance, in front of which a nervous-looking man was waving at him, trying to get his attention. There were also two burly guards standing there....

"Mr. Micheaux!" the man—an intern by the looks of it—squealed as Roland approached. "Thank goodness you're here on time!"

Roland stared blankly, hardly hearing.

The intern was already sweating profusely—as was Roland—"Just go straight down the hall," the intern said, shuffling through some dirty-looking papers. "There should be a dressing room there for you," the intern went on, already looking nervously out of the door for other guests. "Someone will come in and get you ready," he added as an afterthought....

Roland shuffled down the dimly lit hallway, still hearing Rosencrantz's voice resounding in his mind. *Damn Phelps!* What had the man said...? Roland wasn't feeling well at all. The more he tried to think, the more useless his thoughts seemed. Worse, he was going to be on nationwide television within the hour! The thought made him stumble, so that he had to brace himself against the wall.

As Roland shuffled deeper into the building, he got glimpses of the set through an open section in the wall. It seemed suddenly fake: a living room floating in the darkness, surrounded by lights and cameras. Some stage workers rushed past him; and on the set, others were assiduously getting everything in order. In fact, everyone was in a hurry, suddenly striking him as fairytale characters screaming that the sky was falling—but maybe it was! Rosencrantz had summoned him like he was a worthless law clerk....

Roland's gait was now that of a tired old man...and he was lost. He had merely been walking down the labyrinthine passages aimlessly. He tried remembering the intern's instructions, but it was pointless. All he remembered was something about a door down the hall. The sudden frustration drove him to open the first door he saw. He peeped inside, seeing a luxurious dressing room, with a huge dressing table in one corner and a settee in the other. He guessed this was it. After nodding to himself nervously, he stepped inside. He was just closing the door when a woman called from an adjoining room: "Gwen? Is that you?"

Before Roland could say anything, the woman rushed out. Roland stood there frozen, because the woman—a tall, shapely red head whom he recognized immediately as the hostess of the show—came out dressed in nothing but an open robe. Her breasts were showing, as was her pubic hair.

I guess she actually is a red head! Roland thought to himself. His eyes roamed over her shapely body as he waited for her to scream. However, when his roaming eyes reached her face—her *eyes*—he knew he was undone. For the life of him, there was neither shock nor fear in her light green eyes. The way she looked at him, it was as though *he* were the naked one. In fact, as she looked at him, there didn't seem to be any limit to what she might be seeing—or to what she might *be*. For this reason, she suddenly seemed beautiful to him—*wondrous* in fact—

She smiled, breaking the spell. "You're Roland Micheaux, aren't you?" she said. Her voice was strangely resonant—*soothing*.

He paused before he spoke, not yet trusting his voice. He found his jaw muscles unusually tight when he opened his mouth. His mouth seemed too dry. He swallowed deeply, then answered: "Yes." He took another deep breath, then said, "And you're Samantha Dearly."

As she nodded, he suddenly found himself smiling as well, relieved both at his words, and the fact that he had been able to speak. At that moment, she walked casually past Roland and over to the dressing table.

She closed her robe as she walked—but in a way that made it seem as though it hadn't needed closing. It was as though they had always stood before one another like that, either both naked or both fully clothed. She picked up a tube of lipstick and began to apply it. Roland stood there, staring at her in that strange moment. She looked at him in the mirror again and smiled; then:

"Since you're here, would you mind helping me with my necklace?"

"Sure," Roland said, moving with too much alacrity. She handed him the necklace—which was made of flat marble-like plates and joined by three latches—then she turned back around so that he could put it on.

They could see one another via the mirror. She hadn't tied her robe, and Roland could see the smooth, firm outlines of her breasts. He had to loop his hand around her to put on the necklace. Her hair smelled incredible: the scent conjured images of some tropical grove, with a waterfall. It was suddenly as though they were the only ones in the world. She pulled her hair to the side, so that he could have access to her neck...he felt like his head was swimming.

Somehow, he managed to attach the first latch of the necklace. He was moving slowly—fumbling actually. He didn't want it to end. He just wanted it to be them there, forever. While he fumbled with her necklace—and her neck—she inadvertently backed into him, and his erection. He couldn't help gasping at the sensation. *What was happening*?...but he was tired of thinking. He could feel the soft, firm outline of her behind through the thin robe: certainly she could feel him. He looked in the mirror to see her face, but as she was still holding her hair out of the way, her face was averted. He managed to attach the second latch, but she was still there, pressed against his erection. He put his face closer to her hair and inhaled her—took a long deep breath that left him even giddier. God, he didn't want it to end—this strange respite from all the chaos and problems of the world. He would do anything to hold her in his arms. He attached the third latch, but not wanting it to end, he let his hands wander down the warm surface of her neck, to her shoulders, and then from her shoulders, to her back and hips; and she was still there, pressed against him as if they were the only ones in the world.

She let her hair go at last; and for a moment, they stared at one another via the mirror. His eyes were clouded over with longing—and, beyond that, the deep bewilderment of his life. She turned to him then, staring up into his eyes, as if seeing it all; and for once, he didn't hide—*couldn't* hide. She was holding him now, and he pulled her softness to him. He had needed something soft—something *reassuring*. Instinctively, he bent down and kissed her. At first, it was soft...a universe of carefree pleasure; she put her arms around his neck, so that the scent of her perfume flared in his nostrils and made his head swoon.

She was so soft, all of her...but then, her tongue was suddenly wild in his mouth; her arms were like a noose around his neck, strangling him. A side of him, suddenly terrified—suddenly remembering Candice—wanted to push her away and run out of the room; but instead, he grabbed her behind. It wasn't a caress or a fondle; it was a grab. The force of her body against his put him off balance, so that he stumbled back into the wall. It was as if they were fighting one another—at *odds* with one another. She seemed to be biting at his tongue; her nails in his neck and back were like a beast's talons clawing into him. From her throat escaped a groan that was more like a growl: a declaration of war and madness. From his throat escaped a similar noise. It was guttural and horrible; and now that the battle lines had been drawn, it was his turn to push her back. There was the settee to the side: they both collapsed onto it, their struggle not ceasing for an instant. It was as if they would both rend one another to death. Yet, deep within him, he was aroused by the battle: by the internecine war that they had found themselves in. She was clawing at his back more savagely now; he was grabbing her ass with one hand, rubbing her brusquely between her thighs with the other. And then, he was sucking at her neck, tasting her tangy sweat—

She pulled away, either the first to come to her senses, or the first to have burned off the fuel of her lust. She stared up at him; he stared at her, horrified by what he suddenly realized was the horror in her green eyes. The horror was definitely there, although it was clouded by a host of other emotions. In truth, her face wore one of those nebulous expressions that could have been anything from ecstasy to terror. Roland guiltily pulled his hand away from her crotch; he sat up on the settee, and she sat up with him. They were still staring deeply into one another's eyes, searching for the thing that would give meaning to the soupy mix of emotions that bubbled within them both—

All at once, she sucked in air sharply; and as she breathed deeply, Roland realized they had both been holding their breath. Their chests heaved for those first few breaths; but even after their breathing became relatively normal, they still stared at one another, trying to make sense of it all.

"Well then," she said with a laugh that was like a sigh of relief, "maybe we should go on a date first."

Conservative estimates said that there were now at least four thousand angry protesters in front of the hospital—and it wasn't even eight o'clock yet... Mayor Randolph was led to the lectern that had been set up in the hospital's cafeteria. He had spent about half an hour visiting with the wounded and their families, telling them insipid things like, "Hang in there," and, "We'll try to make sure this never happens again." Cameras had been there to capture the entire thing—which had, of course, been the point. Yet, while he said those words and smiled in their faces, the maniac's, "Kill me! *kill me*...!" had been playing in the back of his mind. Demonic images of Maria Santos and the stripper had been there as well, eroding his sanity like acid.

At the same time, his doom seemed so complete that a feeling of calm was taking hold of him. He was like a trapped animal, accepting death; and in truth, when he set off in search of filth all those weeks ago, a side of him had always known this moment would come. Even now, as he looked up from the lectern and saw a crowd of about two hundred people, he was relatively free of panic and terror. He had no more to give, and was now willing to accept rest on any terms they chose—including death.

Maria Santos was standing ascendant before him— literally right in front of the lectern. Her fellow reporters had congregated around her, asking her what she had heard, and who her source was, but she only shrugged her shoulders coyly. Actually, the message from the stripper had been on her voice mail this morning. The stripper was actually a big fan of hers. As soon as Santos heard the message, she had rushed over to the young woman's apartment, practically drooling as she heard how Randolph had supposedly lured the woman to the back alley and attacked her. *Oh no*, of course the woman wasn't a prostitute and didn't do that kind of thing. She was a young woman, barely out of high school, who was trying to survive in New York. She had dreams of becoming a ballet dancer, and Randolph's attack had shaken her so badly that she didn't know if she could go on. There had been tears in her eyes at that moment, as she recounted how Randolph—that towering beast of a man, had attacked her. She had been no match for him, so she had had no choice but to give in and let him have his way....

Emerging from her idyll, Santos smiled and looked up at Randolph. The Mayor was ready to begin his speech, but *she* was the focus of attention. This was her ticket to the big time. She smiled unconsciously, thinking, *No more scraps*!

Randolph shuffled the pages of his speech anxiously. He had a twinge in his belly and a lump in his throat as the audience looked up at him expectantly. It was then that an old thought entered his mind: what if there really were others like himself out there—individuals succumbing to the same demon that had been guiding him. He had once called such men and women soul mates—but these individuals would only be the devil's workmen. He felt like the carrier of a devastating disease. His soul felt *corrupted*. He could feel the hatred and resentment gestating within him—*changing* him. Indeed, now, as he looked out on the reporter corps, he suddenly found himself wondering how many of them carried his disease. If his corrupted soul mates really were running free in the world, then their society was doomed....

He began reading the speech that Dalton had prepared; but while the words rolled off his tongue, his thoughts were elsewhere. His mind went to things that he hadn't thought about in years: the first time he had made love to his wife; the first steps and words of his son; his first idealistic run for office... His entire life seemed to pass him in a blur, as though saying goodbye to him. As for the speech, there had been nothing original in it. It had been so constructed as to sound both compassionate to the families of the victims, and express the outrage of those who had lost businesses and faith in society. He had done it all with the necessary grace. Indeed, the airy tone of his voice had perhaps added a certain poignancy to it. Whatever the case, when he was finished, and it was time for questions, he sought out Maria Santos and pointed to her and her alone.

Immediately, she demanded: "What do you have to say to the allegation that you *raped* a woman last night?"

Incomprehensibly, a glimmer of a smile came to his lips once again.

Now that the moment of truth had come, a feeling of peace and calmness filled him. He would tell them everything now. But what was there to tell? What was the truth? *Rape?* he thought to himself for the first time. Is that how the stripper was going to play it? The reality of the Mayor of New York City going to a strip joint to ask for sexual favors wasn't bad enough? Why did she have to invent lies...? All at once, he felt outraged again; and it was while he was looking down at all of their eager, expectant faces, that he withdrew his neck from the noose and stepped away from the gallows. They stood before him, self-righteously demanding honesty from him, and yet everything about them was dishonest. He stood straighter then.

"Anyone who thinks me guilty of something," he said in an even voice, "I urge to go to a court of law.... You know what really offends me about this nonsense?" he went on in a new, more pained voice. "Right now, dozens of families are mourning their dead and wounded; but instead of working to mollify those losses, and find out the truth about the events of last night, the drive is on finding out if I'm getting laid or not."

Everyone laughed—except for Santos.

While outside the hospital, the forces of self-destruction gathered to hear Botswana Glade's words, Randolph went on: "People have *died*! Businessmen and women have seen their livelihoods literally go up in smoke. The city, at this *very* moment, sits on the verge of mob violence—with men like Botswana Glade fanning the flames of hatred—and the first question I hear is an allegation of sex? With all due respect, madam," he said, glaring down at the suddenly blanched Maria Santos, "you aren't Judge Starr, and whatever young woman you've scraped up from the gutters, isn't Monica Lewinski!" More laughter! "Bring your witnesses, madam. Bring your semen-stained dress if you wish!" Even more laughter! "Bring all of it before a court of law and I'll answer your allegations there and submit to the will of the people. …But right now, this city needs to heal. Botswana Glade is going to hold a rally in front of *this* building. The city needs me to deal with those concerns, not the rumor and innuendo that all public figures are now forced to submit to. We need to *heal!*"

At that, he looked around earnestly, sighed, and began, "Now, are there any *relevant* questions?" A torrent of hands went up, and Randolph began the press conference anew. Maria Santos seemed suddenly haggard. She walked off then; like Marenga at the banquet, she was unable to understand where she had gone wrong—

or how Randolph had managed to thwart her. Yet, unlike others who had been cowed by Randolph's power, Santos left vowing that she would take revenge and bring him down—no matter what.

The three members of the precinct's special drug unit cruised down the Harlem streets, headed for the slum they had finally gotten permission to raid. Riots always had a strong effect on police officers: they were either cowed by the upheaval, or came to the conclusion that they would have to employ harsher methods in the future. Either way, there was always a certain amount of recalibration after the keepers of order saw it dissolve before their eyes.

The three men had on bulletproof vests and black, army-style fatigues. They usually relaxed by joking before a mission—making wisecracks about one another's wives, girlfriends, and penis sizes; but today, they were pensive. Something new and vile was out there: it wasn't only the crumbling tenements, crime, and filthy streets that left them with an uneasy feeling in the pit of their stomachs. Today, strangely enough, the ghetto streets seemed *too* peaceful—as though this were the prover-bial calm before the storm.

"It's *cooking* us," Fred Holtzman said out of nowhere. He was a chubby, bald, slovenly looking cop, about forty-five, who was the philosopher/jokester of the three.

He was sitting in the back seat of the unmarked sedan, staring out at the world with a strange intensity in his eyes. The driver, Michael Colina, a chiseled forty-year-old who had been in the marines for twelve years, glared at him via the rear view mirror, then went back to staring out of the windshield. The man in the passenger seat, Louie Leonard—a bald, pencil-thin cop of forty-seven, with a huge aquiline nose that made him look like a vulture—turned halfway to the back seat and said:

"*What?*"

"The city's a goddamn pressure cooker," Holtzman went on, "...some demon's stewing us. You smell that air—that's like roast meat...the way the upper class Brits cook it. You ever see how they cook the birds they hunt? They tie them up for a couple days—let them *rot* a little. Then they cook it...they like their meat a little putrid."

"*Please,*" Leonard protested, "I'm about to lose my lunch here."

Leonard's revulsion filled Holtzman with a kind of impudent, boyish pride, so he chuckled to himself and sat back in the seat. However, when he looked over at Colina, and saw the man's continued indifference, he felt the pleasure leave him. He hated silence, and something about Colina had always unnerved him—so he quickly went on: "So can you believe that Brooklyn wacko, asking the Mayor to kill him?"

"I say good riddance," Colina grumbled for the first time, "—just get it over with."

"Nah," Holtzman said with a strange glee, happy to have drawn Colina out, "that guy hasn't suffered enough for what he did."

While in Brooklyn, the forces of self-destruction gathered to hear Botswana Glade's words, Colina chuckled mirthlessly, again looking at Holtzman via the rear view mirror: "And what did he *do*?" There was something strange gleaming in his eyes. "Animals killing animals—that's all it was—"

"*Kids* died, Colina!" Holtzman cried.

Colina remained unmoved as he went on, "A rat's a rat—no matter how old it is."

"What the hell's gotten into you?" Leonard was saying now, alarmed.

"This is *bullshit*," Colina cursed, his voice low and menacing, "—*all* of it! Just hours after a riot, they got us out here, busting a drug dealer who's little more than a junkie himself. We're concentrating on the small fish and then we keep wondering why nothing ever changes. This entire system is set up for us to fail. What the fuck are the three of us supposed to do against all this shit. They got us stuck in the basement, with paperwork up to our asses; and they think because they call us the special drug unit—or whatever they're calling us this week—we're going to change something."

"But what can we do, Colina?" Holtzman said to placate him, "—we're just street cops, we don't got power to change nothing."

"Damn right we don't got power!" Colina raged, the veneer of calmness leaving him. "The thieves and robbers and killers—all those scum—*they* got the power. They got it because we give it to them. You know what I seen on TV the other night? There was this story on that crazy fuck, Jasper Kain…turning criminals and nut jobs into folk heroes: that's what we're doing. Crazy scumbags are our heroes. Killers and robbers are role models. Ever listen to rap music? All it is, is glorified crime, with niggers talking about getting pussy and who they robbed. Those are the role models…. All these assholes out there on the streets…creating a beast they can't control…and then they wonder why shit is fucked up—"

"Hey, Colina," said Leonard, in a tone that hinted that he really hadn't been listening, "you sure you don't want SWAT in on this bust? We don't want anything messy—especially with a riot last night—"

"*Fuck* SWAT!" Colina cursed him. "If you're too scared, you can wait in the car and play with your dick while I handle business—and that goes for you, too, Holtzman."

"Who said anything about being afraid?" Leonard said, defensively. "I'm just following orders. The last thing we need is to give Botswana Glade something to harp about. And operating procedure says—"

Colina glared at him, then shook his head: "Listen to you: 'following orders'…'operating procedure.' You think the drug gangs let bureaucracy hold them back? Bureaucracy's the reason the country's falling apart. We got people more concerned with fitting into the system than getting shit done! Everyone knows what's happening out there: we don't need undercover cops and vice squads to figure out where the crime is. All that shit is going on right in front of our eyes, and we're frightened to move without filling out the proper paperwork—in *triplicate*. In the meantime, everything's going to hell! Desperate times call for desperate measures, not 'operating procedures!'"

"All right, already!" Holtzman said, trying to laugh. "For a 'man of action,' you sure do talk a lot!" At that, he laughed again, tapping Leonard on the shoulder, so that the man felt obliged to chuckle along. Only Colina was silent, as he looked out at the streets he hated....

When they finally drove up to the dilapidated slum, it was about eight o'clock. On the front stoop, a youth had been groping some young chick—who giggled coquettishly under his ministrations—but seeing the three white men alight from the car and get their guns and other equipment from the trunk, the youth stopped and watched them warily.

Colina was the first of the cops to step up. "Police," he said, casually gesturing to the badge on his bulletproof vest, "—you live here?"

"I ain't do nothing, man," the youth said combatively.

"Did I accuse you of anything?" Colina said in his

low, strangely caustic voice. He stood there, waiting for an answer from the kid as the other two cops walked over. "—All right then!" he said in response to the youth's sullen silence. "You live here or not?"

"Yeah," the youth said with a sigh, "I live here—so what?"

Colina chuckled to himself, then: "Listen, junior," he said, moseying up to the top step so the kid could see how much bigger than him he was, "that's a *real* bad attitude you got there. I suggest you change it quick." He placed his hand on his holster, conspicuously. "When I talk to you, you listen and keep your fucking mouth shut; when I tell you to answer, you tell me what the fuck I want to hear, you understand me?"

The youth stared at him uneasily, the fire gone from his eyes.

"All right, then," Colina started again. "Now, do you live here?"

"Yeah," the youth whispered, glancing ashamedly at the girl he had been trying to impress.

"What? *Speak up!*" Colina demanded.

"*Yes*," the youth said sorrowfully, bowing his head.

"You have the keys?"

When the youth nodded, Colina gestured with his head for him to open the door.

The youth's hand was shaking when he put the key into the lock; Colina stood threateningly at his back, waiting impatiently. After the deed was done, Colina turned to him and said: "See how smoothly everything goes when you cooperate with the police?" He proffered a loaded smile then, but the youth looked away....

The hallway was hot, dark and smelly, conjuring the feeling of being trapped within a rotting carcass. When they reached the fourth story apartment, they were about to bash open the door with the battering ram, when Holtzman tried the knob and saw the door was open. They entered a small kitchen that was in utter disarray; two huge rats looked at them disinterestedly from the nasty-looking counter, then casually went about their business. Beyond the kitchen there was a small, equally disheveled living room. The three policemen filed stealthily through it and headed toward the open doorway in the far corner. Beyond the doorway, they heard the sounds of a television program. The cops had their guns drawn—

A woman was screaming; after a moment of confusion, they recognized the disconnected—at times *chaotic*—sounds of sex. Colina crept up to the door and peeked inside, seeing a filthy bedroom; on a bed next to the window, a scrawny black man was pumping savagely into a plump Latina who must have weighed about two and a half times his weight. Colina turned back to the other two, who were at his heels, and nodded to tell them to get ready.

When the men rushed in, the suspect screamed out. The officers charged the bed; but with lightning quick agility that no one could believe, the totally nude man leapt from between the Latina's legs and out of the window, onto the fire escape. For a few seconds, they all stared at the window in disbelief. Colina was the first to come to his senses. "I got him!" he screamed, leaping up on the bed to get to the window. The Latina, also coming to her senses, pulled a sheet over her plump nakedness and began to squeal hysterically.

The fire escape looked out on a dreary alley. The suspect was climbing up to the roof. Colina looked up at the man's scrawny buttocks in disgust. "Stop or I'll shoot!" he screamed, but the man was already at the top of the fire escape, disappearing onto the roof. Colina cursed under his breath and began to make haste up the fire escape. He was breathing hard when he got to the top. At first, the man was nowhere in sight, but then Colina saw him about two buildings over. He was leaping from roof to roof. Colina set out after him at full speed. There was a strangely euphoric feeling in him as he chased down his quarry. Soon, the suspect was looking around in a panic—since he had reached the corner building of the block, and had run out of roofs. He looked back at Colina in horror as the officer slowed and started walking up. There was a self-satisfied smile on Colina's face now. The man was still looking around like a trapped animal. Colina waited for him to come to the conclusion that there was nowhere for him to go.

"Get back, or I'll *jump!*" the man screamed suddenly, getting up on the ledge.

Colina stared at him in confusion for a moment, then chuckled at the ridiculousness of the demand. "So *jump* then!" he said with a laugh, pointing his gun at the fool. When the man finally detected the flaw in his logic, he groaned and went to step back onto the roof—

"Get the *fuck* back up there!" Colina screamed, pointing his gun again.

The man was shaking, his eyes seeming on the verge of popping from their sockets—

"*Jump*, you stupid son of a bitch!" Colina cursed him again, while the man began blubbering like a scared toddler. "*Jump!*" he screamed, half-jokingly, "—it'll save me the paperwork! *Jump!*" he raged, as naked fool begin to cry—

"*Colina!*" a voice called then; and looking over his shoulder, Colina saw Holtzman running toward him.

Having gotten that reprieve, the suspect leapt back onto the roof and ran past Colina, toward Holtzman. "He's *crazy!*" the man cried, tears dribbling down his cheeks. "Keep him away from me...he's *nuts!*"

As Holtzman took the babbling man away, Colina watched them in annoyance; but then, all of a sudden, for a reason that even he didn't know, he began to chuckle to himself. At first, his voice was low; but then it became loud and *sick*. Holtzman looked back at him uneasily; the suspect cringed, begging Holtzman to take him away. However, Colina just stood there, his facial muscles still twitching as he looked up at the hazy abyss of the sky.

For Roland, like all of them, the moment of truth was drawing close.

While in Brooklyn, the forces of self-destruction gathered to hear Botswana Glade's words, Roland entered the smaller, less-luxurious dressing room, and sat before the mirror, watching himself in the silence. The face staring back held a combination of horror, disbelief, amusement and triumph. The last twenty-four hours had been a combination of all of those things. What had just happened in Samantha Dearly's dressing room personified it all. It was too dream-like—too much like one of those dubious, boastful letters sent in to men's sex magazines—for him to believe it himself.

Yet, it was while he was staring at himself in the mirror, trying to make some sense of it, that everything went crazy. First, the makeup woman burst into the room. It was a hideous, gypsy-looking crone, who came in mumbling something about how busy and late she was. She reminded him of some bizarre character from *Alice in Wonderland*. Seconds after she appeared, she was twirling him around in the swivel chair and attacking him with a powder puff. He coughed and tried to wave away the cloud of powder, but she slapped his hand out of the way. She was pressing her flabby breasts against him now. The odor of her perfume was pungent in his nostrils—it reminded him of a funeral parlor: it was *too* flowery, as though specifically designed to mask the stench of decay. She kept rubbing up against him as she rushed around—this second combing his hair, that second straightening his tie—

The door burst open then; and, along with the noise of hundreds of people finding their seats, a lanky white man in his mid- to late-twenties invaded the room. By his walk, and the strange, perturbed expression on his face, Roland knew immediately that he was gay. The man walked up to Roland and the woman—who had ceased her ministrations, as if out of respect—and paused dramatically, one hand instinctively going to his hip, while the other brought the writing pad up to his eyes. Apparently, he was shortsighted, because he squinted at it for a moment, while Roland and the woman waited.

"All right, then!" he said in a raspy, stereotypically gay voice. "The super models are late!" he went on, looking at Roland condescendingly, "and you will be second, in their place."

Roland nodded uneasily. He liked to think of himself as a free thinker; other people's sexuality was irrelevant to him; but with these flamboyantly gay men, the very act of pretending that one didn't notice (and as such, didn't care) was inherently farcical—especially since their every action screamed, *"I'm gay!"* Roland couldn't help thinking of the man as a crude caricature of a bitchy woman with PMS. Yet, even as these thoughts passed through his mind, there was an internal voice of censure; and with this internal censure came guilt and uneasiness. Was he a bigot, or was he merely being honest? Maybe the white women who clutched their purses when he passed them on the street were only being honest about being "uncomfortable" around him. Maybe these stupid semantic tricks were an indelible part of the human condition—

"—Make sure you're ready on time!" the producer declared—again, seemingly out of nowhere—so that Roland jumped in his seat. Having made this declaration, the man exited the room like a prima donna leaving the stage. When Roland and the makeup lady were alone, she eyed him critically one last time, shrugged (as though he looked like hell, but there was nothing more she could do), then made for the door. As she was about to open the door, she mumbled for him to go to "the green room" and wait for his turn. He leapt to his feet and went to follow her, but she gave him the look that people gave to stray dogs that they suspected wanted to follow them home, so he slackened his pace enough for her to leave him.

When he opened the door himself, Roland saw how hectic the studio had become. All the restless ticket holders from outside were being let in now. Many of them were tourists from small town America. They came equipped with cameras and autograph books, so that they could impress their neighbors when they got back to their little "in-the-middle-of-nowhere" towns. Roland wandered down the hallway once more—back the way he had come. His stomach clenched as he passed Samantha's dressing room.... He walked on.

Through an open section in the wall, he could see the audience. The ushers were showing them to their seats now. Roland stood there dreamily, while stagehands rushed about and the stage band tuned their instruments and played disconnected, cacophonous bits of music as they warmed up.

He was standing there daydreaming when the original intern came up. The youth was sweating worse than ever. He looked like he was going to have a heart attack! "There you are!" he screamed. "We were looking everywhere for you!"

Roland looked at him with pity. A few years of this, and the kid would be a horrible, ulcerated wreck of a man.

"Wait in the green room," the intern went on. Then: "It's this way," he said, tugging on the sleeve of Roland's jacket. The man led Roland farther down the corridor, and opened a door for him. The square, windowless chamber was spacious—but the dim lighting gave it a depressing quality. Right across from the door, there was a huge TV, before which a man in a dark suit was standing. Between the man and the door, there were two rather long burgundy couches, which faced one another. To the left, there was a huge dining table, with heaping trays of donuts and danishes; and against that wall, there was an entire kitchen, replete with coffee and cappuccino machines.

Roland stepped into the room; and as he did so, the nervous intern (who had been holding the door like a worried prison guard) closed the door behind him. It was then that the man in front of the TV turned around, and Roland saw Botswana Glade. On the screen, there were the images of last night's riot: the video that the bystander had taped. Roland and Botswana Glade stared at one another; and unaccountably, they both stared with a certain amount of antagonism.

"You're that playboy lawyer," Botswana Glade said at last, still scrutinizing Roland.

"My name is Roland Micheaux," Roland corrected him, stepping up. He had intended to shake the man's hand, but he stopped about halfway there, and they stared at one another once more. As Roland saw it, men like Marenga and Botswana Glade were nothing but laughable relics from the 1960s. Their existence was a collective joke, designed either to annoy and reassure whites by their very ridiculousness, or, by that same uncompromising ridiculousness, to shame the black masses and spur them on to mainstream ideologies and aspirations.

Botswana Glade chuckled suddenly in the silence and began: "There are two kinds of successful men in this world, Mr. Micheaux. The first type is the man who will accept anything—who waits around for the alms thrown to him, like a beggar. Such men, if they can make themselves seem desperate enough, and can do a little song and dance for the passersby, can eventually become rich, collecting a dollar here and a quarter there. On the other hand, there are those who go out into the world and, instead of collecting change, *forge* change, demanding success on their own terms."

"Let me guess," Roland said with a smirk, "I'm the former and you're the latter."

Botswana Glade smiled a dead, menacing smile. "Men like you exist only to put people at ease—to make them laugh. You're a well-paid harlequin."

"And why do men like yourself exist?" Roland replied with a smile.

"I'm here to uncover and disseminate the truth."

"*Whose* truth?"

"My own of course!" he said with a laugh; then, sobering quickly—almost *insanely*—he went on, "The truth must always be your own, Mr. Micheaux. Men like you and Randolph get rich by accepting other people's truths. You'll accept *anything*.... There's a war coming, Mr. Micheaux, and men like you are going to be the first casualties. It's always the weak links that break first—"

But just then, the nervous intern again opened the door and poked his head inside, telling Botswana Glade to come with him and wait off-stage. As Botswana Glade walked past Roland, en route to the door and the waiting intern, the man smiled derisively, almost pityingly, at him. "Time for me to forge history," he said to Roland....

Finally alone, Roland walked over to the kitchen and got himself a donut and some coffee. He ate slowly and deliberately in the silence, willing his mind to be still. What else could possibly happen? And what the hell could Rosencrantz possibly want from him...! There was always something waiting in the recesses of his mind...!

The show began about five minutes later. Roland sat in the green room, which, for some reason, wasn't green, and watched everything on the huge screen. All the backstage workers had seemed like chickens with their heads cut off, so he couldn't believe the cheerful, easy tone of Samantha and her co-host when the show finally began. Of course, as he watched Samantha, he was enchanted. It was all so dream-like that a side of him still wondered if their encounter had really happened. As for the show, the first few minutes were taken up by meaningless banter and jokes, while Samantha and her co-host sat on the set and drank coffee. Her co-host, Bart Mitchell, was a perpetually grinning Oklahoman of middle age, who acted way too silly for a man of his age, height and build. He looked like someone who had failed at doing the evening network news, and was now banished to this idiocy. Then there was a moment of suspect, TV outrage, with the requisite gasps, as Samantha related the story in the news that morning, about the man who had run over that kid, shot those people and then been beaten to the brink of death by the mob. They revealed that the man was now conscious and asking to be killed. They also revealed that doctors had found high levels of cocaine in the man's system. During this time, there was, of course, a little gossip about Randolph and Maria Santos; but returning to the "hot" news, they showed the bystander's video, which was showing everywhere by now. Charlotte McPrice was all over the news as well, explaining how Randolph's incompetence was responsible for it all; and then, they showed a video feed from their own sidewalk, and the front of the hospital, where Botswana Glade's supporters were still chanting their slogans. Thirty seconds into all of this, Roland had allowed his mind to drift off....

A commercial break later, Botswana Glade was introduced. He did not smile, and there was only scant applause for him. He talked softly and deliberately for thirty seconds or so. But then, at Bart Mitchell's urging, he went into a lengthy, high-pitched disquisition on the Brooklyn Massacre and the maniac, explaining how the police were devils, and Mayor Randolph was a false prophet and a scared hypocrite. Roland groaned then, thinking to himself: *All these niggers, competing for scraps by stabbing one another in the back*! Yet, as he sat there, listening to Botswana Glade insinuating that there was somehow a conspiracy in all of the random acts of violence that had happened the night before, something in Roland's gut—some creepy, anxious feeling—told him that the man was mad. Botswana Glade, it suddenly occurred to him, was another Jasper Kain; but instead of *shaving* heads, the man wanted to cut them off.

The realization that thousands of people were congregating to hear the man's words, made Roland shudder inside. Indeed, the man's words were even now being broadcasted across the country. Botswana Glade was about to succeed where Kain had failed, and there didn't seem to be anything that any of them could do about it....

Soon, in what seemed like no time at all, it was Roland's turn to be on the air. The nervous-looking intern came running in, yelling that Roland's moment had come, and that he should just "act naturally." Roland was too preoccupied and anxious to be annoyed.

He walked backstage with the youth, fighting to pull himself together. He was to be on the air in minutes—but he wasn't ready! He needed a few minutes to himself—just like at the banquet two months ago! There were too many strange parallels here. On top of that, his mind kept going back to Rosencrantz's summons. He knew he wasn't ready—yet his image would be broadcasted across the country in a matter of *minutes*! He wanted to run away—anything to keep from making a fool of himself! He felt like throwing up! But somehow, he forced himself to be still....

Bart Mitchell was telling a joke as a prelude to introducing Roland. With the Botswana Glade segment over, they all seemed relieved. The audience was boisterous, laughing at anything Mitchell said. Offstage, there seemed to be movement everywhere. Roland's eyes darted around, but his mind was too excited—too *cha-*

otic—to register most of it. And then, the next thing that
he knew, Mitchell was calling his name and some stage-
hand was telling him to walk out, onto the set. He was
in the light now, almost rocked by the wall of applause.
He could barely see—it was so bright! But then, once
again, his eyes focused, and he saw Samantha standing
statuesquely in the same set that had looked so fake this
morning. All of a sudden, it seemed like paradise to
him, because she was there. He suddenly had a yearning
for a woman—not *sex*, per se, even though that was
undeniably part of it... The closeness of a woman—the
trust and love of a woman—seemed either like some
missing link to his joy or an aegis against all that might
trouble him. He was grasping at straws now, trying to
get through this any way he could. Yet, Samantha smiled
at him then, and he was either overcome by hope, or by
terror. She was holding out her hand now, then kissing
him on the cheek.... Mitchell was shaking his hand....

Time seemed to be flying past, like the world outside
a rushing car—or like the world beyond the giddying
splendor of a merry-go-round. For some unaccountable
reason, he felt at ease again. As the show continued,
there was some initial banter about the Brooklyn
Massacre, which Roland navigated by repeating the
same platitudes he had been hearing all that morning.
For the life of him, he was actually doing it! His natural
poise came out of nowhere, and he watched it as if he
were a member of the audience. He waxed poetic on

justice and the state of modern society, before giving a few tidbits about his most recent legal victory to show that justice could in fact be achieved. The applause for him was thunderous—

But just then, the chaotic scene in front of the Brooklyn hospital appeared on an offstage monitor; and as Roland glanced at it, he had a sudden and violent flashback to his father and that day twenty years ago. He felt suddenly lost. Samantha was saying something; but ever so briefly, he was remembering Phelps' perverseness and the enervating strangeness of Candice's sex. He remembered Rosencrantz's terseness and the prospect of losing everything. He was close to the edge. He had made a wrong step, and all of a sudden he was staring into the abyss. Once more, a side of him wanted to rush off—to run away as quickly as he could—but he beat it back with all the savagery that he could muster—

"How has your life changed since you were declared one of the city's ten most eligible bachelors?" Bart Mitchell was asking him now. Mitchell had a smile on his face, and members of the audience began to snicker as well. Roland, still lost in his fears and uncertainties, took a deep breath—which everyone must have taken for coyness. He glanced at Samantha then, and was once again overcome by how exquisite she was. Maybe it was that that saved him. She was sitting there with her legs crossed seductively, smiling back at him, and he nodded his head dreamily before looking back at Bart.

Then, suddenly remembering the man's question about how his life had changed, he smiled and said:

"My life's the same, but the women have gotten more beautiful." The audience burst into applause and laughter then—as did Samantha and Bart. Roland's words hadn't been that witty, but faced with the specter of his father and Phelps and Rosencrantz, he found himself laughing with the rest of them, suddenly desperate to believe in their laughter.

The lights had been turned off by the time Jasper Kain emerged from his drug-induced nightmare. His mind was groggy from whatever Fishman had given him, and it took a few minutes before he was able to retrace the events of the day, or night, or whatever it was outside. He lay unmoving on his cot, now unable to fall asleep. Locked in his cell—which, to his disappointment, wasn't padded, as he'd always heard—the hatred began to bubble within him again. It was hatred like he had never felt before: irrational, *seething* hatred. He had spent his time philosophizing about the difference between chaos and madness, but those differences, if they existed, were meaningless to him now. The entire world had laughed at him, but they would all be brought to pay for what they had done to him. Micheaux, Randolph...*all* of them.

As Kain lay in the darkness of his cell, there was no

way he could have known what was happening to the city—but he felt it in his soul. In his mind's eye, he saw the myriad triggers to "all hell breaking loose": some innocent black kid getting gunned down by the police, for instance; some proto-Rodney King beating, captured on tape—so that the rage would flare up and consume the world like it had Los Angeles. And there, in that orgy of self-destruction, was the horror of Columbine and the sleazy underbelly of some public sex scandal. All that filth and madness combined into one swirling mess, so that Kain laughed out in the darkness at the irony that he was the one in the madhouse. He had tried to talk to them like a man, but they had refused to listen. He had been their only chance at peace, and yet they had destroyed him—*crucified* him— hiding him away in this madhouse like a nightmare thought too terrifying to acknowledge. Even now, they presumed to contain him with locked doors and prison walls: the ridiculousness of it made him laugh out in the darkness.

Kain had *allowed* them to capture him. As he saw it, he had fooled them into believing he was their prisoner. He had allowed them the momentary illusion of power of him—but he saw now that his place was beyond these walls. His hatred of the world had revived him—so that his demonic plan seemed clear to him once again. He had already resolved the means of his escape—and seen the perfection of it. He laughed out loud again, as he saw how easily he could bring their world crashing down. Like wayward children, they had gone astray—but he would put them in their place, like a stern father.

Roland's appearance on the morning show had been a grand success. He felt relieved—*triumphant*—as he headed out of the studio, but then he remembered Rosencrantz....

When Roland got outside and hailed a cab, the world was not only getting hotter, but darker. The heat was like nothing he had ever felt before. And he was so tired of this yo-yoing—of careening wildly from euphoria to horror.... As soon as he was in the cab, headed toward the office, he wrenched off his jacket and lay back in a daze. His shirt and undershirt were already soaked through with sweat. He glanced out at the world as it passed him by, wondering how much more he would have to take. The moment of reckoning was at hand, but exhausted by all that had passed, the only thing he could do was wait for whatever fate had in store for him. He was so very tired now. This was the time to plan and pool his strength, but his mind was like an overworked beast of burden, unable to move—even under the whip of its master.

The dark, smoggy world beyond the cab seemed to be nothing but a projection of his soul. And the thing that had happened with Samantha...there was no sense to be made of it. He remembered holding her breasts—and *touching* her. He had never done anything like that before—and yet, he had never been that turned on before. There was a reckless streak in him: the events of the last twenty-four hours attested to it....

The cab came to a jarring halt; when Roland looked out of the window, he saw he was at the office. He had no idea how much time had passed—he only knew that another moment of truth was here. The world seemed even darker now. Out on the sidewalk, the people moved like exhausted slaves being whipped by some invisible brute. Even the traffic was crawling along—as though the entire world were grinding to a halt. There was a hideous modernistic statue of a man in front of the building. The man in the statue seemed deformed. His mouth was held open, as if he were screaming in agony; his body seemed to be melting—as if he were being devoured by flames. Yet, all at once, Roland saw himself in the statue...

It was about ten o'clock in New York City now; but the later it got, the more the strange dark clouds over-hung the city; and the darker it got, the hotter it got. It was well over thirty-seven degrees Celsius now. Cars with steaming radiators stalled in the middle of the street, snarling traffic all over the city.

The filthy air was barely breathable. One could *taste*

the air—*see* it wafting by. Down the city streets, all the drivers of the stalled cars seemed to be honking their horns at once, cursing the incompetence and stupidity of the drivers in front of them—and the fools who were honking behind them.

It was in this context that the Brooklyn rally began. At least five thousand people were now in front of the hospital, conducting their death vigil. Botswana Glade had been stuck in traffic for an hour, cursing impatiently, along with everyone else—but that only meant the people would be more riled up when he got there. As Botswana Glade neared the scene of what was going to be his triumph, a smile came to his face. *He was ready for war*! There was a thunderous sound raging in him, and even before he looked out of the window and saw all of those animated thousands, he knew that that thunder came from their souls. Sometimes people had to grasp their bestial natures before they could rise with the angels. Botswana Glade would not merely be their instrument of insurrection: like a god, he would be a vehicle for their *resurrection*...

Upon exiting the elevator, and entering the floor occupied by his firm, Roland stopped uneasily. The reception area was uncommonly still and dark. The old receptionist looked up at him slyly—he was certain of it! He nodded to the woman and walked on. His gait was unusually stiff and uncoordinated. His mind was blank when he entered the office area; but looking around confusedly, he saw that there was no one there! The dozens of cubicles were all empty; and the glass-enclosed rooms along the wall, where the partners had their offices, were empty as well! Even the lights were turned off.

"What the hell...!" Roland whispered. But then:

"*SURPRISE!*"

The lights suddenly came on; balloons fell from the ceiling; jaunty party music began playing; and from behind the cubicles immediately in front of Roland, about fifty people jumped out!

While in Brooklyn, the forces of self-destruction cheered at Botswana Glade's arrival, Roland stood there gaping as the people rushed up to congratulate and hug him! Someone put a silly party hat on his head, and he stood there like a simpleton, still trying to make sense of it all. While Roland was looking around confusedly, Rosencrantz came up with a big smile on his face. The old man was gaunt and bald, with an impeccably groomed appearance.

"Congratulations, Roland!" Rosencrantz was saying now. "You did us proud again!" He patted Roland on the shoulder then, and everyone applauded once more. Roland was still in shock; it was at least twenty seconds after they had burst from behind the cubicles that he realized what was going on around him. With the vestiges of a stupefied grin on his face, he saw that Rosencrantz's tone during the phone call had only been a ruse to get him to come to the office for this party. He also saw he had nothing to worry about with Phelps!

He laughed out loud then, overcome by relief. In fact, they were all laughing now, and that laughter rose up in the world, drowning out everything else. He was soaring high now! At someone's urging, Roland began recounting his experiences—sans his encounter with Samantha Dearly—chuckling to himself as he saw their amazed faces. He was acutely aware of the power that he had. And it *was* power: the ability to hold and move people for no other reason than he was who he was.

Roland forgot everything about moments of reckoning and yo-yoing chaotically between euphoria and horror. All he wanted to do was revel in the present: hold onto it like he had held Samantha...

Finally, Mr. Rosencrantz told him to come into his office. "Did Dallas tell you the partnership is yours?"

"Yes," Roland said, slightly unnerved by the intrusion of the man's name.

"Dallas was one of your loudest supporters."

Phelps? Roland mused in disbelief; he wondered if that was some trick on the man's part, but no: it was obvious even to him that he had overestimated the man; and besides, he was just tired of it all.

Rosencrantz smiled coyly at him, then: "How do you feel about handling the Cranston case?" he said, scrutinizing Roland closely. The case, as Roland remembered it, involved a class action suit against a huge conglomerate called Cranston International, which was being sued because its baby food exceeded the allowable limit of pesticide residues. Ten babies had supposedly died from severe reactions to these pesticides. It was an open and shut case, with a potential settlement in the hundreds of millions.

When Roland nodded his head, Rosencrantz smiled and shook Roland's hand.

They both laughed then, like two conspirators. Yes, Roland thought out of nowhere, he definitely wasn't that scared thirteen-year-old anymore! He was moving up in the world now: moving up faster than he had ever thought possible. For an instant, he was overcome by the feeling that nothing could possibly go wrong; but then, just as suddenly and overwhelmingly, came a feeling of panic at the thought that he was tempting fate. It was then that something exploded in the air. Both he and Rosencrantz recoiled violently, turning to the window.

Nicolai Andropov was slow to emerge back into consciousness. For obvious reasons, he was confused as he looked around. He was like someone slowly emerging from a dream, trying to differentiate what was real from what wasn't. He tried to look around, but immediately realized he couldn't move. It was as though his body had been packed in lead. Making do, his eyes scanned the small, darkened room. The lights were turned off, and with the blinds drawn, but the illumination provided by the EKG monitor and other pieces of equipment was enough—perhaps *more* than enough—for him to see. There were tubes and sensors everywhere. He tried to move his head, then immediately put the thought out of his mind as a sharp pain went down his spine. He winced, realizing, among other things, that there was a tube in his nose. And there were others in his arms, and wires of some kind connected to sensors on his chest. It seemed as though he were attached to an octopus...!

His understanding of how he had come to be there—and of what he had *done*—was vague at first. Initially, there were only disconnected images and sounds: ghosts streaking across oblivion. But then, as he saw the mangled body of a kid, and the bullet-riddled bodies of others, he began to see himself in those horrific images. He had *killed* people. He remembered the mob attacking him—and his strange sense of relief that his life was about to end. Why—indeed, *how*—was he still alive? Why had they spared him? Why had the doctors bothered patching him back together? Was it compassion, or the desire to drag out his death?

Indeed, with each passing second, his mind became clearer; demonic images of his rampage became more distinct and horrifying. He wasn't a man anymore—and he knew he would never again be regarded as one. No, it was over, and there was no point in going on. It wasn't that he wanted to escape justice—he only wanted to escape *life*.

In truth, he had been dreaming of death for a long time now. He had dreamt of death as he pumped his penis into that whore, and while he was cruising down those Brooklyn streets. There had been death everywhere; and now, people were dead because of him. Death had brought him to this strange place, and the only option was to again turn to death, in order to complete the circle.

Driven by thoughts of death, he tried to get up—only to once again realize the terrible extent of his injuries. He lay back down, panting and wincing from his efforts. A kind of claustrophobic terror gripped him. What if he *couldn't* move? What if he was paralyzed, and forced to live out the rest of his life in some hospital bed/prison! The thought was worse than the throbbing pain coursing through his body. To be trapped here, unable to move—or to *flee*...his only hope now as death. He wished he would fall back into unconsciousness, so that he would never again have to look upon this sickening world. But damn it, as extensive as his injuries were, he was acutely aware of some demonic strength in him, keeping him conscious! The compassionate Americans would drag out his death for *years*. They would make him *explain* himself, and parade him around like a deformed freak in a carnival—

That was the thought that gave him the impetus to act. He had no idea what he was going to do—but he knew he had to *move*. First, he had to get out of this bed. He took a breath, held it, then, groaning and grimacing, he willed himself to sit up. He was beyond pain now. His broken ribs were like knives stabbing him. He could literally feel sutures in his abdomen bursting! Any second now, he expected the final one to pop, allowing his guts to spill out.

Now that he was sitting up, the tube in his nose made him want to retch. He suddenly realized the tube descended down his throat and into his stomach. He could feel it poking his insides. Panicking, he realized he was passing out—but he did not want to lose consciousness now, only to awaken later. So, he *willed* himself to be strong; he marshaled the last of the demonic strength and forced himself to *move*.

It seemed to take forever before he managed to get his feet to the ground. One of his feet was in a cast; the knee on his other leg was swollen horribly, so that it could hardly bend. It was dawning on him that he would never be able to escape with such injuries, so he pushed himself on purpose, in order to distract his thoughts. The ghosts were still hovering above his head; the mangled corpses of his dreams and aspirations were lying at his feet... He began to pull the tube from his nose. The sensation was...*sickening*. There was a cast on his right arm; his shoulders and back throbbed mercilessly... But he had to keep going; and in a way, the pain was guiding him, insulating him from his thoughts and fears. He began pulling the intravenous tubes from of his arms.... While he was disconnecting the sensors, the EKG went flat.

It was now or never! His first attempt to stand up was futile: the pain was beyond comprehension! He had to suck in his breath sharply to keep from screaming—but even doing that was like having a bomb exploding in his chest. He was forced, by mere self-preservation, to sit down again. Worse, he realized that if the people came in and found him like this, they would tie him down, so that there would never be another chance! *It was now or never!*

It was then that the door burst open and the emergency medical team—along with the officers posted outside—rushed into the room. The EKG, seeming to flat-line, had set off an alarm. The sight of them was horrible. They turned on the blinding light, so that his eyes felt like they were about to explode. The people were coming at him now—yelling nonsense that he couldn't decipher at the moment. As weak as he was, he had to fight them off. An old doctor was trying to push him back into bed. The man was yelling at a young nurse to administer a sedative. There were more arms on him now; how he was fighting them off was anyone's guess, but his only thought was that he *had* to fight. It was probably that demonic strength again. He kneed the old doctor in the testicles, so that the man stumbled back and overturned some of the medical equipment. Yet, all the while, Andropov had his eyes on the young nurse, who was fumbling with the syringe, trying to fill it with the sedative.

It was then that that old thought hit him again: if he couldn't escape, then he had to find some way to end this quickly. In a millisecond, he grabbed the empty syringe from the nurse and pulled the plunger back, sucking it full of air. Then, in the same motion, he jabbed it into his neck, injecting the huge air bubble into himself. He gasped at the sensation—at the horrible pain that left him shuddering and frothing at the mouth—while the medical team looked on in stunned horror. He felt as if his insides were being pulled apart. And then the pain in his chest was like a beast clawing at his heart...he couldn't scream anymore...couldn't *move*. All that there was, was pain...and then a mild sense of triumph as he watched their fading faces, knowing he would never open his eyes again.

The horrified medical team was staring down at him when something exploded in the air. At first, they all recoiled violently, but then one of the officers went to the window and pulled up the Venetian blinds. Andropov's window looked out on the front of the hospital, where Botswana Glade's dais had been set up. Botswana Glade had been making his way up to the dais when the noise resounded in the air. The very foundations of the city seemed to shake. Everyone looked around in horror; and just as the members of the emergency team looked out of the window at all those startled thousands, the invisible thing again exploded in the air. People began screaming that it was a bomb; Botswana Glade's bodyguards had knocked him to the ground and flung themselves on him. People were ready for the world to blow apart—for everything to come to a crashing end—but that was when the heavens opened up and the rain began to fall.

The first raindrops battered the windowpanes and the tops of people's heads like gunshots. Those who were inside, all rushed to their windows then, and looked out at the rain they had spent the last month hoping for. But for those who were outside—even those at Botswana Glade's rally—their first impulse was to run to safety. The raindrops were strangely heavy; in fact, it seemed more like hail than rain. It was only after the people found shelter that they looked out on the world in amazement. The rain was coming down in sheets now—a kind of catharsis for all the madness, all the grief, all the filth...everything that had come with the sweltering heat. The world was purging itself; and for those wonderful moments, everyone was still and no one said a word.

BOOK
TWO

BOOK TWO

THE FETISH SPIRITS

I t was autumn now—the end of October. The heat, and the Brooklyn Massacre, and all the things that had gripped them during the summer, were gone now. For many, they were gone and forgotten. However, like the seasons, the madness came and went. Nature remembered what people forgot; and so, even as the trees shed their leaves and the world prepared for a harsh, cold winter, the madness was still there—beneath the surface.

It was just after five o'clock in the afternoon; but with the changing of the seasons, the sun had already set. There was something depressing about the world now. Nevertheless, Benjamin Thomas smiled as he looked out on the ghetto streets. He was sixteen years old: young and free and *bold*. Even now, as he walked confidently up the street, the cold wind and creeping darkness hardly registered in his mind. Being young, he still believed he could do anything—and that nothing was beyond his purview. His tall, powerful frame regularly motivated dozens of girls to come to his varsity basketball games. His movements seemed like controlled chaos; his speed and agility seemed almost supernatural at times—so that the young girls' fantasies about him often seemed like prayers to a god.

Just then, he spied two remarkable specimens of womanhood across the street. They were standing by a payphone, as though waiting for a call. When they happened to look his way, he waved to them: one waved back; the other, disapproving of such a straightforward show of interest, snatched her friend's hand down and scowled at her. *What a joke it all was*! he thought with a confident smile. Yet, what else was there to think at sixteen years old? To him, getting these young chicks was like pulling a con on a fool who seemed set on giving up her money; rather, the fool didn't just want to *give* it away, she wanted to be *cheated* out of it. If he was straightforward with them, and told them what he wanted to do to their bodies, they protested and became angry; if he told them outrageous lies about love and their beauty, they began giggling and seemed suddenly desperate to give up their bodies and souls to him. This strange mindset had confounded him at first, but it was all part of the game now.

In fact, as Thomas saw it, life was a game, and sex was how you kept score. He had seen it on public television nature shows, of all places. He had seen peacocks doing their mating struts, and bucks clashing heads and antlers to become the alpha male. He had also seen walruses—*huge* beasts—goring one another with their tusks for weeks on end, wasting away and left scarred and deformed...all in an insane drive for a few paltry seconds of sex.

At an early age, he had realized that that titanic struggle was going on all about him. At first, as a seven-year-old, watching the show, *Nature*, on PBS, it had only mystified him—even *bewildered* him; but then, like all the other beasts in the world, at the onset of puberty, it had *excited* him. To him, the women lamenting that men were dogs, were only half-correct. The whole truth was not only that men were dogs, but that women were, similarly, bitches....Yes: he was crude and sexist—but he was unapologetically so, because even the most cursory glance at the world (and at what women, themselves, seemed to want) told him that there was nothing so sexy, as unabashed sexism. For all their cries of wanting a sensitive, feminized man, women dreamed of him when their eyes were closed.

Looking at the two women across the street again, he was like a peacock, flashing his plumage to the peahens. As he waved again, the *other* woman, who had before seemed so dubious about his charms, smiled back—to the outrage of her friend. While the two women argued, he laughed to himself, then continued up the block. Yes, it was all a joke after all.... Later tonight, he had a "rendezvous" with a young woman from his social studies

class. Her mother worked nights—just like his mother—
and it would be so very easy... And then, tomorrow
night, there was the Halloween party on 130th Street.
He could hardly wait for that! Yes, it was all about the
competition—the *game*—so the entire house of lies was
still exciting. He was like a young lion, still practicing at
hunting, not yet having to face the realities of the
hunt—the life and death implications of survival....

When he reached his tenement, he jumped up onto
the stoop; then, like a playful antelope testing his
muscles, he bounded into the building. The graffiti-
coated front door was off its hinges again...entering the
hallway, and beginning to ascend the steps, his expression suddenly soured. That old Dominican woman on
the first floor was always cooking some pungent stew.
Today, it smelled like dirty socks and garlic. He held his
breath and hastened his steps, hoping to reach his
fourth-story apartment before he lost consciousness.
Between the second and third stories, the burning in his
lungs became too much for him and he exhaled forcefully. He attempted to inhale, found that the stench was
even more nauseating, and held his breath again. As
such, he was a little dizzy when he reached the fourth
story. He rushed to get his keys ready, so that he could
dart inside the apartment and take his first untainted
breath. However, when he looked up, he saw not only
that the entrance was open, but that the door, itself, was
lying on the floor. He froze, still standing there with the
key in his hand.

Inside, it seemed as though a hurricane had been unleashed. The kitchen cupboards were all open, their contents spilt like animal entrails. The furniture was all either overturned or heaved into some unlikely position in the room. His mother, he realized after a few seconds of shock, was bent over, searching through the rubble. She was still only dressed in her nightgown. She stood up and stared at him in the unfocused way of someone who was still in shock. She was a short, plump woman of middle age, who had worked hard all her life and had either been left wiser or beaten and morose by the entire struggle. Benjamin was her only child, and the only remnant she had of his father—who had been killed sixteen years ago, in a financial transaction involving heroin. As she stood up and stared at her son, she seemed ten years older—as though something so terrible had happened that it had drained the life from her. Thomas unconsciously flinched at the sight of her. She seemed suddenly haggard—*decrepit*. He rushed over to her, clasping her by the shoulders:

"Mama!"—he looked around with wide, unbelieving eyes—"We get robbed?" His darting eyes eventually came back to her. "You all right?"

She shook her head, as though still in shock. "The police," she managed to say.

"*Police*!" The word made a queasy feeling wash over him.

"They were here..."—she looked up at him ominously—"looking for you."

"For *me*!" he said with a nervous laugh.

His mother's face remained grave: "Some special drug unit...said somebody called Benjamin Thomas was some kind of drug lord. You're wanted for twelve counts of murder."

"*Me*?" More hysterical laughter escaped from him.

"*Of course it ain't you*!" she shouted in annoyance, life finally seeming to creep back into her. "I told them that!" she said angrily. "It's an obvious mix-up. They said you were five-eight and two hundred and eighty pounds, with a bushy beard and a scar on your forehead! You have to go down to the police station and clear this up."

"Now?" he whined, "I was gonna go out—"

"*Fool!*" his mother cursed him, gripping him by the lapel of his jacket with one hand, while waving the other threateningly. "Didn't you just hear what I said to you? Don't you see that broken down door lying there? It's there because the police threw it there when they came rushing in with their SWAT team! You see all this *shit* on the floor! That's there because they emptied out all the drawers, cupboards and closets, looking for your drug stash! You see these goddamn welts on my wrist!"—and she shoved them in his face— "That's from wearing handcuffs for three hours while they asked me where the drugs and money were! This is *serious*, and you worried about getting some goddamn *pussy*!"

"—I'll go, Mama," he said quickly, suddenly ashamed.

"*Damn* right you'll go!" she cursed him again. "All you

young fools," she started in disgust, "...as soon as you grow two hairs on your balls, you lose all your goddamn sense!" She looked up at him with a snarled lip then, going on, "I'm going to tell you one thing, son, and I hope it serves you the rest of your days." She paused then, staring ominously into his eyes before declaring: "Pussy ain't *shit* to get!"

Charles Marenga was dying, and he knew it. He couldn't walk up a flight of stairs without becoming dizzy. He had a paunch and plump, stubby limbs; and he was dying, as he knew they were all dying. The feeling was vague yet unrelenting as he emerged from sleep and looked out of the plane's window. His ears were still stuffed up from the air pressure, and his body was cramped from the irregular position in which he had fallen asleep; and these things, combined with the drowsiness of his mind, and his strange thoughts about death, left him wondering if he was still dreaming. He stared out of the window for about two minutes before he realized what he was seeing. It was nighttime, but New York City's glittering skyline was like an inconceivably huge Christmas decoration. He felt suddenly small; and for a moment, the skyline reminded him of all the stars and constellations he had seen in the African sky. His mind went back to the tent in the middle of the Sahara, where, for the first time in a long while, he had felt peace. Besides his guides, there had been no other humans around for two hundred kilometers: no noisy cities, no traffic-clogged streets...and for a little while, there had been an extraordinary feeling of peace within him. However, he was back in New York City again. All his old fears were returning now; old wounds were reopening; the sick feeling in his soul was taking hold again, so that he sat back in the seat and closed his eyes.

Yes, his five-month tour of "The Motherland" was over. He had gone to Africa in search of life, but Africa had destroyed him—just as it had destroyed generations of would-be adventurers and missionaries. In a sense, his five-month tour of Africa had been nothing but an impromptu study in world philosophy. As he visited the various countries, he had seen the wreckage of Capitalism and Socialism...of Colonialism and Revolution, of Dictatorship and Democracy...of *every* hackneyed idea the world had ever conceived. He had driven across Africa, seeing the beautiful mixed with the ugly; the strong with the weak; the old and traditional, sprinkled haphazardly with that which professed to be new and modern. He had seen things that he had never even conceptualized before, along with scenes he could have seen from his stoop in Brooklyn. He had seen everything in Africa, because this, as everyone was saying nowadays, was a *global* world, where a blip on the Malaysian stock market had last week caused the New York Stock Exchange to drop one hundred and fifty points. There was an interconnectedness about everything that was unfathomable—and yet more real and telling than all of their whiny movements and philosophies combined. A disastrous devaluation of the Philippine Peso meant that a factory in Portland, Oregon was going to be moved to Mexico: it didn't make sense, but it was going on all around them. In a second-rate hotel in Brazzaville, he had not only been able to view that story on CNN, but the latest details of Mayor Randolph's sex scandal. In the face of all of these new realities, and hundreds more that he couldn't even conceptualize as yet, nothing seemed real anymore.

The startling interconnectedness had no face—no soul, no motives. He and his constituents had spent their time romanticizing the power and selfishness of some cult of evil (white) men. However, the interconnectedness was incapable of caring if its victims were black, if they were women, if they were Jews, or homosexuals, or *whatever*. Job seekers were moving from state to state on the whim of investors in foreign lands, who decided to consolidate factory production in China. These realities were beyond race, beyond gender, beyond culture—beyond even class!

Yes, he was different now—*changed* inside. Africa had given him of glimpse of the human existence. He had seen the *vastness* of it, and now he felt small and petty in the face of it all. He felt *old*... And he was afraid—not only of the world, but *himself*. He felt suddenly soulless: not simply that his soul had been drained, but that there was something evil within him. Indeed, now as he looked out of the window, he couldn't help thinking that he was bringing this newfound evil with him. He didn't feel like a man anymore. He wasn't merely an exhausted traveler: he was an instrument of evil. The devils of Africa had infected him, and now he was bringing his disease to America....

Shaking his head, Marenga chanced to look down—and noticed something sticking out of his carry-on bag. Distracted, he bent down and pulled on it, so that the rest of it emerged. It was a hideous, snarling fetish doll that some official in Namibia—or was it Swaziland?—had given him. It was only about twenty centimeters long, but its head was two-thirds of its body. He frowned at the hideous, snarling face, his mind blank; but in time, he was amazed to find himself relaxing. As contradictory as the notion seemed, the fetish was somehow a testament to the end of superstition. It was now a kind of tourist souvenir, making fun of the beliefs that still held millions. The official that handed it to him had worn an Armani suit and driven a Mercedes-Benz. Marenga found himself thinking that maybe one day their society would view the fetishes of Western beliefs in a similar manner—with a good-natured wink, and the acknowledgement that they had once allowed themselves to believe in something idiotic.

Thomas walked broodingly outside. He was still somewhat numb, but he had the sense that his pride—or whatever passed for his manhood—had been seriously breached. Then, as his mind cleared, the idea of the police—images of them breaking the door down and storming into his home, handcuffing his mother and screaming threats and demands at the half-dressed woman—tore at something more vital in him. What good was manhood when such things could happen? He felt suddenly weak: his usual confidence was gone, replaced by a feeling of vulnerability and helplessness that almost made him want to cry.

He *hated* the police! They had frisked him a couple of times, jumping out of their cruisers and ambushing him—claiming, when they found nothing incriminating on him, that he had "fit the description" of some miscreant in the neighborhood: some villain that they, as forces of justice, were in the act of apprehending.... Nothing brought on hatred like a feeling of helplessness: the knowledge that you had been wronged, and that there was nothing that you could do to rectify it....

He walked down Malcolm X Boulevard with these thoughts and uncertainties fluttering in his mind. Or maybe it was only a presentiment that his life was about to end.... It was about half past six now, but it seemed like the darkest night. The wind seemed suddenly biting, as though winter had come and entrenched itself while he wasn't paying attention. He zipped up his Knicks jacket and walked on, a little hunched over against the wind. On the corner of 125th Street, a crowd had gathered. He was so preoccupied that he would have passed them and gone on his way, except for the fact that the crowd was so big that he couldn't pass without going into the street. For some reason, the people were laughing hysterically; and it was as this laughter pierced the air that he looked up and saw they were listening to a bum with a shaggy beard. The bum was standing on a crate, gesticulating wildly and making strange facial expressions that left the people howling—

"...We got churches out here saying that if we do wrong we'll go to hell," the shabbily dressed man said in a preacher's intonation. "*Fools,*" he went on, "where the fuck they think we are now!" The crowd, which was composed mostly of young black men, laughed appreciatively. "They say if we endure this hell without causing a fuss we'll go to heaven. *Crazy!*" the man screamed, waving his hands violently. "There ain't no way out of here! And no matter how much you bend over for the devil, all you'll get in return is a worn out asshole!" Even Thomas snickered at that one. He stepped in closer, suddenly forgetting about his errand. The man on the crate was scrawny and disheveled, but there was something hysterical in his eyes. No one would have guessed it, but behind that bushy beard was Jasper Kain! Without his huge, ridiculous Afro, which he had shaved entirely off, he looked altogether differ-

ent; and after the media frenzy, everyone had forgotten
about him. Even his escape had received only minor
attention (probably because the media had been obsessed
with Randolph's sex scandal).

Whatever the case, while Kain's homily continued,
Thomas noticed the man had helpers: two other black,
middle-aged bums, and a white kid of college age, were
handing out pamphlets. When the white kid came
around, Thomas took a pamphlet. It read: "Manifesto
of the Sons of Kain." Thomas chuckled to himself and
put the pamphlet in his pocket for later amusement—

"What the hell do you want peace for!" the man
boomed. "This ain't no time to be pacified! This is
hell that we're in, so burn, baby, burn! Feel that hot
brimstone on your ass, and know that you're in the
presence of the last true nigger!" The people again
howled approvingly. "I'm not here to put you at ease, to
enlighten you, to show you the way to peace and understanding!"

"—Tell them, brother!" screamed one of the toothless
bums, to everyone's delight.

"No, I'm here to *fuck* your head up!" the man screamed,
to more gales of laughter. "If you're at ease, I want to
scare the *shit* out of you!"—Some people were laughing
so hard that they were crying—"I don't got the spirit of
God coursing through my veins, I got pure evil in me.
I'm not here asking for donations...to get you to repent
your sins...none of that shit! I'm here to scream in your

goddamn ears till your eardrums burst! I ain't looking
for converts; I'm here so that you'll walk away saying,
'Fuck you, nigger!' Yea, yea...!" he said, while half the
crowd doubled over with delight. "I want to infect
whatever goodness you have left: to put you on that
cosmic plane of pure evil. I ain't one of those preachers
you see on TV every Sunday morning, got God on their
tongue, but the devil in their soul. I'm *pure* evil! Yes,
brothers and sisters, evil is the last pure thing left on
this earth! Evil is the last thing that God has deigned to
let our corrupted minds understand. Ha, hey!" he laughed,
an insane gleam in his eyes. "This ain't the Church of
the Immaculate Conception; I ain't one of those Jheri-
Curl-wearing, Cadillac-driving, store-front preachers
who tells you to give up your cash. This is the Church
of Shit and Stale Piss, and I'm here to burn in you like
a bad case of gonorrhea—"

But at those words, the annoying boop-boop of New
York City police sirens sounded at the curb. Everyone
turned to see two white officers step out of a police
cruiser. For some reason, Benjamin Thomas froze; but
everyone else was soon laughing as the strange preacher
and his disciples darted down the street, laughing
insanely.

"All right, break it up!" The policemen were yelling
now. The crowd of young black men looked at them
sullenly—with hatred even. As the two policemen stood
before them like overseers, the people grumbled and

went on their way. Remembering his errand, Thomas thought about going up to the two officers and telling them what had happened, but that would have required too much personal interaction.

Sighing, Thomas set off for the police station with a weary step. He wanted it all to be over, so that he could go about his life—the great game—and find solace in its simplistic rules. He smiled wistfully as he walked, thinking that after he was through setting the police straight, he would stop by that young chick's house and, to use the jargon, "hit the skins."

The theme music for Maria Santos' new network show was being played; the director was counting down from five to one, as Santos stood on the set triumphantly. When the theme music ended and she was given her cue, she smiled cordially and began: "Welcome, friends. It is through your will that we have been granted this vehicle to bring the stories of America to you, *the people*. You are the soil from which we draw nutrients, and in which we are anchored. In other words, America, this is your show. This is the vessel of your thoughts and hopes and ambitions. We are here to get back to that old adage that made America what it is today: The customer is always right. We are your servants, more susceptible to your will than your congressman, your mayor, the president, even! You have to wait years to cast your vote and show them how you feel; but you only have to wait milliseconds to show us your will, by simply changing the channel. We are your means of empowerment. We are your voice! As such, we don't think ourselves presumptuous in calling this show, simply, *America*. It is about all that makes us great, and all that keeps us from greatness.

"This being so, who better to have on the inaugural show, than one of America's suddenly rising lights: Councilwoman Charlotte McPrice. Through her famous line, 'We're Americans, damn it!' we have all been reminded of our place in the world. Suddenly, people are putting those words on bumper stickers; those words now regularly appear in television shows and movies. People all over this country are using those words in their daily conversations! In those few simple words, she has tapped the vital courage that is America, and we are all grateful.

"Let us not waste any more time," Santos went on, beginning to walk over to the couches on the set. "Here she is, America: Councilwoman Charlotte McPrice!"

The theme music began again. There wasn't a studio audience, but there was suddenly the sound of applause. McPrice walked out in a red business suit with her usual statuesque self-possession. She was made for television: made for *America*. She and Santos laughed and hugged one another as the piped-in applause waxed in the air.

The police precinct was a grim place, which looked dirty and dilapidated from the outside, and even more so from within. It looked like one of those asbestos-polluted old places, with crumbling walls that forever looked as though they needed to be painted. The special drug task force, one of Mayor Randolph's new programs to "get tough on crime," had its office in the basement. The place, to put it succinctly, seemed like a rat hole. It was dimly lit, and the furniture was old and rickety— actually discarded relics that had been stored down there when the officers upstairs got new things. The rat hole had been busy an hour before, when the unit returned from an unsuccessful bust. The SWAT team and forensic specialists, whom they had dragged along, had shouted recriminations against the members of the unit, saying how they had wasted their time just to frisk an old woman. Only the three members of the unit were left now—mostly to finish the paperwork. Detectives Holtzman and Leonard sat morosely at their desks. Colina stood in the corner of the basement, by the small window near the ceiling, looking up at the dark world. All three cops were silent until Holtzman looked across at Leonard and said:

"Hey, Louie, you think Randolph really fucked that stripper chick?"

The bone-thin Leonard looked up from his paperwork with pursed lips, apparently giving it thought. "Of course," he said with a grin, "wouldn't you? Why else would he refuse to deny it?"

"I don't know: she seems like a gold digger to me. Notice how she ain't go to the police yet? She just keeps appearing on the air, crying on cue, talking about how innocent she was."

Louie thought about it for a while, then shrugged his shoulders. "Hey, Colina," he called across the room, "what you think?"

However, the man only stood there with his back turned.

"You still got your panties in a bunch about that bust?" Holtzman said, laughing uneasily.

"I'm telling you," Colina started, turning around threateningly, "*that* was the place! That cunt mother of his was hiding him—saying all that bullshit about how he didn't come home from school yet!"

"You *sure* that was the place?" Leonard put in.

"Of course I'm sure!" Colina shouted at them. "Didn't you see it in that bitch's eyes. I don't trust *none* of those fuckers. The police force was meant to keep order among people who *want* it—not *those* people... Stab you in the back the first chance they get... Fuckin' *rats*, all of 'em—"

"What the hell is eating you?" Holtzman ventured. There was a note of alarm in his voice; he looked at Leonard, seeing the same bewildered expression.

"What's with *me*?" Colina went on. "We just gonna turn our backs and try to forget that a murderer's out there?"

"Calm the fuck down, Colina," Holtzman said nervously again.

"Don't tell me to calm down! I ain't some goddamn rookie!" he raged, his face turning deep red. "I've seen too much on these streets to not know what's going on!"

"All right, damn," Holtzman said with even more forced laughter. "You seriously need to get laid, pal," he said, shaking his head.

"*Fuck you!*"

"Well, I never said I was offering!" he joked, at which Leonard—who usually tried to stay out of these arguments—laughed as well.

While the two men laughed, and Colina glared at them, the phone on Colina's desk rang. Scowling at the other two, he walked over and picked it up. "Colina!" he belted into the phone. But then his eyes grew wide as he listened. A moment later, he banged down the phone and ran toward the stairs. The other two stared expectantly at him—

"It's *Thomas*!" Colina said, rushing past them, "—he's waiting upstairs!"

The other two first looked at one another in disbelief, then leaped up and rushed after him. What could it mean? They were all running up the stairs now, as though Thomas might escape their clutches again.

"Where is he?" Colina yelled to the desk sergeant when he reached the waiting room. He had a look of madness in his eyes, exacerbated by the fact that he was panting and flustered from his run. The sergeant looked at Colina warily before gesturing toward the kid in the corner of the empty waiting room, who was reading a magazine. Colina rushed over to the kid, just as the other two cops arrived. As Colina approached, Thomas stood up.

"Look, I didn't do nothing," Thomas barely managed to say, before he was shoved back into the seat.

"Shut the *fuck* up!" Colina exploded as he towered over the kid. Then, "Where'd you hide it?"

"Hide *what*?" For some reason, Thomas laughed—

Colina hauled him up by the lapels, then heaved him against the wall, putting his forearm to Thomas' chest. "You son of a bitch," he cursed the kid, "stop *fucking* with me!"

"Colina!" the desk sergeant screamed, while Holtzman and Leonard looked on in shock.

"Look, man...!" Thomas started, but Colina punched him in the ribs then, so that he fell to the ground, wincing in pain.

"He don't even match the description, Colina!" Holtzman yelled from where he stood.

"*Fuck* the description!" Colina cursed. "*This is him*!"

"Yo," Thomas started, finally getting his wind back, "I didn't do *shit*, man!"

"Shut up!" Colina barked; and at that, he kicked him—

"I *knew* it!" a woman suddenly screamed. They all turned to see a plump black woman come in dressed in an all-white nursing aide uniform.

"Mama..." Thomas moaned from the ground.

"Something told me you bastards would do this!" she screamed at Colina. She ran up to them then, and pushed Colina aside, so that she could get to her son; but Colina, incensed, and in no mood, slapped her in the face, so that she fell heavily to the ground. Then, as though some animal instinct had been unleashed in him, Thomas leaped up and punched Colina squarely in the jaw. As Colina crumbled to the ground, Thomas jumped on him, raining wild blows on the man. However, as Colina remembered a trick from his old Marine days, he grabbed Thomas' arm; and, twisting it, he flung the kid to the side. Colina leapt to his feet a millisecond before the enraged Thomas. The kid went to charge, like a bull; but all of a sudden, something exploded in the air. At least, it seemed like an explosion in the closed quarters of the waiting room. Soon thereafter, Thomas fell to the ground with a loud thud. Only Thomas' mother seemed to have understood what happened, because she screamed out. Leaping up, she, too, charged the gun-toting Colina with all the hatred and madness of her son; but after another explosion, her unmoving body fell on top of her son's. In the horrible silence, they all started down at the bodies; but it was obvious, from the way that those sightless eyes stared off into the distance, that they were dead. Colina stood triumphantly then, the wild look of battle still in his eyes as he replaced the gun in his holster. The others stared on in disbelief—in *horror*, in fact. Colina looked over at them nonchalantly; then, suddenly annoyed by their expressions, he screamed:

"Well, *you* saw them! They came at me like *animals!* I had to shoot them: it was self-defense!"

Finally on the ground, Marenga and the hundreds of other passengers hurried down the passageway that led to Immigration. The process went smoothly enough: the middle-aged white man behind the desk looked at Marenga's passport, peered at his face with dawning recognition, then stamped his passport. At that, the man grunted equivocally and waved Marenga on.

While in Harlem, the Thomases lay lifeless in their own blood, and the seeds of hatred and madness began to sprout from that blood, Marenga followed another passageway, which led to the Customs Department. Just before Customs, there was the moving belt that brought out their luggage. He waited for his baggage with a mind that was still numb from his trip. He moved listlessly toward the Customs Officer after he had grabbed his bags, hardly even bothering to look up. The officer was a tall black man in his late twenties. There was a military precision about the man as he simultaneously searched through Marenga's bags and interrogated him.

"How long were you out of the country?" the man demanded.

"Five months," Marenga answered distractedly.

The man glanced at Marenga's passport, double-checked the name and picture, then went on: "Visiting Africa, Mr. Marenga?"

"Yes, sir," Marenga answered, suddenly annoyed with the entire process.

The man grunted and went back to unloading Marenga's clothes. As the man stacked Marenga's folded underwear on the metal table, Marenga grimaced—not in shame, but in further annoyance.

"Anything to declare?" the man inquired.

"No, sir."

Just then, the officer took out the fetish and shook it, hearing something rattling within. "What is this?" he demanded.

"It's a fetish," Marenga said curtly, in a tone that suggested that only a fool wouldn't know what it was. For some reason, a scowl came over the officer's face as he watched it; and unaccountably, that expression pleased Marenga.

"What's in here?" asked the Customs Officer, shaking it again.

"I don't know," he said, testily.

"I have to open it."

"There's no way to open it," Marenga said, his annoyance growing. "It's *glued* on."

"I'll have to break it, then."

"You can't break it!" Marenga said, outraged. "A dignitary gave it to me in Namibia"—*or was it Swaziland?* he thought.

However, the Customs Officer only chuckled, a wry

smile coming over his face. "I *can't* open it?" he said with a laugh. And then: "Maybe you should step this way, sir."

"What!" Marenga exploded.

"Gather your things and step this way."

"What the hell is this about?"

"You have given me sufficient cause to suspect that you're smuggling something—"

"Don't be ridiculous! I'm—"

"I don't care *who* or *what* you are! Here, *I* give the orders. Get your things and follow me...or we can do it the hard way." Having said that, he nodded to two armed officers.

Marenga groaned in frustration, then grunted for the man to get it over with. The man loaded Marenga's things onto a cart, then wheeled them down an adjacent corridor, while Marenga followed testily behind. He was taken to a moderately sized room with a huge metal table in the middle of it. Besides that, there was nothing else in the room, save for one of those huge mirrors that no doubt had an observation room on the other side of it. Two young white officers came in; Marenga stepped to the side. One of the officers started unloading Marenga's bags, while the other officer busied himself trying to crack the fetish open.

The original black officer stepped up to Marenga then, and said, "Take off your clothes, sir."

"*What!*"

"Take off your clothes!"

Marenga was in a dream—a *nightmare*, in fact. He disrobed in a daze, mesmerized as he watched the two other officers ravaging his things.

Marenga, now shirtless, was loosening his belt now. He looked up at the black officer as he unzipped his pants: *You worthless young nigger!* he thought to himself. The man stood above him with the same military precision. He noticed the hatred in Marenga's eyes, but that recognition only produced a grunt of pleasure from him.

Marenga looked on as the last of his things were thrown in a heap on the steel table. He was standing there in his underwear and socks now; the black officer stared at him, his face like stone. With a gesture, the man told Marenga to remove his underpants. Marenga stared back at the man with the same harsh intensity. He pulled down his shorts: *Is this what you wanted to see, faggot!* he thought. The man's gaze hadn't moved from Marenga's eyes. They stared at one another, the hatred exchanged between them. The officer smiled, then said, in a voice that only he and Marenga could hear:

"It's niggers like you who make things hard for all of us."

Marenga couldn't move! The extent of his rage made his breath get caught in his throat. He felt suddenly weak, grimacing at the arrhythmic thumping in his chest. All of a sudden, it was as if an icy finger were clawing at him; he gasped at the first touch, then bit his lower lip to keep from screaming, as the ice turned to fire. *You piece of shit!* he went to curse the smug officer, but he had to suck in his breath when the pain in his chest gripped him like nothing he had ever felt before. The sensation was twofold: first, there was the sensation of an explosion within, then there was the even more debilitating feeling that the world was being sucked into him. All its pain and sorrow and violence and destruction, was being sucked into him, so that he almost collapsed from the weight of it.

He wasn't merely having a heart attack—he was the conduit for a world on the verge of blowing itself apart. He felt it all at that moment: the Thomases, Kain's madness, the self-destructive anger of *millions*...it went on and on, filling him up until he felt that he was going to burst. He panicked then, not at the thought of death, itself, but at the thought of dying like this, before the grinning officer—

With a final blow of his baton, one of the white officers broke the fetish in two and allowed the contents to fall onto the table. All three officers gathered around the object and its contents as Marenga stood to the side, with his drawers around his ankles, willing himself to live. The officers stared at the sandy substance on the table for a while; the black officer bent over and put his finger to it. First, he sniffed it, then he dabbed it on the tip of his tongue. His face soured. Another officer repeated the procedure, a frown coming to his face: "It's sand," he said.

The black officer looked back at Marenga, still smug. "Well, I guess everything's fine here, sir," he said, unapologetically. "You may leave now," he went on, but there was biting condescension in his phrasing. The two white officers left; the black officer stood by the door, watching Marenga.

The old man looked around at all that had been undone, and then finally at his flabby body in the reflective glass. He felt so...*unreal*. He stood there naked, wounded, raped, able to think of nothing but vengeance. He looked over at the black face of the officer at that moment, hating not only it, but the entire country and ethic that had spawned it. It seemed as though his entire life had come down to this moment. It was no longer even a matter of him having wasted his life, but of life, as he had known it, having wasted *him*.

While in Harlem, the stunned police officers gathered around Colina and his victims, asking what was to be done, Marenga was enveloped by a kind of boundless, rampaging hatred. He looked at his bloated, sagging, middle-aged body, again feeling something new and horrible growing within him. The sensation was almost orgasmic in its intensity, leaving him shuddering and light-headed. Africa had been a five-month orgy; his life before that had been foreplay; and now, at last, with this final spasmodic thrust, he had reached the fulfillment of his lust: pure, maddening, insatiable hatred. His soul cried out for vengeance...but he wasn't strong enough yet. Within him, was the will to rip all of their heads off—but he had to bide his time. First things first, some palliating demon kept whispering in his ears. Yes, they would all come to feel the hell he was carrying around in his soul, but he had to get out of here first—escape to fight and kill another day. He took a deep breath to steady himself, then he began to put on his clothes.

The black officer still stood at the door, watching his every movement with a look of amusement. Marenga took his time, fighting not to betray the depths of his weakness... At last, he gathered up his things, saving the fetish for last. Very meticulously, he scooped up the grains of sand, pouring them back into the crack in the skull, as if the sand were blood. It was then that he turned around to look at the officer. The man stared back at him indifferently; then, as he saw that Marenga was ready to leave, he exited the room and went about his business.

Alone, Marenga put his bags back on the cart, holding the broken fetish tenderly, as though it were a baby. Then he pushed the cart outside, and past the black officer. The horrible new feeling was still growing within Marenga as he walked through the terminal tentatively. In his arms, the hideous face of the broken fetish seemed even more grotesque, now that it was cracked in two; but all of a sudden, that very repulsiveness was his only hope. He had once thought of the fetish as a testament to the end of superstition; but as he walked through the bustling terminal, and toward the exit, he was suddenly desperate to believe in all the dark magic it was supposed to embody. He gripped it, willing whatever heathen spirits it had once channeled to return and serve him. It was as he stepped out into the chilly New York night air, and saw one of his young aides waiting with his car, that Marenga knew, with a horrible certainty that brought a quivering grin to his lips, that justice would be delivered onto this place, and that they would all pay for what they had done to him.

Little did Roland Micheaux know that the seeds of his destruction were being sown in the events currently taking place in the city; but the lifecycle of seeds can be anywhere from a few minutes, to decades—even centuries....

Roland was now waving at the hundreds of people at the press conference. Dozens of flashbulbs exploded in front of him as he stood on the podium. At his back, were Rosencrantz and some of the petitioners of the class action suit. As the head of the legal team that had gotten Cranston International to settle out of court for a landmark eight-figure sum, Roland was the focal point of the excitement.

"We have achieved a great victory for America today!" Roland declared. "It is a long-overdue victory for the consumer; and in this case, it is the most innocent and susceptible of consumers: our children!"

While in Harlem, other officers came running to investigate the gunshots, only to see Colina standing proudly before the corpses of the Thomases (like a game hunter), Roland's audience erupted with wild cheers.

Rosencrantz patted him on the back then, and unconsciously licked his lips at the fifty million dollar fee that was coming to the firm. Roland was unquestionably a star now—there was no denying it! When the question and answer period began, even the reporters—as jaded as they were—looked up at him with sudden awe. And then, after the press conference, scores of people came up, wanting to shake his hand and ask him further questions; but finally finding a use for the rest of the legal team, Roland deflected those questions onto them. Rosencrantz, seeing him sneaking away, shook his head and laughed.

"Where you off to again!" his boss asked.

"Another appointment, sir," he returned with a cheeky smile.

"Who is this mystery woman you're always running off to?"

"Mystery is the spice of life!" Roland said obliquely, bowing to them all and taking his leave.

While in Harlem, the fidgety policemen decided that the first thing they had to do was take Colina into custody, and Colina took out his gun and told them all to back away, Kain and his men trudged down the dark side streets of the ghetto, toward their hideout. Kain had met these men—with the exception of Maury Feingold, the Jewish kid who fancied himself an anarchist—at a homeless shelter. There had been hundreds of them, languishing either in chaotic madness or the debilitating kind of freedom that came with having nothing. Kain could have built an army, if he had been so inclined....

As for Kain, as insane as he obviously was—or "mentally ill" to use the modern, politically correct phraseology—the idiocy of the state's psychiatric bureaucracy had made his escape a breeze. Also, the extent of his madness had probably given him the strength to appear sane. Some voice had constantly been in the back of his mind, telling him when to smile and what to say and how to allow himself to be treated by the condescending psychiatrists and attendants—who had been easily manipulated, because their ultimate fantasy was that they had the ability to cure madness. A few teary, heartrending episodes by Kain, in which he regurgitated his doctor's theory about his mother not loving him and asked the doctors if they thought that the society would ever forgive him, had been more than enough to get himself transferred to the minimum security wing of the facility. There had been three group sessions a day, in which several other blubbering idiots spouted drivel about their lives. Kain had invented similar stories, sometimes barely able to keep from laughing at the convoluted nonsense that came out of his mouth. All the while, the philosophy of blessed self-destruction had been working itself out in his mind. After a week of these teary sessions, Kain had made his escape by posing as an orderly. Given severe state budget cuts, the minimum-security prison had turned into a no-security prison at certain times of the night. Kain had timed it all so perfectly that he was strolling through Times Square before he was even missed.

While back at police headquarters, Colina cursed them all, accusing them of having surrendered the streets to scum, Kain and his men continued their trek down the cold, dark, tenement-lined streets. Just then, one of the old black men, known as Crazy Eddie, exulted: "The people like us!" flashing one of his infamous toothless grins.

As Kain turned into an alley, he casually declared, "Forget the people."

"Yeah," Feingold added, "*fuck 'em all*...!" He had been a freshman philosophy student only two weeks before, doing a report on homelessness. He had interviewed Kain, and had never been quite right since. Of course, he had left school and turned his back on his parents' comfortable home in the suburbs of Connecticut, in order to overthrow the world and bourgeois society.

Whatever the case, it was about a second or so after turning into the alley that they saw a heavyset white man in a trench coat. The man's smile was smug, especially seeing the momentary shock on the faces of the men before him. Kain and his men instinctively leaped back, but the white man only smiled and shook his head.

"Maury," began the sleazy-looking private investigator Feingold's parents had sent after him a week ago, "you *forced* me to do this!" At that, he took a .45 out of his coat and pointed it in Kain's direction. "This man," he said, gesturing derisively at Kain, "just escaped from the goddamn *looney* bin! He was the *Hair Jacker*, for God's sake!" When that seemed to have no effect on Feingold, he exploded: "Your parents are worried about you, kid! This isn't normal!" he said, looking over Kain's followers. "Goddamn, couldn't you have joined a frat like everyone else—have a couple of orgies, do some drugs...! Shit, *whatever!* This is crazy! Look...okay, the pressure of school was too much for you. Perhaps you can take a year off, then go back to the university—"

"Get the hell out of here!" Kain screamed, finally coming to his senses.

"I'm holding the gun!" the private investigator pointed out, "*I* give the orders."

"I'm not going *anywhere* with you!" Feingold screamed at the man.

"You're coming with me, kid," the private investigator informed him with a sardonic laugh. "We can either do this the hard way, or the easy way. Either way, I'm bringing you back home."

Kain laughed softly then, at which time his followers joined in.

"What the hell is so funny!" the investigator demanded.

"Do you really think that you are in charge of this situation?" Kain said.

"Let me see," the man said sarcastically, "I'm holding the gun. That seems to put me in charge."

"You put too much faith in the threat of violence, Mr. Weiss."

"How the hell did you know my name!"

"That's of no consequence. The matter at hand is that you would like to take young Feingold back to his parents. I know how you can do that with the least possible trouble."

"What are you talking about?"Weiss said, suddenly suspicious.

"How would you like to bargain for this boy's soul?"

"His *what*?"

"You heard me correctly, Mr. Weiss. I'm offering you the means to win his soul."

Weiss couldn't help laughing. "Who are you supposed to be, the devil?"

"As far as you and you clients are concerned, I am. All you have to do is come with me and we can get this over with."

"To where?"

"Are you afraid, Mr. Weiss? We are unarmed, frail and insane: you are sane, relatively healthy and armed."

Weiss continued to look at him suspiciously. He knew that he should just take Feingold and go, but something about Kain intrigued him. His curiosity had been piqued. "You still haven't told me where."

"The place you've tried to follow us to for the last few days—without success, I might add." Weiss' eyebrows rose. "This is a chance both to solve a mystery and win young Feingold's soul."

"And how do I 'win' his soul?" Weiss said with another sardonic smile.

"You win simply by matching your sanity against my madness. You have faith in sanity, don't you? You believe in a rational world, don't you, Mr. Weiss?"

"And what if I do?" Weiss said in the same joking manner.

"Well, I believe in chaos and madness—and the malleability of the human soul. I believe that given a chance, most people will choose madness over reason. This is your chance to prove me wrong."

Weiss laughed heartily then. "You're good, Kain," he said, nodding his head. "I can see how young Feingold got his head fucked up by you. But see, I don't give a shit about philosophy—and I don't let nobody fuck my head up. The only thing I really care about is getting paid—and that happens when I bring back this kid here. See, as you noted before, I'm armed, and unless you've totally fucked up this kid's head, I think that if I point this gun at him, he'll come with me."

302 D. V. BERNARD

However, Kain only laughed again. "Either you're already mad, or you're a fool, Mr. Weiss. Certainly you don't propose to *shoot* young Feingold, here. That would preclude you from getting paid—which you stated before was your only motivation. So, obviously, the threat of violence is not going to suffice here." Weiss looked unsure for the first time. "Moreover, even if you managed to get him away from me, you'd be taking back an enemy, Mr. Weiss. Are you going to handcuff him in the trunk while you drive? Obviously you haven't given thought to everything. I'm offering you the chance for his *soul*: the opportunity to bring back a pacified mound of putty, ready either for your hand or the hands of his parents. I'm sure his parents would compensate you double if you managed to complete such a feat."

Weiss was still looking at him suspiciously—and now with confusion and a certain amount of alarm. "What would I have to do?"

"All you have to do is come with me—prove to me that reason is more powerful than madness."

But Weiss' instincts began to exert their force; and shaking his head, he blurted out: "You must be *mad* if you think I'm going anywhere with you!"

"I *am* mad," Kain said, matter-of-factly. "I've never denied that. Come on, Mr. Weiss: the night is getting cold. And you still have the gun, don't you? Certainly you still trust violence."

"*Damn* right—and I trust getting paid even more!"

Kain smiled. "...I am understanding you better, Mr. Weiss," he went on, in the same calm manner. He reached for his pockets then—

"Don't move!"

"Relax, Mr. Weiss. I am unarmed." At that, he brought out a huge wad of one hundred dollar bills.

Weiss' eyes bulged! The man stared, entranced: he had to shake his head to break the spell. "Where'd you get that money!"

"That's of no consequence, Mr. Weiss. All that matters is that you want it. So, let's sweeten the pot, as they say. You said before that you only care about getting paid. I have, here in my hand, ten thousand dollars, Mr. Weiss." Weiss looked at it again. "Feingold's parents are only paying you two thousand—"

"How the hell did you know that!"

"That, too, is of no consequence, Mr. Weiss. Let's stick with the matter at hand. Prove to me that your reason is superior to my madness, and I'll hand over not only Feingold, but this wad of cash."

"I could just take them from you!" he said, uneasily.

"Could you?" Kain said with a laugh. "If you thought you could, you would already have done so. The fact of the matter is that you relied on the threat of violence alone." He gestured to his followers then. "Do you really think these men care about life and death? They are the dregs of society, Mr. Weiss. They have slept on sidewalks on the coldest winter nights; they have eaten out of garbage cans. Do you really think that your pointing a gun at them is going to make a difference? Now," he said to the suddenly fidgety Weiss, "you may be able to shoot one of us, but the rest of us would be on you.

"No, Mr. Weiss," Kain said with a sigh, "you didn't think this through at all. Indeed, the only reasonable thing to do, is come with us." He waved the money again; Weiss looked away from it uneasily. "If you have any faith in yourself—and your reason—then you'll come with me." Not even waiting for a response, Kain calmly walked past Weiss, who still stood there with his gun drawn—but with a trembling hand. Kain's followers walked past next; and after they were all about five paces away, Weiss began to follow them, looking haggard.

While in Harlem, Colina finished up his tirade and fired his gun above the heads of his fellow officers—so that they ducked and scattered—Maria Santos smiled at her guest and said: "...So, are you looking forward to your big debate with Mayor Randolph tomorrow night?"

"Of course," McPrice replied, smiling. "I always look forward to a chance to prove myself the better man!"

While Santos and her guest chuckled at the witticism, the piped-in audience clapped uproariously.... A commercial break later, the next guest was the woman accusing Mayor Randolph of rape. After they sat down,

Santos held the woman's hand compassionately in order to give her the courage to tell the story that everyone had already heard dozens of times.

While in Harlem, Colina declared that they would never take him alive, Roland walked into his dark condominium and shut the door quietly behind himself. There was a candle burning in his bedroom. Roland tossed his briefcase on the couch and walked toward the light with a smile on his face. He began to undress now, tugging at his tie and throwing off his jacket. When he reached his room, he saw Samantha lying on his bed seductively, in only a teddy. There was something exotic about her as she lay there, under the flickering wick of the candle. Soon, he was in her arms; her mouth was on his, her tongue searching wildly. He needed her desperately—it was beyond desire: it was *need*. Being with her was like a narcotic. He craved it: felt, in moments of forced depravation, that he could kill for it if necessary.

While in Harlem, Colina darted from the precinct house, and fled into the night, Samantha let out a moan. Roland moaned as well. Soon, he was inside of her, and she was clawing at his back. They seemed like two beasts thrashing—*fighting* one another. She liked to be choked and slapped and cursed, and all kinds of improbable things; and during those subsequent moments of discomfort, he would think, with a gnawing unease, of his father raping a white woman, and Phelps' perverseness... But the next time that he saw her, everything would be forgotten, and he would again lose himself in the extremes of their sex.

While in Harlem, Colina jumped into a police cruiser and zoomed off, Kain led his men and the private investigator into a virtual wasteland. The buildings had been razed, as though in preparation for new construction, and everything was in huge piles of rubble. Weiss was still following at a distance, with his gun kept at his side and his finger on the trigger. As there were very few streetlights here, Kain and his men were only dull silhouettes against the darkness. Weiss lost himself in the act of following Kain; his immediate fears and concerns were dulled by the act of putting one foot in front of another. However, when Kain's men opened a manhole cover and began to file in, something in Weiss' gut churned. He walked up warily, watching as the men descended into the dark hole. The only one who remained outside, was Kain—and he presently gestured for Weiss to come closer.

Weiss walked up uneasily, saying, "What is this?"

Kain smiled then, saying, "If you've characterized me correctly, then this is the gateway to hell, Mr. Weiss."

Weiss looked down into the darkness.

"Don't tell me you're afraid, Mr. Weiss."

"I ain't afraid!" he said defensively. "I just ain't stupid, that's all."

"That's right, you aren't. Therefore, if you don't come now, then you lose everything: Feingold…the ten thousand. These sewers go on forever: you'll never see us again."

"I could still take the money from you!" Weiss countered, but Kain only laughed again, still with that disconcerting calmness.

"If you search me, you'll find that I have no money, Mr. Weiss. It's on young Feingold's person. So, you see, you really have no choice. Do you want to go first, or should I?"

Weiss' mind was working furiously! "I could tell the police where you are! Those people in the looney bin would love to know where you are!"

"Right you are, Mr. Weiss," Kain said with another laugh, "—but if you were going to do that, you would have done it days ago. The fact of the matter is that you want to get Feingold on your own—*without* help. That way, you not only get the credit, but all the money. There's a reward for me, but you're not the kind of man who gets his collar like that: like a frightened kitten. You want to be the one in control: the one to subdue his victim, not the one who hides behind a bush and then goes in to collect the reward after the police have done the work—"

"I could just take you in now!" Weiss continued, his voice rising unsettlingly.

"Of course you could," Kain conceded, "but then you wouldn't succeed in your goal. I would be in jail, and you would get the five hundred dollars they are offering for my return, but you would never see Feingold again—and there is the ten thousand, which you would never see again either. So," Kain continued, "are you coming or not?"

Weiss looked totally distraught. His every instinct told him to be that scared kitten Kain had mentioned, but Kain had touched a sensitive spot; and seeming to come to the conclusion that there was no choice, he blurted out, "*You* first!" pointing his gun again. Kain shrugged his shoulders and complied. Weiss followed a few seconds later; but when he put his hands on the rungs to descend into the dark, cramped smelliness, he was alarmed by how much they shook. Looking down, he couldn't see anything! His gut was telling him that it was a trap, but for the life of him, he couldn't stop—couldn't *think!* He was more than three-quarters of the way down the rungs when the trembling in his limbs became so severe that he lost his grip and slipped. He had been holding the gun in his hand, but it fell along with the rest of him; and before he even knew it, he was lying in the sludge, groaning and disoriented. There was a dull light down the corridor. From that dim illumination, he realized Kain and his men were standing above him; a millisecond later, he became aware that he had lost the gun! He went to grope around in the filth for it, but Kain turned on a lantern then, saying:

"Get up, Mr. Weiss: I have your gun here." Kain's face looked horrible in the lighting—as did Weiss'! However, that was when Kain calmly handed the gun to Weiss. Weiss grabbed it eagerly, and pointed it at Kain again, but the man only laughed. "You're the one with the gun, yet you're the one who's shaking." Then, gesturing with his head, he continued, "Put that gun in your pocket and follow me. Such ridiculous things are of no use where we're going."

While on the Harlem streets above, Colina fled into the night, able to think of nothing but taking revenge on the world that had betrayed him, Weiss did as told. He didn't so much comply as surrender—and he was still shaking. They walked for another five or so minutes—down labyrinthine passages that Weiss realized he would never be able to navigate on his own.

In time, Kain and his men entered a little nook in the sewer; Weiss followed them warily, like a sleepwalker unable to awaken from a nightmare. Actually, they were now in the basement of an abandoned, sealed off building, which could only be reached through the sewer. Kain switched on a light then, and Weiss flinched when he saw everything that the bulb illuminated. The place was replete with everything from electric lighting and heating, to full living and dining room sets, a television (which had been left on) and a refrigerator—all of which Kain had had his men procure using certain disreputable means.

"What the hell is this place!" Weiss demanded, looking more distraught by the second.

"Have you already forgotten why we're here?" Kain said, laughing again. When Kain laughed, his men automatically chuckled along, like his chorus. "This is where you will match your sanity against my madness, Mr. Weiss—and win ten thousand dollars." Kain nodded to Feingold then, and the youth took out the wad of bills and held it up for Weiss to see.

Weiss again looked away nervously; and with the light, he could see his clothes at last: he was totally covered with sewer sludge. He realized, again, that he had no idea where he was—and nobody knew where he was either! How could he have been so stupid! That was when a sound came from the corner of the chamber, where there was a closed door. Someone or something was banging on the other side of it!

"What's in there!" Weiss demanded.

Kain smiled enigmatically then, saying: "One of your colleagues, Mr. Weiss: someone else who puts his faith in sanity."

Before Weiss could respond, Kain and his band walked over to the door and fought to open it (it was locked with a huge bolt). Weiss followed numbly behind; and when the door was finally open, a bone-thin, disheveled white man stood in the doorway. However, at the sight of Kain, the man retreated. There was a dim light inside the small, windowless room, and a small cot, on which the disheveled man now sat, looking up at Kain warily. The walls were unpainted bricks and the entire thing reminded Weiss of a dungeon. There was a pungent toilet in the corner—or at least a commode. Kain entered the room and stepped up to the man calmly; Kain's men made space in the doorway, and Weiss stood there with them, staring inside in disbelief.

While on the Harlem streets above, Colina ran red lights and zoomed down crowded city streets at eighty kilometers an hour, Weiss looked into the room, seeing that the elderly man—the *prisoner*, by the looks of it—was covered in nothing but rags and muck. The man had a bushy, disheveled beard, scraggly hair and a wild look in his eyes—all of which spoke to long captivity and madness—

"How long are you going to keep me here, Kain!" the man suddenly cried.

"What?" Kain responded, laughing again, "—don't like the accommodations? They're the same ones you kept me in when I was in the Institute."

Yes, believe it or not, that man was Dr. Fishman, Kain's one-time psychiatrist. Three weeks ago, learning that Fishman was going to a psychiatric conference to receive an award, Kain had gotten a limousine and posed as the driver. Like all egotists, Fishman had inwardly believed the luxury was his due, so had stepped into the vehicle without thinking it odd or taking time to take stock of his driver. While they drove along comfortably, Fishman had taken a drink in the bar of the limousine; and twelve hours later, he had awoken in this small, windowless room.

"Kain," Fishman pleaded, "this has gone on long enough. What do you intend to prove?"

"That madness is superior to reason. All you have to do is realize this, and I'll let you go."

"Okay," he said, "madness is superior to reason."

"Nice try," Kain taunted him, laughing, "but you're still acting rationally."

Fishman swore then! "I know what you're trying to do!" he screamed then, "but it's not going to work."

"Of course," Kain said sardonically. "I forgot you know everything."

Fishman groaned, raking his hand through his filthy hair in frustration. Then, in the calmest voice he could muster: "As I've been telling you, Kain, this isn't about me, but about *you*—and your delusions. It's about your failure to see the problems of your life as your own doing. You're trying to punish me now—like you tried to punish all those people whose heads you shaved—"

"I'm doing to you exactly what you did to me!" Kain returned. "You kept me in a room no bigger than this, claiming that you were trying to make me sane—to *cure* me. Now," he said with a sardonic chuckle, "I claim to want to drive you *in*sane!"

"Kain," Fishman tried to reason with him again, "this is kidnapping!"

"It's exactly what you did to me! You think I *wanted* to be in that room!"

"You weren't well, Kain—you *still* aren't! The law said—"

"Don't try to use that cop-out on me!" Kain raged. "You claimed to be an expert on madness—now let's see if you know what madness is! I'm keeping you exactly as you kept me. If you had intended to cure me of madness, then you don't have anything to worry about!"

"I didn't keep you in filth!" Fishman couldn't help but scream. "This is all about *revenge*, Kain!" But catching himself, Fishman sighed and took a deep breath. "...Look, Kain, you shaved those heads to get revenge on the world. It was nothing but acting out, because you felt so impotent to change the world. You're *harmless*, Kain—but bewildered by your harmlessness: the fact that no one fears you; no one rushes out to carry out your will—besides these homeless bums," he said, pointing at Kain's men. "I've said it before, and I'll say it again—no matter how long you keep me here. We both know that you don't have a violent bone in your body, Kain—"

"Then why did you back away when I entered the doorway?" Kain said, laughing mordantly. "What is that I see in your eyes, if not fear?"

"...Kain," Fishman said from the depths of his frustration and exhaustion, "if you were violent, you would have *killed* all those people, instead of simply shaving their heads. You need *help*, Kain. Come back to the Institute with me now. In your heart, you know you're not well."

While in the outside world, members of the media heard the first reports of Colina's shooting spree over the police scanner, and rushed to investigate the story, Kain shook his head resolutely. "I've told you already, Dr. Fishman: there is only one way out of here, and that is for you to understand madness: to be *cured* of sanity! To get out of here, you have to understand what madness is—"

"*Stop saying that!*" Fishman couldn't help himself; and then, in a lower voice: "How long are you going to keep me here?"

"I'm not keeping you here: you're keeping yourself here."

Fishman raked his fingers through his hair again. It was at that moment that Weiss, who had been looking on with a blank, uncomprehending expression, suddenly realized that Fishman's desperation foreshadowed his own fate. He was snapped back into consciousness then, acutely aware that he had to defend himself. He grabbed for his gun, but then frowned and looked down at his pocket in horror—*it wasn't there!*

Kain laughed out then; and at that moment, Weiss looked around to see Feingold holding the gun on him.

Weiss had been so engrossed in the goings on of the room that he hadn't noticed he'd been pick-pocketed! Feingold gestured with his head, then pushed Weiss into the room when he stood there in shock. Bewildered, he sat down on the cot, next to Fishman, looking up at Kain in horror.

"I'll be back in a day or so, gentlemen," Kain said as he made his way for the door. But then, remembering something, he nodded to one of his men, and the latter handed over the shopping bag he had been carrying.

"Here are enough groceries to last you a couple of days, gentlemen. Maybe during that time, you'll have an epiphany and come to understand madness." The two men looked on in horror, unable to move; and then, the door was closed on them, and they were alone in the putrid darkness, and Kain was gone.

While in Harlem, six police cruisers chased after Colina, and backup from neighboring precincts was called for, Charles Marenga sat in the back seat of his Mercedes-Benz, staring out of the window. His aide was driving him home now, but Marenga's mind still coursed with chaotic images of death and vengeance.

They were presently driving past a public housing development; and as Marenga watched the decaying buildings that he, himself had once campaigned for, his upper lip unconsciously curled in disgust. Inside those buildings, he imagined the graffiti-covered corridors, with their stench of stale urine; he saw the young and innocent losing their lives in gunfights and turf battles. As the images played nightmarishly in his mind, he wondered how many of his people had been victimized by his best intentions.

While in Harlem, news helicopters rushed to capture the police chase, the world outside Marenga's window seemed like an open wound that needed to be cauterized. He had spent his life trying to corral his people into a critical mass, but true power wasn't about numbers: it couldn't be amassed, like coins in a purse. A heaping pile of muck and filth was an awesome sight—but it was still only a pile of filth. There was a kind of alchemy to power that had always eluded him. He had spent his life trying to turn lead into gold; and while his heaping pile of filth may have scared his adversaries into building these horrible housing projects, it was clear to him now that filth could only produce filth.

While in Harlem, Colina's car ran through an intersection, running over a half-deaf old woman who hadn't heard the sirens and helicopters, Marenga was on the verge of something horrible. He didn't believe in alchemy and fairytales anymore; but outside his window, he saw the will of god—not the God in the heavens, but the god of filth. The god of filth fueled their ambitions and desires. It told its worshipers to want more and more; the only way to receive its blessings was to spend!

spend! spend! That was their amen and hallelujah. They were "happy" so long as they kept on consuming: kept buying houses and cars...paid for junior's college expenses and went on a yearly vacation. Luckily their god believed in credit, because their strange happiness was burying them in debt. The debt made them slaves to their jobs—but god told them they were happy, so they believed...at least for a little while. And what were recessions and depressions, but low points in their collective religion, when the people were too doubtful to spend? What priests called faith, economists called consumer confidence; and it was both of their jobs to keep it going, so that their religion could prosper and draw more converts. And emerging markets were being discovered every day: vast, fertile plains of new converts to their religion—new *buyers*! Just look at the soaring national debts of the developing countries: yes, they had caught the spirit, too! And just like Americans, they were all whiners—worshippers who were caught in some sick paradox between showing their strengths and their weaknesses, with the sickest of them realizing, in time, that their greatest strength was their weakness. This was how one got aid: be like Russia and claim that if aid weren't given, then the fragile edifice of market capitalism would crumble, and some reactionary extremist, some *infidel*, would seize power—

Marenga had to get some fresh air!

While in Harlem, seventeen cars and three helicopters chased after Colina—and the order went out that Colina had to be stopped at all costs—Marenga bellowed:

"Stop here!"

The aide looked around confusedly. "Sir?"

"Stop here: I'm going to walk home!" He was only about two kilometers away from his brownstone...and he had to get outside.

"But, sir," the youth pleaded, even as he pulled over, "the streets aren't safe."

"Listen to yourself!" Marenga said in disgust. "Are you afraid of your own community now!" As soon as the car stopped, Marenga practically jumped out, onto the dark, tenement-lined streets that held his people. The aide looked back at him anxiously, but: "I'll see you at home!" Marenga bellowed with a violent expression that made the youth drive off in terror.

However, as soon as the youth was gone, and Marenga was alone in the cold night air, he felt the pain in his chest return. He felt dizzy, too, so that he retreated to a stoop that was almost totally blocked by pungent bags of rotting garbage.

While in Harlem, Colina came to the conclusion that he wasn't going to get away—and, like Andropov months earlier, he looked around for a means of ending his life—Marenga sat down heavily on the stoop, clutching his chest as the pain consumed him. It was the same feeling: there was both the sensation of an explosion emanating from within him, and the feeling that all the pain and madness of the world was being drawn into him. He looked out on the world then, as the moon rose above the eroded gray bricks of the tenements; and for an instant, there was the fantasy that he was the city: that he was the world, and that if he died, the world would die with him.

While in Harlem, Colina took out his gun and put it to his sweaty temple, Marenga sat in the gutter, waiting for death. The pain in his chest was a sign from the heavens, and all he could do was tremble with joy as he received those blessings.

While in Harlem, Colina finally pulled the trigger—and his car flipped three times, before ending up on some hapless spectators on the sidewalk—Marenga's chaotic thoughts seemed to match the arrhythmic thumping in his chest. Yet, he sat back at that moment, peacefully aware that he was dying. After a few moments, he looked up with blurred vision, seeing the city again; and it was so repugnant to his senses that he knew, all at once, that the city would be his legacy: that the city had been his lover and his progeny, and that he would survive in it after his corporeal form was gone from the world. The city was being ripped apart, just as he was being ripped apart. Grinning, he was ready for all of it to disappear into the nothingness, like a bad dream.... Yet, after a few more seconds passed, he realized the pain in his chest was becoming duller; his labored breathing was becoming more regular. Unaccountably, he felt himself growing stronger. When he saw he was not going to die tonight after all, he nodded his head grimly, accepting his fate. The god of filth had showed him the truth about the world; as a true believer, Marenga was suddenly reassured that god would make all the infidels pay for what they had done to him; but like a prophet from the Bible, he knew he would have to endure more horrors before god's will was done. He got gingerly to his feet then, and began to stumble home.

Kain had taken his men outside, to the abandoned lot that still held the rubble of the buildings that had been demolished. To keep themselves warm, the four of them stood around a huge fire. They had put pieces of wood—broken beams from the building and old furniture that had been discarded with the rubble—into a drum and set the contents on fire. They stood there, holding their hands up to those flames in silence, suddenly melancholy. Or maybe it was only Kain.

"Let's all get drunk," he began, taking a bottle of cheap whiskey from his coat, "for tomorrow, we'll be sane again." He took a swig, and passed the bottle to Feingold, who was to his right. "God created drugs for a reason, my sons," Kain went on. "He clouds our minds, so that we can see clearly; He drives us insane, so that we can know what logic and reason are. He puts us in the darkness, so that we can know the light. Seize the darkness within, and you'll see; embrace insanity and the road ahead will be made clear; seep into confusion and senselessness, and you will discover the meaning of the universe. Yes, get drunk, my sons. God loves drunkards and lunatics—they are the last true followers of His will—"

But just then, by which time the bottle had come back to Kain, a figure emerged from the darkness at Kain's right. They all turned to look; but before anyone could say or do anything, the man—a disheveled old bum in an army jacket—raised his sledgehammer into the air and brought it down squarely on Feingold's head. The sound was sickening—like a watermelon hitting the ground. Feingold fell heavily to the earth, right next to Kain. Seeing the kid die, the other bums ran away screaming. However, Kain only stared on casually while the man with the army jacket placed his sledgehammer down nonchalantly and stepped up to the drum to warm himself.

Kain looked at the man with pursed lips. "Pardon me, sir, but why did you do that?"

The man looked up as though only now noticing him. "I was cold," he answered tersely.

"I see... Care for a drink?" he said, handing over the bottle.

It was approaching ten o'clock now. The events surrounding Colina's flight were quickly becoming myth—as were the actors involved. However, for some reason, the news hadn't reached City Hall as yet. Mayor Randolph sat at his desk, staring unseeingly at a chart of financial figures. A precursory glance at the scene would lead the viewer to believe that he was hard at work, but the fact of the matter was that he was day-dreaming—*dawdling*, in fact. He could have gone home hours ago, but he stayed here, wary of the lonely empti-ness of Gracie Mansion. Since his sex scandal broke, he had withdrawn from the world. Every magazine seemed to have an article on him; every news broadcast had some tidbit about his depravity. He was now a punch line in situation comedies...but the scandal had reached a kind of stalemate. A good scandal needed a constant stream of sordid details—but it had been a while since anything new and provocative emerged in Randolph's case.

The fact of the matter was that the stripper had lied to him: there weren't any cameras in the strip joint, so it had all come down to her word against his. She didn't even have any stray semen to blackmail him with. She seemed to realize that Randolph wasn't going to give her anything, but this only made her more bitter and self-destructive. She had gone so far that she was trapped in her own media frenzy. When Randolph watched her on TV, crying like a baby, he almost felt sorry for her. Feminists were lining up behind her now, congratulating her for refusing to accept victimization, but it was all a farce.

As for the rest of his life, his divorce had been finalized a month ago: he had put up no fight. His marriage was behind him, as was his strange mid-life crisis...and his political career. The election was only days away and he was trailing Charlotte McPrice by forty points.

He had given his bodyguards the night off once again, and settled himself in his office, somehow finding solace in the silence. In fact, for the last few nights, he had slept in his office. After the violent upheaval of the summer, everything was settling back—not the way it used to be: just settling. All the matter was there—for matter was indestructible—but everything was dust.

Just then, the phone on his desk rang. He first looked at it with indifference; then, as it continued to ring, he looked at it with annoyance. There was a hideous jack-o-lantern next to the phone—he looked at the snarling face strangely for a moment; but coming to his senses, he picked up the telephone receiver gruffly: "Yes?" He listened for a while, then a dumbfounded expression came to his face: "Who?" He listened again, but still seemed not to believe what he heard. At last, he said: "Okay, escort him in."

He sat back in his chair then, still somewhat confused. He looked at the clock on his desk and thought to himself, *I wonder how he knew I was still here?* It was while he was thinking this, that he got up and began to pace the room. Happening to look up, he noticed the huge abstract painting on the far wall. It had been a gift from a rich constituent. He walked over to it distractedly and stood before it, his face creasing. He had had it for a month now; and every time he watched it, he became more convinced that the artist had merely slipped and splattered some paint against the canvass. Somehow, it was worth well over five million dollars. That meaningless conglomeration of colors—

"It's a piece of crap, isn't it?" a voice ventured from the doorway.

Randolph turned around abruptly, only to see Marenga standing in the doorway with a guard. Marenga looked strangely aged since the last time he had seen the man. The sight of the man triggered recollections of how Marenga had laughed at him that day, and Randolph's face unconsciously creased. Yet, despite all that, there was something about Marenga that wasn't quite right—which disarmed him somehow. Marenga, known for his dapper suits, now wore a disheveled black suit that looked like it had been worn thin by use. The man's collar seemed not simply undone, but as though it had been ripped open. His entire shirt was damp and discolored with sweat; and his tie was pulled to the side—as though he had wrenched it loose in a fit of suffocation....

Forty-five minutes ago, Marenga had set off for home, wanting only to leap into the madness; but two blocks later, whether it was a pang of conscience, or his last iota of humanity, his soul had rebelled. He had looked about desperately for something to fight off the

madness; and finding nothing else, his mind had proffered Randolph. His coming here had been yet another
last-ditch effort. He had hailed an oncoming cab and
jumped in, sensing vaguely that Randolph had the tools
to outwit his stupid thoughts, and make him right again.

"You an art lover?" Marenga ventured then. He sounded
winded—as though he were laboring for each breath.

"I like beautiful things," Randolph answered him
suspiciously; nevertheless, seeming to put the bulk of
his apprehensions aside, he nodded to the guard, so that
the two men were left alone. "—So, I take it that you
didn't come here for the art," Randolph said, curtly.

"No, I came to talk to you."

Randolph gestured for Marenga to take a seat in front
of his desk. "What about?" he asked, sitting down; but
at the same time, he frowned as he watched Marenga's
rickety gait—and the feeble way the man took his seat.

"Don't worry, Randolph," Marenga said with a melancholy laugh, seeing Randolph's apprehension. "I'm not
here on business—or at least, not business as you know
it. I have no recriminations to make—no ultimatums—I
simply want to revive that long-forgotten art: conversation."

Randolph frowned—not so much at Marenga's words,
as Marenga. The man still sounded winded—and he
was sweating profusely. Randolph went to ask the man
if he was okay, but he realized he did not really care.
"Conversation?" he said with a bemused smile.

"Yes, talking: not repeating slogans, or stating positions, but genuine conversation. You know what I mean, don't you?"

Randolph pursed his lips, staring critically at the distress written all over Marenga's face. Then, "Yes," he said with a wry smile, "I know what conversation is."

"I want to start," began Marenga, "by apologizing to you—for all the arguments I started with you: all the strife I nurtured...for *all* of it."

"What's this about?" Randolph said, suspiciously.

"I have no agenda, Randolph," Marenga said, solemnly. "Nobody is ever going to know that this conversation happened.... No, wait," he started in a new voice, "I lied: I *do* have an agenda...to hell with it," he said as though exasperated with the stupidity of it all. "I'm giving you *one* chance," he said with more urgency, "—you...the city. I'm giving you this chance to stop me."

"Stop you from doing what?" Randolph said in bewilderment.

Marenga looked at him then—looked up with eyes that had been attuned to the brutal will of the city—and it was all there. On some level, he knew about the Thomases; he saw the feverish reports on the twenty-four-hour news channels; he saw the great mobs all congregating to the scene of the crime, their outraged voices at first demanding answers, then only blood. He saw it all in a flash of light that was so brutal to his senses that he felt dizzy afterwards. He stared into the bewildered contours of Randolph's face, desperate to get his bearings—and to stop the world from spinning. When the man's face finally came into focus, he sighed in relief, but seemed even feebler now. He spoke up quickly, as though time were running out:

"I'm giving you a chance to save yourself," he whispered at last.

"What?" Randolph said, suddenly wondering if Marenga was mad.

"The city's about to tear itself apart!" he shouted.

Randolph got up nervously and went over to the wet bar to mix a drink. He thought about calling the guard; but for some reason, a sense of morbid curiosity got the better of him. When he looked up, Marenga was staring at him intently; Randolph gestured toward the bottles of liquor, but Marenga shook his head. After pouring himself a drink and taking his first sip, Randolph ventured: "So, what's this all about?"

Marenga had been waiting patiently; he nodded before going on, "Something's coming, Randolph, and if you don't stop me, I'm going to be at the head of it." Randolph looked on, utterly lost. "Right now," Marenga continued, "it's gathering strength...I can *feel* it," he said, gasping for air after every few words. "We're at a strange place in history, Randolph. It's make-or-break time for all of us.... I left five months ago because I felt it then—I felt my own place in it. But I'm tired of it all, Randolph: all the preordained, senseless struggles—all the meaningless political wrangling. This is the calm before the storm. I've *seen* things—"

"What are you talking about?" Randolph said with a mixture of alarm and curiosity.

"Like I said," Marenga continued, desperately needing to make Randolph understand, "we all have our roles to play. I have a role, you have a role...we're all taking part in it. The world's connected, Randolph, but connected by meaninglessness." Randolph's face creased even more. "Now is the time to question it all, Randolph—to *stop* it, if it can be stopped. This is our *last* chance," he said, looking as though he were going to collapse at any moment. "We can't just sit around anymore: it's complacency that's killing us—"

"What the *hell* are you talking about, Marenga?" Randolph said at last, losing all patience.

"It's our *last* chance!" Marenga screamed, on the verge of hysteria.

The words echoed horribly in the chamber; Marenga was looking at him imploringly, but Randolph only sighed to himself, thinking, *Marenga is mad!* Strangely enough, his first impulse was to laugh vindictively—the way Marenga had laughed at him—but he was suddenly weary of the entire thing. "Look, Marenga," he said with another tired sigh, "maybe you should leave—"

But Marenga was laughing now. He shook his head and chuckled softly to himself, while Randolph stared at him, frowning. "You think I'm mad, don't you?" Marenga said then.

"Yes," Randolph answered, simply.

Marenga laughed even harder, his entire body jiggling. Something about it was contagious, so that Randolph, despite everything, began to laugh as well. Suddenly, he just felt silly—and even Marenga's madness didn't matter anymore. While he shook his head and chuckled to himself, he walked back over to his desk and sat down heavily. "Okay, Marenga: you're mad, I'm mad...we're all mad. Why are you *really* here?"

Marenga was still chuckling softly to himself. He seemed totally drained now. "I guess the madness drove me here," he said, to which they both began to chuckle once again. "Misery loves company: I guess madness loves company as well," he said, snickering.

However, as Marenga's laughter sounded in the closed quarters of the room, something within Randolph broke, and he found himself remembering the thought he had had during his weeks of filth: that there were other warriors like him out there, fighting the same battles that he fought—soul mates of a sort, who had all been brutalized by the realities of the world. He remembered his own madness; he remembered how, at the announcement of the Brooklyn Massacre, a part of him had been certain he had sensed it—had been at *one* with it. He sobered suddenly:

"...What are you feeling, Marenga?" he started in an anxious tone. "What's got you so upset?"

After a final chuckle, Marenga shrugged his shoulders, then began: "I hate the world, Randolph. It's as simple as that." Having said that, he paused and looked at the man earnestly. "I hate everyone and everything in it...I'm *tired*, Randolph. I'm tired of everything. I'm an old man, looking back on my life and hating it all. You said I was mad—and maybe I am—but I've never been so sure in my life that something's out there...something *evil*. I can *feel* it. I may even be the source of it," he said quickly, "...and I came here to *warn* you—"

But all of a sudden, Marenga looked up sharply, his eyes narrowing: "Now I see what's going on here!" he began with a laugh. "You've sensed it, too, haven't you!" Randolph shook his head feebly. "You're the Mayor— you've lived through it all. You've seen it all—and *felt* it!"

Randolph sighed to himself, unable to see the use of denying it or confirming it. He just sat there with a blank expression on his face, suddenly drained. "Why'd you come to me, Marenga? Why *me*?"

"I needed another lunatic to talk to," Marenga said with a smirk, but neither of them laughed this time. The joke was suddenly stale; and beyond the ease that had been built up between them, they sensed the harsh, sobering realities of the world.

"What happens now?" Randolph asked then, but Marenga only looked toward the windows—and the dark world of chaos beyond them—wondering the same thing himself.

The media had somehow gotten access to the surveillance video from the police precinct's waiting room. In the morning, those images of death and madness would adorn all the papers and news broadcasts. Multi-page spreads were already being coordinated; network specials documenting Colina's insanity were already being considered. Heads were going to have to roll for this, or so the media were saying. Yet, those images were already becoming sacred icons. Faithful worshipers watched Colina's rampage and genuflected to the heavens.

Feingold was dead. The kid lay amongst the rubble at Kain's feet, his blood still seeping out from the crack in his skull. "...The only way to get rid of all evil, is to kill everyone," Kain said, desultorily. He had been talking nonstop for the last fifteen minutes or so. He and the murderous bum were the only ones there. The latter was still drinking Kain's bottle of whiskey, ignoring him. Actually, when Kain handed over the bottle, the man had considered it his, and had never passed it back; and Kain, engrossed in his disquisition, had forgotten about getting drunk.

"The search for purity in a profane world can only lead to madness," Kain went on, while the bum stared unseeingly into the flames. The man had put a turned-over garbage can next to the fire and was sitting on it, while he held the bottle of whiskey in his arms like a newborn baby. Kain had remained standing, like a professor before a student. He continued, "I was just telling my men that we were all going to be sane in the morning. I believe that each one of us has a choice if he wants to be sane or not. Sanity is socially prescribed, you know. So it's possible for the society to be insane and the madman to be the most logical thinker....

"The doctor at the madhouse I was in said that I was harmless—said I would never kill. Now, as I see it, if the only surefire way to get rid of evil and live in a pure world, is to kill everyone, then I would have to be killer, wouldn't I? I would have to seep into chaos and *kill*. So, the big question is if I have it in me or not—a *killer*, I mean.... I know what *they* say sanity is: I've got to figure out if I'm willing to live with that—or to *die* with it. Those are my choices....

"You drunk yet?" Kain said, looking down at the bum; the man took another swig, still staring into the flame as though mesmerized. "No?" Kain went on. "That's good. It ain't right to kill a man when he don't know what's coming. You ain't really killed until you can look into the eyes of your victim and tell him what you're going to do. That's *real* killing. Now, when you think about it, you didn't kill my disciple like a man. You snuck up behind him—did it like a *coward*. I'm gonna kill you to your face—tell you all about it before you die. We should all kill the cowardly killers among us. Even in the Old West, they understood that you don't shoot a man in the back. You 'call him out' as they said—shoot him out in the open, like a *man*. We've got an entire world of cowardly killers. They kill you behind your back; and after you drop dead, they act like they had nothing to do with it. They'll drain your soul—*everything*—like a parasite. Suck you dry...! Kill you like cancer—from *within*... Attack the vital organs: entrench themselves in everything you need to survive, until the only way to get rid of them, is to cut out your cancerous liver, kidneys—all the things you need to survive. Horrible way to die—even worse way to live. That's what they do today—*underhanded* killing....

"But I'm gonna help you out, 'cause you see, *this* kid here"—and he pointed at Feingold—"he's trouble. He's two things a poor black man should never deal with: he's rich and he's white. They already sent a detective after me. When this kid ends up dead, they're gonna come looking for me, not for you. They're gonna try to kill me in their old, underhanded ways. They'll bring me out before their cameras; first, they'll suck out my guts, maybe chop off my tongue—*figuratively*, I mean— let me starve: waste away. After all that, they'll probably sentence me to the death penalty: kill me twice. That's all the death penalty is—killing dead men...*superfluous*. So, the way I see it, I have days, probably hours, before they begin that slow, painful death on me. Now *you*... you've already set it all in motion. Time's ticking...and there doesn't seem to be any way out of it. The only thing to do, as I see it, is to find out the truth about the world before I go. I've figured out most of it by now, but I'm not sure about some vital things. Somehow or another, it all rests with what that psychiatrist said. Either I'm a killer or I'm not. Either I'm able to do what it takes, or I'm just a joker, like everyone says....

"Put down that bottle now," he said with a deep sigh, while the bum, still ignoring him, took another deep swig and blinked drowsily at the flames. Kain picked up the sledgehammer then. At the motion, the bum watched him indifferently; then, as Kain raised the sledgehammer above his head and began his swing, the man screamed out, his face highlighted horribly by the flames.

THE MUSIC BOX

These were the last moments of Roland Micheaux's life. He sprung up from sleep, searching the darkness for the source of the shrill noise. For an instant, the dream projected itself onto the waking world—and he saw himself as a thirteen-year-old, running away from his father. For a moment, he was lost—and the shrill noise was still in the air. As the dream world faded away, he searched the darkness frantically, caught in some bizarre fight or flight impulse—

A hand appeared out of the darkness! In a deft movement, the shrill noise was cut off; and as Roland stared into the darkness, the world finally began to make sense. He checked the hands on his luminescent wrist watch (which said that it was just after three-thirty in the morning), then he stared into the darkness as Samantha got out of the bed, yawned, checked the pager that she had just turned off, and headed for the bathroom. Exhausted by the strange early-morning struggle, he groaned and fell back onto his pillow.

While outside, the story of the Thomases began to take on a life of its own, Roland sighed. Turning his head, he watched his girlfriend's retreating silhouette. In the bathroom, she turned on the light, and he took in the entire length of her smooth, creamy nakedness. He liked the idea of their sordid lovemaking, contrasted with the sweet, "all-American girl" image that was broadcast over the airwaves. All at once, he was madly in love with her—or at least with the *thought* of her. It felt so good to lie there, knowing that there was love in him and that he didn't have to work at it. In fact, his love was like the exhaustion that came after a hard day of work, when everything was complete and the only thing to do was rest. This new peace was like a wonderful dream, so that he felt like laughing out in the darkness. He remembered the Cranston International case then—and his ascension into the stratosphere....

The sound of his girlfriend starting her shower brought him out of his reverie. He smiled unconsciously, remembering their first chance encounter. Yet, two months later, theirs was still a relationship of trysts. They met at cabins for weekend rendezvous; they left coded voice mail messages for lunchtime sessions and after-work meetings. There was something thrilling about the secrecy—and the *silence*. They made it a point to talk only sparingly. They didn't know what the other's favorite color was, or their favorite food. A touch was all that they needed; entire conversations were to be had with a facial expression, a gesture or a kiss. Sometimes they didn't even have sex at all, but instead lay for hours in one another's arms, saying nothing with words, but exploring vast universes of possibility with touch. With their busy lives and their high profiles, there was something wonderful about the silence and secrecy and, at times, bestiality. It wasn't even that anything would happen to either of them if their, for lack of a better word, affair, were ever discovered. It was just that they couldn't stop the fantasy of danger; and that after all this time, they were loath to change the comfortable syntax of their relationship.

After a few minutes, Samantha came out of the bathroom, turning off the bathroom light as she came. She was dressed in a pair of jeans and a blouse (both of which she would change at the studio). She came over to him and straddled him playfully, kissing him on the forehead. They stared at one another for a while, both of them smiling. Outside, the wind was howling softly. It was so perfect—so *peaceful*. His love for her waxed high again; but this time, he needed it to be real—needed it to be more than some panic-stricken impulse.

She kissed him on the lips now, then got up to leave. He turned his head and watched her disappear into the darkness. He wanted to call her back and tell her his feelings, but there was no rush: there was always time...

Still smiling, he closed his eyes and went back to sleep... However, a few minutes later, just as the dream world was about to envelop him again, the phone rang. He sat up and stared at it: at first with annoyance, then with alarm, because rarely did anyone get good news at four in the morning.

He picked it up: "Yes?"

"Mr. Micheaux?"

"Sam?" Roland said with a frown. It was the doorman.

"It's that woman again," he said ominously, "—and that kid."

Roland lay there for a good three seconds before it hit him. "Candice?" he said, more to himself than the doorman. The doorman groaned to give his assent. *What the hell...!* Roland thought, warily. He hadn't seen Candice since the last time Phelps went on his sex binge. The thought of Phelps repulsed him; and the mere thought of the meaningless, self-destructive sex he had had with Candice—not to mention the sex that Phelps was probably *still* having with her—was nauseating. Some more seconds passed; a side of him considered telling the doorman to say that he wasn't there—but that wouldn't work, as she was no doubt standing right in front of the doorman. Seeing no other way, and suddenly remembering Mindy, he sighed. "...Send her up, Sam."

He got up in a daze, put on a robe, then went to the living room, where he turned on the light and sat down on the couch. *Has Phelps been drinking again?* he wondered. Probably. He and Phelps hadn't exchanged anything beyond the standard salutations since they had had that talk all those months ago. Now the man's weirdness was impinging on his life again. He had neither the time nor the patience to enter that again. As such, by the time Candice rang the bell, he had worked himself into a fit of anger. He walked to the door in four brisk strides, his face stern and his jaw tight. But when he opened the door, his jaw dropped. Candice was crying: she was a *mess*! She looked as though she had just been in a fight; her left eye was swollen and her hair looked like a disheveled bird's nest. Little Mindy seemed exhausted and dazed. The little girl was in pink, fluffy bunny pajamas, replete with huge floppy ears and bunny slippers. She smiled vaguely at him when he opened the door, but otherwise seemed ready to fall asleep.

Roland quickly brought them in and sat them on the couch. Mindy looked tired beyond reason. "Come on, sweetheart," he said, taking her from Candice. "You can sleep in here." At that, he rushed her off to the guest bedroom. The little girl lay like a sack of potatoes in his arms. In the room, he took off her slippers and placed her underneath the covers. She closed her eyes soon thereafter and went to sleep. The feeling of anxiety was still growing within him when he went back outside. Candice was balled up on the couch, rocking herself. Roland was going to ask her if she wanted something to drink—some hot chocolate maybe—but the sight of her made him put all that off.

"What happened!" he demanded. When she seemed not to hear, he went up and touched her shoulder. She recoiled; for a moment, she looked like she would scream, but then, seeing that it was only Roland, she came to her senses. He repeated the question in a softer voice. She stared at him for a while, then burst into tears.

"He's gone *crazy!*" she cried.

"Phelps?"

She nodded, like a child forced to admit a horror.

"What did he do?" Roland asked, uneasily.

"God!" she cried. "You don't know what he's like!"

Don't be so sure! he thought to himself.

"He said if I told, he would report me to Immigration…"

"He make you have sex with him?"

"No!" she said in frustration, as though that were too trivial a thing. She seemed to be fighting to find a way to make him understand. Then: "He makes me watch—"

"Watch?" Roland said with a frown.

"He puts me in the closet, then…he brings in Cindy… and then they…" She looked up into his eyes, unable to say the rest.

Roland nodded his head, looking away. *Still up to your old tricks*, he thought. "How long has this been going on?"

"A couple of weeks. It's not normal…the things they do! Sometimes he ties her up! Sometimes I think he's going to *strangle* her!" Remembering the things Samantha cried out for, Roland winced. "And his back is all scratched up. He likes her to do it!" Roland groaned, feeling slightly ill. "But tonight…" She stopped short, wringing her hands anxiously.

"What happened?" Roland managed to whisper.

"Tonight he had me watch as usual. They were doing it, and then, all of a sudden..." She started biting her fingernails; Roland pulled her hand from her mouth. "...All of a sudden," she went on, "he tells Cindy to go get something from the closet, where he had placed me! I couldn't move! Cindy came walking up to me— that stupid, trusting woman!" she cursed her. "She does anything he wants...! She walks up, opens the closet and sees me standing there! I still couldn't move! I was just in shock! As soon as she sees me, she screams! I scream, too! And then, all of a sudden, she starts punching me, calling me all these names. At first, I was so shocked, I couldn't move. But in the background, I hear Dallas laughing—that son of a bitch! I hear him laughing, and I knocked her back. That skinny woman: she couldn't do me *nothing*! I slapped her back and went for him! I was gonna *kill* him!"

Roland groaned.

"I leaped at him...and he was still laughing, as though it's all a joke. But that bastard soon had me held down, like he always held down Cindy. The way he was laughing, I thought he was gonna take me right there, but I saw Cindy then. She was still standing by the closet, kind of in shock like. Things were working in her mind, you see! Hearing Dallas laughing, and seeing him over me like that, she realized it was *him* who had me in there! All of a sudden, she grabbed a lamp and hit him in the head with it. It would have knocked out a normal man, but it only weakened him enough for me to push him off. Next thing I know, he springs at Cindy, blood gushing down his face...*God!*" she cried.

"What happened!" Roland demanded.

"I just ran—ran for my *life*. Somehow, I remembered that little girl, Mindy. I grabbed her from her bed and ran with her...ran for my life. And all the while, I still hear those two fighting!"

"You should have called the police!"

"Police!" she said, outraged. "And tell them what! I ain't even legal here since I stopped going to school! They wouldn't listen to me. And besides, those two freaks...it's all a game to them! If you had seen some of the things I've seen them do...!"

"What about Cindy?" Roland asked anxiously.

"What about her?"

"You don't think she's in danger?"

"Not any more than usual."

Yet, Roland was still concerned: "You must have felt there was some danger—since you took Mindy."

"I took Mindy because I have some decency!" she said, hotly. "One day that child is going to grow up and realize what her parents are. If they haven't corrupted her by then, then God help her!"

Roland sighed to himself, still deep in thought. "So what's going to happen now—since you won't go to the police?"

"That's why I came here," she said, looking up at him.

"Me?" Roland laughed nervously. "What do you expect me to do?"

"Do whatever you want," she said in an offhand manner. "I'm not going back. I just needed someplace to leave Mindy. I'm leaving town."

"*What*? Where are you going?"

"I have a cousin in Boston. I've had enough."

Roland sighed again. "Well, I guess you're right..." *And she has been through a lot*, he thought to himself—and most of that because he had introduced her to Phelps. He couldn't help feeling somewhat responsible.

"Look, Candice," he said in a new voice, "I'm sorry... if I had known how Phelps was—the *full* extent of it—I never thought it would go this far."

However, she only shook her head, as though it were too late for any of that now. He looked at her, trapped between ineffectual guilt and the urge to push everything to its natural conclusion—whatever that was—and get the entire thing over with. Whatever the case, there was something about this that was not right, and it spurred him toward the latter state of mind. "You *sure* Cindy is okay," he said again.

Candice only laughed, shaking her head as she said, "If you had only seen half the things I seen..."

"Well, all right," he conceded, uneasily. And then: "You can sleep in my bed. We'll figure everything out in the morning."

She nodded and left him. Still, as he looked at her retreating form, an icy finger seemed to go up his spine. It was then that he remembered today was Halloween; and that the day, and the coming night, were set aside for the celebration of death and mischief.

Marenga didn't look well as he sat in the back seat of the cab, but he was strangely at peace...maybe not peace yet, but he was satisfied that he had tried his best. With respect to Randolph, he didn't know if anything had been accomplished; even now, their conversation blurred into one long tirade, free of conclusions and prescriptions. They had talked for five hours in all, discussing the nature of the world, the 1960s, the nature of "the struggle," even the chances of the Knicks winning the title this year... But no matter what happened, at least he had talked to someone and let out the proverbial steam. He felt like a man again....

The cab stopped and Marenga paid the turbaned driver before getting out gingerly. He was exhausted, and the knowledge that he was going to sleep well filled him with simple joy. Unfortunately, just then, he looked up and noticed there were four news vans in front of his house: all the major networks were there! Seeing him, the news crews rushed out to greet him, at first seeming like attackers. He unconsciously took a step back, but they were already upon him, yelling, "Have you heard!"

"...Heard what?" Marenga said, looking at them as though they might still attack him. It was then that several of them began talking at once—about Colina and the Thomases. Something about them reminded him of drunkards vomiting up their guts. And then, when they were finished, they shoved their microphones into his face, as if expecting him to return the favor and vomit up his guts as well.

Marenga only stared at them for a moment—stared *blankly*—while they trained their cameras on him and waited anxiously. He felt like he was going to faint: not from the news, itself, but from the wave of revulsion that went over him. Whatever peace he had had, left him entirely, so that he felt suddenly empty. "Let me just have a few moments to collect myself," he managed to say at last. They begrudgingly made room for him, and he walked up to the house, still in a daze. Yet, once he was free of them, he shuddered, remembering his strange evocation of the fetish spirits.

Roland had intended to stay up for the rest of the night; in fact, Candice's story had been so unsettling that he had doubted he would be able to sleep at all. He had turned on the television and lain on the couch, watching the chaotic images surrounding Colina's rampage. Even in the middle of the night, people had already begun to gather at the police station where the

Thomases had been killed. The camera crews had captured their rage; their chants had already filled the air as they called for justice and vengeance. And maybe, something about the chaos had called to his soul, and coaxed him to sleep, like the devil's lullaby.

Either way, just like the last time Candice came over, he opened his eyes to see her standing before him. At first he thought that it was a dream, because it seemed exactly the same as the last time. The only thing was that she wasn't totally naked this time: she now had her underwear on. Also, the television was still on; and highlighted by those scenes of violence, Candice looked like a ghost. She bent over him and caressed his face. Her hand was warm and soft—almost soothing—but her touch was suddenly revolting. She bent lower to kiss him, and he pulled away quickly, sitting up. He was panting for air, seeming terrified as he stared at her. She frowned, looking at him confusedly; and against the backdrop of the chaotic television images, she looked like a mournful spirit. He had an impulse to turn on another light, so that she could again seem like a human being, but—

"Don't you find me attractive anymore?" she said, staring at him in confusion.

He hated that question. "...I just don't want to, Candice..." He didn't know what else to say.

"It's Dallas, isn't it?" she said suddenly.

"What?"

"It's because I let him...touch me."

"I don't care about that—"

"But you always wanted me before."

"Candice..." He took a deep breath, searching for words that never came.

"You don't think that I'm good enough for you, do you?" she said, hysterically.

"What are you talking about?"

"You just wanted something cheap and meaningless—"

"*What*?"

"You're like all men: a *user*!"

He had a sudden impulse to laugh; but seeing the tears in her eyes, he was unable to move a muscle. She ran off then, back into his bedroom. He stared at her in disbelief, wondering what the hell had happened to her. Where was the poised, confident woman he knew from the night of the banquet? What had Phelps done to her! She didn't even talk like a human being anymore, but like some cliché romance novel character.... Still, he was guilty as well—and maybe he had used her: not with calculation, as wronged people liked to think in retrospect, but, perhaps worse, as a convenience.

Yet, she had used him as well; and before she had bitten off more than she could chew, she had no doubt tried to use Phelps, too. They were all guilty of making stupid decisions; but worse than that, instead of dealing with their stupidity honestly, they comforted themselves with the self-righteous delusion that they had been wronged.

By the time Marenga arrived at the Harlem police precinct where the Thomases had been murdered, it was a little past five in the morning. He had been chauffeured over to Manhattan by the same aide that had picked him up from the airport. He had sat in the back numbly, while six news vans followed his car, and the young aide ranted about outrage and justice.

Botswana Glade was already on the scene, with about two hundred of the more diehard protesters. Things were clearly getting out of hand. The mob had congregated in front of the police precinct's entrance—which had been barred with a steel partition. People were standing on top of cars, yelling a hundred different hateful things at once. Some were holding makeshift signs; some had baseball bats and machetes. In the meanwhile, police reinforcements could be seen congregating down the block, getting on their riot gear.

When Marenga's car stopped at the curb—followed by all the news vans—Marenga didn't really have any intention of venturing out. In fact, he had found himself wondering what he was even doing there. Yet, the invisible hand of fate drew him out of the vehicle and onto the pavement; and as he did so, there was an almost horrific cheer from the mob. Or at least it seemed horrific to Marenga's ears. It was as though those cheers were eroding something inside of him, acting as a kind of acid on his soul.

Botswana Glade came up to him then, patting him on

the back. The man's eyes gleamed with excitement. There was something *insane* about it—as though Marenga had been dropped off in a colony of madmen. He instinctively wanted to flee, but he was suddenly surrounded—engulfed by the mob. Botswana Glade said something to him then; but with all the chanting and chaos, the words were lost. People were chanting Marenga's name now; and as he looked at their excited faces, he realized that he was now, somehow the epicenter of their madness.

It was then that the police announced a warning over a loud speaker, to the effect that the protesters were having an illegal gathering and that this was their last chance to disperse. As expected, this was met with defiant screams. The uproar rose in the air like nothing Marenga had ever heard before. He again felt it eroding something in him, *changing* him. And at that moment, he sucked in his breath sharply, feeling the terrible pain return to his chest. It felt as though someone had just stabbed him in the heart. In fact, there weren't words to describe the pain, which left him screaming out and disoriented. Since he was already in a screaming, agitated mob, his screams were easily overlooked—

And soon, there were pops in the air, as the police reinforcements gathered down the block released teargas canisters. Still, even as the acrid gas burned Marenga's eyes and made him choke, the pain in his chest rose up to shield him from the goings-on of the world. He stood there stiffly, jostled by the mob as people began running for cover and fresh air. He was lost in the chaos, waiting for the pain to encompass him fully and end his life. That was when he felt an arm on him, pulling him through the mob; and when he looked up, he saw the same young aide. All Marenga could do was follow. In fact, he wondered how it was that he was still standing. A side of him had been waiting for death—not with horror, but with the expectation of the peace to come. Indeed, when the aide put him in the back seat of the car, Marenga was disappointed—since the pain in his chest was subsiding. Death seemed like a cruel temptress then, who refused to give him any release.

A few moments later, the aide took the driver's seat, and asked Marenga if he wanted to go home. Marenga thought about it for a while, then shook his head, saying, "No, the media will be wanting a statement."

Outside, the chaos was like a boulder tumbling down a mountain, setting off chain reactions. Mayor Randolph sat in the semi-darkness of his office, trying to figure out what Marenga had done to him. All that he knew was that something was gestating within him, opening his mind to new possibilities. Things were clearer to him now. There was something out there—just as Marenga had said. Something was coming, and he and Marenga—and countless others—were soul mates, whose destinies would be defined by the upheaval....

Strangely enough, he had been finding some measure of peace in the darkness, but now that a new day was at hand, everything seemed to be coming to an end. The sun was fighting its way through the Venetian blinds now. Horizontal lines of light were cutting across his face. A normal man would be squinting by now, but Randolph just stared ahead in a daze, oblivious. Beyond the Venetian blinds, there were the muffled sounds of traffic—and *life*. It was almost as if those blinds were a stage curtain; and that beyond them, the production company was busily getting everything ready for the show.

The door to the chamber opened suddenly; the entrant took several quick steps into the room before stopping abruptly—

"*There* you are! We've been looking *everywhere* for you! The guards thought you had left!"

As though just waking up, Randolph looked away from the window and turned toward the door. While he was doing so, he again noticed the hideous jack-o'-lantern on his desk. The snarling, fanged face was facing him; his eyes passed warily over it before coming to rest on the young aide.

"How long have you been here, sir!" Radix demanded.

"Radix?" he said, squinting at the man. "...Since last night—"

"You know about the Thomas thing? It's all over the news!"

Randolph grunted noncommittally.

"You *have* to know about it!" he said in disbelief. "A policeman killed an unarmed, innocent black kid *and* his mother last night—*in* the police station...you haven't heard?" he said again. "The cop went on a rampage, running over three other people ... !"

Yet, Randolph only chuckled to himself, going back to staring at the window as though the aide's revelation had been a trifle. This strange reaction unnerved Radix, so that he continued: "It's a *major* crisis, sir! It's all over the news! We have to act quickly on this! We tried to reach you...! Everyone thinks you're hiding. Worse than that, not only is that bastard Marenga organizing a march, but McPrice is milking this for all it's worth. With the election just *days* away, you can't appear ineffectual on this...! And then, there's the debate tonight...!"

Randolph was still staring unseeingly at the window.

Radix stepped a little closer to the desk, his voice lowered as he asked: "You all right, sir?"

Randolph chuckled softly. "I *felt* it, you know," he said with a strange kind of pride, "—just like the last time."

Radix was utterly confused—and a little scared, too. That incursion into the private realm had unnerved him. He retreated back to business, his voice cracking slightly: "We tried to reach you," he repeated. "Is your pager working...? Even your bodyguards didn't know where you were." Randolph was still staring unseeingly; the aide's voice grew more unsteady and panicky. "You *have* to act quickly, sir!" And then, when all else had failed: "You're the Mayor of *New York City*!"

Randolph chuckled a strange, sardonic laugh: it was horrible in the silence.

The aide stepped in a little closer to the desk, but cautiously, the way someone approached a strange dog. "You all right, sir?" he repeated, almost whispering now.

Randolph laughed again, but there didn't seem to be any mirth in it. "...Just tired." He shook his head then, again noticing the hideous jack-o'-lantern. Some well-meaning constituent had no doubt provided that monstrosity as a Halloween gift: people were always giving him useless things... Randolph sat there, with a strange, far-off smile on his face; and then, abruptly, he looked away from the snarling face and up at the aide, saying, "You spend so much time trying to keep the monsters at bay—"

"*Sir?*"

"That's all I've been for the last four years: a dragon slayer, hired to keep the city safe from the monsters... Marenga was right—"

"*Marenga?*" Radix shouted at the mention at the man's name—

"You just get tired, that's all," Randolph concluded, before going back to staring at the window.

"...Sir, I'm..." He was shaking.

The smile was still on Randolph's face: it looked like an etching left by a sharp knife in a mound of putty. It didn't seem to convey anything at all; if anything, it demonstrated a horrible emptiness within.

"Monsters, Radix," he started desultorily, as if finishing off some dialogue that had been going on within himself. He turned from the window and faced the young aide: "You can't stop them—not in this place. Maybe it's better to let a couple through, so that people remember what monsters are: what *evil* is."

"...Sir?" He was really getting nervous. His mind shot to something, and he went to it desperately: "Can I get you a drink, perhaps?" He rushed over to the wet bar in the corner of the room. "...You've been up all night, you say?" he squeaked as he poured out a drink.

"Monsters, Radix..."

"...Sir..." He was so unnerved that he gulped down the contents of the glass himself. The biting whiskey in his throat steeled his courage: "*Sir!*" he belted; the loudness of his voice took him aback, so that he made a conscious effort to lower his tone as he continued: "You have to get it together! We're in the midst of a *reelection* campaign!" He stepped up to the desk again, forgetting about the drink he was to bring: "Sir, your big debate with McPrice is *tonight*: this could be it for us—our *last* chance. And, on top of that, there's this Thomas murder...and the public relations nightmare with the police department—not to mention the rally that Marenga's planning to protest it. He's planning to march right down here in a matter of hours! He'll be outside your window,"—he pointed to it with a trembling finger—"calling you a *coward!* We have to *plan* for all this. This is D-Day, sir... !"

Unfortunately, the urgency sounded feeble in the silence. Neither of them moved nor said a word for a good five seconds. Randolph had gone back to staring at the window, but he sighed at last, saying, "Do what you must, Radix."

At that, the aide nodded and rushed out, somehow managing to convince himself that things would be fine. Yet, the Mayor still sat there thinking about monsters.

Roland's dream opened up like a sinkhole beneath him, and then he screamed out as he was tossed back into consciousness. Like before, the horrors of his nightmare followed him into the waking world. It sounded as though a million people were laughing at him. He burst upright—but the morning sun was so brilliant that he almost immediately had to shut his eyes. That millisecond, however, was enough for him to get his bearings. The television, he remembered, had been left on. He was lying on the couch: the television was on a console against the wall; and as the French doors were at an oblique angle to it, the glare was blinding. His girlfriend's show was on. Some general morning perkiness was in progress, with his girlfriend's high-pitched adolescent giggles drowning out her co-host's pompous, coughing laughter.

Candice and Mindy! He remembered them suddenly. His dream had been about them—and Dallas and

356 D. V. BERNARD

Cindy... He realized, with a feeling of frustration, that he couldn't recall any of the dream's details. He shook his head, trying to get his bearings.

Did Candice and Mindy really come over last night? That seemed like a dream, itself. In fact, needing proof that it had actually happened, he got up and jogged over to the guest bedroom. He opened the door cautiously, grimacing slightly when he saw Mindy sleeping peacefully on the huge bed. The things Candice had said came back to him. *Shit!* Maybe something really had happened to Cindy....

Trembling slightly, he closed the door and returned to the living room. He had to get in touch with Phelps and make sure everything was all right. He flipped through his address book, and was about to pick up the phone to call Phelps, when he looked over and saw the door to the master bedroom was open. From where he was standing, he saw that the bed had been made, and that there was nobody there. He put down the receiver and walked over to the door, suddenly numb.

"Candice?" he called, but there was no answer. He went hopefully to the bathroom, but there was nobody there either. On his way back out, he noticed a note lying on the pillow. He snatched it up, then read it through twice. It said:

I left to get the early morning train to Boston. There was no need to wake you—you've done enough already. Her sarcasm made him queasy. *Deal with the Mindy situation any way you wish. I've had it. Good luck, Roland. Tell Mindy goodbye for me. It always amazed me how something so pure and sweet could have come from something so polluted. Goodbye.*

Candice

As he stood there with the note in his hand, he had the same creepy sensation from last night—when he watched Candice retreating into the darkness. He was being entangled in something horrible—he was certain of it! Returning to the living room, he picked up the phone and dialed Phelps' number, but the line was busy. *Shit!* He felt trapped. He had always prided himself on his reason; but all of a sudden, he felt *doomed*. He walked stiffly over to the French doors, needing desperately to clear his mind. On the television, Samantha and her co-host were laughing again. He ignored them.

The view from the French doors usually calmed him, and he needed that desperately at the moment. There was something enlivening about being twenty stories up, able to look out on vast sections of the city. As his view faced lower Manhattan, he could see the Empire State Building and the World Trade Center; to his left, were the Manhattan and Brooklyn Bridges—and, of course, Brooklyn. The view was magnificent! The sky was bright, making even the New York air seem inviting. He opened the door with a brisk motion, and stepped out onto the balcony. It was the end of October and there was a definite chill in the air; but as he stood on the balcony, he found it refreshingly crisp.

Twenty stories below him, the cars moved fitfully

along the streets. The muffled sounds of the city—
honking horns and far-off police sirens—wafted up at him,
sounding like whispers in the silence. The view usually
enlivened him, but as he watched the people making
their way down the sidewalks, they suddenly seemed
like ants. It wasn't even the illusion of size that came
with his great height—they just all seemed so locked
away, and *mindless*. The entire thing reminded him of
being a child again: of visiting his grandmother on the
bayou and looking down at the ants as they rushed out
into the world to follow their programming. Roland
shuddered, then grimaced as he thought about Candice
and Phelps. He just couldn't get over this malaise—this
weird feeling that something was terribly wrong—

He suddenly remembered the story Candice had told
him that night in the parking garage—about killing her
uncle over sex! All at once, new, horrible possibilities
flooded into his mind. What if Candice had done something to Dallas…? Nothing seemed right anymore.
When he first moved here, the city had seemed like a
great experiment—like the ultimate test of human
potential and frailties. Once, that had excited him; but
lately—in stolen moments, between all his rushing
about and success—it had begun to strike him as somewhat barbaric. Just last week, walking down Broadway,
it had occurred to him that if one were to go for a kilometer in any direction, one would go from heaven to
hell and back again: from luxury condominiums to slums

decaying in the face of decades of neglect and abuse. Go for a kilometer in any direction, and one went from stories of triumph, to stories of inconsolable despair. Yet, that seemed to be the trade-off in a place with so much possibility. It seemed that there couldn't be great highs unless there were abysmal lows. Maybe there were such highs in this city only because there were so many people willing to risk the depths. The high rollers could be found in the penthouses and slums alike; but more troublesomely, at least to Roland, the cautious and indolent were also tenanted in those places. There they all were: players in a game where the only tangible rule, seemed to be chance—

A cold breeze made him shudder—or maybe it was only a cold realization. Whatever the case, he pulled on the lapels of his robe, and retreated into the warmth and comfort of the condominium. The television was still playing; exhausted, he plopped himself down on the couch, and stared unseeingly at the screen. It was probably a minute or so before he even became aware of what he was seeing. The news segment of the show had come on. The anchorwoman, Wendy Wu, an Asian American, was talking about how Thomas and his mother had been shot for nothing. A case of mistaken identity, and the madness of one policeman, had resulted in the deaths of six people. On the screen, there were now images from the previous night. There was video from the surveillance camera at the police precinct.

Colina was shown gunning down Thomas and his mother, then his speeding car was shown darting down the street, hitting pedestrians and eventually flipping over, into a crowd. While those images played, Ms. Wu talked about the unrest that had already been spawned by these events; and then, on the screen was a video recording of the hundreds of angry people who had congregated in front of the Harlem precinct house, yelling for justice and revenge.

All these scenes passed Roland in a blur. He watched them numbly, wondering, vaguely, if this might all be a dream. Now, Wu was talking about how minority leaders were calling for a shake-up at the Police Department. Roland stared at the screen without really seeing or hearing. The next thing he knew, Marenga was on the screen. It was a tape from the riot, right after the police dispersed the mob with tear gas. Marenga had set up an impromptu press conference down the block from the precinct, standing there like a waif in his rumpled suit. His eyes had still been red and teary from the gas—and he had been so weak that he had to lean against a parked car to support himself. It had been as though he were in shock; he had talked in a slow, rambling whisper that was haunting; and Roland suddenly felt himself being drawn into the depths of the man's soul—

"Some say I'm a rabble rouser," Marenga had said, "but some things are so egregious that no man—no *person*—of conscience can stand idly by and do nothing.

I call on all people of conscience to march on this city, demanding justice! There will be a rally today at City Hall!" he announced, before adding, "Some say that I am inciting violence, but the violence has always been there—it is only that we have been fooled by the illusion of peace...."

Roland felt as though his head were going to explode! ...And there was still Dallas to deal with. He felt like he was being pulled apart in every direction. He groaned.

Wu was back on the screen again, talking about how the Mayor couldn't be found, and about the upcoming debate...and Randolph lagging badly in the polls; and then, McPrice was on the screen, her face florid as she declared that Randolph was missing in action and a coward—

And then Wu came back on again, then other commentators, then images of angry blacks and policemen... Roland didn't know how much more he could take! Somehow, it wasn't simply that he was watching a news report, but that they were invading his mind—his *soul*. He felt powerless against them. The television had the omniscience of God: the ability to be everywhere at once. It swept down into the souls of millions of people. One moment, it brought felicity and joy; the next, it unleashed inescapable wrath. The next news item was coming on now. It was a report on Mayor Randolph's sex scandal. Roland couldn't take it anymore! All the churning madness was ripping him apart. Seeing the remote control on the coffee table, he practically leaped at it and switched off the television—

But then, when he was sitting on the floor in the sudden silence, he felt lost again. He felt empty—*drained*. All at once, he was desperate for his girlfriend. It was the same feeling he had felt last night: he wanted to lose himself in her touch. Yet, as a media personality, he was suddenly wary of her. Strangely, he found himself wondering if he even knew her. She belonged to that sensationalized world of gossip and scandal and violence and ruined lives. She was like some high priestess, manipulating the faith of true believers. It was Samantha's job to make light of it all—to laugh it all away over a cup of coffee. He had never really taken time to find out if she actually was like her on-screen persona. It had never seemed to matter before. Besides, part of him had probably always been a little terrified of knowing. Last night, he had been overcome by a feeling of love for her; now, he found himself wondering if theirs was even a relationship where love was applicable. It occurred to him that everything left unsaid was unreal. Maybe he had wanted that unreality once, but those times seemed at an end.

As for his girlfriend, maybe he had never wanted to know her before because he had never wanted to risk hope or fear or rejection. Their relationship, it suddenly seemed to him, had been like the city, itself. It had been everything and nothing, presenting both the possibility of self-fulfillment and self-destruction. Perhaps neither of them had wanted to gamble and find out which it was. He was nodding his head now: once Samantha was done with her show, he would tell her that he loved her. Then, he would sit down and talk with her. He wanted that more than anything at the moment—

"Uncle Roland?" an uncertain little voice called at his back.

Roland whirled around and stood up, seeing Mindy looking out confusedly from the doorway of the guest bedroom. She smiled when she saw him, seeming relieved; and seeing that relief and trust, something in Roland was reassured as well. The trust of children: how *wondrous* it was! He got up and went over to her; she came up to him as well, leaping up into his arms as she always did. She was still in her bunny pajamas, and the huge ears poked him in his eye. Still, he laughed along with her, suddenly relieved.

"Where's Candice?" she asked as he twirled her playfully in the air.

"Candice had to go away," Roland answered obliquely. And then:" Are you hungry?"

Before she could even say anything, he was carrying her over to the kitchen, holding her above his head as if she were an eagle. She giggled with delight at the sensation. But after he placed her at his hip, so that he could open the refrigerator, they both saw, at once, that it was empty—except for some ice cubes.

"Wow," said the little girl, "you must not eat a lot!" As the little girl began to laugh, he found himself laughing along with her.

"How about we drop by a deli on the way back to your parents' house. We can't let you go home hungry, can we?"

"No!" said the little girl, raising her fist triumphantly at the declaration.

Someone knocked the front door while they were laughing.

Instantaneously, Roland stopped laughing. It wasn't necessarily uneasiness—just the strangeness of it. He put down Mindy and walked over to the door. It occurred to him that it could be Phelps—just like the last time— but then he realized that if that were the case, the door-man would have called him. More likely than not, it was one of his neighbors coming to announce a tenants' meeting, or some such nonsense. He was so sure of this that he didn't bother to check before opening the door.

However, when he opened the door, he saw a middle-aged black man in an odd, mismatched outfit that was too big for him. The man had a clean-shaven head, and a bushy beard that nonetheless allowed Roland to see his grin.

"...Yes?" Roland said.

"Breakfast delivery, sir," the man said in a singsong voice, suddenly producing a huge picnic basket. Mindy came up then, looking at the man in awe. The aroma of freshly baked pastry filled the doorway, and the demands of Roland's belly left him confused for a moment, but he shook his head.

"I think you have the wrong apartment."

"You *are* Roland Micheaux, aren't you?"

"Yes, but I didn't order anything."

"You sure? You're quite a busy man—maybe you forgot."

The strange thing was the gleam in the man's eyes. It suddenly occurred to Roland that the doorman wouldn't let a deliveryman upstairs without calling—especially one who looked like this man. "How'd you get up here?" he demanded.

"I took the elevator."

"Did you pass the doorman?"

"Of course," the man said with a singsong laugh. "How else would I be able to get up here?" Then, bypassing Roland, the man opened the picnic basket and bent down to Mindy, showing her the heaping pile of freshly baked pastry. There were also containers of eggs and bacon, and coffee and juice. The man was like some fairytale character tempting a woodland child, and the little girl couldn't resist. She squealed out and grabbed a huge danish, sinking her teeth into it. It was so big that she couldn't open her mouth wide enough—

"Mindy!" Roland cried in alarm; but at the man's urging, she grabbed the picnic basket—which must have weighed half her weight, and made haste to the couch. There, she sat down to devour her breakfast.

Roland watched it all in disbelief; when he looked

back at the man, he was somewhat disconcerted by the pleased look on his face. "Well," Roland began, not quite knowing what to say, "what do I owe you?"

"What do you owe me?" the man said, laughing cryptically. "Now that's an interesting question."

"—Just let me get my wallet," Roland said, suddenly flustered. He turned and went into the room to get his wallet; but halfway into the room, he became aware the man had entered behind him—and that he was closing the door!

"I didn't say you could come in!" Roland said with rising alarm.

"There's no need to fear me, Micheaux," the man returned, still calm and carefree.

Something about the way the man had said that triggered something in Roland. "...Do I *know* you?"

The man laughed with a strange twinkle in his eyes, saying: "Who can say? This is New York City—who knows who you pass on the street?"

Roland stared at him with a frown. "...Do I *know* you?" he said, more to himself; but as he said it, his eyes widened and his jaw dropped. "*Oh my God!*" It was Jasper Kain!

They began to arrive in front of City Hall by six o'clock in the morning: a mere handful of the more diehard elements. They carried their banners and chanted their trademark, "No justice, no peace!" However, as they were few in number, their voices seemed feeble—if not comical. Traffic zoomed past, drowning out their voices; apathetic passersby hardly even seemed to notice them. What made it even more comical was that the police commissioner had stationed a thousand riot police in front of City Hall. Reporters and camera crews had also arrived on the scene. They had stood around like kids impatiently waiting for the matinee to start. Like children, there had been a perverse side to them, which hoped that the show would be as gruesome and spectacular as advertised....

By eight o'clock, however, the handful of protesters had grown considerably. At first, a steady stream had made that handful grow to a respectable two hundred or so. Their once feeble chants became genuinely raucous—if not fearsome. The policemen became visibly anxious. They had been given orders to avoid all unnecessary conflict—especially with the election near and so many people watching—but things seemed to be spiraling out of control. The media had been warning of potential violence all morning; by then, they had been darting around the scene like a swarm of bees collecting nectar. By eight, it had been impossible for passersby to walk past indifferently. Instead, they had stopped and looked at the spectacle—or made a point to walk to the other block for safety's sake. The growing crowd had soon spilled out into the streets. Traffic had slowed to a crawl; cabbies had been seen screaming and banging their horns in frustration, adding a cacophonous undertone to the chants for justice.

By nine in the morning, it was beyond anybody's expectations. There were at least five thousand people there now, and there weren't any signs of the tide slowing. There were reports of local subway stations being packed with people coming to protest—on top of the usual rush hour traffic. There were at least half-hour delays on all trains; there were even reports of fights breaking out in the overcrowded trains and buses. Something was going to happen: everyone seemed to know it. Some came only for the show, and could not care less about the Thomases. School kids—many of whom had already planned to be truant for Halloween mischief—showed up to watch; the unemployed and homeless gathered around, their life's frustration somehow encompassing the injustice of the Thomas murders. A good percentage of white people had also showed up: old-time socialist sects, idealistic college students and marginalized homosexual groups, who saw any action against "the system" as a step in the right direction. And there were some who came out in their Halloween costumes, dressed as Count Dracula and other such noted historical figures. Who knew why the hell they were there?

Whatever the case, the wary police were placed between City Hall and the crowd. Officials were frantically calling for backup. Maybe a good ten or fifteen thousand people would come when it was all said and done—maybe even *twice* that. As for that growing crowd, their chants were now not only deafening, but *maddening*. Drums had been brought out, adding a rhythmic urgency to the chants. People danced as they chanted. It would have seemed like a party, were it not for the fact that their voices were so angry—so *vitriolic*. Their hands were waving violently in the air as they stood in front of City Hall, packed in like sardines. Many of them were covered with sweat and half hoarse from screaming. They didn't seem so much as protesters, as a tribe of African bush warriors. One could imagine them with spears in hand; with the drumming and the chanting, it all seemed like some pagan ritual: a prelude not to words, but to war.

One of Randolph's aides shuddered at the sight, then turned away, saying, "God help us when Marenga gets here and *really* stirs them up...!"

...But Randolph was alone now. There was to be a press conference in a matter of minutes, and his aides were giving him a few moments to clear his head. Everyone was worried about violence, but as Randolph stood at his office window and looked at the growing crowd, he didn't so much feel anxiety as a strange sense of excitement. Maybe there would be another riot, but he wasn't worried in the least. It was all out of his hands now. This feeling went against every political impulse that was left in him, and it was perhaps this realization that gave him the impetus to laugh—and to laugh with genuine mirth....

The door to his chamber opened after a soft knock, and Radix appeared in the doorway. "It's time, sir."

Randolph nodded his head and followed the aide out. Other aides, and members of his cabinet, were in the hallway waiting for him. They all seemed agitated. As they began to walk along with him, they asked him questions about how he was feeling, and if he had memorized the statement—things that suddenly seemed like trifles to him. The people around him seemed like gadflies now: he had an impulse to swat them away— which brought a slight smile to his face.

The press center was packed and noisy. He still didn't know how he felt.... When he entered, the room became as still and quiet as a cemetery at midnight. The only noise seemed to be the shutters of cameras. He sighed imperceptibly, stepping up to the podium. The chanting from the crowd outside could be heard if one listened carefully. He saw no one; he stared down at the speech that his aides had written, his voice too soft and unin-spired as he read:

The NYPD is the finest police department in this nation. Crime rates have been in freefall over the past few years. Rapes and robberies are down; people are beginning to feel safe on the streets again. Still, the police department, like all bureaucracies, has always had its rogue element: has always had those whose only interest has been self-interest. There have always been those who wanted to take justice into their own hands; and, perhaps worse, those who have wanted to take *injustice* into their own hands. Yet, in our eagerness to apprehend these rogue elements, we must not become guilty of their crimes. We must not usurp the very justice that we claim is our goal. Right now, the forces of chaos are amassing outside this very office, demanding that we rush ahead blindly. We must be deliberative and stoic, as all proceedings of justice must be. This is the way that we have survived as a nation so long: not through the mob instinct, but through the careful pursuit of justice. Lest anyone misunderstand me, let me be clear here: justice, when it finally comes, will be as harsh and uncompromising as is necessary, but it will be justice.

When he was finished reading, he stood there, staring at the paper, not quite sure what to do next. Then he remembered, in a strangely off-hand manner, that this was supposed to be a press conference. He looked up, seeing the torrent of raised hands and realizing that he was to be asked questions now.

"—Do you feel responsible for the Thomas shootings, Mr. Mayor?" yelled one reporter.

Randolph just stared: not necessarily at the reporter, but out, generally, into space. "Responsibility? Is that what all this is about?" There was an earnestness to his voice that was close to bewilderment. He thought it over for a while, and then he sighed. "I guess so," he mused. "...Someone to explain why the monsters come: to explain away the fears." His aides were suddenly whispering furiously behind him. "*Responsibility?*" he said, laughing out horribly, the way an old drunk laughed, oblivious of what was being said and who was listening—

The next thing he knew, his aides were coaxing him away by the shoulders, while his press chief stepped to the forefront, saying: "The press conference is over."

Roland backed away in horror!

"Don't look so alarmed, Micheaux," Kain said with a chuckle. "I'm not here to do you any harm—not yet, anyway," he said with a mischievous wink.

"*How...?*" Roland managed to whisper. He felt suddenly faint. He studied Kain's face closely: the beard had thrown him off; and without that ridiculous Afro, Kain looked totally different. The voice was the same, though. He should have realized it at once—

"I'm *sane* now!" Kain said, laughing. "Well, at least, I'm sane *enough!*" he corrected himself. He took a step into the room and Roland instinctively retreated a step.

"How'd you get past the doorman?" Roland demanded again.

"Where there's a will, there's a way," Kain said with a mysterious laugh. "...Don't look so worried, Micheaux,"

Kain said with a smile, as he sat down beside Mindy. The little girl had spooned out some of the bacon and eggs onto a Styrofoam plate and was wolfing that down as well. Kain took a donut from the basket then, still smiling as he said: "I'm only here to talk, Micheaux."

"—About what?" he said anxiously, still trying to recover his poise: to get over the fact that Jasper Kain was in his house!

"I came to tell you that I can do anything now," he said in a strange, euphoric voice. And then: "Sit down, Micheaux," he said in his usual calm tone, "—you're acting as though I'm a stranger. Sit down: we're all friends here. Why don't you have a croissant," he said, putting it on a Styrofoam plate and handing it over to Roland.

Roland took it cautiously, a side of him wondering if the man had poisoned it; then, feeling overburdened by the weight of it all, he sat down on the easy chair, which was at a right angle to Kain and Mindy. He felt a little uneasy about the little girl's proximity to Kain, but she was like a dog chewing its bone: perfectly heedless and carefree. In the meanwhile, Kain was watching him calmly, waiting patiently for him to get settled. When the man nodded in encouragement, Roland, despite himself, took a bite of the croissant.

"*See*, it's good, isn't it?" Kain said, grinning.

While at City Hall, the angry crowd continued to grow, Roland grunted noncommittally, still not quite able to believe what was happening.

"Here's a cup of coffee to wash it down," Kain added,

fishing it out of the picnic basket. "It's just the way you
like it: cream, no sugar."

Roland stared in awe, wondering, as always, how the
man could possibly know that. Kain stood up then, and
handed the cup to Roland—who took it wordlessly and
sat there in a daze. Then, "Here, young lady," Kain said
to Mindy, handing her a container of orange juice.
Roland watched it all, acutely aware that the world was
mad.

"How did you get out?" Roland managed to say.

"Bah," Kain said, laughing and shaking his head, "you
concern yourself with too many trivialities, Micheaux.
The matter at hand is that I've come to tell you something wonderful."

"What?" he whispered, still holding the croissant timidly in one hand and the cup of coffee in the other.

"I have looked within myself and feel neither fear nor
regret," Kain said with the strange enthusiasm that had
unnerved Roland from the onset. "In fact, today is a
great day, Micheaux. Remember that when they ask you
about me."

Not this again! he thought to himself. Still, despite
himself, he ventured: "Who's going to ask?"

"The media, of course. I'm sure you'll be a witness at
my trial—"

"*What* trial?"

"All in due time," he said with a laugh. "As for repre-
senting me at the trial," Kain nonchalantly went on, "I've
learned from the last time I counted on you. I'm not

presumptuous enough to believe that a man like you, who has achieved so much success, will deal with the likes of me. I'm sure your firm won't even let you do pro bono work anymore. You're too valuable—winning two hundred million dollar lawsuits. Nah," he continued, laughing strangely, "you're too much of a success now."

What the hell is that supposed to mean? Roland thought to himself. It was again as if the man knew him—had seen into his deepest dreams and fears. Roland frowned: had the man been studying him, *stalking* him, perhaps!

However, there was now a look of serenity in Kain's eyes, as he looked over at Roland and continued, "There is no such thing as evil, Micheaux. That's what I discovered last night. That's what I've come to tell you. There's no good, and no evil: those are just arbitrary things created by society. All that there is, is action and reaction; and one day, when the universe exhausts itself, there'll be nothing left."

"Kain," Roland said from the depths of his exhaustion—mental and otherwise—"what does any of this have to do with me?"

"Because you're the center of it all."

Despite his best efforts, Roland couldn't help smiling.

"How can you still doubt it?" Kain said in surprise. "Haven't you seen the news?"

"Kain..." Roland started, trying to ignore the sudden uneasiness that came at Kain's mention of the news, "why did you come here?"

"I came to tell you about last night."

"Then tell me already," he said impatiently.

"I did something that restored my faith in myself. Now, all the illusions have been washed away, and I have been made pure. I have infinite faith in myself now."

"Faith to do what?"

"Faith to bring sanity back to the world," he said, laughing.

"Sanity?" Roland said mockingly, "I thought you were trying to save us with madness?"

"Ah," Kain said joyously, "—but just as the truth is beyond good and evil, it's also beyond madness and sanity. I see that now—after last night. You're as sharp as ever, Micheaux!" he said as if genuinely impressed. "I'll try to be more precise in the future. As I said before, all there is, is action and reaction—so our task is to push them to take the right actions. That's a commendable plan, isn't it?"

"I suppose," Roland said confusedly.

"Good, so I have your blessing then?" he said cheekily.

"Do you really require my blessing, Kain?"

"Right you are, Micheaux!" he conceded. "Maybe 'blessing' is the wrong word. 'Acknowledgment' seems better."

"So, you want acknowledgment?"

"Of course, isn't that what the psychiatrist said at the trial: I was desperate for attention because my mother hated me and my father wouldn't play baseball with me... But everybody wants attention, don't they? Everyone wants to do something that nobody will ever forget. We all want that, don't we?"

"I suppose."

"But most of us are afraid of the consequences—afraid to *act*: to take the steps that are necessary."

"But you're not afraid?" Roland said, trying to gauge Kain's intentions.

"Not anymore."

"Not after last night?" he asked, pointedly.

"Right."

"And what did happen, Kain?" Roland said again.

"...I *killed* someone, Micheaux."

"*What!*"

"I took the final plunge... I just wanted to tell you—so that you'd know."

"...*Get out*," Roland whispered.

"What?"

"Get out...*please*. Just leave me alone, Kain... I never did anything to you," he said in a desperate voice that he barely recognized as his own. "Why are you doing this to me? I never did anything to you," he said again, looking as though he were going to cry. "Leave...*please*."

"...Very well," Kain said with a sigh, getting up. "I'll leave, Micheaux, but that changes nothing. You won't be able to run forever."

"Just leave, *please*..."

Kain nodded, then he left. Roland didn't look up: he merely listened for the sound of the closing door. Only after the man was gone, did he look around. He needed it all to be over. He couldn't take it anymore—not Kain, not his worries about Phelps and the chaos of the world... He needed it all to be over.

"Mindy," he called to the little girl then.

"Yes, Uncle Roland," she said with a mouth full of food.

"Get your things together—it's time to go home."

Nestled in his Brooklyn brownstone, Marenga was getting dressed for the rally. A television was playing in the corner of his room, showing the entire Thomas controversy and his tirade on the injustice of it. There was also a scene from City Hall, showing the massive crowd that was gathering to hear his words. He looked at all the churning chaos and chuckled to himself, not with pride, but with an acute awareness of how ludicrous his place in it was.

There was something sinister growing in him, and he had no defense against it—he didn't *want* a defense against it, in fact: he only wanted to surrender. He wanted to hasten whatever evolutionary dead end was their collective destiny. Now, it was no longer even a matter of him hating them for what they had done to him—but worse, for what they had done to themselves. He had lost his faith in humanity—and *irretrievably* so. He had gone to see Randolph, hoping desperately that the man could point out some error in his reasoning. He had gone, in short, hoping to be *bested* by the man, but had instead found someone who had long been disarmed. The only thing left to him, was surrender.

Just then, there was a deferential knock on the door. Still staring at the television and buttoning up his shirt, Marenga bellowed, "Come!"

A youth with dreads and a colorful dashiki entered the room. He was technically an assistant, but Marenga considered him and the five or so others, who lurked around in support of "organizing the people" apprentices at best, and sycophants at worst. Marenga used to scour the ghettoes assiduously, trying to court such youths; but as of late, he had begun to think most of them hopelessly naïve. *Everything had changed!* Youths whom he had once praised for their diligence, he now found either unimaginative, in that they spent their time trying to recreate the mythical activism that had existed during the 1960s, or "slaves of the past," who did all that they could to assert their "African Heritage" when, in many instances, they had never even been out of the country. The youth standing before him was of the latter sort. Marenga glanced at him with a certain amount of derision, then looked away.

"We're ready to leave for the rally, sir," the aide began.

Marenga grunted equivocally and went back to staring at the television as he put on his tie.

The apprentice didn't know whether he had been

dismissed or not; he decided to risk the latter and start a conversation. He ventured: "We're going to make history today, sir."

Marenga looked up at once, slight annoyance showing on his face. "No one *makes* history. It is not a contrivance." He went back to getting dressed. Abashed, the sprig went to leave. "Always know your terms, sir," Marenga called after him. The youth stopped and looked back sorrowfully; Marenga, went on: "'History' is a serious term: use it wisely."

"Yes, sir." Bowing his head, the youth once again went to leave.

However, something about the youth's obeisance shamed Marenga, so he called him back. "Look, there are two notions of history: one as something that people write in books, and another as something that writes *people*. Both are, in their way, correct, but only one is not corrupted by human idiocy. Some say that 'History is made by the victors of wars,' but that is foolishness. History—*real* History—can never be controlled, or even steered. History is pure violence. It is a *killer!* It does not care about right or wrong: about victor or vanquished. History is a *beast!* It is beyond the need for maintenance; it needs no nutrients to survive. It does not *plan*; it does not launch attacks. It has no conscience— no *hesitation... brutal.* Even to say that it destroys is foolishness when you think of it. To it, destruction *is* construction. It effaces with the same uncompromising violence as it gives birth. It is what gave us life and what will kill us. History, my friend, is *God*. You and I, Mayor Randolph, the *Thomases*, even: we're all irrelevant to it. Some pray to God for deliverance and hope; but God— *History*—is incapable of answering prayers. Those that History today showers with benevolence and felicity, it will tomorrow torture." He chuckled to himself. "Now, that's some fucked up shit!" The youth laughed along and nodded, even though he had perhaps understood about two percent of what Marenga had just said.

Marenga was strangely cordial now as he tapped the dumbfounded youth on the shoulder and said: "We're all victims here. But I'm thinking about a time that must inevitably come. Martin Luther King talked about the Promised Land and Mountaintops and all kinds of wonderful things. I know: I was a young man listening to him—*hoping* with him. As a man, I realized that History was beyond hope. For a while, I became a revolutionary. I listened to Malcolm X and read Lenin, but even they were misled. Those who waited and hoped, saw a benevolent God; implicit in the message of the others was a vengeful, just God—or *no* God. There is a God, but it does not care about hopes or justice. Yes, like King said, one day we will climb to that final Mountaintop and find peace. Like him, I cannot even begin to conceptualize how it will be done, but there will have to be a war: a *revolution*, in fact!" He chuckled sardonically at the word; the dumbfounded apprentice affected a simpering grin. "It will be a revolution like no other. I'm not talking about fighting against people or *regimes*, but *History*. I'm not here saying *love* God. I'm saying *hate* it! That's our enemy: History. I'm standing here, as powerless against it as everyone else. But there must inevitably come that time of change. And as nothing is as violent as History, we will have to fight it with equal violence and brutality. We will have to forget that we are human beings! We will have to *kill* History: to *murder* it, with neither conscience nor hesitation; without ideology or hopes of justice or victory. The revolution, my friend, will be against our very existence!" He stopped and narrowed his eyes at the quailing youth, then he lowered his voice to a whisper: "Find a way to do that *and* survive, and you'll have the power of God, Himself."

Charlotte McPrice had been busy all that morning, coordinating a campaign that now seemed unstoppable. With Colina's rampage headlining the news—and social unrest breaking out on the streets—she had given a press conference earlier, repeating the charge she had been stating for months now: Randolph's incompetence was dangerous for the city—if not criminal.

She now stood before the window of her private office, staring out on the Hudson River with a sense of quiet triumph. The open door at her back led to a larger chamber, with was filled with about fifty volunteers and campaign staffers. They were busily answering phones and carrying out all the little tasks that would guarantee her ascension.

At that moment, Wisinski, her campaign manager, entered the doorway, but stopped short, just to stare at her. He did that often, always with awe in his eyes. His was the kind of objectification that the feminist streak in women castigated as demeaning—but which the feminine streak often craved. In any case, McPrice's back was still to him as she stared dreamily out of the window. Now, as he stared, the rays of the morning sun reflected off her shiny hair, producing the momentary illusion that she had a halo. *And maybe she is an angel*, he thought, only half-wistfully.

As for McPrice's followers in general, many were undeniably drawn to her sexuality—not so much in the sense of wanting to have sex with her (though there were many who did!) but in the sense of wanting to be cloaked and protected by her. Hers was the sexuality of a god; and in just the same way that it was impossible—if not sinful—to think of Jesus Christ having sex, there was a similar disconnect with her. She was flesh, and yet seemed beyond the needs of flesh. For some, this contradiction made her perfect.

Still smiling, Wisinski stepped into the room, announcing: "We're up to a forty-five-point lead in the polls!" Barely looking away from the window, she nodded; a faint smile graced her lips. Wisinski was just about to make a joke about Randolph self-destructing (and that stripper crying about how he had raped her), when the phone on her desk rang.

Wisinski stopped in front of her desk, while McPrice walked over to the desk as well and answered the phone. Wisinski stood there smiling, thinking that he would tell his joke when she was finished; but he could tell, by the cloud that came over her face, that her husband was on the other end of the line. McPrice wasn't saying anything: she just listened and stared blankly at her desk with a troubled expression. Wisinski could almost hear the husband spewing one of his post-binge excuses, replete with many blubbering exclamations of love and sorrow. Wisinski's face wrinkled then, and he felt something unmistakably dark coming over him. Maybe it was the violence of the city that possessed him, because he suddenly found himself thinking, in that presumptuous way of men, that he would do whatever it took to protect her. Even as the evil thoughts filled his mind, he nodded his head, as if he were receiving a message from God.

Roland took a cab to Brooklyn Heights. He could have driven his Benz—which he usually kept in a parking garage—but the thing about driving in New York City was that the benefits and convenience of the vehicle were canceled out by the inconvenience of traffic and finding parking (and, of course, the reality of driving in New York City).

These were the last moments of Roland Micheaux's life. Yet, death was not like in the war movies, with the dying hero mumbling some courageous drivel into the ears of a heartbroken comrade. There was no way to die courageously; because the courageous, numbed by duty, never really saw death. To them, death was a triumph. They went into it with their eyes closed and their minds numb, like coma victims. Even fear, when it was strong enough, brought on this sudden blindness; so that to a certain extent, the fearful never truly saw death either. Death, when it was seen and felt, came slowly. Just like Kain had said, it greeted its victim cordially and whispered all of its secrets in its victim's ear. It made everything clear and plain; and in that final moment, when everything was seen, there was death— and *only* death.

While at City Hall the outraged masses chanted their slogans, Roland sat in the back of the cab with Mindy. They were entering the block of Phelps' brownstone now. During the ride, the little girl had prattled on the whole time. Among other things, she had informed Roland about a girl from her preschool called Melissa, whom she thought selfish and rude. Apparently, Melissa wanted all the toys for herself; and for this reason, none of the other kids would play with her. In addition to this, Mindy informed him that she had acquired a new doll, which could soil its panties, burp and spit up the green, disgusting goop that was spooned down its gaping mouth. To Roland's alarm, she produced the abomination and made him kiss it!

They were alighting from the cab now. Phelps' million-dollar brownstone was on one of those strange, pristine New York City blocks, with oak trees and the veneer of suburbia; and five blocks over, there were slums. It was the same old thought: the city was everything and nothing...

Roland paid the Ukrainian cab driver and the latter rushed back to Manhattan. Roland watched the cab disappear in a cloud of exhaust, then he looked up at the three-story brownstone, feeling uneasy again. Even Mindy seemed ill at ease. Looking around, Roland realized the block was just too quiet. He took Mindy in his arms again, then walked up the stairs to the entrance. Why was he feeling so strange... ? There were cardboard Halloween decorations on the door, with glossy cartoon monsters, and a huge sign that read, "Trick or Treat." It all seemed eerie in the silence. His hand lingered over the doorbell before he pressed it. He laughed at himself nervously. He waited about fifteen seconds, straining his ears to hear the hoped-for sound of approaching footsteps within—but there was nothing. He rang the bell again. *Shit*! Where the hell could they possibly be? Now what? He could bring Mindy home with him until her parents showed up...and call the police. Those were possibilities... But while his mind went over the irksome complications, he instinctively put his free hand on the doorknob and turned it. *It was open*! He stared unbelievingly. He called in a tentative voice: "Cindy? Dallas?" There was no answer. He felt really...*strange*; for some reason, his heart was beating violently in his chest.

Just then, he thought he heard something inside. He strained his ears to confirm it. "Cindy? Dallas?" Still, there was no answer. He was sure that he had heard something inside. He pushed open the door and stepped in, calling their names again. Part of him was praying that they would answer him—so that he could laugh out in relief and go home to fantasize about making love to his girlfriend—but something wasn't right here. Instinctively, he put the little girl down and told her to wait there. He crept deeper into the house: through the living room, with all of the Phelps' glittery trinkets and baubles, and through the luxurious dining room. He was coming upon the main bedroom. The door was slightly ajar. He stopped abruptly: someone was definitely crying within! *God!* He stood there indecisively, listening to the quiet sobs on the other side of the door.

He fortified his courage—or whatever was needed to go on—then pushed open the door. As the thick drapes had been drawn, the room was dark. The only illumination came from a light in the bathroom—which was directly across the room from where Roland was standing. The huge bed was perpendicular to Roland and the bathroom door. It was because of this placement, and the scant lighting, that Roland didn't immediately see Cindy. She was sitting on the floor, next to the bathroom door. She looked...*wretched*. It had been her sobs that he heard! He rushed over to her. Her hair was a mess; her nightgown was ripped, exposing her breasts—

"Cindy!" He touched her skin—she was cold! She was in shock! She was staring ahead...and, as though in slow motion, he followed her eyes. She was staring unseeingly at something on the floor; Roland looked down—a *body!* And *blood!* It was Phelps! Roland rushed over to see; but when he did, it was as if years of his life were pulled into some abyss. There was a gaping hole in Phelps' forehead! The man was lying there naked and bloody, his sightless eyes staring into space. Shit! *Phelps was dead!* There was no doubt about it. Roland recoiled as the realization hit him, scurrying back to Cindy. The sickly sweet smell of blood was nauseating. With the sight of Phelps, and the smell, he was sure that he was going to throw up—

But just then, he chanced to look down, noticing the gun in Cindy's hand; and when he finally understood what had happened, he shuddered. Maybe she had been sitting like that for hours—*since last night!* He looked at her, his mouth gaping. "Cindy," he called, but she was still catatonic. "Cindy!" he yelled. "*Cindy!*" Finally, he shook her violently; and as though suddenly seeing him, she screamed out. It was the most bloodcurdling scream that he had ever heard! He scurried away, almost to the foot of the bed, by Phelps. Her eyes were wild—full of madness. To his horror, she was pointing the gun at him! She fired...! After the explosion, he sat frozen for a moment, trembling. Somehow, it had missed—actually going out of the bedroom window. For a moment, neither of them moved; there were no sounds. But then, footsteps could be heard coming down the hall. They turned their heads and looked toward the door. Hearing the shot, Mindy came running into the room, where she stopped, unsure. Yet, seeing her daughter, Cindy started crying uncontrollably. There was something horrible in the woman's eyes now. Coming to his senses, Roland suddenly realized she was raising the gun again! Mindy had taken a couple of steps into the room, but stopped abruptly again. Cindy was aiming the gun at her daughter! Roland grabbed Mindy and darted for the exit. The thundering report from the gun came, hurtling past his ear. He didn't stop—he *couldn't* stop, in fact. Another report came...! All that he knew was running. The inside of the house passed him by in a flash. Outside, the neighbors, who had no doubt heard the scream—if not the shots—were staring. He darted past them as well. He was numb—*terrified*...thinking only of escape. Even when he got outside, he couldn't stop. He was running not only from Cindy, but everything he had ever fled. He was on automatic pilot, totally disconnected from what was passing before him. The little girl was crying at his shoulder—*screaming* in fact—but as he fled, he was only peripherally aware of her as well.

Marenga and his aides were driving to the rally in a rented limousine. They were going in style. About seven of them were sitting in the back, on two long seats that faced one another. Sitting across from Marenga was his second in command, Botswana Glade. Apparently, the man had started up some bizarre Unitarian church in Harlem while Marenga was away. As they rode along, the man explained why God was vengeful but just. He was holding a copy of the Koran in one hand and a copy of the Bible in the other. He also wore a big golden cross around his neck, and had a crescent moon pinned to his lapel. Marenga watched him with a frown; then, with equal dismay, he looked at the aides.

In addition to the dreadlocked, dashiki-clad youth, whose name was Clarence, there was a short, gaunt youth that they called "Bright Eyes." The latter's sight was so bad that his thick glasses made him look like one of those "bug-eyed" aliens. Another aide, an ex-convict called "Bush Dog," was a huge, muscle-bound man with a scar over his left eye. He never smiled and rarely talked, which gave Marenga the creeps. Yet another one was brilliant, but had a nervous tic, and sometimes squealed out various expletives when excited. A side of him wanted to laugh—since they were all part of the cosmic farce. Yet, another side of him just wanted his eyes to close and his mind to cease its ramblings.

Marenga was coming full circle now. As a child, growing up in segregated Kentucky, he had felt pity for the wretched around him; as a young man, coming to the city, he had looked at those wretched people and been outraged. Now, as a middle-aged man, passing into old age, he looked at the wretched state of his people, and felt an inexplicable kind of contempt for them. Their lives were meaningless—and he had wasted his own life trying to make meaning out of that meaninglessness. The only thing left to him now was revenge. Everything seemed clear to him now: he hated them all, but once the cosmic farce reached its conclusion, they would all be dead—

Marenga winced as the pain in his chest returned. A dizzy spell gripped him as well, so that he felt disoriented and nauseous. All at once, he realized that he was sweating profusely...*just a little further*, he said to himself. He wanted to make sure that everything was in place, then he would gladly die.

They were coming upon City Hall now. Thousands of people were chanting their hate-filled slogans; policemen were standing their distance, looking ominous. There were even vendors, selling hot dogs. Looking out on it all, Marenga was somehow reassured. Soon, all those thousands would listen to his tirade, embrace his hatred, and riot—

But then, in a panic, he realized that might be the extent of it. For a moment he was stupefied by his oversight, seeing that this event alone might not be enough: that there was still more to do, more hatred to spread, more cattle to prod into stampeding. *Shit*, when would it end...!

It all rested on him, but what could he possibly do to ignite the flames of hatred and madness within them? Words weren't enough. With words alone, it would all die out in a week or so. After some patronizing remarks from "the powers that be," and the necessary passage of time, the blacks would lose their outrage, the larger society would tire of this story, and the stage would be set for the next stage of the farce. He was suddenly terrified that it would never end: that God would laugh in his face one more time and keep the farce going forever, like a stale joke that everyone was compelled to laugh at.

The intensity of the crowd's chants grew as the limousine approached its epicenter. Having gotten word that Marenga was arriving in the limousine, the crowd began chanting his name. They had assembled to hear his words; but as he stared out on them, he wondered what there was to say that hadn't been said before... Oh God, he felt *sick!* It wouldn't be enough—nothing he had planned! It would just keep going on! He felt horribly weak all of a sudden; worse, parts of his body now seemed to alternate between numbness and biting pain.

He needed to lie down, but his aides were excitedly getting ready to disembark. The car was stopping now; the door was opening, and his aides were helping him out.

People were cheering louder now. God, he felt *horrible!* How was he even standing? People were patting him on the shoulder. He wanted to run from them: their closeness, their smiles...their *numbers*...everything about them repulsed him! For a moment, he feared they would lynch him like some escaped slave.... It was over: the struggle...*everything*! ...*Oh, God, he felt horrible*. He felt old and tired and *sick*! He wished he were dead; and just then, the pain exploded in his chest. In his mind, the blast was like a nuclear bomb, disintegrating everything in its path, rending flesh from people's bones, turning bricks and skyscrapers to dust...but in reality, he merely collapsed to the ground.

They all watched Marenga collapse. A hush came over everything. It was Botswana Glade who yelled, "Get an ambulance!" A cascade of voices went through the crowd, with people asking what had happened. Someone somewhere—or maybe there were several people at once—yelled out that "they" had "gotten" Marenga. Soon, the air thundered with a cry of outrage like nothing they had ever heard before. The cry coursed through the crowd, like a current flowing through a wire. They had *killed* Marenga! This wasn't the time

394 D. V. Bernard

for shock or mourning: this was the time for outrage!
Someone threw a bottle at a policeman; a police car
got its windows smashed. Tear gas canisters were
released. People seemed to be running in every direction at once. People were getting *trampled!* Screams of
panic and agony joined the shouts of outrage that had
been in the air all that morning. There was madness
everywhere. Luckily, someone had the presence of
mind to pick up Marenga and toss him into the limousine. It was Bush Dog. Coming to their senses, the
other aides jumped in as well. Marenga wasn't even
moving anymore. Botswana Glade screamed for the
driver to go faster—but with the chaos outside, it was
impossible to go fast without running someone over.
Nevertheless, as the seconds passed, and their impatience
grew, the limousine hit things; they heard screams as
the vehicle went over apparent speed bumps in the
road—but death was all about them then, so there was no
point in stopping to see what had happened.

Officers Flanders and Mucelli were driving down
Atlantic Avenue in Brooklyn. Flanders, the older and
fatter of the two, was proud of the fact that there had
been a Flanders walking the beat in New York City
since 1899. Of course, few policemen in New York
walked beats anymore, and Officer Flanders certainly
didn't do much walking at all. As a nineteen-year vet-

eran, his pendulous gut and multiple chins attested to a lifestyle of sitting in a police cruiser all day and making frequent stops at the local donut shops, delis and pizzerias. Something about him was redolent of a huge hog basking in the filth of its sty. He was fond of saying that after so many years on "the force" he had seen everything and was surprised by nothing—which was another way of saying he was dense. At the moment, he had a young charge: a rookie, into whom he was to instill the essential mindset of the New York City Police Department. Unfortunately, young Officer Mucelli was not only in awe of his mentor, but eager to learn. Flanders was driving, his huge gut brushing against the steering wheel. After only a few weeks, Mucelli was already well on his way to mastering that "I don't give a shit" expression and attitude of hardened veterans. He was sitting back in the seat, chewing a wad of gum with the slothful indifference of a cow chewing its cud. Every once in a while, he blew a gigantic bubble and nonchalantly looked out on the world with a kind of Clint Eastwood squint. Needless to say, he was in heaven.

"Pizza?" ventured Flanders.

"What? Pizza Hut? Sicilian? What?"

"C'mon, pizza's pizza," the veteran said, groaning.

"I mean, you got your different varieties. You got your thin crust, your deep dish, your—"

"All right, already: we'll go to Geno's."

"What? *Again*? He don't cook the crust long enough."

"What do ya mean!"

"His crust is raw—"

"I been eating there thirty years! I been eating pizza before you were even sucking your mama's tits!"

"—All right, all right, we'll eat at Geno's. I'll just ask him to leave mine in a little longer."

Flanders watched him askance; he was about to unleash a string of expletives when the radio came on: "This is a general alert! The rally in front of City Hall has escalated into a riot!"

"What the fuck did I tell you!" Flanders yelled, his face turning purple. "Didn't I tell you this was gonna happen!"

The report went on: "Marenga is reported to have collapsed before the riot ensued. An assassination attempt hasn't been ruled out!"

"*Oh shit!*" cursed Mucelli.

"Be advised that flare-ups are possible, given the emotional nature of the event. Do not, under any circumstances, have any unnecessary engagements with the minority community... !"

"That asshole, Marenga!" cursed Flanders. "A goddamn troublemaker. I bet he *faked* it!"

"You think so!" the rookie ejaculated, still awed by the veteran.

"Sure," he said with confidence, "I bet they faked all that shit, trying to prop themselves up. And that fucker Thomas wasn't even as innocent as they was saying.

Them guys is always made out to be choirboys after-wards—no matter what the fuck they done. *Bullshit*! Marenga's to blame for all of it; and that bastard Randolph is gonna let him do whatever he wants—'cause he scared of losing the election. *Politics!*" he said in disgust. "As cops, we're the ones forced to clean up other people's shit. They don't care about us. It's us against *them!*"

Mucelli nodded nervously, his eyes wide. But just then, the radio went off again:

"Attention, all cars in the vicinity of Brooklyn Heights and western Brooklyn, be on the lookout for a young black male between six feet and six feet three inches tall, dressed in jeans and a leather jacket. His hostage is a white three-year-old girl, dressed in what was described as a pink Halloween costume. The suspect was last seen running down Atlantic Avenue with the hostage. It looks like a burglary that went wrong. He entered the house and shot the couple, before taking their daughter. Officers are advised to exercise extreme caution: the suspect is assumed to be armed and dangerous!"

"Shit!" both officers yelled in unison.

The only thing that made sense to Roland now, was running—and even that was more of an impulse than a thought. Terror darkened the world and obscured everything around him, like a cold, fine mist. There was no escape—no *relief*—and every few moments, residual images of Phelps' corpse wafted back into his mind. Phelps' unseeing eyes...! Cindy's dementia...! People made way for him as he ran down the blocks: they could see the madness in his eyes....

Someone was crying! He had been hearing crying for a while now, but it had seemed so far away. All of a sudden, it was loud—*piercing*! He grabbed for his ears. He stopped. Mindy? Somehow, he had forgotten he was carrying her. She was crying—practically *screaming*! He hugged her, only then coming to his senses. He instinctively patted Mindy softly on her back, telling her that everything would be all right. Yet, the words didn't even register in his own mind. Looking around, he saw that he was on Atlantic Avenue: a wide, busy, four-lane boulevard, lined mostly with greasy-looking auto repair business. On the upper stories of these buildings, there were apartments of the low-rent variety. He had only gone about a kilometer and a half, and yet everything had changed. On his side of the street, there were tenements of the type he had left in Louisiana. In one of the tenements, an old woman watched him warily from a window; when he made eye contact with her, she quickly closed the blinds and disappeared. He felt suddenly weak. He must have run at least ten blocks—and those at full speed. Images of the scene again confronted him and he saw them with new horror and understanding.

Phelps was dead! God! His legs felt weak beneath him. He remembered how the neighbors had seen him running out of the house—and with Mindy in his arms! Somehow, he had become embroiled in...a *murder!* He leaned against a telephone pole, his eyes wide. His mouth was so desiccated that he couldn't swallow: he gave up even trying. After spending so much time in a daze, his mind was now alive with new terrors. First, he had to call the police and tell them what had happened. Yet, he was trembling. Mindy was still sobbing—he patted her back nervously.

He was looking around for a pay phone, when he saw a police cruiser driving down the block! What luck! He ran to the curb and started waving for the car to stop. There was a feeling of desperation in him that was so acute that he felt as though he were going to cry. He had to clear this up: it was all a misunderstanding. The police were stopping; the men were getting out—practically *running* out. He opened his mouth to explain—

"Put the girl *down!*" an old, fat cop yelled. Roland, in his preoccupation, didn't notice that the man had drawn his gun from his holster.

Roland put Mindy down—though she began to cry again and clambered to be held. The cops were coming over; Roland again opened his mouth to explain—

"Keep your hands in the air!" yelled Officer Flanders.

Roland did as told, and he did it without thought, falling deeper and deeper into the abyss. That was when

Officer Flanders grabbed him and threw him against the police car. Roland was beyond shock! "We got you, you bastard!" the old cop hissed, while his partner stood to the side with his gun drawn.

What the hell...! was all Roland could think as the cop put his baton to the back of his neck and began frisking him.

"You shot that couple and took their kid!"

"*What?*" Roland managed to squeak.

"Thought you'd ransom the little girl off!"

"—No! ...Wait...*What!* I can explain!" But he couldn't. He was shaking...stammering, just like any other scared nigger.

Not finding any weapon, the enraged cop hit him in the back with the baton. Roland didn't feel the first couple of blows—he had already been in shock. Then, all at once, images of the Thomases flew through his mind. And then, there was the whole Rodney King thing, framed against a black, unreal backdrop. Some dark impetus made Roland whirl and ram his elbow into Flanders' jaw. The old cop grunted and took a step back, but he recovered quickly, letting his baton swing again. Roland ducked and it rattled against the top of the car. Undaunted, the old cop rushed Roland, heaving his bulk against the man. However, Roland let his fists fly, hitting the man with a solid right to the temple. The man grunted and relented a little; and seeing his chance, Roland brought a vicious knee up into the man's mid-section, before unleashing a well-timed left cross that caught the man in his jaw.

Now, the young cop, alarmed by the changing fortunes of the battle, raised his gun with a trembling hand, waiting for a clear shot. No sooner did he think this, than he heard something explode. Everything stopped. The battle between his partner and the suspect ceased. Flanders, whose back was to him, froze, his spine arching. And then, for some reason that the young cop did not initially understand, his partner dropped heavily to the ground. Unfortunately, death in reality was not like death in the movies—where everything was quick and clean. The old cop began squealing out, flopping about like a fish tossed into a basket. His mouth was now frothing with a combination of blood and mucus. In fact, there was blood everywhere now. With the man's screams, it was all as sickening as it was maddening.

After what seemed like minutes of watching the sick dance on the sidewalk, Roland and the young officer stared at the supine body with an acute sense of horror, because it was clear it was dead. At that moment, they looked up at one another with the same expression in their eyes. They stared for perhaps two or three seconds, neither of them able even to breathe. The young officer looked down at his gun, realizing, perhaps for the first time, that it had gone off—and that he had killed his partner!

Roland was the first to come to his senses. He bolted.

Seeing Roland running off, the young officer nervously fired his gun at him—but he was trembling so badly that his aim was way off. Once again, Roland ran without seeing and without thought. He felt like screaming: something was blaring so loudly in his ears that maybe he was.

Only running seemed right now. He darted across the wide, busy boulevard—almost getting hit twice— then he ran down a side street. This mindless fleeing made him feel as though he were caught in a loop in time. He ran for about another block, and then darted into an alley, hiding behind a dumpster. He was beyond shock. How much time had passed, he had no idea. What had happened was still too vague and menacing for him to name it. All that he could grasp was the horror. Everything was spiraling wildly out of control, and there seemed to be no way of stopping it—

There was someone over him! Looking up, he saw Mindy standing before him. She was crying as she stood there, still holding that repulsive little doll; but for a moment, he was possessed by an impulse to kill her: to rip her to *shreds*! ...But she was crying again; and as he saw the scared innocence in her eyes, the mad impulse receded, leaving only terror. *What had come over him!* He had only felt the impulse for an instant, but it had been there. He felt sick and drained. Seeing Mindy's tears, he grabbed her, hugging her tightly. Thankfully, the numbness soon came over him again.

While in lower Manhattan, crowds were still being dispersed with tear gas and rubber bullets, Botswana Glade walked out of the hospital, looking drained. It was around noon, but it seemed much later. The sun seemed to be fleeing—darting toward the horizon as if it were terrified of shedding light on the world. The wind picked up, and the slight chill that had been there before, became more biting. People pulled their lapels and bent their frames to the wind. This was Botswana Glade's posture when he and the other aides stepped out of hospital door and down the steps.

The reporters seemed to leap out of nowhere. He inadvertently took a step back—as if muggers had just leapt out from behind a bush. He stood there, in shock, while the twenty-five or so members of the media yelled questions at him.

While on television, at that very moment, all the major stations had helicopter views of scenes from the riot, with people running in every direction and clouds of tear gas in the air—not to mention people looting businesses and firing guns at one another—Botswana Glade stood before the reporters, trying to make sense of what they were saying. At last, he took a deep breath, his voice faint and flat as he said:

"Marenga is in surgery now—the doctors think it was a heart attack—possibly a stroke as well." He went to leave.

"Do you feel any responsibility for the riot?" one of

the reporters yelled. Botswana Glade stopped in his tracks, looking back with the same uncomprehending expression. The reporter went on: "So far, at least five people have been trampled to death; dozens of others have been taken to the hospital with various injuries. And there were reports of several stabbings and shootings, not to mention property damage and police officers."

As though regaining consciousness, Botswana Glade reeled, his horse teeth becoming prominent as he lashed out: "You going to blame this on *us*! The only thing that this nation seems to understand is *violence*! This nation was *built* on barbarism: on the notion that the strong take it all, and that you fight for everything. There is no peace in this place: only submission to power... I'm almost *sure* they did something to Marenga."

"What are you implying?"a reporter demanded.

Botswana Glade was fired up now: "I'm not *implying* anything! A black man—a man that this nation has always hated—has conveniently fallen just before he was about to make a crucial speech to a crowd of angry black people. What does that say to you!" At that, he walked off with his aides. Yet, as he took his leave, it occurred to him, for the first time, that they *were* his aides—and that it was all his now.

Reports of the riot were everywhere—on every channel. All the chaos and madness was rising up again. It was a drug, and they were all addicted. Now, a new story was hitting the airwaves:

"We have a breaking story from an exclusive Brooklyn Heights neighborhood. A little girl has been kidnapped—and her parents shot...one killed." There was a camera crew at the scene, showing the half a dozen police cars and vans in front of the house. *"The husband is confirmed dead, with multiple gunshot wounds to the head and chest. The wife was raped and shot in the head, and is now in critical condition at a local hospital. Neighbors heard screams and gunshots; when they came out to investigate, they saw the assailant running from the house with the couple's three-year-old daughter in his hands. The assailant is described as a black male about 6' to 6'3" tall, with jeans and a leather jacket. The little girl is white with blond hair, wearing a pink bunny..."* Someone handed her something; she looked a little confused.

"And we have yet another update. A few blocks away from the house, the same assailant shot and killed a police officer." She paused for a moment after reading this, as though unable to believe it. *"Details are sketchy, but apparently two police officers, who had just heard an advisory on the shooting of the couple, came upon the assailant as he was fleeing with the little girl. After confronting him, a scuffle ensued, and somehow the assailant got one officer's gun and shot the officer's partner. That partner has been...confirmed dead."* Her voice was a little shaky.

"The police are advising people in that area to lock their

windows and doors and avoid all confrontation with this man. If you spot him, call the police as soon as possible, as he is obviously armed and dangerous..."

"Why did this have to happen now of all times!" yelled Mayor Randolph's chief aide, Abraham Levin. About a dozen voices were now raised in panicky conversation. Randolph and his entire cabinet were now in a fortified sub-basement of City Hall. They were sitting around a huge conference table—with the exception of Levin, who was pacing at Randolph's right. Also to the right, there was a huge television, on which the events of the outside world were being shown. The volume had been turned off, but that only made the scenes more unreal.

"First the Thomas thing," Levin began again, "and now a riot! What are we going to do about this, Alex?" Levin asked as he stood above Randolph, panting. As always, Levin reminded Randolph of a vegetable; today, it was a squash. The man always looked unkempt: his beard always looked shaggy; his eyes always looked beady behind his thick glasses. Moreover, Levin was one of those balding white men who insisted on combing his few remaining hairs over his scalp. Levin's were slicked down with grease that made his entire scalp seem to be oozing. Randolph unconsciously grimaced.

"—*And we have that debate tonight!*" Levin added, to

which all the other aides and cabinet members shuffled in their seats and looked nervously at Randolph.

Still, despite everything, Randolph's only reaction was an equivocal groan as he shrugged his shoulders.

"*Come on*, Alex!" Levin raged at Randolph's reaction. "Get it together, man!"

All the other aides and cabinet members stared at him in the uneasy silence; but unmoved by Levin's tirade, Randolph looked past the man—and toward the television, where hundreds of people were having a standoff with a column of policemen in riot gear. The mob was throwing bottles (and whatever else they could find) at the police. It reminded Randolph of Palestinian boys throwing stones at Israeli tanks. Somehow, it struck him as a farce; so that his face wore a strange smile when he looked back at Levin.

"What the hell has happened to you, Alex!" Levin said, taking a step closer to the table; his face turning an oily mauve now. "Get it together, man! This is *politics*, not the goddamn rosary society! We get shit done." Randolph stared at the man with blank eyes. "That's why people put us here. We get shit done that they don't want to do for themselves or are too lazy or *stupid* to do for themselves! That's all politics is! We keep people content—by making them think their problems are taken care of—"

Randolph's eyes lit up: "Maybe they should do for themselves for a while."

Levin retreated a step, looking as though Randolph had just declared himself the Antichrist. "What the *hell* are you talking about...!" He was so enraged that he shook. But then he sighed and took a deep breath to calm himself. "Look, the pressure's got us all a little crazy. After you're reelected, you'll go on a vacation and get everything cleared up. You'll see: it'll be like the old days. And I know you don't want to give all this up," he said, flashing a toothy grin that showed his crooked, coffee-stained teeth and swollen, purple gums. It was supposed to be ingratiating, but it was repulsive. He was now talking in that annoying, singsong voice that people used with their disagreeable toddlers, declaring: "You get to meet foreign dignitaries and movie stars... you're the Mayor of *New York City*, for God's sake! Wake up, man! There are people who would sell their *souls* to be where you are."

Randolph chuckled then; on the screen, there were now scenes of people breaking the windows of a department store and rushing inside—

Levin's smile evaporated. He seemed uncertain for the first time. "Look," he said in a more anxious tone, stepping in front of the television so that Randolph would acknowledge him, "just rest, okay. Your big debate is tonight...*God*!" he whispered as the immediacy of it confronted him. "Look, just clear your head for a couple of hours—go in the back and get some sleep or something. We'll deal with the spin on the riot. Later on, when your head's clear, we'll come back and coach

you for the debate... Or maybe," he started with a hopeful voice, "with the riot, we can cancel the debate."

But at that, Randolph spoke up. His expression was
inscrutable as he shook his head and said: "No, there's
no reason to put it off."

Levin looked at him oddly, nodded his head with a
certain amount of uncertainty, then went over to talk to
Radix.

Half an hour had passed with Roland crouched behind
the dumpster in that alleyway. He had tried to think of
what to do next—and to retrace how he had reached
this place to begin with. It was amazing how quickly
time passed when every road led to death; and as much
as he tried to make sense of what was going on around
him, his jumbled, panicky thoughts had only added fuel
to the fire. In fact, he had started walking again, hoping
to distract himself from his thoughts.

There was a side of him that instinctively wanted to
go to the police. Logic told him to do it—but every
time he tried to consider it, his mind went to the dead
cop. The man would have beaten him to death if given
the chance. Roland saw that now. And then, there were
the Thomases. The police had killed the kid when he
turned himself in at the police station! They had even
killed the kid's goddamn mother! ...And they had been
innocent, too!

No, things had gone too far: if he tried turning himself in, they would only kill him. ...But how was he going to get out of this? A strange feeling of hopelessness was growing within him, mocking his every precaution—his every *thought*. The only thing that made sense for now was hiding. He went anywhere he could hide: down alleyways and up the relatively deserted industrial district along the East River. It was getting colder; but even though he had taken off his coat and balled Mindy up in it to hide her, he couldn't really feel it. The little girl lay in his arms quietly, overcome by the same shock as himself. Twice, her doll had fallen from her fingers as she stared off in a daze. He had had to go back and pick it up for her. As for himself, he didn't even know what he was thinking. All that he knew—like Andropov and Randolph had known before him—was that he had to hide. Everyone seemed like a potential attacker. The paranoia was deep in his veins: everything was suspect—

For the hundredth time, his mind drifted to thoughts of to Phelps' corpse and Cindy's madness. Explanations eluded him—*reason* eluded him. He felt like a monster that had been concocted in a madman's laboratory. The villagers were after him now—*tormenting* him. But he patted Mindy's soft, little body then; and at least for the moment, it calmed him.

How unreal it all was: he was an accused murderer on the loose, and yet this little girl was in his arms, somehow keeping him within sight of his sanity. Feeling her little body was a reminder that things could, in time, be all right. It was proof that he was still a human being: that if she could find comfort in his touch and in his words, then he wasn't yet a beast—a *nigger*. He needed her desperately at the moment, and there was something unspeakably shameful about that...

There was a pay phone ahead; seeing it, his mind suddenly went to his girlfriend. He quickly picked up the receiver, shoved in some random coins from his pocket, and called her cellular phone number.

"Sammy?"

"Roland!"—she seemed relieved—"I was trying to reach you. Is your cell phone working? I thought you were caught up in the riot! You want to get together later?"

"Sammy...where are you?"

"I'm still at the studio." She sensed something in his voice. "Roland?" she said, suddenly uncertain.

"Sammy..." But he didn't know how to begin. Everything seemed to want to burst from him at once. He almost cried in the face of it all; he bit his lower lip, trying to hold back the tide. "Sammy," he blurted out, "something's happened."

"Roland?" It didn't sound like him at all—it sounded pathetic.

"God," he whispered. He didn't know where to begin. And then: "I'm sure it's been on the news—"

"What? *The riot?*" She lowered her voice. "Were you in *that?*"

"What riot...? No...there was a murder—"

"Rol..." she seemed to run out of breath; she took a deep breath, and then: "What is it? You're *scaring* me."

"God," he whispered again. "I'm sure it's been on the news: a couple in Brooklyn Heights—"

"What! ...How were *you* involved?"

"The police think I did it." She gasped. "They're *after* me. They think I did it!" he repeated.

"Turn yourself in!" she said quickly. "*Explain* everything..."

"They want to *kill* me!" he pleaded, his voice sounding pathetic again.

"Roland..." but then her voice trailed off, as though the full extent of it were just reaching her. "You have to give yourself up—they won't hurt you if you're innocent..."

He listened to her voice, desperate to believe. However, while she continued talking, not only did he remember the Thomases: he had an image of himself in handcuffs. He saw his mug shot all over the news—*just like his father*! He saw himself being led away in manacles, joining the nightly parade of jailed niggers on television! That was worse than death: worse than what they had done to the Thomases! He thought about the people at work seeing it. His innocence was irrelevant: it was their *seeing* it...and he would never get a major case again—

"No," he breathed into the phone. She had been talking at that time.

"...What?"

"No," he repeated. "...I *can't*." Again, he couldn't explain it to her: there was just too much. "I want to clear this up...but without...*handcuffs*." That was the closest he could come to explaining it to her. "I want them to know that it was all a mistake...and then, I'll turn myself in."

There was silence on the other end, as though she were thinking something over. At last, she said: "Do you really have that couple's little girl?"

"Yes!" he said in exasperation. "She's here with me, but it's all a misunderstanding. I didn't *kidnap* her. I didn't *kill* anyone ...It's so...*silly*." He couldn't think of a stronger word, and this was suddenly frustrating to him.

There was another long silence. "What about the police officer you shot?"

"*What!* I didn't *shoot* anybody!" he squealed.

"Where are you now?" she demanded.

He looked around, seeing the 59th Street Bridge about two kilometers away. "I'm in Queens—by the 59th Street Bridge."

She was still thinking. "Look, we have a sound stage in the city, on 47th Street—you met me there once, remember?"

"Yes, but..."—he grew suddenly timid—"people will *see* me—"

"No one will see you!" she snapped, her voice suddenly on edge. "It's small—*rarely used*. I can leave the door open and get the guard to take a break."

Silence: he couldn't think straight.

"Look," she went on, "I can get your side of the story on the air...and then you can turn yourself in, like you said."

He thought it over for a while. "Yeah," he said, suddenly brightening. "That's all I wanted—just to *explain*."

"Then I'll see you," she said, her voice all business. "I'll get everything ready." She went to hang up—

"Sammy," he said before she put down.

"...Yes?"

"I love you..." There was silence on the other end; he went on quickly. "I was going to tell you this morning... I know it's a weird thing to say—with all that's going on...I wanted to tell you this morning, like I said.... I want us to talk, Sammy: to *know* one another...there's so much—"

"Just come over," she said, curtly. "I'll get everything ready."

After she put down the phone—that is, while he stood there, listening to the dial tone—he didn't want to admit it to himself, but there had been a horrible coldness to her voice. In the face of everything that had just passed, maybe he *couldn't* admit it.

The city wasn't yet on fire, but it seethed; and in that wild churning, there was the possibility of combustion. Botswana Glade had gotten about five blocks away from the hospital before making the driver turn around;

besides, with the riot, traffic wasn't going anywhere. Many of the reporters had stayed at the hospital, waiting restlessly for news on the cause of Marenga's collapse. Reporters hated waiting, but they hoped that their waiting would be worthwhile. Many of them would have to make live reports for the five and six o'clock news broadcasts, and they hoped that they would have something new to say. Still, they knew all the tricks. News didn't have to be new—it didn't even have to be *news* for that matter—it only had to be newly packaged. It was like adding seasoning to meat that was going rancid. If all else failed, they could always make hot dogs.

Whatever the case, the reporters were upbeat as they milled about their microwave vans, but when Botswana Glade's car pulled up, a sense of euphoria took hold of them again. They were like a pack of dogs that ran to their master upon his return from a long journey. They jumped about him, seeming desperate to put their paws on his chest and lick his face. Botswana Glade looked resplendent as he stood on the curb, surrounded by his aides. His bony chest was puffed out as he heroically looked from side to side, ignoring the reporters' questions. Now, *this* was news! Fifteen reporters had their microphones shoved into his face; ten cameramen clambered for the best positions, and just as many sound crews maneuvered huge microphones above his head. Finally, at the height of the tension, Botswana Glade's voice suddenly boomed:

"A war has begun, and there is no turning back! This

is obvious from what is going on in the streets, but it is in the air as well—in our *souls*. A vigil is going to be held on this very spot"—and he stamped the pavement with his size fourteen shoes—"until Marenga recovers! And you had all better *pray* that he does," he warned. "We can no longer sit back as this country kills our prophets and leaders. My supporters and I are here so that none of this will be forgotten: not Thomas and his dear mother—not any of the people that that insane cop ran over—*and not Marenga!*" We will not be coaxed into forgetfulness about what has happened here today.... And it's funny how a story about a murderous black man breaking into a white couple's home has emerged just when people were about to see this nation for what it is—"

"What are you saying?" demanded a reporter.

"I am very clear in what I am saying," Botswana Glade continued, annoyed by the interruption. "I am declaring war against this country!"

"How do you respond to those who say you are fanning the flames of racial conflict for your own ends?"

Botswana Glade chuckled through a scowl, and then, "I didn't start this fire!" he hissed. "This fire has been raging for centuries." He laughed, as if some joke had just occurred to him. "If I fan it toward your house, it is only because I am tired of seeing my own community being burned. You alone have the means of putting out this fire. You seemed reluctant to do so when I was the only one being burned. Maybe you will be more willing to act when your own house is ablaze!"

Roland rushed across the 59th Street Bridge; with the cold wind blowing off the East River, his body was as numb as his mind. He was able to think of nothing but Samantha. He was lost in the darkness, and she was the light.... At most other times, the view of the Manhattan skyline would have been spectacular, but now it seemed like a hurried charcoal sketch. The sky was darkening quickly—as if all the light and *life* were being drained from the world. He had always hated the coming of winter. With its long, dark days, the season had always seemed like a coffin's lid closing about him.

The temperature had dropped precipitously in the last few hours. The icy wind howled past his ears; every few moments, a gust threatened to push him over the banister, and into the churning waters of the East River. Once, for just an instant, he found himself wondering if that would be so bad....

As he walked, ghost images of murder and madness kept leaping out at him. He held Mindy close to his chest, trying to keep her warm as the biting wind dug into him. He knew he couldn't keep the little girl out in this weather much longer, so her needs guided him. As for Mindy, she seemed content as long as he held her. She still grasped her little doll in her hand, but her eyes were blank.

Roland lost himself in the act of putting one foot in front of the other. Once, a man had passed him on the bridge; Roland had stopped, his mouth gaping as he stared back. For a moment, he had been sure it was

Phelps! But then, with a shudder, he had shaken his head at all the things that haunted him, and continued on his way....

When he reached Manhattan, he sensed immediately that something was very wrong. He knew nothing about the riot—besides Samantha's vague exclamations—but he sensed that something horrible had happened. There were police officers everywhere! At first, paranoid thoughts fluttered through his mind—about the entire world mobilizing to bring him down. However, when he looked into the people's eyes, he saw their panic—as if they had seen, or were expecting to see, the devil. They moved with a nervousness that was extreme even for New Yorkers. As for traffic, it was all hopelessly snarled. Drivers were cursing and honking their horns; people sometimes seemed to be jogging, in their haste to get off the streets. Everywhere, there was motion and sound—but something about it reminded him of an intricate music box, with millions of dancing figurines. Someday, the music would stop, and all the figurines would be frozen in place; and there would be a horrible stillness while God decided whether to crank up the box again or close the lid over all of their heads....

For some reason, he was thinking about his grandmother and the summers he used to spend at her home on the bayou. No, he knew exactly why he was thinking about her: the old woman, with her wizened skin and missing teeth, had been his respite from the world. She had lived in the Louisiana swamp, like a voodoo queen; and he had fled into her power every summer, desperate for the protection of her magic. He remembered how she used to wander out into the swamp at night by herself, without fear of snakes and crocodiles, and all the other things that had terrified his childish imagination. Somehow, she had always been *beyond* fear. Even now, he could see her sitting on that rickety rocking chair on her porch; he remembered the vague outlines of her parables, and scoured his mind to relearn those sacred truths. Indeed, as he walked the city streets, he could almost hear her pigs squealing in the background, and feel the warmth of the Louisiana sun; all around him, he saw oak and mangrove trees, with their lavish, fur-like covering of Spanish moss. What was strange, too, was that she had had an ancient music box, and that he would sit in front of it for hours at a time, watching the figurines dance....

The policemen—primarily traffic cops—were at many of the intersections, diverting traffic from downtown (which had received the brunt of the damage from the riot). Roland kept his head low and held Mindy tighter, not knowing whether that was for her or for him. Either way, rationalizations were of no use to him anymore. His girlfriend was off in the distance: his only hope. She was once again that high priestess, conferring grace and delivering him from his sorrows. He would get all of this craziness cleared up, and then he would talk to his woman about love and the future. A fairytale world was taking shape in his mind now; an entire kingdom rose up before him, with a beautiful princess and a courageous prince. There were hardships in the way, but the conclusion was clear—was *preordained* by heaven and the rules of fairytales.

As he walked along, his yearning for Samantha became a kind of madness within itself. All that he wanted—all that he could *think* about—was grasping her body close to his. He was almost running now. Some phantom energy fed his muscles and he found himself jogging down the streets....

The studio was a huge, nondescript building in the middle of one of those strangely peaceful side streets. Now that he was finally here, he lost his drive. He stood outside for a moment, looking up and down the block uneasily. There were hoards of people at the intersections, but none down the block. He looked up at the building again. It was a single coat of dark green paint—even the windows had been painted over. He just felt uneasy—*unsure*. It occurred to him that he still had his wallet—and that he could flee. All at once, getting to Samantha seemed wrought with too many perils—even for a courageous fairytale prince like himself. He could go to the ATM, get some money and flee down to Louisiana—or wherever. His grandmother was dead now, as was his mother; still, there had to be places of ease and freedom out there, into which he could flee. Only flight seemed to make sense now. Yes, there were thoughts—*fantasies*, in fact—of rectifying it all; Samantha still shimmered in his imagination as a princess, he didn't trust the world anymore. For Samantha's plan to work, he would have to rely on countless people—most of whom he had never met. He realized, suddenly, that trust required hope—and that there was only darkness within him.

He hesitated for a moment, as these doubts went through his mind; but in the end, the fantasy of Samantha was the only thing that he had. In a contradictory sense, the fantasy was the only *concrete* thing that he had. Looking up, it occurred to him that she was waiting inside of the building. The reality of her bridged the gap between fact and fantasy, and he found himself stepping forward.

When he opened the huge door, he saw that the guard post was unoccupied—just as Samantha had promised. And the place was warm: this at least was inviting. At the little desk in the corner, where the guard was supposed to be, a note was written out to him in huge block letters. It read: "ROLAND, WALK UP TO THE 2ND FLOOR." He stared at it for a moment; even Mindy, as he held her, stared at it—even though she couldn't read. A weird feeling of déjà vu coursed through him. The building seemed too quiet as well—just like Phelps'. The impulse to run again seized him, but it was countermanded by the palliating image of his girlfriend—and the realization that he was spent. He needed this to end. He needed to rest and put this all behind him; and now, the fantasy of settling everything once again swelled up in his mind, so that there again seemed to be no choice. *I've come this far*! he chastised himself.

Either way, a side of him was numb as he walked up the dark, dusty staircase. He didn't want to think anymore. His steps sounded horrible in the silence... The staircase led up to a huge sound stage. The door was open, and he stood in the doorway, in awe of all that he saw. He took Mindy out of his jacket now, and placed her on the ground, holding her hand. The room before him was *cavernous*. The ceiling was perhaps two stories above him. They used to shoot soap operas here, and the sets were still up: a living room scene, several bedroom scenes, a kitchen scene, a business scene... A side of him was alarmed when he saw people moving about inside; but then, deep into the room, he saw his girlfriend! She and a few others were standing next to a living room set. Roland's heart soared. All the cameras were being put in place and checked. There were also flickering video screens.

Roland took a few steps toward them; as he did so, everyone stopped and stared at him. He felt...*unreal*. Mindy clambered to be held again, so he put on his jacket and took her in his arms. He began walking toward Samantha then. Everything was so strange... Somehow, he was now standing with his girlfriend and the rest of her crew. He was aware that there were several people around him, saying things to him, but he wasn't entirely aware of what was happening. Somehow, Mindy had been coaxed out of his arms. They had given her something sweet to eat.

He felt arms on him, leading him toward the set they had prepared. He went to panic at this, but then he saw his girlfriend ahead—always just out of his reach, like a carrot dangling before a donkey's lips. They made him sit down on one of the sofas. It was too soft and he felt as though he would become stuck in its cushions. He forced himself to sit up on the edge of the sofa... His girlfriend was still just beyond his reach, staring at him with an expression that he could not gauge. They hadn't touched, nor had they spoken. They just stared. He couldn't read whatever was in her eyes, and this made him feel horribly lonely... The lights were blinding; the technicians were making the final adjustments now. His image appeared on one of the video screens, and he was aware, suddenly, of how wretched he looked. He hadn't shaved that day; there were lines under his eyes, and his lips were quivering slightly. He felt like a scared rat in a cage. He looked at his girlfriend, but she just seemed so far away—so *very* far...

A Latina, whom he recognized vaguely as Maria Santos, was going to do the interview—or so Roland guessed when the woman came up and shook his hand. She had a strange gleam in her eyes, which unnerved him. He glanced at his girlfriend, but she was staring at the floor and hugging herself—as if she were cold. Mindy was sitting on a chair not too far away from his girlfriend, staring ahead in a daze as she gnawed on a chunk of cake. They had covered her in a blanket—

Roland was suddenly aware that Santos was talking to him. He looked up nervously, realizing that the interview had begun. "—What?"

"What is your name?" Santos asked again.

"Roland: Roland Micheaux," he said in an unsteady voice. He cleared his throat.

"And why are you here?"

"I'm here..." He looked over at his girlfriend; she looked away when he met her eyes. "I'm here"—he lost his train of thought; he looked back at Santos, who was staring back with an encouraging but ultimately patronizing smile—"I'm here because I'm innocent."

"Innocent of what?" she chimed.

Roland had a sudden impulse to punch the woman in her stupid, smiling face. He stared at her, frowning. It was then that she sighed loudly—somewhat *dramatically*—before going on:

"You are in fact here, are you not, to claim that you weren't responsible for murdering Dallas Phelps in his house and then raping and shooting his wife, Cindy Phelps. And," she added for theatrical emphasis, "the murder of a police officer—not to mention, the kidnapping of Mindy Phelps, the couple's daughter."

Roland felt sick; he was suddenly aware that sweat

was pouring down his face. He opened his mouth to say something, but nothing came out.

"Do you have any violence in your past?" Santos asked him, her eyes narrowing, as if she were laying a carefully placed trap.

Roland shook his head, and then: "No, I'm a lawyer"—some of the stage hands laughed; Santos smiled, and then:

"Do you think that your father's life has affected you?"

It took a while for him to digest what the woman had just said.

"What? ...I..." Roland felt paralyzed. He looked around in dismay, perhaps searching for his girlfriend; but just then, his eyes landed on the video screens off camera. On one of them, was that scene from his recurring dream: him as a scared thirteen-year-old, being escorted through the sea of reporters. They were showing his father's mug shot now and running news items from all those years ago.

Roland became aware he could not feel his body anymore—it was as if his consciousness were floating away. Movement became sluggish; words sounded as though they were being slurred by an alcoholic. But then, the rage suddenly caught fire in him. It expanded within him so quickly that he burst upright. The feeling of betrayal hit him. He looked over at his girlfriend, but she only stared back, her eyes blank. Either implicitly or explicitly, she was one of them.

"What is this!" he demanded, looking around desperately. "Stop this! Stop this *now*!" It was then that he realized that Santos had fled—disappeared into the darkness. Off camera, everyone seemed to be inching away. He frowned, just then noticing some figures creeping up in the darkness. *Policemen*! His eyes darted to his girlfriend, the rage bubbling to the surface.

"It's for the best!" she yelled out, already retreating into the shadows. Yet, he couldn't deal with that now. The dozens of figures were still advancing.

He was backing away now. "No!" he kept repeating. He tripped over the coffee table of the set and landed on the ground. A phalanx of police officers emerged at his back. Their faces were hard and set. On the video monitors, the documentary on his father's wasted life was still going on. He didn't know where he got the strength or will, but Roland whirled and darted at the policemen who were coming at him from behind. He was so quick that he was upon them before they could react. He leapt at two policemen's feet and threw them to the ground. However, as soon as he was to his feet, a policeman grabbed him from behind—and two more approached from the front. Instinctively, Roland used the policeman who had grabbed him as leverage, and kicked both of the approaching policemen in their heads. Soon, they were splayed on the ground, with the others he had knocked down previously. His was the strength of the Devil. The cop was still trying to hold him, but with a vicious elbow to the temple, the man was on the ground and Roland was free. One of the policemen he had just knocked down was trying to get to his feet: Roland kicked him viciously in the face and sent him to the ground. He then leapt over the entire pile and darted into the darkness beyond the blinding lights of the set. The policemen were still trying to corner him, but he outflanked them all by leaping over a luxurious bathroom set. He was in the clear now. Mindy had been roused from her daze by all the commotion. She started running toward Roland, but Samantha grabbed her and held her. The little girl was screaming out for 'him, but Roland was running now. He leaped over two sets and outdistanced the confused police by a good deal. He was running back toward the entrance; but after a few strides, he saw that policemen were emerging from it as well! It was strange, but he didn't panic. Some dark avenging angel must have been whispering in his ear, because as soon as he saw the policemen, he went into action. He grabbed a stool from the kitchen set that he was currently in, then ran toward the wall, perpendicular to both groups of advancing policemen. They thought that they had him cornered against the wall, but when he was close enough, he threw the stool.

For an instant, the illusion took them all aback. It was as though he had broken the wall with his throw; but in fact, he had thrown the stool into one of the huge, painted-over windows. It shattered, letting in the dwindling daylight. In two steps, Roland was in the window, looking down. It seemed as if he were going to commit suicide; the policemen slowed, telling him to come back inside of the building, but Roland had spotted his goal. He was at the back of the building, looking down on an alleyway. The huge dumpster, piled high with garbage bags and empty boxes was two stories below. Before he could even think, the avenging angel told him to jump. He was in the air and there was a gasp from everyone inside the building. For a moment, there was an unbearable silence, in which the only sound was the pained cry of the little girl as she screamed, "Uncle Roland!" And then, there was the loud crash of Roland's body as it hit.

Some policemen rushed to the window, expecting to see his body splattered against the ground, but they only stared on in disbelief—then *rage*—as they saw Roland scrambling out of the dumpster and darting down the darkening alleyway.

Roland ran, but it wasn't as before. He darted down the alleyways and side streets, but he wasn't running from anything anymore. He had a sudden impulse to laugh out triumphantly, remembering how he had eluded all of those policemen. But then, just as quickly, he remembered his girlfriend—and her *treachery*—feeling everything unraveling.

He had been running for several minutes, but now he slowed and began walking. Just around the corner, was 42nd Street. There were hordes of people—all walking along with that strange uneasiness. That was the thing about New York: no matter what happened, a block or two away, it was always as though nothing had happened. The world was constantly negating itself; lives were constantly being destroyed and disappearing into the nothingness.

At first, watching the people around him, he was again overcome by the urge to flee; but at the same time, he knew that the best place to hide, was in a crowd. He joined the throng that was headed west, toward Broadway. The feeling of loneliness and isolation hit him hard then. He had nowhere to go and no friends to turn to. It was cold out now and he shivered in his jacket. The reality of what had just happened hit him again, and his previous numbness came back. They really believed that he could have done it! His girl-friend...all of them: they *believed* it! It was not even a matter of if he had done it or not: it was that they thought him *capable* of it. He was desperate for the avenging angel to return and guide him—but it was gone, leaving him stranded in this wasteland. The numbness was enveloping him now. Maybe he was freezing to death and didn't know it....

He was passing by an electronics store, which had several television sets in its display window. He thought that he had imagined it at first, but there it was: his father's mug shot! And then, in the next instant, there was a picture of him—he recognized it from his news conference the day before. He stopped before the display window, unable to move. He couldn't hear the television, but he didn't need to hear, because he was watching Maria Santos' interview at the sound stage! *They had already aired it!* He looked like a lunatic on the screen, and then he was running from the police, toppling over furniture... He saw himself wrestling with the policemen and fighting with them like an animal in a cage.... It was as though he had blacked out while standing there, because when he came to his senses, he was watching scenes from the riot today. However, he didn't know that: it just seemed like his childhood memories were being projected onto the screen. He swallowed deeply and with effort. It was over: the story on the news, his life...*everything*. Roland walked on.

Kain had said that the world was going to end; as Roland looked up to find himself in Times Square, with its flashing billboards and giant screen TV, he couldn't deny it anymore. On that giant screen, nightmare images of the day's riot played. In fact, all around him was that world of chaos and madness. He was a wanted criminal now—a *murderer and rapist*, like his father before him. Still, unaccountably, a smile now came to his lips. It was with pride that he recalled how he had struggled with and outmaneuvered all those policemen; as he revisited the image of the bullet-riddled policeman lying at his feet that afternoon, the madness seized him completely, and he laughed out loud.

Presently, as his gaze returned to the giant-screen TV, he saw his image looking back at him from on high, like some sinister god. They were running that special report again, describing him as the latest version of evil incarnate—a murderer, cop killer, rapist...There was definitely no going back now—no way to reclaim his fairytale existence of wealth and fame; and as the bridges to his humanity had been burned, he found himself freed in a way that was at once wonderful and horrible. Like Adam of the Bible, the power behind the universe had turned him away from Paradise; but unlike Adam, he left not with sorrow and the hope of redemption, but with a newfound hatred for the power of God—which he saw flickering on the giant screen before him. All his life, he had fought the inevitable. He had fled from his father's murderous act—and from everything he had ever known. He had fought his way to the upper crust of society, and yet he still found himself in the same place he would have been had he stayed in the ghetto. *He was a nigger....*

SURRENDER

By eight o'clock that night, the riot had been subdued—but the violence remained in the souls of
the people, gestating into something else as the
hours went by. And it wasn't even like the last time,
when they had Andropov to embody their rage. Colina
was dead, and Marenga was comatose, and the Thomases
rose up as martyrs to all the injustice and oppression in
the world. The violence seeped into the hearts and
minds of those watching it on TV; and by now, images
of the riot were being broadcast all over the world:
scenes of people breaking into stores; people fighting
with the police and one another; people lying around
dazed and bloody, or dead...and then, there was the
image of an old white woman being kicked and punched
by a mob of black youths... It was all sickening to watch,
but they couldn't help but surrender their souls to it.

"Smile and wave your hands, Mr. Mayor," an aide
said as they exited the car, and Randolph stretched his
lips taut over dry teeth. He was being hustled through

the crowd now—toward the studio where the debate was to be held.

Back at City Hall, about half an hour ago, he had given a statement to the press. He had made empty statements about peace, order and justice; but after the day's violence, and all that had passed, the crowd seemed like ghosts from the riot. Cameramen and reporters cluttered around him, yelling what seemed to be gibberish. He didn't want to hear what they were saying anyway.

Beyond the media, the hundreds of bystanders and protesters seemed to surge toward him. Some were cheering and stretching out their hands to be shaken; others were booing, holding up banners that he couldn't read without his glasses.

Finally, he was pushed through a side door, which was hastily shut behind them—him, four aides, and two bodyguards. The crowd was gone now. The crowd's cheers and boos faded away, as did its images. It was warmer and darker inside the studio. He felt an urge to remove his trench coat, but he was quickly being hustled up some stairs now, swept along by the men that propped him up by the armpits. He let them lead him. It was all out of his hands anyway. Everything passed him by like the crowd, hardly even registering in his mind. The realization that he was to have a debate in a matter of minutes was first met with alarm, then, a millisecond later, with the same apathy as everything else.

This was what his life had been like for the last few years: this almost mindless running around. It seemed so much like a tiresome game to him now. Where there had once been excitement and hope, there was now just...he didn't even know what. The first Mayoral election seemed like a lifetime away. He had somehow been able to lose himself in the thrill of competition and the fallacy that all that the city needed—all that the *world* needed, in fact—was the right man. The people who had gathered in droves to hear his speeches had believed it as well. Bewitching them all had been the myth that one man could manifest bravery and thoughtfulness and moral uprightness in a population lacking in all three; and that such a man could not only embody the society, but also be a kind of crutch for the masses. It had been the myth of rugged American individualism: the fantasy of some hired gun being able to "clean up a town." It all seemed like so much shit to him now; but four years ago, buoyed by the cheers of the hopeful masses, he had fought his way into office, believing that he could "make a difference." He had stepped into the office of his predecessor—whom he had lampooned as being corrupt and indifferent to the needs of the city—only to look up and find himself speaking like the man, doing the same things that he, himself, had campaigned against. He had done to his opponent what McPrice was doing to him; and in time, someone else, basking in McPrice's ignominious defeat at the hands of the city, would be doing it to her as well. From the vantage point of his new-found apathy, he could see it all clearly now. It had truly been him against the world. For months, maybe *years* now, it had been a simple matter of survival.

His marathon conversation with Marenga came back to him then. When Marenga was leaving, the man had turned to Randolph and said, "I respect you, Randolph. You are an honest man, even though you have dishonest ideals."

"Isn't that a contradiction?" Randolph had said with a smirk.

"Not at all. You want to have integrity when you deal with others, but you lie to yourself all the time. You lie to yourself, so that you can keep on lying to them."

"And what do I lie about?" he had said, trying to sound flippant, even while a sense of alarm began to build in him.

"You're an easy man to read, Randolph," Marenga had said, chuckling. "You have everyone else fooled, but not me—not anymore, anyway. You're not that easygoing, glib character that everyone thinks you are. The only reason there is hope for you yet, is that you aren't at peace: you aren't complacent. You and I aren't men of peace," he had said with a strange laugh. "We're men of violence—of *war*. We're *killers*, Randolph: soldiers in a kill or be killed world...."

They hustled Randolph into a crowded dressing room, where he was again the focus of attention. Levin was there, looking insecure, but nonetheless smiling his crooked, repulsive smile to give Randolph confidence. They sat Randolph in a chair that faced a large mirror with bright light bulbs around its perimeter. He squinted...The lights were hot... He wrenched off his coat... There were aides everywhere, yelling instructions. He heard none of what they said. A stoic-faced white woman applied makeup to his face.... He stared at his face in the mirror: it looked grim and old. He was only forty-eight years old, and yet he seemed haggard...

Someone poked her head in the doorway: "Only a minute until air time." It was a young black woman, just out of college, but Randolph couldn't remember her name at the moment. She had worked hard; but as Randolph got up, he had already forgotten her face... No matter...

"All right, it's show time!" the perpetually sweaty Levin yelled.

Everyone made way for Randolph, now shouting his or her support.... White faces, black faces, Latino faces, all smiling and clapping—but he suddenly detested them!

"Try to smile more, Mr. Mayor," Levin yelled, but Randolph could do nothing but walk along, feeling the strange revulsion rising in him. He made his way out to the dark studio, where the spotlights always blazed in his eyes, making him squint—and look deceitful. Three objects seemed to float on islands created by the spotlights. There were two lecterns and a desk. Everything else was cast in black; and he could only see silhouettes moving in the darkness, where he guessed that the cameras and studio technicians might be. He squinted and saw that his opponent and the moderator were already at their places. The moderator was sitting at the desk, which faced the two lecterns. His opponent was at her lectern. Everyone had been on time, but Randolph.

They acknowledged one another's presence with dignified nods of their heads. Ed Muskie, the moderator, was a gaunt, desiccated white man about sixty, with a completely bald head that shined in the bright lights. Charlotte McPrice looked incredibly young and vibrant. Everyone called her the progressive poster woman. During the last election, they had had a nickname for him, too. It had been something ludicrous like: The Trailblazer. All of that was yet another part of the farce—it didn't matter at all....

As he stepped to the stage, everything about him—his every action, his every thought—seemed futile and self-destructive. The feeling of panic again tried to exert itself, only to be beaten back by the feeling that everything was beyond his control. His opponent's victory was imminent, and yet that didn't bother him in the least. He knew it as he looked at her. McPrice had a forty-five-point lead in the polls...she was going to be the first female Mayor of New York City, but that would be yet another meaningless milestone of humanity. She seemed strong, and was certainly glib and optimistic—just as he had been. And yet, a side of him couldn't help but pity her. It was indeed time for change, but Randolph knew that if she won—*when* she won—she, too, would be riding the beast, holding on for dear life.

He stood behind the lectern, his face grim. The television crew was now whipped into a frenzy, with a voice, whose face he could not see in the bright light, yelling that there were only ten seconds until air time.

"Welcome everyone," Ed Muskie said when it was time, "to the final Mayoral debate between incumbent Mayor Alexander Randolph, and Councilwoman Charlotte McPrice—or is it Councilperson?" he asked McPrice with a smile.

"Councilwoman's fine," she answered. "I'm not afraid of being called a woman." To this, there was applause from off stage, where her supporters and aides looked on eagerly. McPrice and the moderator chuckled with one another for a while; Randolph, who stood there stiffly, felt like a contestant on a game show.

After formerly greeting them both—a presentation for the television audience—Muskie went over the rules of the debate. McPrice looked on eagerly while Randolph only stared ahead. Muskie was now telling Charlotte that she had three minutes to make an opening statement, and she put on her business face, beginning:

"We live in a city that is facing many problems from

many sides. The most poignant example I can give is the fact that there was a *riot* in front of City Hall today, ladies and gentlemen! There is disorder and panic on the streets as I speak. Today alone, two police officers were killed because of this social unrest—not to mention dozens of innocent bystanders. What we need is stability and order and *prosperity*, not sex scandals and riots!

"Four years ago, we were promised an end to many of our social and economic problems. We were promised *more* jobs; we were promised *better* education; we were promised *safer* streets; but what have we gotten? Look around you, people of New York: we have scandal after scandal; crime is worse, education is stagnant or in decline: the very buildings in which our children go to school are decaying; and for this, your taxes and mine have been increased to outlandish levels by the present administration. Faced with these facts, the action ahead seems clear.

"We have to get away from the laughable bungling of the present administration. We need a Mayor who will be tough on crime, who will lower taxes...! We need a Mayor who will bring back the standards of education that we grew up with, and which made America the greatest nation on earth! We cannot pussyfoot around the issues—or go missing in action! *We must attack*! And I am the woman to lead that attack.

"Tonight is Halloween," she continued in a lower, more pained voice, "and all around our great nation,

innocent children are going out to play make-believe—
to *pretend* to scare one another; but in this city, our
children are already scared! They don't need make-
believe to be afraid—because for them, there are real
demons out there. It is time that we make it safe for our
children to play make-believe again; and I tell you,
people of New York City, *I* am the woman to do it, and
now is the time to start!"

There was wild applause to this. Randolph had been
staring at his lectern blankly, lost in all the contradictory feelings. He looked over at McPrice now, a side of
him wondering if she believed all that nonsense. He
nodded his head unconsciously: she believed it; she was
beyond all doubt—just as he had been. Her shrill words
were still with him, so that he shook his head to drive
them away.

There was a long silence after the cheers subsided,
and everyone stared expectantly at Randolph. He had
memorized his statement, but it all seemed like so much
drivel to him now.

"Mr. Mayor?" the moderator was saying, over and over
again; as though coming to some decision, Randolph
nodded to himself and looked up from the lectern.

"Yes, okay, Ed," he said with something strange
glittering in his eyes. "Everything's fine," he went on to
reassure them all, but a hush came over everything
nonetheless. He seemed calm, but the tone of his voice
took them aback. Then, when he became tired of fight-

ing the thing rising within him, he sighed deeply and shrugged his shoulders, letting it all go.

For some reason, he smiled as he looked over at McPrice again. "She's right: she's absolutely right," he said with a shallow nod of his head. It was said in a voice that he almost didn't recognize as his own. It was calm and peaceful—the voice of his very distant past— and he was both overjoyed and shocked to find it again. "I've done absolutely nothing during my tenure," he continued, as a collective gasp went through the audience. He was staring ahead blankly, nodding to himself as he heard the words reverberating from his lips. "Crime *is* rampant, good jobs are scarce, schools do graduate illiterates and delinquents...I'll go further than Ms. McPrice," he went on, his voice coming quicker. "I *deceived* everyone last election"—the studio was buzzing with voices now; his own voice instinctively rose to counter them— "but only because you wanted me to: only because you *wanted* to be deceived!"

"—Mr. Mayor!" the moderator exclaimed.

"No, I'm fine, Ed. I'm only now becoming sane again." He looked at his opponent; she stared back with disbelieving blue eyes. "Yes, all of that was very true. I wish you well, madam."

"—Mr. Mayor!" Muskie burst out again, but an euphoric smile came to Randolph's face as he felt the burden being lifted.

"No, Ed, everything's fine. I'm not so much concerned

with her winning, as with our losing...and we're *all* losing!" He almost had to shout over the audience now. "'Get tough on crime?'" he said with a frown, "'Lower taxes'?" he said, chuckling. "...Yes, we're all losers...."

"W-We're going to go to a-a commercial now," Muskie was saying, but Randolph was already walking away, ignoring all of the staring faces and questioning voices. He walked away from it all, chuckling all the while.

It was about eight-thirty when Roland Micheaux looked up from his daze to find himself stumbling down a nondescript city block. It was unbearably cold. The people he passed on the street walked with quick, hunched-over gaits to protect themselves from the biting wind. However, as he was still in shock, Roland felt nothing. He walked with a careless stride, baring his chest to the wind.

The streets were unusually empty—at least for New York. Most of the businesses—the eateries and delis and grocery stores—were closed. The upheaval of the riot was in the air, so the people fled to the safety of their homes. Watching them, Roland couldn't help but be reminded of all that was lost to him. He had no home to return to now: no friends... The police—the *world*, in fact—knew all about him now, and would be waiting for him if he tried to go back to the condo. Everything that he was—or was *supposed* to be—was being dissected by the media. Everything was returning to the nothingness now—his life, his love. It all disappeared so quickly and completely that he began to suspect that none of it could have been real in the first place.

Samantha...she had tried to *kill* him: had *betrayed* him! The thought mocked him as he somnambulated across town; but with his growing numbness, the pain was only a dull ache now. He was beginning to feel the freedom that damned men felt. It was the same sensation that Kain had felt when he bashed the man's head in with a sledgehammer. There was nothing that he couldn't do now, because there was nothing to go back to. What could they possibly do to him that they hadn't already done? For those few moments, walking along the cold city streets, all fear, all hope...*everything* that had shaped and guided him, was short-circuited, and he was free.

He was strangely at peace, but it was a peace nourished by hatred and the realization that his life was over. Even if he could find some mystical way to return to his former life, he no longer had faith in the world. He was like Dorothy in "The Wizard of OZ." He had looked behind the curtain and seen the true power behind the workings of the world; and now, all the illusions were torn away. Where there had been magic, he now only saw the crude manipulations of men; where there had been order and justice, he now saw random acts of violence....

He was on the eastern side of Manhattan now. He saw a police car and abruptly stopped, staring at it intently; but even then, he stared not with fear, but with a kind of morbid curiosity, wondering what was going to happen next. When the car passed him by and disappeared down the block, he only shrugged his shoulders and continued walking. He knew it was only a matter of time before they cornered him. He knew there was no escaping it; but as the hatred rose in him, he swore, right then and there, that when his time came, he would stand before the world with the defiance that his father should have had, and be that unbroken, unrepentant nigger.

When he reached Lexington Avenue, he randomly set off toward the north. His hands were like ice, and his jacket seemed porous; yet, he wasn't shivering. All his reflexes seemed to have been switched off... There were slightly more people walking the streets here—notwithstanding the fact that there had been a riot downtown just hours ago. As he had thought before, if you travelled for a few blocks, the city went from heaven to hell and back again, contradicting itself. He looked into the faces of the strangers who darted past him in the darkness, thinking: *These are the ones who are going to kill me.* Out here on the streets, they were all locked away within themselves, avoiding eye contact and conversation—as though fearful of what they might do to one another. It was in their homes and offices and meeting places that they spread their rumors and lies, and carved up their victims. He had an impulse to grab one of them right now, while he or she was defenseless on the street, and yell, "I am Roland Micheaux!" He smiled, suddenly gripped by the fantasy that he was some kind of suicide bomber, strapped not with sticks of dynamite, but with hatred. When he set off the bomb, they would all be sucked into the cosmic explosion; the entire society would come crashing down around him (just as Kain had said), and Roland would be at peace. He was giddy with this fantasy now, telling himself he would grab the next person he saw. The adolescent joy of it waxed in him for a moment, so that he was drunk with the thought of it. However, the next person to approach him was a white woman with a little girl who instantly reminded him of Mindy. He froze in the middle of the sidewalk. The woman, seeing him standing there, staring at her, sped up, clutching her daughter close as she darted past him.

He suddenly felt cold—and alone. He walked on, now bending like everyone else to protect himself from the wind. He was trembling at last... He shuffled down the street; a few passersby, taking him to be a drunkard, gave him wide berth. *What did it matter*...? Seeing a subway station, the prospect of warmth and protection from the wind was like a beacon to him. It was only when he was halfway down the stairs that he noticed there was a commotion ahead. Two teenagers were beating up a scrawny man, who was lying on the ground. The man was cursing and screaming, and the youths laughed while they kicked and punched him. Without thought, Roland walked down the stairs—again with that disconcerting calmness—and nonchalantly pushed the youths away from the man. The two boys, unfazed by Roland's interruption, laughed out merrily and ran toward the street.

Roland was just going with the flow now. He was free at last, and if the boys had stabbed him, or blown his brains out, it would not have made a difference. The boys' victim, a bum with a shaggy beard, was still moaning on the stairs. Roland bent down to help him up, but when the man turned his face to the light, Roland gasped!

"What took you so long!" Kain said, grinning as he stood up.

Officer Mucelli stared at the interrogating lieutenant blankly. He had been lying to them for hours now—but the more he lied, the more he felt doomed. Either way, there was no going back now. Presently, the young officer was sitting in the interrogation room of the police precinct, facing a one-way observation mirror. As he took a glance at it, the face staring back at him was sallow and craven. Standing above him, was Lieutenant Craig Ericsson, whom everyone called Eric the Red, because of his red hair and Viking-like ruthlessness against his enemies. At the moment, however, the inter-rogation had a conversational, affable tone; several times,

Ericsson, like most of the other officers in the precinct, had expressed his sympathy that Mucelli's partner, a "beloved veteran of the force," had been killed. Everyone was rallying around Mucelli; their questions didn't so much seem accusatory, as tools to understand what had happened; but young Mucelli had no choice but to be uneasy—especially after what he had done....

"Okay," the lieutenant said for about the fifth time that hour, "tell me the entire story again."

Mucelli picked up the glass of water before him and took a long swallow. His hand was shaking, and this alarmed him. *Keep it short and simple*, he thought to himself. *Add nothing; take away nothing that you've already given*. He cleared his throat and began: "Flanders and I were driving in the cruiser. First, we heard about the riot at City Hall, then we got the all-points bulletin on a man fleeing from a crime scene with a hostage—"

"You mean," said Ericsson, "Roland Micheaux."

"Yes, sir. But then, nobody knew who he was. All they knew was that a black man was seen fleeing from the house with a little blond girl, just before the police found her parents shot."

"Okay, what happened next?"

"Well, since we were in that area, we were on edge."

"So you were expecting something to happen?"

"We're cops—we always expect something to happen."

Ericsson smiled; Mucelli felt a little relieved, so that he smiled as well before going on:

"We recognized Micheaux right away: he was carrying the victims' daughter."

"Did you call for backup?"

"No, sir. Everything happened so quickly. We looked up, and there he was. We got out of the car and told him to freeze and put the girl down."

"And then what happened?"

"Officer Flanders went up and started frisking him."

"Then?"

"Then, all of a sudden, Micheaux just *attacked* Flanders. It was like he went *crazy* or something. He smashed Flanders against the car—"

"And where were you at that moment?"

The panic surged in him! "I came up and tried to restrain Micheaux."

"Was your gun drawn?"

He swallowed. "Yes, sir."

"So, this is when Micheaux got the gun from you and shot Flanders?"

"That's about the time, sir. Everything was happening so quickly."

"Did Micheaux hit you?"

"He knocked the gun from my hand—"

"So, while he was fighting with Flanders, he reached over and knocked the gun from your hand—"

"He knocked me down, sir!" he said suddenly. *Shit*, he had forgotten that from the last recital. Micheaux had to knock him down—how else could he explain being out of commission when the shooting occurred.

"So," Ericsson started in an unconvinced tone, "Micheaux knocked you to the ground, beat off Flanders long enough to reach down and get your gun, then shot Flanders?"

"Yes, sir."

Ericsson stood before him in the same dubious air. Mucelli forced himself to look at the man—to not avoid eye contact like criminals always did. "Wait here," the lieutenant said then, walking out of the room.

Mucelli made it a point not to look up: not to stare at the mirror, behind which he knew the investigators were looking at his every motion.

He felt sick to his stomach as he waited. He wanted another drink of water, but he was afraid of how much his hand would shake when he held the glass. He sat with his hands in his lap, waiting in the silence of the room.

When Ericsson entered the observation room, his captain and a lieutenant from the internal affairs department were sitting there. The captain had a chubby, grandfatherly face, but the internal affairs officer always reminded him of a Gestapo agent. The man had a pale, attenuated face and he always had the stench of cheap cigarettes about him.

"What do you think?" Ericsson said after closing the door. He addressed himself to the captain.

"What do you mean?" Captain Miller answered in an

annoyed tone. "The kid just saw his partner shot by some kidnapping, raping psycho. What am I supposed to think about that?"

"But is that *all* that happened?" he said, glancing over at the internal affairs officer—who stared back with indifferent bloodshot eyes.

"What the hell are you implying?" Miller demanded.

"I don't know," Ericsson started, the discomfort showing on his face. "Something's wrong here—*very* wrong. I just came from the room where they are holding the little girl that Micheaux supposedly kidnapped. She's not asking for her mommy or daddy. Who is she asking for? 'Uncle Roland.'"

"So fucking what!" the captain exploded. "So he had a bond with her—*big* deal! Most of the kids that are abducted are taken by someone they know. Micheaux worked at the same firm with the girl's father; half the kids that are raped, are raped by someone they know!"

"Stop that!" Ericsson couldn't help himself. "There was no sexual abuse of this child—"

"Only because that fucker didn't have time!"

"...I don't know," Ericsson said uneasily. "Something stinks about this. Who was Micheaux going to ransom the girl to—he supposedly shot both her parents. Besides that, we just got an anonymous report that it was Mucelli who shot Flanders—"

"What the fuck...! You gonna believe an anonymous report! Mucelli is a goddamn *hero!*"

"Now wait a minute—"

"*You* wait a minute!" Captain Miller began, turning a deep red. "His partner was gunned down *right* in front of him... You know, that's the sick thing about this country: it's getting so that people don't respect cops no more—don't trust or respect authority. *That's* why there was that riot today; *that's* why two fine cops got killed and dozens wounded! This is the goddamn mind-set of these people! They believe a criminal before they believe a cop! You said something's wrong? *Damn* right something's wrong! There's a lunatic wandering the streets and we're in here accusing a fine young officer! *That's* who we should be questioning: that scumbag who shot two upstanding members of the community. On top of that, he had the *nerve* to kidnap their kid and kill a police officer. This case is shut as tight as a consti-pated asshole!"

Ericsson sighed then, glancing through the observa-tion mirror at Mucelli: "I hope so—for all our sakes."

No more scraps for Maria Santos! What a wonderful day this had been: a riot, an exclusive interview with a murdering, raping celebrity, and now the Mayor's strange resignation. She took a certain amount of pride from the thought that she had helped to bring Randolph down—whether or not that was true.

She was being cued for broadcast now, hardly able to

restrain her excitement as she stood on the set of her show and stared into the cameras that would broadcast her image to millions. Her interview with Roland Micheaux, put on the air just minutes after the fact, was already a national story. It had been there just in time for the local and network evening news broadcasts. A rising star was now a murderous, raping lunatic on the run: it was perfect for mass consumption. Americans loved successful people; but more than that, they loved to see successful people fall from grace. It was the national pastime. Even as the madness of the riot died down, Roland Micheaux rose up to take its place.

Everything was in place for her ascension. She had introduced the murderous Roland Micheaux to the world, and she intended to be there when they hauled him in—or gunned him down. She had men hunting Micheaux in Manhattan now; crews were on standby, like SWAT teams ready for the fight of their lives.

And then she was on the air, waxing poetic about the horror of the riot, and Mayor Randolph's cowardice, and the fact that Roland Micheaux was a kind of metaphor for the city and everything that had happened: a glittering star who had been poisoned by evil.

"Roland Micheaux was on a long spiral down into crime," she began. "The evil was *bred* within him— nourished by the same madness that gripped his father over twenty-five years earlier. On the outside, he was a successful lawyer: an upstanding member of society—

gregarious and handsome. He was even rated one of the ten most eligible bachelors in the city! That was the illusion that he showed us all, while within him, the evil was stirring. That murderer is out there now," she continued, "—still on the loose; and just as we have to put this city and country back on the track of justice and order, so too we have to bring in Roland Micheaux: *by any means necessary!*"

Roland's face was blank and pale. The uptown four train was in the station when they got down to the platform; they had to run to make the train—but the moment the door closed behind them, Kain turned to him and laughed out loud.

"So, the great Roland Micheaux is a nigger, too, just like the rest of us!" The man then proceeded to laugh insanely for the next few minutes—while the express train made its way from 59th Street to 86th Street. The crowded Harlem-bound train was filled mostly with blacks and Latinos. With Kain's loud cackling, Roland realized everyone was looking in their direction! Even those who were trying to ignore Kain were glancing at them surreptitiously to see what was going on. There was not even one empty seat in the car; and this density, combined with Kain's apparent inability to be discreet, began to eat away at Roland's sanity.

At the first stop, 86th Street, Roland wanted to dash

outside and run from them all. However, Kain gripped him by the arm—as though he were a prized possession—and pulled him to the middle of the car. They bumped several people, who turned and looked at them with annoyance. Roland tried to keep his face averted, but with each passing second, he felt the madness building.

"Well, welcome to the nigger brotherhood!" Kain said with a grin, as he stood facing Roland's panic-stricken face. "The madness has come at last—just as I said it would!"

When Kain laughed again, practically everyone in the car again looked to see why the *hell* the man was making all that noise. Roland felt as though he were going to throw up! The speeding express train was rocking back and forth now, as it zoomed uptown. Roland was overcome by an insane impulse to pull open the doors and hurl himself onto the electrified tracks! Just then, the express train zoomed past 96th Street in a blur. Roland felt as though they were going too fast: that the world was going by too quickly, and that they were all running out of time—

"Now we can stand together, my brother," Kain continued, "stripped of hopes of belonging and delusions of success. In fact," he went on, "we weren't made for this world, my brother. Like sons of God, we emerged fully formed, with that sacred knowledge within us—but without the power and magic that made men follow Jesus. Still, being dutiful sons, we were desperate to prove

ourselves worthy of Our Father's love; we thought that
if we proved ourselves, the power and magic would
come… But Our Father disowned us—refusing to give
us His name, His love, His trust… and we were left to
fight for ourselves in a world dedicated to our destruction…*God's Bastard Sons*!

"But the madness has come at last!" Kain yelled
euphorically. "And beyond this seeming chaos, Paradise
awaits." Roland put his index finger to his lips, futilely
gesturing for Kain to be quiet. "Everything is coming to
fruition: all the hatred, all the chaos—all the seeds sown
by this society!

"Didn't I predict it all, Micheaux!" he said, tapping
Roland on the shoulder; and not only did Roland flinch
at the man's touch: he shuddered when he realized Kain
had used his name! "…Yes, Micheaux," Kain continued,
as Roland looked on in stunned horror, "all the great
men are seizing their madness today—you, Randolph,
Marenga…and where the great lead, the rest must follow. Only in madness can there be peace and unity!"

Roland felt the first stream of nervous sweat trickle
down his face. When he glanced up, several people
seemed to be scrutinizing him closely—*as if they recognized him*! He had the feeling that he was falling
through space: that solid ground was miles below him,
and that when this hurtling journey finally came to an
end, he would be splattered against the ground. Like
the last time Kain cornered him, he had reached the

point where he knew he couldn't listen anymore. To survive, he would have to *silence* Kain. He felt himself on the verge of strangling the man—doing whatever it took—to keep the man at bay.

However, seeing that murderous will building up in Roland, Kain only laughed out. "Yes, my brother, let that nigger hate set you free!" The man began cackling then; and as that horrible laughter sounded in the cramped space of the car, Roland knew his only chance was to get the hell out of there! He looked around for a means of escape, but the express train zoomed past 116th Street, going nonstop to 125th Street.

Roland's mind was a convoluted mess. The train was finally slowing down as 125th Street approached. Kain was still chuckling to himself. Roland's only thought was to flee the moment the doors opened. He needed to get away from all these people—

Someone opened the door between cars, and a wall of sound entered the car. Roland happened to glance in that direction as two black transit cops entered the car. He felt as though his intestines were knotting themselves! Kain laughed suddenly—*defiantly*—just as the train entered the station and began its rapid deceleration. The cops were looking in their direction; Kain was laughing even louder—*laughing like a madman*! The cops were walking over; Roland looked in horror from them to the cackling Kain. He had a sudden urge to knock the man senseless—

But then, the train came to a jarring halt and the doors burst open. Roland bolted for the door, bumping into an old woman; Kain ran after him, still laughing.

"It's Roland Micheaux!" Roland heard someone scream.

Roland was darting through the crowd now: he ran up the steps with Kain hot on his heels. The cops were yelling now, but Roland couldn't hear—couldn't *think*. All that there was, was running. He jumped over the turnstiles and ran outside, numb to everything. Kain was right behind him, giggling insanely; the cops were still hot on their trail, but once outside, Roland looked about the Harlem streets indecisively, not knowing which way to go—

"Run, nigger!" Kain said with a laugh. "I'm not ready for you to get caught yet!" The man tugged at Roland's arm then, and they ran down the street. Roland couldn't see anymore; Kain was in the lead and Roland let himself be led by the man's madness. A police car was coming down the street, going in the opposite direction from them. But when the cops spied them, they made a hasty U-turn and began pursuit, their siren blaring. As though by instinct, Kain turned down a relatively narrow one-way street. A truck had taken up half the street, and the rest was backed up with cars waiting for the light to change. The police car had to slam on its brakes to keep from hitting the truck. However, with its velocity, it slid, blocking the street as it ended up sideways.

As for Roland, all that there was, was running. He had

been running all his life, and it seemed as though it would never end. They ran for perhaps another five or so minutes, but it seemed like an eternity. They were now running along the wide expanse of Malcolm X Boulevard, seeing blocks lined with the usual tenements. Loud music was coming from one of the buildings—a party. There were people in Halloween costumes standing outside, on the stoop. Kain darted into the building; Roland followed the man, numb to the world. Outside, he heard the sirens coming—

"Run, nigger!" Kain encouraged him, cackling again. They ran into the hallway. The party was on the first floor, and the door to that apartment was ajar. Kain pulled Roland toward the door, while outside, the sirens stopped in front of the building. The party was dark and packed, with dozens of costumed forms moving erotically in the darkness. The air was stale and musty— since there were too many people. Kain led them through the party. The partygoers were just kids, most of them. However, they were drinking beer, and a few joints were being passed around. Everyone stared at Roland and Kain—they were obviously out of place: both were panting for air and sweating. They looked like *killers*.

Kain held Roland's arm and pulled him hastily toward the back of the apartment. People made way. At the back, Kain pulled the window open and hopped outside—into the back alley; Roland followed him, and the two disappeared into the darkness.

Everyone was staring quizzically at the scene, when, all of a sudden, the front door burst open again. Four policemen ran into the dark room with their guns drawn. Several people screamed; the kids holding the joints tossed them to the floor—

"Where'd they go!" a ruddy-faced policeman roared. He entered threateningly; everyone made way, but remained mute. The policeman grabbed a quailing kid by his costume—a toga—practically ripping it off. The kid was in shock, standing there with only his drawers on; the cop flung him to the side, going farther into the room with his gun still drawn. The other cops followed suit, screaming questions and demands that nobody seemed able to decipher. Who did it, nobody could say for sure; but somehow or another, a beer bottle was thrown in the dark room, hitting the ruddy-faced cop in the jaw. In that dark chamber, a gunshot suddenly rang out—an involuntary reaction to being hit, perhaps. And then, all of a sudden, people were running and screaming; there was another gunshot, and then another as the panicky screams pealed in the air; and everywhere, there was madness.

Randolph had walked out of the television studio and into the cold night air. For a while, there had been no more worries about struggling to hold on; no more worries about what he *should* have done, but didn't; no more worries about what he *wanted* to do, but couldn't. For once, the world had had boundless possibilities. He had walked at a brisk pace, letting his legs and instincts guide him. A cold, biting wind had been blowing through his thin suit—but since he had had no worries, nothing had seemed to matter.

Like Roland Micheaux, he had known there was no going back. He had seen no point in thinking about how many people he had just impacted by his desertion of it all. That was what had worn him down these last four years: the reality of how many lives he was impacting; and, worse, the reality of how many lives remained unchanged, no matter what he did.

After an hour and a half, he looked up to find himself in Harlem. His hands were numb from the cold, and his teeth were beginning to chatter, but none of that mattered when he wandered into his childhood neighborhood. He was not initially sure where he was—since he had ceremoniously razed the two city blocks a year and a half ago, in order to make way for new construction. Standing before the cheering crowd, he had promised that by the end of his term, it would be a thriving community, with businesses and new housing. However, now, as he looked around, he saw that it was still a wasteland. The original financing had fallen through, and no other banks seemed interested in funding the venture. There were few streetlights here, so the piles of rubble were only dull silhouettes, standing ominously in the cold night air. Besides his chattering teeth, and the wind as it whizzed past his ears, there were no other sounds in the air. He was about to turn around and leave when he noticed a huge sign beneath one of the few streetlights. It read:

YOUR TAX DOLLARS HARD AT WORK
Making Our Community Safer and Stronger
Another Community Project
By Your Mayor, His Honor:
Alexander J. Randolph

Randolph stared at it for a long while, as if unable to get the meaning of the words and why he would be connected to them. Around the razed blocks, there were waist-high, wooden police blockades. They were the quickly assembled kind, which were put together by the fitting of slots. After being exposed to the elements for a year and a half, a few of them had begun to rot. Everything seemed to be coming to an end—either through natural decay, or the unpredictable violence of men.

Bewildered, he pushed aside one of the police barricades and began to stumble through the dark piles of rubble. His pace was slow now. Did he really play on these streets as a child? Where were all of the colors and joyful sounds that he remembered? He walked on, willing himself to remember the people who had lived here.

He stumbled over something soft. In the darkness, he looked down at the ground, trying to figure out what he had stepped on. He bent lower, frowning—but when he finally realized what it was, a muffled shriek escaped from his throat, and he backed away in horror. *It was a body!* Actually, it was Feingold's corpse. It was lying where the bum had left it; and a few meters away, was the bum's corpse, lying where Kain had left it. Randolph stumbled over the second body as he backed away from Feingold. He cried out again when he saw. There were two dead men at his feet; and yet, in his state of mind, those two corpses weren't simply men that had been killed the day before. This was a graveyard he was in—a graveyard of dreams! He had personally reduced these blocks to rubble, and now all the restless spirits were emerging from their graves.

As he descended into madness, he saw the ghosts of his past everywhere. His mother had succumbed to breast cancer two decades ago, but she now stood before him in a tawdry outfit; his sister had met her end through an AIDS-infected heroin needle, but now she was reaching up her hand, as though to claw out his eyes. Out of the abyss of his past, only his brother, Roger, was still alive—but Randolph was backing away again. As the madness tightened its grip, he saw hundreds of playmates and lovers and passing acquaintances, who had met their end through the streets. All of them were reaching out their hands like zombies. He had desecrated their graves, and they were going to drag him down into their hell to take revenge—

He turned and bolted for the sidewalk! Twice, he fell to the ground and scraped his legs on exposed metal rods, but nothing would stop him. He was running for his life, seized by the kind of terror that only the insane knew. The world of men was somewhere out there—beyond the police barricade. The ghosts were still hot on his heels; they merged with the images and sounds of the day's riot, so that it was if all of hell's demons were after him.

In his terrified haste, he tried to hurdle the barricade at the curb—but his trailing foot hit the top, so that he found himself toppling through the air. He screamed out when he saw he wasn't going to make it, then he grunted as he fell heavily to the ground. He lay there for a moment, still trembling as he panted for air and winced from the pain...but there was silence again. Looking back confusedly at the rubble, he saw nothing but shapeless silhouettes; he heard nothing but the wind. He got slowly to his feet and looked around longingly. Eventually, he limped off, his mind numb...

On the next block, there were again streetlights and the tall, inhabited tenements that he had known from his youth. Nevertheless, there was nothing here for him. He walked on, still shivering—from the cold and the thought of spirits. He went on like this for about ten more minutes, letting himself get lost down the blocks of his former life. He was limping down the sidewalk when sirens suddenly blared behind him; he barely managed to turn his head before speeding police cars blasted past him. He almost fell to the ground as he whirled. The next block was Malcolm X Boulevard; suddenly and inexplicably, the air filled with the crisp pops of gunfire.

He stared ahead, squinting as the cars' emergency lights blinded him; their blaring sirens deafened him. Yet, the effect of all this chaos was strangely hypnotic. Mesmerized, he looked on as people on the next block suddenly began to empty out into the street. Some of them were almost run over by cars. In fact the people were running for their lives, screaming and darting for cover as more gunshots sounded in the air. Now, police officers were fighting their way into the building, pushing past the fleeing people. Yet, still hypnotized, Randolph found himself slowly walking in that direction.

Some of the people were running toward him. Indeed, they were running in *every* direction. The people—*kids*, he realized—began to congregate on the street when they saw they were out of immediate danger. Besides, many of them had left their coats inside, and were shivering in only their Halloween costumes. Some of those who had run out soon collapsed in the middle of the street, succumbing to gunshots. People gathered around them, yelling for help as police officers ran about. Randolph was standing shoulder-to-shoulder with the people now; and overhead, it seemed as if every windowpane framed an eager face or faces. It was all a spectacle, and even Randolph found himself being drawn in. There were probably two hundred people on the street with him now—and hundreds more were coming out from the surrounding buildings. There was death in the air, and it was both repellent and attractive to all. People were jostling for better views of the dead and dying now—Randolph included. Half a dozen bodies now lay on the pavement and in the street—several others were on ambulance stretchers, getting ready for departure. Some moved and cried out; others lay still, in positions that one only saw amongst the dead.

Ambulances and more police cars were arriving. Randolph again had to squint to protect his eyes from the glare of the swirling red and blue lights. Police officers were yelling for people to stand back. Paramedics moved quickly from one body to another, trying to discern which ones still had a chance at life. Then, all at once, a woman's voice pierced the air:

"Jimmy! *Jimmy*!"

People were moving out of the way; Randolph looked to see a voluptuous black woman about thirty-five, who was dressed only in a pink bathrobe, slippers, and curlers. Her face seemed to be fresh with the shock and despair that was slowly draining from other people's faces.

"Where's my son!" the woman cried when she burst to the front of the crowd. She got no answer. Everyone was silent, including the policemen. However, she was soon wailing, having to be held back by two policemen, because she finally saw her boy's corpse lying on the sidewalk. At first, she cried hysterically; but then, gripped by the strangeness of the moment, she turned to the crowd and wiped her eyes with the wide sleeves of the robe. "He wasn't a bad child," she said; and right there on the bloody sidewalk, above the sirens and amid the flashing lights, she gave the eulogy, and everyone listened; and even those who didn't know the boy, stood solemnly and nodded along to her words.

Randolph was feeling the biting cold again. His fingers were fully numb, but he wasn't shaking anymore. Like everyone else, all he could do was listen to the woman's words. A nearby ambulance took off suddenly; and as its siren blared in the air, the woman burst into sobs. Randolph needed to leave this place. He went to walk away when the woman suddenly noticed him and frowned.

"*Mayor*?" she said in disbelief, her eyes wide.

Randolph froze, looking at the woman warily. Whispers cascaded through the crowd as his presence was announced.

"Mayor, what's going on here!" the woman cried in despair. Randolph opened his mouth to speak, but nothing came out. "We thought you was gonna stop this kinda shit from happening!" the woman screamed.

There were people all around him now, he realized. He tried to hide his fear with a nervous smile...but they were all around him now, and there was nowhere to go! More voices cried out:

"...That nigga ain't done *shit* for us. What the hell he doing here... Probably looking for votes...!"

Harsh voices rang in Randolph's ears; then suddenly, he found himself being pushed, tugged and punched. He guarded his face with his numb hands, feeling himself being hit all over—in his ribs, in his thighs, in his back, in his neck; but all of the blows were dull, actually bring sensation back to his numb body. The voices waxed in the air, until he thought that there were *thousands* around him, all wanting a piece of his flesh to pummel. He dropped to his knees, feeling blows raining down on him as they had rained down on Andropov. Yet, just then, he was pulled up gruffly. He thought that was the end for him; some angry screams punctuated the air— but the blows had stopped. He looked around confusedly, realizing that the police were leading him away now.

"Yeah, you got the police to protect you, but who *we* got!" a defiant voice screeched. Randolph looked up to see the woman in the bathrobe, her tears gone. Her face was disfigured into a scowl, as were the faces of most others. The half dozen policemen fought their way through the crowd and toward a patrol car. When they reached it, they pushed Randolph into the back seat and slammed the door shut. Two white officers got in the front and drove off as quickly as they could. They inched their way through the sea of undulating bodies; the people outside the car glared and yelled and shook their fists. Randolph closed his eyes; but even with his eyes shut, he kept seeing the angry faces of the people who were no longer his. He was fleeing from it all now, and he was happy for it. He became aware that he was hyperventilating, and consciously took some slow, deep breaths—

"Mr. Mayor?"

Randolph looked up, realizing that the young policeman in the passenger seat had been talking to him for some time now.

"Yeah?" Randolph said, distractedly, as he looked out of the window again. Outside, there were more angry faces.

"Do you want us to take you home, sir?"

Randolph stared at the man absentmindedly again. He nodded his head after a while, still taking deep, slow breaths. The car was finally free of the crowd now. The angry voices faded from the air, but they still resounded in his mind. That was when the young officer spoke up again:

"Where *is* your home, sir?" the man asked. He was only asking for directions, but Randolph stared at him for a long while before chuckling to himself and lying back in the hard, uncomfortable seat.

As they ran, Kain laughed at the chaos they had left behind: Roland only ran. He no longer really believed the things happening around him were real. Something had been short-circuited in him. He could see and smell and *feel*, but he couldn't really process anything anymore. He followed Kain because his mind offered no other alternatives. Indeed, when Kain opened a manhole cover and began to lead him down one dark, smelly sewer corridor after another, Roland could see the rats and filth, but his mind produced no thoughts, no fears—no *reactions* to any of it.

Presently, as they trudged through the muck, Kain laughed and looked back at him. His voice was both calm and menacing as he said, "I'm not going to let you out of my sight, Micheaux. I want to be there when they put a bullet in your head."

When Roland cringed, Kain only laughed.

"Don't worry, Micheaux," the man went on, patting Roland on his shoulder, "they'll definitely want you alive—to show you around like some kind of freak at the carnival. After all you've done, they'll have to make an example of you, boy: rape, murder, kidnapping...and now, inciting a riot!" At that, Kain began to laugh like a second-rate cartoon villain; yet, even then, Roland was so numb that all he could do, was follow....

Eventually, Kain led him to a side chamber, where he had his hideout. Roland looked about confusedly at the basement chamber. The reality of the place—its existence in the sewers—was as surreal as everything else. The TV was still on; and as the volume was on mute, images of the day's violence seemed more fantastic somehow. While Roland stood passively on the threshold, Kain walked over to the TV and turned up the volume. However, the first words that Maria Santos said were: "Roland Micheaux is a menace to society!" There was a split screen, with Maria Santos on one side, and one of her roving reporters on the other. The reporter was in front of the building that Kain and Roland had run through only fifteen minutes ago.

"Two kids have been killed," the reporter cried, "and a dozen wounded, including police officers."

Maria Santos was so enraged that she shook as she declared: "We have to get Roland Micheaux behind bars as soon as possible—before he causes any more damage!"

Kain switched off the television; and the sudden silence shocked Roland back into consciousness. He felt suddenly faint, but managed to stumble over to the couch. The day's events flew through his mind as he collapsed onto the couch. Some of the springs were exposed, and they dug into him, but he only stared up at the ceiling. "This can't go on," he whispered after a few seconds. He nodded his head as the truth confronted him. "—I have to...turn myself in—"

"*What*!" Kain said in disbelief. He was still standing by the television.

"I'm turning myself in," Roland said more forcefully, sitting up on the couch.

Kain scrutinized him with pursed lips, then shook his head, saying, "You're no fun, Micheaux. You give up too easily—"

"This is a *game* to you?" he said, finally seeming to come to his senses. "People are *dead...kids*!"

However, Kain only shook his head sorrowfully

again, saying, "You were just a fatalist all along," he lamented, "—waiting to be screwed. I should have seen that before—wouldn't have wasted so much time on you. You weren't *worth* it."

For some reason, Roland laughed. "Sorry to disappoint you," he mumbled under his breath.

Kain tried to reason with him: "You *can't* turn yourself in, Micheaux—not yet."

"That's right: you haven't had your fun yet," he said with a sardonic sigh.

"You just need time to clear your head—this is no way to go out, is it?"

"...All those kids at the party," Roland whispered, shaking his head as the reality of it hit him again. He sat back on the couch, staring at the ceiling. "I can't let anyone else die—"

"*Fuck* everyone else!" Kain raged, so that Roland flinched. "You're just like me, Micheaux," the man went on, "—driven by *hate*!"

"What the hell are you talking about!"

"You wanted to show them all, didn't you? The world, I mean—after they killed your father. That's why you were so driven to be successful—you wanted to show them that you weren't what they were saying. All those years, studying hard with hate in the back of your mind, you only wanted to step above them and say: '*Fuck you all! I made it anyway*!' There was no choice but to show them all—no matter the cost. All the self-sacrifice, the drive! There was a *killer* in you, Micheaux— you didn't care about nothing but winning: showing them all! You probably even hate your job, don't you?"

Roland couldn't think about that now: he shook his head wearily and looked away. When he sat back on the couch, the exposed springs gored him again—

"You liked the money," Kain went on. "You wanted the status; but at the end of the day, you hated the job and everything it represented: all those frivolous lawsuits—"

"What difference does it make!" he cried in frustration.

Kain's eyes had a strange gleam in them as he whispered: "Hate *is* everything—"

"I don't care!" Roland said in desperation—he had needed to speak up: to do anything to drown out Kain's voice, but:

"That's right—one thing at a time," Kain cooed to him. "You need to think, don't you: to clear your head—"

"Shut up!" Roland begged. "Just keep quiet!" He got off the couch and began pacing nervously.

"Yes, I'll be quiet," Kain went on in a singsong voice. "But first, if I may, let me suggest that we both change our clothes—there's a bin over there with some extra clothes. We need something to throw the police off."

"I'm turning myself in, remember," he said, feebly, "—what do I need a disguise for?"

"That's right," Kain placated him, the way someone

talked a raving lunatic off a ledge, "you're turning yourself in, but you want to do it on your own terms, don't you? You just don't want anyone to grab you off the street, holding you there like a criminal. You want to walk to the police precinct with some dignity: do it like a *man*!"

Roland stared at him hopelessly, realizing how thoroughly the man knew him—and how easy it was for him to be manipulated. It was at that moment that the two men locked in Kain's dungeon started banging on the door.

"—What's that!" Roland gasped, instinctively horrified. There was a terrible urgency to the banging; the door seemed like a supernatural barrier, to some demon dimension.

"*Ah*," Kain said with a laugh as he turned toward the door in the corner. "How's that for perfect timing! I almost forgot." And then, to Roland: "Come over and I'll show you."

"What's in there?"

"The answer to all your questions, Micheaux," Kain said inscrutably. "Behind this door..." he took Roland's trembling arm and led him up to the entrance "is everything you've been running from all your life." Roland was beginning to lose his will again, and this alarmed him. He felt giddy and sick by the time they reached the door. Kain was just about to open it, but then he laughed in a self-deprecating manner, as though he had forgotten something vital. "Oops," he said then, taking out Weiss' gun from the small of his back. (Roland looked on in horror!) "Can't be too careful," he said, winking at Roland.

When Kain pulled open the door, the effluvium of the place made Roland back away: he almost retched; and then, the two filthy white men scrambled out, onto the floor of the basement, their chests heaving.

"*What the hell....!*" Roland squealed.

"Let me handle this," Kain said, still with his disconcerting calmness. All Roland could do was stand there, feeling himself being devoured by the (un)reality of the two men on the ground—and of everything else...

"Okay," Kain started then, addressing the panting men, "have you figured out what madness is yet, Dr. Fishman? How about you, Mr. Weiss?"

Weiss seemed even more out of sorts than Fishman. The psychiatrist was so thin and frail that he conjured images of Nazi death camps; but while Weiss still had his girth, he had cracked in one night. The man could do little more than stare mutely, with the eyes of a dog that was both terrified of its master and willing to do whatever its master wanted.

"—Please..." Fishman begged, beginning to sob on the ground.

"You've had three weeks now to come up with an answer, Dr. Fishman—you're not proving to be a good student."

"We'll do whatever you want!" he begged again.

"All I want—all I've *ever* wanted—is for you to tell me what madness is. Do you want to live, Dr. Fishman? I'm beginning to think that you have some death wish—you definitely won't last much longer."

"*Please!*" Fishman cried again.

"Answer the question!" Kain raged, and he cocked the pistol and loomed over the sobbing doctor threateningly. "Do you want to live?"

"Yes!" cried the doctor.

"You desire to live, and yet you can't tell me what madness is? Do you want to live?" he demanded again.

"Yes!" Fishman cried.

"Then, what is madness!"

"I don't know!"

"I'm really losing patience with you, doctor!"

"There is no answer!" Fishman cried in desperation. "No matter what I tell you, you tell me I'm wrong. There is no answer!" he said through his sobs, "—you probably don't know yourself!"

Kain laughed at the assertion, shaking his head. "Then, you're saying that madness is unknowable?"

"...Yes," he said, unsure, willing to do anything to appease Kain.

"*Wrong!*" Kain raged, cocking the gun again. Fishman screamed; the previously mute Weiss began mumbling something to himself. "Do you know that you want to live?" Kain demanded again.

"Of course I do!"

"Then how can you *not* know what madness is...!" Kain was silent for a while, then he took a deep, ominous breath. "Last time, doctor," he said, now bending down and squatting on his hamstrings, so that the gun was practically touching the frail doctor's trembling head. "What is madness?"

Roland wanted to do something, but he was frozen in place; he had the sudden idea that all his substance had left him, and that even if he tried to tackle Kain, he would only fly past the man, like a vapor—

"What is madness!" Kain screamed.

Desperate, Fishman cried, "Wanting—wanting to live!" And as he said it, he closed his eyes tightly, averting his face, as though expecting the thundering report of the gun, but:

"Congratulations, Dr. Fishman," Kain said, smiling. He stood up slowly now, and stood staring down at the doctor. "Madness is wanting what you can't have."

Fishman began crying uncontrollably, because the logic of the words told him that he was a dead man. Kain looked back at Roland then, and nodded; Roland could only stare. While Fishman's cries filled the chamber, Kain turned to the doctor and began raising the gun. Roland braced himself for the horrible sight, but:

"You may go now, Doctor," he said in a calm, almost indifferent, voice. "Take Mr. Weiss with you."

Fishman stared at him, wondering if this was another perverse mind game. However, Kain was walking away now. As he was leaving the room, he gestured to Roland with the gun: "Come, Micheaux, there is much work for us to do yet."

If Kain had kept the television on for five more seconds, he and Roland would have seen it all. Maria Santos' cameras had been on the faces of the crowd, showing one dark, brooding mass. The people of Harlem had still been in shock. The police had put up a barrier to keep them at bay; in the meanwhile, officers had gone about the grim task of detailing the crime scene.

However, in time, the people's shock turned to outrage. Someone started yelling about what had been done to the Thomases and Marenga. The same thing was happening to them now! The police were killing their children—exterminating them like *rats*—and even the goddamn Mayor, a *black* man, didn't give a shit about them! The outrage grew until several people began yelling across the barrier at the police. Field commanders were consulted, and these cautious men advised their subordinates to break up the crowd—and move the people along before they became violent. Unfortunately, when the policemen began telling them to move on, the people of Harlem only yelled back louder. One enterprising officer took out his baton; but in trying to goad a screaming black man into compliance, he only stoked the outrage further. This officer got punched in the face; and then, a millisecond later, the whole angry mass ran through the police barrier. Sometimes people revolted because an injustice was too egregious to go unchallenged. Sometimes, when people revolted, the trigger, itself, was irrelevant—like the proverbial straw that broke the camel's back; sometimes people revolted because of what they had lost; sometimes people revolted because they had nothing to lose. There were those who made a conscious decision to revolt, and those who surrendered their wills to it, so that they could claim afterwards that they had had no choice. For the people on the Harlem streets, the precise reasons probably did not matter anymore. All that there was, was a world of action—and Maria Santos' cameras were there to capture it all. Tomorrow, or the day after that, or the day after that...there would be consequences; but now, as cries and gunshots rose in the air, there were only actions and reactions.

Marenga regained consciousness about two hours after he opened his pale, soulless eyes to the world. Because of his corpse-like expression, those gathered around—doctors, policemen and Botswana Glade— thought that he had sustained brain damage. The chief doctor was in the process of checking Marenga's vital signs when his previously blank eyes looked up quizzically at the man. The doctor gasped.

"Do you know your name?" asked the doctor. He was an old white man with a benevolent face; and over the man's shoulders, Botswana Glade and the police detective hovered, like relatives looking into a crib to hear a baby's first words.

Marenga wanted to curse the man—to scream that of course he could understand—but he was too weak. He barely managed to nod.

"What's the last thing you remember?" the man asked again.

Marenga went to say, *Wishing you all dead!* but curbed himself. "...Rally," he whispered at last.

The old man smiled in relief, before ominously adding, "The police are going to have to ask you some questions now."

Marenga grunted.

The detective stepped up now. Maybe it was the residual effects of his heart attack, but the detective's face struck him as a plate with a repulsive dish. His lips were like greasy sausage links; his nose was like a half-eaten carrot; his eyes were like rotten eggs; and the entire dish was swarming with some nasty-looking gravy, which Marenga in time discerned to be the man's perspiration. The man walked up with a macho swagger and declared:

"I just want to fill you in on what has happened since your fainting spell at your little rally." Marenga scowled at his tone. "First, a riot broke out, right in front of City Hall; then, some raping, murdering lunatic ran off with a little white girl; and when confronted by a cop, he shot him. In the resulting police chase through Harlem, there have been several other deaths—"

"Yeah!" Botswana Glade exploded at the detective's

mention of Harlem, "and you can bet your *last* dollar that we'll be organizing another rally tomorrow in Harlem for all those slain and wounded kids! And don't think we forgot about the Thomases, you bastards!"

The detective fought his every impulse to remain calm; he turned back to Marenga: "Look, Marenga, things are *tense* out here, and something major's going to happen if all of this isn't resolved. There have been little skirmishes going on all over the city; and on top of everything, the Mayor quit!" At these last words, Marenga showed interest for the first time. However, that was when Botswana Glade broke in:

"What do you expect him to do about it! You want him to sweep it all under the rug, don't you? Want him to make some stupid ass, Rodney King, 'Can't we all get along?' statement before the press? This is all your doing!" Botswana Glade roared, his horse teeth bared threateningly: "Don't try to make us responsible for your mess, you bastards!"

"Now wait a *goddamn* minute!" the detective yelled back at last. "You're the ones who started this mess, with your goddamn rallies!"

"You evil devils!" Botswana Glade squealed, "...always putting blame on somebody else!"

"—*Enough!*" the doctor yelled. "Both of you get the *hell* out of here! This is a *hospital!*"

Botswana Glade and the detective looked at the doctor confusedly, scowled as they looked back at one another, then left begrudgingly. The doctor nodded to Marenga and left as well; but when they were all gone, Marenga closed his eyes contentedly and chuckled to himself.

All the media stars were out tonight. Maria Santos was almost hoarse by now. The scenes of the riot—of all the riots—were before them now; and her screechy homily on the bestiality of their society was everywhere. Her homily encompassed Randolph's desertion, Roland Micheaux's murderous rampage, Marenga's irresponsibility, Botswana Glade's maniacal agenda—everything and everybody, it seemed.

On another channel, Botswana Glade was standing outside Marenga's hospital. "This should be seen as an attack on the black community!" the man shouted, his horse teeth bared to the cameras. "First the Thomas murders, and now this..."—he searched frantically for a word—"*Raid*...! Yes, the people are justified in rebelling against the police! Their raid on those young kids in that party was ill-conceived and simply *racist* in origin! This kind of ambush—and it was exactly that— would *never* have happened in a white community. Never would you have police officers firing into a crowd of innocent white kids. But this kind of thing happens on a daily basis in our community!" he raged, waving his bony hand in the air. "Moreover," he continued, his eyes boring into the camera with new contempt, "were it not for the fact that reporters and policemen were searching desperately for a black man who had supposedly harmed some of their own—not only a cop, but a rich white family—and that our weak-minded Mayor happened to stumble into the mess, we would not be hearing about any of this! It's time for us to forge a mandate for action! There will be a rally in Harlem tomorrow! It is time for us to mobilize and put an end to such attacks, by exercising our constitutional right to protect ourselves...!"

At the same time, in Brooklyn, Captain Miller, the man in charge of the entire Roland Micheaux manhunt, was on the air as well. He stood on the steps of police headquarters, giving a statement to the press. About a dozen uniformed police officers stood in the background as he declared, "Recent events have not, in our opinion, shown a pattern of police brutality, but, on the contrary, a pattern of brutality *against* policemen. First," he went on, raising his hand threateningly in the air, "there was Officer Flanders' murder by that killer and rapist, Roland Micheaux; and now, once again, we have an incident, instigated by Roland Micheaux, where the policemen were attacked by a mob—simply because they were trying to bring this madman to justice. That was the only reason they fired: they were *defending* themselves! And now, we have a riot, with people attacking the police directly! In view of these events, many officers have been contemplating going on strike to show this city our worth—"

"When?" yelled a reporter.

"We will decide that tomorrow—after the memorial for Officer Flanders and all the slain and wounded officers who fell over the last few days." He looked into the camera ominously now. "One man, Roland Micheaux, has caused all of this. The quicker we get him off the streets, the better we will all be. Just ask Officer Mucelli here," he said, putting his arm around the young cop at his side. "He dealt with that killer firsthand. This is a *real* hero here!"—Mucelli looked like he was in shock; his face seemed *haggard*—"Yes, here is a man who went out there and did his job!"

A reporter asked: "How are you feeling, Officer?"

Mucelli leaned over to the microphone timidly: "Fine, sir."

Miller beamed; but then, another reporter asked, "If all the policemen go to Flanders' memorial, won't there be a shortage of officers to control the possible unrest tomorrow if Botswana Glade and his supporters get out of hand?"

Miller snorted in disgust, then went on: "If the choice is between paying homage to our fallen brothers, and putting out our necks for people who don't care about us, then we choose to pay homage..."

And of course, McPrice was there. She was back at her upper west side office, answering questions from the assembled reporters.

"What do you make of the latest events, Councilwoman?" a reporter asked.

"Well," she started with a sigh, "without a doubt, they call for change—especially in terms of leadership. The final result, in terms of innocent deaths, was unfortunate, but let us not forget the facts here. As I have been told, the police went to arrest that maniac, Roland Micheaux, who was even then running from them. A mob attacked the police officers, and they defended themselves. The final result of that pursuit is unfortunate—even *tragic*—but the thing is not to fight ourselves. We have to get that fugitive to justice—lock him behind bars with the other homicidal maniacs. In this instance, we might even get a chance to use the death penalty. After all, Roland Micheaux has killed twice; and, in the midst of all of this," she added in a pained voice, "let us not forget that Cindy Phelps is still in a coma from when he shot her in the head. Let us not forget that a scared little girl might have to grow up without her mother. No, Roland Micheaux and misguided, self-absorbed men like Marenga—and his lackey, Botswana Glade—are the cause of all of this strife. Combine that with weak leadership from the Mayor, and you have a dangerous situation. We cannot constantly go on blaming the police for everything. They are doing their job, which is fighting crime, and we must support them if we expect to have a lawful society...."

Lieutenant Ericsson had watched the captain's press conference on the steps of police headquarters, then gone back to his office with a rising sense of alarm. While in Harlem, tear gas was being used to disperse the angry crowds, he sat in the darkness of his office by himself. The initial forensic report on Flanders' crime scene, and the murder weapon, had come back half an hour ago. Flanders had been shot in the back, which didn't make sense, since he and Micheaux had supposedly been fighting hand-to-hand. According to Mucelli's testimony, Micheaux had had Flanders up against the car, so how in the hell could he be shot in the back...! However, the really troubling thing was that there were no fingerprints on the gun—not even Mucelli's! It had obviously been wiped clean; and since Micheaux certainly hadn't wiped it before throwing it to the ground and running off, that left only one person: Mucelli!

Ericsson had said before that something was very wrong, but he was only now beginning to see the full extent of it. Just before his captain's press conference, he had been reading the statement of the doorman at Micheaux's condominium. According to the man, Mindy Phelps, the little girl that Micheaux had supposedly kidnapped, had been brought in the night before by the nanny—something that had happened at least once before. Micheaux had left his house with the little girl the next morning, about eight in the morning. Another report from a cabbie said that he had dropped them both off at the Phelps home about 8:45 that morning—five minutes before neighbors heard the gunshots and saw him running away with Mindy. However, as the coroner had told him at the crime scene, Dallas Phelps had been dead for *hours*. According to Micheaux's doorman, the man had been at home all night with his girlfriend; and before that, he had been at a news conference! Those were all practically *air-tight* alibis—unless there was something Ericsson was missing. It was still possible that Micheaux had shot Cindy Phelps, but the gun had been in her hand when they found her; and as Micheaux had fled from the scene with such haste, it was doubtful that he had planted it on her! On top of all that, there were only two sets of prints on the gun—both belonging to the couple—so it was looking more like a murder-suicide all the time. The only thing that kept Ericsson's doubt alive was the fact that Micheaux had run. The man had run for some reason—run for *blocks!*—and in Ericsson's experience, innocent men didn't run like that. Maybe things would be clearer if they could only find the missing nanny—whom some were suggesting Micheaux had killed, or who had been an accomplice. The doorman had mentioned that she was a mess—and had come in the middle of the night, as though running from something. They had found a cryptic letter back at Micheaux's condominium, written by the nanny, in which she said that she was leaving for Boston and that Micheaux could "handle the situation" any way he pleased. Obviously something had happened—but *what?*

Ericsson groaned in the darkness: he didn't like this at all! He was waiting for the final forensic report on the Phelps home. That was why he was still there. They had found semen all over the place: hopefully some of it was Micheaux's—or at least, not the husband's. With all that had happened—and all that seemed on the *verge* of happening—Ericsson was almost *hoping* that Micheaux had done it!

There were still about half a dozen reporters at Charlotte McPrice's office. It had been a busy night, with the Mayor quitting and all the riots. Most of the reporters had stood around to ask her follow-up questions and ingratiate themselves with the woman who was now, for all intents and purposes, the Mayor of New York City. After answering her last question, McPrice waved to them all and wandered off into her private office. They all watched her go, each one admiring the graceful precision of her movements.

I wonder where my husband is? she wondered when the door was closed behind her. It wasn't that she really cared: she was only concerned that he wasn't out somewhere, getting drunk. Yet, even that might work for her at this point: portray her as a woman who could overcome her husband's weaknesses. And she certainly had!

In time, she would have to divorce him, but she had plenty of time to think about that. For now, nothing could stop her. In a matter of days, she was going to win the election and become the Mayor of New York City! She was just about to smile to herself when she heard a knock on the door. The prospect of another interview was loathsome to her, but she was a pragmatist.

"Come in!" she called, turning around just as two plain-clothed policemen entered the room.

The sight of their badges left her nonplused for moment, and there was a look on their faces that she couldn't quite gauge. Their expressions were a strange combination of respect and dread as they walked up to her. She frowned.

"Good night, ma'am," one started, bowing his head reverentially.

"Hello, officers," she ventured, aware that this was just a polite prelude to something much more weighty and troubling.

"It's about your husband, ma'am," the other one added.

What has he done now? she thought warily, just as the first policeman sighed sorrowfully, saying:

"He's dead, ma'am."

"*What!*" She was actually shaking; she took an unconscious step back and rested against her desk. Her mind was suddenly sluggish. She hadn't loved him—at least, not in the last few years—but still...! "How?" she whispered.

"He was shot, ma'am—seems like a suicide, but it looks suspicious. We're still conducting an investigation."

"What happened?"

"He was found in his car. It was parked in an alley behind the bar where he was drinking. Nobody even heard a gunshot."

She nodded her head, but hadn't really heard.

"We're sorry about this, ma'am," one ventured.

"Yeah," added the other. "The body is down at the morgue, if you want to see it."

She nodded vaguely, but her mind was numb.

"We liked what you said on the air. You always support cops: we need that right now."

She nodded to them as they bowed their heads and left. Her husband was dead! She didn't know what she was feeling. It wasn't exactly grief; still, there had been good times—before the man she had fallen in love with turned into a coward and a drunkard. Maybe that was the thing to be mourned. She sat down on a couch to think about it all, just as someone knocked on the door again. Before she could say anything, the door opened. It was Wisinski. He stepped up to her quickly, excitement gleaming in his eyes; she rose to hug him.

"How are you doing? I guess you've heard the news?" he said when they disengaged. His eyes were still gleaming with excitement.

She frowned unconsciously, but went on: "I'll be all right. I just can't believe he's gone."

"Well," Wisinski said with contempt, "he *deserved* to die."

"Nobody deserves..." But she again looked at him, seeing the strange excitement in his eyes. They stared at one another then: she searching and he letting her see. Finally seeing, her breath got caught in her throat as a cold shiver went down her back. She went to sit back down, but Wisinski took her hand and pulled her up again. She was staring at him the way someone stared at a stranger—at a *killer!*

"Come now," he said, supporting her weight and steering her toward the door. "I told the press to stick around: you have another announcement to make. Now *nothing* can stop you!" he said excitedly, as McPrice shuddered.

While the police dispersed the last of the crowds with tear gas and rubber bullets, Botswana Glade palliated them into strategic retreat by vowing that tomorrow would be the day of reckoning. Randolph found himself walking up to his brother's upper west side co-op. His brother was the only thing that remained of his youth. Now, as Randolph pressed the intercom button for his brother's apartment, he couldn't feel his fingers anymore. It had been a twenty-minute walk from where the policemen had let him out. Randolph had walked the blocks slowly, stiffly, feeling the frigid air in his bones.

He did not exactly know why he had come here—just as he did not know why he had walked into the mob—but it was clear to him now that something self-destructive was guiding him.

He took his numb finger away from the button and waited. He was standing in front of a glass door, which had a cardboard cutout of Count Dracula with a caption that read, "Happy Halloween." The room beyond the glass had a luxurious aura about it. There was a plush couch and two antique armchairs, all situated on an exquisite oriental rug. The light from the lamps reflected off the tan upholstery, giving the room a golden quality. There were also some rubber plants and palms in the corners: a perfectly arranged scene. Yes, his brother, Roger had done well for himself after his stint in prison. The man had gotten his life back on track and was now a CPA, of all things. Maybe that, too, was why Randolph had come: to find out the secrets of his brother's magic. The man was happily married, with two beautiful kids.

Randolph looked at his watch. It was just past midnight. Maybe Roger was already sleeping; maybe Roger's wife and kids would be awakened as well; maybe Roger wouldn't be glad to see him after all. Where would he go now? He didn't want to be alone tonight—and he certainly couldn't go back to Gracie Mansion. He wasn't the Mayor anymore—he had given all of that up: had *fled* from it—

"Yes?" said a husky voice over the static of the intercom.

"Hello—*Roger*?—it's Alex!" he said, too loudly.

"*Alex*...! Thank God...! Come in!"

There was a loud, buzzing noise; Randolph pushed the door and stepped in cautiously, as though expecting something to break. The abundant heat of the chamber engulfed him at once. There was a momentary burning sensation on his exposed skin, which made him think that he was on fire. Still, he was relieved beyond reason to be out of the cold—and ostensibly away from ghosts. It was only after he entered the elevator that he found himself wondering what he was going to say to his brother. They were on good enough terms. They met for the big holidays: Thanksgiving, Christmas...birthdays. Still, since the summer that Randolph found out the truth about the world, there had been a certain stiffness between them. Randolph, distrustful of everything from that world, had never really accepted his brother back into his heart—even after the man began to make a success out of his life. In a sense, his temple had been destroyed that summer, and he had never been able to find another god. It seemed so obvious to him now—but the truth usually was.

Roger was standing in the doorway of his apartment when Randolph emerged from the elevator. The man was in a bathrobe, gesturing for Randolph to come. His brother was a plump man of average height, who had just turned forty-five.

While all over the city, people were being taken to hospitals and police stations by the droves, Randolph looked at his brother's concerned face, realizing that their positions had switched: that now his brother was the success, and he was the failure. Randolph walked toward his brother slowly, still arguing whether or not he should have come—

"I saw everything on TV," Roger said when Randolph was close enough.

"Lucky for me then," Randolph tried to joke. The men stared intently at one another for a weird moment.

"—Come in, come in," Roger said suddenly, as if coming out of a spell.

"Don't want to be seen in public with me, huh?" Randolph said, again trying to joke, but neither of them laughed.

They entered the living room. The lights were off, but the television was on, showing a news channel. Maria Santos was everywhere.

"Maybe I shouldn't have come over," Randolph found himself saying.

"Don't be ridiculous—"

"Did I wake you up?"

"Naw, I was watching television." However, there was still uneasiness between them. They stood staring at one another; and then, needing something to do, Roger turned and locked the front door. "I was just going to make some hot chocolate," he was saying now. "You want some?"

"Sure."

Roger gestured again, and they walked toward the kitchen. Just then, Roger's wife poked her head out of the bedroom, her hair in curlers. "Is everything all right, honey?" she asked.

"Everything's fine, Mary," Roger answered; and then: "It's only Alex."

"Oh...Alex," she said, sounding unsure.

"Hi, Mary," Randolph greeted her.

"Hi—you all right?"

"Yeah... I'm fine."

"Go back to sleep, honey," Roger said.

"I'm sorry if I woke you up, Mary," Randolph apologized.

"Oh, it's okay," she said, vaguely. "Good night."

"Pleasant dreams," Randolph said, and both men watched her head disappear.

Randolph was feeling uneasy about intruding again, but Roger was gesturing him to the kitchen now. Randolph sat down heavily at the kitchen table, while his brother put on the kettle.

"...So, you saw me give it all up, huh?" Randolph said sarcastically, trying to smile as he looked down at his well-groomed fingernails.

"I saw lots of strange things tonight."

"Yeah...me too."

After the uncomfortable silence, Roger went to the cupboard to get some mugs. Then, sitting down in the seat across from his brother, "What happened tonight?"

496 D. V. BERNARD

he began cautiously. "I mean, what have you been going through? First the divorce, and now this. What's *driving* you?"

"That's a good question, brother," Randolph said with another chuckle.

"...What are you going to do now?"

"What is there to do...? I won't starve, if that's what you mean."

"You really don't want to be Mayor anymore?" he asked incredulously.

"I don't know what the hell I want," he said in an offhand manner. "That's the most honest thing I can say to you. I just know I'm sick of it all. It *sickens* me...I don't want any part of it."

"What *really* happened tonight?" Roger said again, this time in a more ominous tone.

"Death," Randolph returned. "Eventually everyone looks up and sees death standing there; when that time comes, your only choices are surrendering to it, or running for dear life."

"Which did you choose?" his brother asked.

Once again Randolph chuckled to himself, but his brother only looked on warily.

"...You need a break from everything, Alex," Roger started, now convinced that his brother was having a nervous breakdown. "...Look, I, myself know how hard you worked. I've seen you...all my life—"

"You happy, Roger?" Randolph said abruptly, looking at his brother critically.

"What?"

"Are you happy? Are you *fulfilled* by your life?"

"...I suppose—*yeah*.... Why?"

"I just needed to know."

"Look," Roger started in a more determined tone, "we're not kids anymore, Alex."

"No, I guess we're not." And then: "I just came from our old neighborhood," he went on quickly, as if admitting a sin. "It's all in ruins now. There was going to be a development there, so I had it all destroyed." He laughed strangely. "Maybe that's the only way...nothing was ever built on sterile ground—there was always something there before: something that had to be destroyed to make way for progress."

Roger looked at him for a long while, a side of him terrified—either of his brother, or the world that could do this to the man who, for Roger's entire life, had been a kind of god—

The kettle began to boil; and a millisecond later, the kitchen door burst open as Roger's five-year-old daughter entered the room. "Daddy, I'm hungry," she complained, rubbing her eyes; then, looking up and seeing Randolph, an astonished smile suddenly came to her face: "Hi, Uncle Alex!" she said, giggling as he picked her up and put her on his knee.

"Worry no longer, my dear," Randolph said as he tickled her, "—feeding the hunger of little kids is what us grownups are for."

Kain and Roland snuck out of the sewers, emerging onto a dark, empty block. Roland could still hear Fishman's desperate cries in his mind. Sirens were blaring a few blocks away; every once in a while, he swore he heard gunshots and people screaming—

"Where the *hell* are we going?" Roland said abruptly.

"We're going to turn ourselves in," Kain responded flatly. "Isn't that what you wanted, Micheaux?"

"...Yeah," Roland said, surprised and confused. He looked over at Kain warily: "You're going to let me?" And he glanced uneasily at Kain's hand, because the man still held the handgun.

Kain only laughed softly; he looked at the gun as though he had forgotten about it, then put it in his pocket. "There, Micheaux—feel safer now?" And then, still smiling in his inscrutable way, he went on, "I've never forced you to do anything against your will, Micheaux—except maybe to listen and look, and draw conclusions from your observations. We all have free will—even the slaves among us. We all have power over that one vital thing: if we live or die. You have chosen to die."

Roland stared at him for a while. In frustration, he cried out: "What the *hell* do you expect me to do, Kain? You think I can go back home and act like none of this ever happened!"

"Here, Micheaux," Kain said, handing him the gun.

"I don't want it—"

"*Take* it!" Kain demanded, so that Roland held the thing tentatively. "There, Micheaux," Kain said with a menacing look, "now you can blow your fucking brains out! You want to die? *Die!*" While Roland stood there fidgeting, Kain grabbed Roland's hand—the hand with the gun—and began putting it to his temple. "*Do* it!" he raged, while Roland instinctively tried to fight him off. "*Do* it!" Kain demanded, until Roland began to sob, like Fishman had sobbed.

"Look at you!" Kain raged. "Your head's so fucked up, you're rushing to be some goddamn martyr. *Look* at you!" he went on in disgust. "Dreaming about going out in some cinematic, 'Disney Movie of the Week,' 'I want to do what's best' scene. Be *real*, Micheaux! You're a *nigger!*" Roland shook his head feebly and unconsciously. "You were never nothing but a nigger to them! Let the world fuck itself if it wants! Smell the madness in the air now: people wanting all kind of things they'll never receive—things they can't even conceptualize: justice, revenge, order, peace...*all* of that. They turned your goddamned life into passive entertainment, and yet you hate yourself so much you want to sacrifice yourself to them! You think you'll be at peace if you turn yourself in, Micheaux? You think that all of a sudden everyone will start loving one another? *Fuck* society!

"Your life is nothing but a passing news blurb, to be forgotten in a week's time. You think you're at peace with turning yourself in, but don't confuse peace with

500 D. V. Bernard

death—with *suicide*! Always fight death, Micheaux—
even if all you can manage is a couple of seconds. Make
death take you like a *man*—don't let him trick you into
doing the work for him. Death is a lazy bastard,
Micheaux. Most of the time he doesn't even have to lift
a finger—we're too easily tricked into doing his work
for him!"

But in that world of random violence, it was then that
a young black man came up behind them. Actually, it
was a youth, no older than seventeen. "Yo!" he called,
and when Roland and Kain looked around, they saw that
the youth had a revolver pointed at them.

"Gimmie *all* your shit!" he demanded. And then, seeing Roland holding the gun: "Drop it!"

Roland did as told. It was as if time were going in
some maddeningly convoluted loop, because he felt like
was back at the parking garage again, being robbed by
Lamar Smith.

"Back away from the gun!" the youth screamed again,
and Roland and Kain complied. Roland's entire body
throbbed with the pulse of his heart. Every time he
thought that it was over, it was only just beginning!
When Roland and Kain backed away far enough, the
youth picked up the gun and put it in the small of his
back; then, "Gimmie your shit!" he screamed again.

"'Gimmie your shit?'" Kain said, laughing with a
frown. "Now is that any way to ask for something?
Whatever happened to, 'Your money or your life?' At
least that had some style—"

"Shut the fuck up!" the youth screamed, but he was instinctively taken aback by something in Kain's eyes. "I ain't playing!" he said, maybe more to himself than them. "Gimmie *all* your shit!"

But Kain only laughed and turned to Roland, saying: "Here is a perfect specimen of society, Micheaux: a mind so corrupted by unattainable desires that—"

"Shut the *fuck* up!" the kid screamed hysterically. "I said, give me everything you got!" Then, suddenly recognizing Roland, the kid's eyes bulged. "I *know* you! You're that nigger on TV! I bet I can get money for you!"

Kain snickered: "These are the fools you're trying to defend, Micheaux: a thief wanting to turn you in to the police for a reward."

"Keep quiet, old man!"

Kain shook his head and smiled to himself; and then, as though remembering something more relevant to his time: "Come on, Micheaux," he said, grabbing Roland's arm and leading him away, "we have work to do—"

"Don't move!" the kid screamed, pointing the gun with a trembling hand, but Kain continued to pull Roland along. "*Stop!*" the kid yelled, but Kain ignored him; and Roland, caught in a world of indecision and horror, was pulled along like a swimmer caught in the undertow. It was then that the kid's gun went off; a moment later, Kain fell to the ground, going through the death throes on the filthy sidewalk. The man died like that old, fat cop had died—*horribly*. Yes, time was indeed following some maddeningly convoluted loop, because Roland and the kid stared down at Kain like Mucelli and him had looked at Flanders. Still, it was as though the kid had taken Roland's place in the loop, because he bolted first. For a moment, the only thing Roland could do was stare at Kain's unmoving body; but soon, the madness of the night—*of his entire life*—seemed to drop on Roland's head. The weight of it crushed him, but it also freed him in a way he had never thought possible. Whatever Kain had meant to him—had become to him in the last few hours—the man's sudden death sparked something in Roland that was raw evil. From some terrible place within himself, the rage escaped and burst to the surface like an erupting volcano. The kid was halfway up the block, but as Roland took off after him, the power of hell seemed to fuel his muscles. The kid kept looking back in horror, because Roland was like a demon pursuing him. The kid ducked into a side street; looking over his shoulder, he saw that Roland was only a few steps away! He aimed the gun and pulled the trigger; but somehow, miraculously, it jammed. And then, seeing that Roland was upon him, he let out an involuntary yelp as he was tackled.

There were no boundaries for Roland now; and so, he used all of his strength and will when he knocked the kid into a wall. The sound of the kid's head knocking the brick was blunt and horrible—*sickening*—but Roland couldn't hear anymore. He was pummeling the kid's unmoving head with his fist now. "*Nigger*!" he yelled as he smashed the kid's front teeth and broke his nose. "*Motherfucker*!" he screamed as he began pounding the kid's unprotesting head into the pavement.

He was in the middle of picking up the kid's head to smash it into the pavement, when he remembered Kain: remembered the strange bond they had somehow managed to forge; he remembered his mother and grandmother, and all the people he had ever professed to love; he remembered his pride and hope, now unrecognizable and useless to him; and then, with the last ray of light provided by his sanity, he saw himself, perched over the kid's bloody corpse like a vulture. The words he had called the kid were still resounding in the air. With a shudder, he got up. The kid was dead—there was no doubt about it. His hatred had driven him like nothing had ever driven him—just like Kain had said; and for the second time in his life, he had killed a man with his bare hands! The hatred had driven him and intoxicated him, but the high was fading away now. The hatred had been like heroin. At first, it had brought him to the heights of ecstasy; but now, as it left his system, it rendered his insides. He needed something to salve the pain—but that was all that addiction was: a desperate attempt to find some equilibrium between the highs and lows—between ecstasy and agony. *Kain*! Remembering the man, Roland backed away from the corpse and ran back the way he had come. How far he had fallen, that Kain was all that he had to stave off the pain…! Yet, a block away from where he had left Kain, he stopped. Hundreds of people were screaming, running down the block in terror! There was smoke in the air— tear gas—and four police riot vans were pursuing the people down the street, followed by police cruisers. Roland stared at it all, not knowing what to think. The world was chaos personified, and he seemed to be the source of it. He was a killer after all. Indeed, he was everything they were saying. Once, as a child, he had hoped to find his father an unrepentant nigger—just as bad as everyone was saying. Now, as he watched the people fleeing from the police, he knew *he* was that nigger. Only he could unite all the niggers behind him; only he could incite them to rise up against all the things they hated—and all the things that hated *them*. He had killed, and he wanted to kill again—*needed* to kill again—in order to ward off the cries of his addiction. However, when the thoughts reached his inner consciousness, he shuddered and scurried away—like a thief startled by the light.

THE MULTI-LIMBED BEAST

The world was awakening, but it was awakening to the same nightmare. Randolph awoke abruptly. He sprang up from the couch and scanned the strange room to get his bearings. Two children were lying on the floor; their backs were to him as they watched the huge television. On the TV, a bizarre cartoon character was doing something with other bizarre characters. Randolph stared at the screen for a few seconds, trying to make sense of the show, but it was impossible.

At any rate, he finally remembered he was in his brother's home. He went to lie back down; but as soon as he did, everything that had happened the night before came back to him. He sat up abruptly on the couch, bewildered. He felt sick. From the grandfather clock on the other side of the living room, he saw it was a little after seven o'clock. Roger's eight-year-old son was changing the channels now, holding the remote control in an authoritarian manner. His sister, not yet fully cognizant of the inequality inherent in their relationship, sat patiently, more interested in her doll than the television.

Randolph glanced at the screen, just as there was a brief glimpse of a crowd. There were hundreds of black people, with faces contorted by rage. Botswana Glade's face appeared for a millisecond; but then Joel, Roger's son, quickly changed the channel, so that two sweaty, entangled professional wrestlers appeared on the screen.

"Change it back!" Randolph yelled from the couch. Both children bolted around, surprised to see him up. Joel changed the channel.

"—Yes," Botswana Glade was saying, already surrounded by hundreds of people, "we are going to march down the street, and nobody's going to stop us!"

Randolph cringed, just as the scene changed back to the television studio. The anchorman, a white man who looked as though he had just come out of high school, looked into the camera uneasily and went over last night's riots. While he talked, the screen showed all the damage. Nine people were supposedly dead now; dozens of stores had been looted... Randolph stared at it in a daze, breathing shallowly. Perhaps two minutes passed with Randolph sitting there like that; and then, the anchorman continued:

"Charles Marenga is out of his coma and alert, but we haven't been able to speak with him—"

I've got to get the hell out of here! Randolph thought as he sprang up from the couch and tossed aside the blanket that had been covering him. He was wearing his pants and undershirt; he got his shoes from under the couch, then grabbed his shirt and jacket, which had been placed on the loveseat—

"What's going on!" Roger said, running out at the commotion.

"Everything's crazy!" Randolph said as he hastily buttoned his shirt.

Now, the anchorman was talking about the police rally that was going to be held at City Hall.

Roger's wife came out then, dressed in only a housecoat. "Is everything all right?"

"No," Randolph said, grimly, "—not at all."

She too stared at the television in silence. There was a report on the death of McPrice's husband now.

"You have an extra coat for me, Roger?" Randolph asked, remembering that he had left his at the TV studio.

"Yeah," Roger answered distractedly, going to the hall closet. But then he stopped, venturing, "Where are you going, Alex? Maybe I should come with you."

"No," Randolph said quickly. And then, in a lower voice as he looked back at the television: "Your family needs you."

Somehow, Roland had fallen asleep—or passed out. He was lost in another recurring dream—a nightmare about a man dying in the gas chamber. When he first had the dream twenty years ago, the man had been his father. Now, he saw himself...strapped into the death chair, veins bulging from his neck as he tried futilely to hold his breath...!

Roland cried out as he awoke. He looked about frantically, seeing that he was in one of those ugly, asphalt-covered city parks. The morning sun was pale and lifeless—just like the one from twenty years ago—and he shook his head to purge his mind of those thoughts. He couldn't remember how he had come to be in this park, but his body slumped when he remembered the events of the previous day. He saw Phelps' corpse, and that fat cop going into death convulsions; he remembered his image on TV, as he scrambled about Maria Santos' set. He grimaced. He had seen too much—*done* too much—and now there was no going back.

He got up from the park bench then, stretching and moaning. As blood began to flow to all of his numb parts, and sensation came back to his limbs, he looked about the park again, seeing how filthy it was. Dog droppings, food wrappers, and broken bottles were everywhere. There were slums and abandoned buildings on the streets surrounding the park. He never thought he would find himself in a place like this again, yet here he was.

He was about to sit back down and brood on these thoughts when he detected something in the air. He looked around confusedly. The sound was coming from down the block; mesmerized, he walked out of the park, so that he could look down the street. As he stood on the curb, the rumbling sound grew louder. Still numb from the cold, he shuffled to the end of the block, and stood at the corner, looking to his left; and there, before him, was a tangled mass of blackness. Hundreds—no, *thousands*—of black people were walking up the middle of the street! He took an unconscious step backward, but froze after that one step. The people spoke with one voice, but it was a madman's voice. He was not able to make out their words: they just rumbled in the air, like inarticulate thunder. Yet, like thunder, they told him a storm was coming.

The people in the street were about one hundred meters away from him now. They didn't even seem like individual people anymore—but as a multi-limbed beast, plowing down everything in its path. He knew, at once, that there was no stopping it. Yet, for a strange moment, he exulted at that. Would it be so bad to destroy everything—to toss this entire mess into some cosmic wastebasket and start over? He was about to smile; he again saw himself as the unrepentant super nigger of last night—

But the police, he suddenly noticed, were across the street, walking down the sidewalk. They were quietly stalking the beast: more policemen than he had ever seen in his life! And now, suddenly, every window seemed to frame a gaping black face. Some people were coming out of their tenements, and standing on their stoops; in time, some of them became entranced by the call of the beast, and joined the tangled procession. This was how the beast grew, Roland realized with a shudder. It was almost upon him now! The beast was coming up the sidewalk on his side, and if he didn't move, he would be trampled. He could smell its scent in the air. It was as strong and acrid as the musk of bitches in heat. It was young and old, male and female: a huge hermaphroditic orgy.

The beast was now so close that he could decipher its voice. "Justice, peace, war: *decide!*" the thing chanted. Common sense told him to run as far away as his legs would carry him—but another (*stronger*) voice told him to surrender. He had been running since yesterday, and he was tired. He had been running all his life, in fact; and for once, instead of running away, he wanted to delve into the fire. He closed his eyes, and stepped into the midst of them—like a diver leaping off a cliff. At first, he was jostled about; there was a moment of terror when he thought he would be trampled; but in a matter of seconds, his numb legs got the rhythm of the march. The people around him were screaming and waving their hands wildly. His own limbs still felt numb; his mind was light and somnolent—but it felt good, somehow, to lose himself in the belly of the beast.

Marenga had his hospital bed up on an incline, and was watching a Saturday morning cartoon as he ate his breakfast—some gelatinous swill that was supposed to return him to good health. He felt more tired—more *exhausted*—than he had ever been in his life. He could barely move his arms up to his mouth to feed himself. The nurse had started to feed him, but he had been annoyed by her presence; and she, a white woman, had been resentful of having to attend to him, so they had reached an agreement between themselves. His chest still ached—after all, they had sliced him open to operate—but there was a strange kind of peace about him: perhaps a *horrible* kind of peace.

Suddenly, the door opened and a man entered. Marenga looked over at the man and smiled, saying, "I was wondering when you were going to come."

Randolph stepped in quickly; he was breathing deeply, as though he had run all the way there. "So you know why I'm here?" he said as he stepped up to Marenga's bed.

All of Marenga's movements were slow and deliberate: the movements of an old, wounded man. He lay there considering Randolph for a while; then, still speaking softly and hoarsely: "You want me to control Botswana Glade?" Randolph nodded. "I was watching him on the news this morning," Marenga went on, gesturing to the TV on the far wall. "I got sick of it," he said, laughing in an offhand manner, "so I turned on cartoons."

"—Can you do it?" Randolph asked eagerly. "Can you stop Botswana Glade?"

Marenga only chuckled at him, before taking another spoonful of the swill. "I couldn't stop him even if he wanted to be stopped. It's beyond even Botswana Glade now: the *people* want this... As it is," he went on, his voice getting hoarser, "I have no control over Botswana Glade anymore—especially now as he's tasted power."

"Yeah, I suppose so," Randolph said vaguely.

"And you can't stop them either," Marenga warned, after clearing his throat. "They hate you now—want nothing more than to rip you to shreds. I've seen the news," he said, looking at Randolph intently, "—saw the end of the debate last night—"

"That doesn't matter," Randolph said quickly.

"Nevertheless," Marenga went on, "your words at the debate required courage. Hopefully they'll eventually come to understand what you meant."

"They understand enough to vote me out of office," Randolph replied sardonically. And then, to get them back on track: "We have to do something, Marenga."

"Like what?" he said with a bemused smile. "The time when you and I could have stopped this has passed, Randolph."

"Look, Marenga, I know you're tired—you're *sick*—"

But Marenga laughed out then, saying: "You have no idea how sick I am."

"Stop being so melodramatic," Randolph jibed anxiously, "the doctors say you can make a full recovery."

Marenga looked at him, as if to show Randolph how

drained he was: how *dead* his eyes were—and *soulless*. "...You know what I did when I heard about the riot after my rally? I *laughed!* I've never felt such peace before—*never!* You're here to try to get me to stop what's going to happen, when my only reason for living is to see it all come to pass—"

"You don't really believe that!" he said in alarm.

"Don't I?" Marenga returned with a laugh. "Not only do I believe it, but so do you!"

"—*What?*"

"This is the time for revenge," Marenga said with an insane gleam in his eyes. "They had their chance to do right, but didn't—now, *fuck* 'em!"

"...Marenga," Randolph whispered in bewilderment.

"It's down to the wire now, Randolph. Time to face reality. No more illusions!" But at that Marenga began to cough uncontrollably; there was a glass of water on the night stand, and Randolph picked it up and brought it to Marenga's lips. There was something strangely tender about that scene, with Randolph holding the back of Marenga's head as he helped the man to drink the water. "...Thanks," Marenga said at last.

They were both silent for a while, perhaps a little embarrassed by their strange intimacy. Whatever the case, Randolph sat down on the edge of bed, his back to Marenga. They sat like that for a while, both brooding in the silence, until:

"We have to do something," Randolph repeated,

turning around and looking at Marenga imploringly. Marenga looked over at him and shook his head in bewilderment. "...You still love them, don't you?"

"What?"

"The people out there—the ones who are killing you. They annoy the hell out of you—*disappoint* you, perhaps—but you still love them."

"*What*... ? Of course not. Look," he went on quickly, as if fighting to put his thoughts together, "we have to do something... We've got to stop them. No matter what has happened, we can't act out of hate: can't surrender to it. They are human beings, Marenga—"

Marenga was about to laugh sarcastically when he happened to glance at the television. A special report had come on during the cartoon. On the screen, a sea of black people—perhaps tens of thousands of them!—could be seen marching down one of the streets of Harlem. The point of view changed, and now a lanky white reporter was standing on a side street; and over her shoulder, one could see the passing mob. The reporter's hand trembled as she held the microphone. She kept looking over her shoulder, as if terrified the thing would attack her. She had to scream to be heard above the chanting crowd. Randolph grabbed the remote control and turned up the volume.

"...This thing was both spontaneous and planned," the reporter continued, "—instigated by racial activist, Botswana Glade. As far as we know, they intend to march to the sight of last night's..."—she searched fran-

tically for the right word, her lower lip trembling—
"*incident* here in Harlem. Botswana Glade said that this
would happen, but nobody could have guessed the
scope..."

The scene changed to a television studio, where a
skinny black anchorman seemed oblivious of the fact
that he was on the air. The stillness of the newsroom
seemed abrupt and bombastic. The anchorman was
looking offstage, like he was receiving some new information. He suddenly looked directly into the camera.
"We now have a reporter within the march, itself,
alongside its supposed leader, Botswana Glade."

The scene changed. Suddenly, the viewer had the
sensation of being engulfed in a sea of writhing bodies.
The camera kept bounding up and down, as though the
cameraperson were running along. The loud voices
could now be heard clearly, chanting: "Justice, peace,
war: *decide*!" Their many fists were raised defiantly; their
voices were thunderous. An athletic-looking white male
reporter was holding a microphone before Botswana
Glade's indignant face. Botswana Glade had been
shouting to the reporter—no one could *just* talk anymore—before the scene switched to him. Randolph
leaned in closer.

"...Injustice demands action!" Botswana Glade roared.

"What do you say to those who would say that this is
nothing more than inciting a riot?" the reporter yelled
back.

Botswana Glade thought for a moment, then: "Maybe

we need to have a riot every once in a while," he said in a voice that was almost peaceful." Randolph looked at Marenga with alarm, but the man only shrugged his shoulders and took another spoonful of the swill. "We need justice any way we can get it," Botswana Glade went on. "The end justifies the means, as they say. If this society can only understand, and be moved by, the realities of war, then it is in those terms that we must speak! Justice, peace, war: *decide!*" he continued chanting, with the others.

The reporter was still running along, trying to keep up—trying, Randolph considered, to keep from being trampled by those behind him.

The reporter looked into the camera now: "There you have it," he said, out of breath. "Now, back to the studio..."

Randolph was nibbling his lower lip anxiously. The anchorman was talking over images of the scene, noting how the police had so far tried to maintain their distance. The man kept repeating that the situation was tense and unstable—stating the obvious. He revealed that off-camera, many officers were saying that they were not going to risk their lives if a riot broke out; others seemed to want a confrontation to re-exert their authority after the weaknesses of Randolph's term in office—

Randolph anxiously got up and started for the door.

"Where the *hell* are you going!" Marenga demanded.

"I have to stop this," Randolph said vaguely, looking suddenly haggard.

"Don't do anything stupid!" Marenga called after him, but Randolph was already gone. Marenga shook his head.

Something brutal had happened to Charlotte McPrice. She had been sitting in front of the television all night; and yet, she had done so without seeing. Her husband was dead...and her campaign manager was somehow responsible for it. She had spent the first couple of hours in shock and panic; but about four in the morning, she had been honest enough to admit that much of her reaction had nothing to do with what her campaign manager had done. Rather, what left her unsettled was the realization that she was willing to live with that. In fact, a side of her had exulted in the fact that she was free of him. ...And she hadn't called the police either. She could have easily exonerated herself by turning Wisinski over to the police—yet she had done nothing.

She had had a perfect soul before. Fighting her way to the top of the mountain, she had been a tireless warrior for justice, willing to fight any battle. She had been able to endure it all, because she had been pure. Now, as she sat on her couch and stared at the special report on the march, she felt indecisive for perhaps the first time in her life. There was a poison working its way through her system. A normal person would call it guilt; but for someone as pure as Charlotte McPrice, this was like being tossed from grace. Why wasn't she calling the police? Again, she hadn't done it because, on some level, she approved of what Wisinski had done. In fact, she was now an accessory to murder! She didn't know which horrified her more: the fear of being publicly ridiculed and punished for this crime, or the prospect of living her entire life with this stain on her purity. She tried to think of her options. Would the police figure out that it hadn't been a suicide? And if so, would they be able to trace it back to her?

Yet, even these thoughts mocked her! When had she ever thought about hiding behind a crime—and *benefitting* from it! Now, she was like the rest of them: like all the people she had lampooned and chastised...like Randolph! All that lay before her was learning to live with it—going through life with this knowledge of herself—or telling the world and losing everything.

She put her hands to her face, and, for the first time since she heard of her husband's death, she cried. They were tears of mourning, but for *her*, not her husband. She was so lost in her grief that she didn't know when the two policemen had entered her study. They were the same men from the previous night; she flinched when she saw them.

"We're sorry, ma'am," they quickly apologized in unison. Both men were in their dress uniforms now, and as she stared blankly at them, one of the officers explained: "We were heading to the memorial service, ma'am...just wanted to tell you that we are almost convinced that your husband's death was a suicide. There is no evidence that it was a robbery or anything else, since all of his money was in his pocket. And since there haven't been any threats to his life...well, it looks like suicide, sorry to say. We even found a note."

They handed the handwritten letter over to her. It read: "I'm not worthy of my wife." McPrice almost screamed out hysterically: those words were so obviously Wisinski's! "I'm a sinner and I can't go on!"

When she looked up from the note, one of the officers ventured, "It *is* his handwriting, right?"

McPrice stared at it, frowning. Believe it or not, it actually was his handwriting.

Wisinski had probably made the man write it before killing him. McPrice looked back up at the officer and nodded her head.

The officer nodded his head grimly. "I know it's no consolation to you...."

However, she only sighed. "Thanks, officers," she said then, her voice faint. Once again bowing to her, they left. She stared at their retreating forms, feeling sick to her stomach. Wisinski walked in then: he had spent the night in the guest bedroom. Seeing him, she knew this was her last chance to do right—to call the policemen back and tell them all what had happened—

but she realized, at once, that it wasn't in her. Her hurtling flight from the apex had come to the end, and her broken corpse was now sprawled against the rocks at the base of the mountain.

Seeing her sitting there dejectedly, Wisinski came up quickly. He kneeled before her then—the way someone kneeled before a queen—grasping her hands. She cringed at the sight and touch of him, but he was so insane in his joy, that he didn't seem to notice or to care:

"Did they tell you the good news!" he exulted. "Now, nothing can touch you!" She looked at him with the same horror as last night; and like Andropov and Randolph and Roland and Marenga before her, she wondered how in the hell she had come to this place...

Young officer Mucelli hadn't slept in thirty hours now—and he didn't expect to sleep anytime soon. Every time he closed his eyes, he saw Flanders falling to the ground; with his sleep deprivation, he was beginning to see the scene when his eyes were open. He feared he was slowly going mad; but like Roland, he had come so far and done so much that the only thing to do was wait for his fate.

He was getting dressed for the police rally/memorial service now, putting on his dress uniform. He just had to hold on a bit longer, then everything would blow over. At the rally, Mucelli would be in the first row, of course—with the rest of the dignitaries. And nobody suspected him—or at least nobody that mattered. There was only that bastard, Ericsson.

Mucelli was booked for Maria Santos's show that night. She and hundreds of others were calling him a hero now. The sickening irony left him somewhat queasy; but again, it was too late to do anything about it. He just had to keep going—

There was a knock on the door. *That must be my ride*, he thought, taking a deep breath to calm himself. "I'm coming!" he bellowed, glancing at himself one last time in the mirror before walking to the door. He had affected a calm, reverential expression before opening the door; but after he opened it, and looked into the eyes of the man standing on the other side, all of that fell away. Ericsson's eyes bored into him; Mucelli stood there in shock, fighting not to panic. He had a sudden impulse to rush at the man and beat his brains out...! He opened his mouth to say something—he didn't know what—but Ericsson stepped boldly past him then, and into the room.

Mucelli closed the door softly, seeming suddenly frail. When he turned to face the man, Ericsson was still staring at him the way someone stared at a piece of filth. Ericsson began by ceremoniously holding up a plain manila folder:

"Let me tell you about the final forensic report I have in my hand here," he started, "—and some of the conclusions that I've come to." As though losing his strength, Mucelli moved over to the couch and sat down heavily; Ericsson walked over as well, but remained standing. "First of all," he continued, "the semen inside of Cindy Phelps was her husband's alone; second, Dallas Phelps was dead for hours: *way* before Micheaux got there—several people corroborate that. Dallas Phelps was in fact killed the night before—most likely by Cindy Phelps, whom he raped. And why do I say that? The only fingerprints on the murder weapon were hers and her husband's. They had fought over the gun... she won. Furthermore, it was his skin alone that we found beneath her fingernails: more evidence that they were the only ones involved in the struggle. As far as I can tell, they fought the night before; frightened by this fight, the nanny left with the little girl, and went over to Roland Micheaux's house. They used to have a relationship, so this explains their connection—and why she would turn to him for help. But," he said, walking up and stopping before the blanched Mucelli, "who shot Cindy Phelps? We've all been saying Roland Micheaux. However, the angle of the gunshot wound to Cindy Phelps's head is consistent with a self-inflicted wound— which is to say that after killing Dallas, and shooting at Micheaux, who had just then come to return their daughter, she tried to kill herself. When she fired at Micheaux, he ran away—was so traumatized by it, that he probably went into shock. I doubt he had any idea he was still holding the little girl as he ran all those blocks. Now," he said with a dead smile, "does any of this make sense to you, Mucelli?"

Mucelli had been staring on in a daze, but now ventured, "I guess so, sir."

"You *guess* so?" Ericsson said with a smirk. "Since you have the answers, what do you suggest I tell the commissioner?"

Mucelli opened his mouth, but nothing came out. Ericsson went on: "From all this, it looks to me like we've been chasing an innocent man, Officer Mucelli. What do your keen senses tell you?"

Mucelli couldn't move—couldn't even manage to look up anymore.

"And then," Ericsson went on quickly, "there is the question of your partner." Mucelli looked up in horror! "I was wondering if Micheaux did that either. What do you think about that, Officer Mucelli?"

Mucelli was breathing shallowly now, his face seeming drained of blood and life. Ericsson stepped up to him threateningly then, screaming, "*You* did it, didn't you!"—Mucelli cringed against the couch, looking like a scared dog—"*You* killed Flanders by mistake, but weren't man enough to admit it!"

Suddenly, Mucelli burst into tears, hiding his face like a terrified child; Ericsson stared down at him, still hoping, somehow, that he had been wrong about it all. Unfortunately, Mucelli's tears confirmed his worst nightmares. All that he could do was stare at the man in horror.

"Justice, peace, war: *decide!*"

Roland was pulled along with the rest of them. He felt like he had fallen into a serpent pit. Every inadvertent touch seemed like a prelude to death. He walked along numbly and mutely, while tens of thousands of them vented their hatred of the world. How long he went on like this, he couldn't say for sure; but eventually, when it was about ten in the morning, the mob finally began to slow. The mob was now making a right-hand turn onto Malcolm X Boulevard. *Thousands* of people were already there! Camera crews and speakers had been set up—as if it were a rock concert or something. Pushed along, Roland found himself on the left-hand side of that huge boulevard—and was content to stay where he was— when he all at once found himself being jostled again.

Now, everyone seemed eager to get on the right-hand side of the street, where a dais had been erected. This block seemed to be their destination. Panicking, he suddenly realized he and Kain had fled down this block the night before. The police had chased them into that building over there! The realization brought a flood of memories and fears. *He had to get out of here*! He had ridden the crest of the wave as long as possible: now, it was time to escape before he was thrown to the rocks....

Unfortunately, the current was taking him to the right; people were amassing around the dais. Microphones and speakers had been set up, and everyone was desperate to get a good spot. He was being jostled about in the crowd now. There was no way to turn back—or to stay where he was—but from his vantage point, the next block seemed to be clear. It occurred to him that if he continued to go straight, he could escape the crowd. It meant fighting the flow of the crowd, but it was his only choice.

He was coming level with the dais now. A man had alighted it, and was now waving to the people below; the crowd, responding to the man's gestures, began cheering. The din of them was horrifying. Roland felt like a leaf in a whirlwind; he was giddy and nauseous— but he had to keep fighting. There were cameras across the street from the dais. Roland passed beneath them as he fought his way down the block.

Helicopters were hovering overhead—some from television stations, and some from the police. He imagined the scene from above—the *chaos* of it. Tens of thousands of people, stretching along the entire length of the boulevard... The protest march was becoming a shuffle now; soon, they would all be locked in here like sardines, *suffocating* ... !

But when Roland finally passed the dais, and was about five meters from the end of the block, he realized, with a start, that there were thousands of police officers in riot gear amassing at the end of the block! With the

crowd shuffling for space, Roland hadn't noticed the
policemen until he was practically on top of them. He
turned his back abruptly, his heart racing. His only
hope was that they hadn't noticed his face in the sea of
enraged blackness. For all intents and purposes, the
police were making this a dead-end block. They, too,
had anticipated where the march was going to end, and
were now taking up defensive positions. There was
nowhere for Roland to go now: nothing for him to do
but to wait...but wait for *what*? What was he to do after
this? What were any of them to do? The old numbness
was coming over him again. The air felt charged, as
though lightning would strike at any moment. He
looked around in bewilderment, looking at the thousands of people. Some were sitting on the cars parked on
the curb—anywhere there was space...and thousands
more were coming! So many people...the air was filthy
with them. There were speakers on roofs, and in open
windows. Botswana Glade had prepared well, Roland
thought, just as the man began gesturing for the crowd
to be still and silent. Roland took a sneak peek over his
shoulder: the police were still amassing, trapping them
all like rats.

"Yes, we're here—we're *finally* here!" Botswana
Glade's voice boomed over the loud speakers. The voice
reverberated in Roland's chest...and then the cheers:
tens of thousands of them...the noise left him trembling.
It was a good two minutes before Botswana Glade could
speak again. The cheering had a domino effect, spread-

ing down the blocks, soon to reach people who were seven blocks away! They cheered, even though they couldn't possibly know what they were cheering for. Again, Roland nervously glanced back at the police. They were still amassing, with more blue and white cars pulling up all the time—

"We here," Botswana Glade roared when the cheers had died down, "and ain't *nobody* gon drive us away! We gon *stay* here"—he had to yell over their cheers—"till we good and ready to leave!" Once again, the deafening cheers spread down the blocks; the people looking out from their windows screamed and waved as well...

"Yes," Botswana Glade started in a more solemn voice, "right here, in front of this very stoop, three brothers and sisters—*children*—died; and four more are on the verge of death as we speak! Right *here*, this happened, but let us not be fooled into thinking that this is an isolated event!" The crowd groaned, feeling his words. "No, sir! That's what those devils like you to think. *Remember the Thomases!*" The crowd roared! "Every time these crackers get caught with their hands in the cookie jar, they cry out: 'It was only this one time!'" he mimicked them in an effeminate voice that made the crowd burst out in laughter. "Well," he continued, "we ain't fools! Yeah, we caught you this one time, but how many cookies did you eat *before* we caught you!" The applause rose and crested, like a wave; Roland had the sensation of drowning—

"Those devils always playing their tricks! Pacifying us

like it ain't nothing! Well, devil," he screamed, "we will no longer be appeased by your silly lies! We've got *God* on our side, and got sense enough to know that the strength of God will always win out over the devil's lies!" The crowd was in a state of euphoria once again; Roland couldn't move.

"I'm not here to whip you into a fury!" Botswana Glade said, even while the cheering crested above his head. "I'm not here to instill the mob instinct in you, like the media are saying!" People laughed. "I'm here to *bore* you, because this event is nothing new! It has happened before—and it will happen again unless we do something to stop it! I'm not here to outrage you by pointing out the excessiveness of the force that was used by the police last night—and *every* time they come into our community! On the contrary, I don't have to say anything! I don't have to point *anything* out! We *all* know! Many of us have known for most of our lives! There will be an inquiry, a few cops will be punished... blah, blah, blah... This is nothing new! I don't have to whip you into a fury, because that fury has always been there, and will be there until this ceases once and for all!" The cheers roared in the air: roared like *thunder!* "You don't need me to tell you, brothers and sisters!" Botswana Glade went on. "I didn't drag you out of your homes! You came because you know what they're going to do; and you are here to finally put an end to it!"

Botswana Glade barely managed to take a breath, when—

"Please, stop this!" a voice suddenly cried. Everyone was confused, because although it boomed in the air like Botswana Glade's, it hadn't come from him. It had come, Roland and thousands of others realized a millisecond later, from the police-blockaded side of the boulevard. Even down the blocks, the cheering had dwindled to almost nothing. The euphoria, as fragile as it was, scurried away, leaving only surprise and confusion.

They all turned to see where the voice had come from; and there, standing on the hood of a heavily armored riot van, was Mayor Randolph! The van, fitted with huge speakers on its roof, was right on the edge of the crowd—actually, just a few meters away from Roland! Randolph was still holding the microphone that had allowed his voice to be heard above their cheers. "Mr. Glade!" he cried again as the stunned crowd looked on. "Please, I beg you, put an end to this craziness! This is the *last* thing our people need!"

Botswana Glade had been taken off guard like everyone else, but he allowed himself to smile now. He looked over the crowd with an exaggerated gaped mouth, and people laughed at his feigned disbelief. "Why, Mr. Mayor," he said, in a singsong voice, "what might *you* be doing here?"

The crowd laughed.

"Please, sir—"

"Yes!" Botswana Glade was shouting now. "We should have expected this! What was I just talking about?

Pacification? Well, here is Mr. Uncle Tom-House-Nigger, himself, here to tell all us field niggers that we shouldn't do nothing to harm dear old massa."

The crowd was laughing a mirthless kind of laughter.

"Look at this bastard," Botswana Glade went on, pointing a bony finger across the multitudes to Randolph, "...still got his police protecting him! If you're too scared to come in the black community without your mommy holding your hand, then go back home!"

The cheering became something vicious—

"Look, let's just talk about this!" Randolph begged again. "I'm not here as the Mayor. I'm just a man now, here without the police—without the threat of violence—without *power*—"

"You here to talk?" Botswana Glade said with a bemused expression that made the crowd break out laughing once again. "Well, then, if you're here to talk, then that's a different matter. Come on up here, brother!" Botswana Glade mocked him. "That's right: if you're a man like you say, leave those police and come up here—walk though this gathering of people you claim to represent, and come up here!"

"—All right," Randolph said at once, to everyone's surprise. People had just been about to break out laughing when Randolph got off the roof and pushed aside the barricade, so that he could make his way through the crowd. There was a terrible kind of tension in the air. In the people's eyes, the hatred of the Mayor was clear: it contorted their faces into scowls; some were whispering to their neighbors, asking if "that nigger" was actually going to do it—

"Pardon me," the Mayor said to the first person in his path, who begrudgingly made way with a snarled lip and a grunt, and then he began to inch through the crowd. Soon, Randolph would come upon Roland; and for a moment, Roland panicked at the realization that the man—his mortal enemy of the last few years— would recognize him and turn him in—

"Yes," Botswana Glade laughed mordantly, "come right up, Mayor: we want to hear everything you have to say." He had tried to joke, but the laughter was suddenly flat and forced. There was a new intensity within the crowd now. To Roland, they seemed like snakes about to strike; and just then, as Randolph was on the verge of coming upon him, a husky black man tackled Randolph and began raining blows on the man. The people around Roland cheered as Randolph was knocked to the ground. Roland stared down at the thing that was literally happening at his feet, feeling empty inside. As for the crowd, only the sickest of them wanted to cheer, but it was as though none of them could stop the thing growing in their souls. If Roland had had any faith in humanity left, it was gone now as the husky man pummeled the Mayor and the surrounding crowd cheered and whooped like animals.

"—Stop it!" Roland cried out then, but his words

were lost in the cheers. He balled his hands into fists, gnashing his teeth in frustration and madness: "*Stop* it!" But still, he was ignored. In desperation, Roland tried to grip the man and throw him off the Mayor, but the crowd was inadvertently pushing him back as they clambered around the fight. In fact, with all the whooping, his efforts were easily lost in the chaos. It was then that something occurred to him: an idea born of madness—maybe not even an idea, but the old impulse to push everything to its conclusion and get everything over with. Without thought, he shoved some people out of the way and made haste to the police barricade—which he leapt over. Soon, he reached the riot van, grabbing the microphone that the Mayor had left on the hood. The riot police had actually retreated when the crowd began mauling the Mayor, so Roland had free access as he leapt onto the roof. It was then that he screamed at the top of his lungs:

"*It's me: Roland Micheaux!*" His voice was so forceful that those nearest to the speakers were literally blown back. The crowd was again thrown off track by a new voice. They looked up in confusion as Roland repeated: "It's me: Roland Micheaux! It's *me!*" he screamed as people gasped and whispered and frowned, trying to see from themselves. "...Roland Micheaux," he said again, "—the *killer*...!"

Now, it was their whispers that had a domino effect throughout the crowd. Tens of thousands of people were asking their neighbors if it was really Roland Micheaux. Even the police, who had maintained their distance when the husky man attacked the Mayor, were craning their necks now. Roland Micheaux—the cop killer: the cause of all of this! Even they couldn't believe it; but: "It's me, the killer!" Roland screamed, confirming it again.

And now, as though his name had hypnotized them, dozens of riot police began to approach the van. The man on the roof was their quarry—they had been chasing him for over a day now; and here, of all places, they had finally found him. The people in the crowd didn't know what to do—even Botswana Glade was in shock. As they looked at Roland's face, they saw something horrible there—an emptiness so vast that it seemed like would swallow them all—

"I'm Roland Micheaux!" they heard the man say one last time, just before he began to laugh with a sick, empty kind of laughter that was like weeping. He laughed before cameras and all the gaping faces, realizing that his death was complete. And yet, despite his utter emptiness, a side of him was thankful that nobody he loved was there to see it. The world was something that he was indifferent to—there was no hatred left. He stood there limply, so that the microphone slipped from his fingers and tumbled off the roof—

But just then, one of the policemen in riot gear grabbed Roland's ankles and pulled him off the roof.

He hit his head on the roof as he fell; and then, after having the wind knocked out of him by the fall, he was swarmed by dozens of officers. People still stood about, stunned; but it was when the police began to club Roland, that a horrible scream erupted from within the crowd, breaking the trance that had kept them in check.

Those policemen, hypnotized by the name of Roland Micheaux, had made a grave misstep: they had assumed that the mob's fire had gone out for good; when in truth, Roland had only distracted them. Outraged by the same brutality they had come to protest, they attacked the policemen. The eruption came at last; and as he lay on the ground, beneath the chaotic surge of thousands, Roland closed his eyes and listened to all the violent explosions. In their haste to rip the officers to shreds, the people were trampling Roland now. He could literally feel his bones breaking and his organs being crushed! His hurtling descent from the heavens came to an abrupt end, and he lay splattered against the filthy street. At that very moment, Officer Ericsson appeared on TV, relating the story of Roland Micheaux's innocence—and Mucelli's duplicity. But it was too late by then: both for Roland and the city.

EPILOGUE

Years seemed to pass; but years, to a child, were lifetimes. Roland found himself living random scenes from his life. One moment, he would be with his grandmother on the bayou, then with his mother in the Louisiana slums; then, he would be a man, ascending to the heights of success and fame. Yet, just as he seemed be on the brink of some breakthrough, he would be a toddler again, living with both of his parents, in that strange preconscious bliss known to all children. Reality didn't matter anymore— just as time didn't matter. Love and hate—and all the other emotions and sensations—blurred into one, so that he saw at last that life was meaningless.

Yet, as the years passed by, strange, incomprehensible scenes began to filter into his consciousness: a nurse standing over him; strange men touching him; strange voices reverberating from the heavens...and then they would fade away, and he would find himself reliving random scenes from his meaningless life—

But then, one day—ostensibly after centuries had passed—he found himself playing in the park with his mother. It was a sunny, wondrous day. She was holding his hands, and they were dancing in a circle together—going faster and faster, until his legs left the ground, and he was *flying*. He went around and around, with the world as a blur, and only his mother's smiling, euphoric face as a reference point—

The scene ended abruptly, and the next thing Roland knew, a white man was peering into his eyes. Roland's first instinct was to flee, but it was as if he had been bound in lead. There was a horrible sluggishness about him. Everything seemed to be moving in slow motion—and *warped*. The white man's face was a misshapen oval—like reflections of faces in spoons; the man was saying something, but it was so resounding that it only rumbled inarticulately in the air. And then, seemingly after more years had passed, the man stepped away. Now, some other men came to the fore. Roland stared at them, hopelessly lost. They were saying something, but their words only resounded in the heavens once again. The original man—the *doctor*, it now occurred to him—was checking him again; Roland's eyes were pulled open; impromptu auscultation was performed on him. He lay there, staring up at the strange man—and at the three others, who seemed just as strange. Of the latter men, two were black, and one was white. The white man was in a police uniform; the two black men were in robes, as though they were patients. All were middle-aged and haggard—

Mayor Randolph! Roland finally recognized one of the

men. What was he doing here? The man had a bandage around his head; his face was discolored and swollen, and his hand was in a sling. Frowning, Roland realized the other black man was Marenga! The man was standing there with the help of one of those walkers that old women used after they had broken their hips. The third man was...the Police Commissioner? Roland couldn't remember the guy's name, but he looked as though he hadn't slept in days. The doctor, who had just finished checking Roland's vital signs, was staring at him with concern. He loomed above Roland again, repeating some resounding gibberish several times before—

"...Can you understand me?"

Roland looked up excitedly when he deciphered the words.

"I think he's coming around!" the doctor said to the others. He looked back at Roland: "Can you understand me?" he asked again.

"Yes," Roland managed to say—even though his mouth felt horribly dry. He glanced down: both arms were in casts; his left leg was in traction; his neck, he realized as he tried to turn his head to look back at the men, was in a brace. As he emerged back into consciousness, all of his broken and bruised parts began to ache—or rather, he became aware of the pain. He grimaced. Nevertheless, the men before him suddenly seemed relieved; the doctor looked over his shoulder at the others and beamed.

"You've been in a coma for two days now," the doctor said, turning back to Roland. "But you should make a complete recovery—"

Roland had a sudden flashback to the rally—all of those rampaging thousands...!

The Police Commissioner stepped up now; Roland cringed at the sight of him, but the man quickly said, "We're not chasing you anymore, Mr. Micheaux. We realized that you weren't involved in any crimes—but too late."

Marenga chuckled sardonically; the Commissioner looked back at him nervously, then went on: "There has been social unrest for two days now—riots, looting, fires...and in all five boroughs. It's even spread over to New Jersey, Connecticut, and Long Island."

Roland smiled unconsciously: *Let it burn!* he thought.

Randolph stepped up now: "After the initial"—he seemed to search for the right word to describe Botswana Glade's rally—"...after the initial disturbance, when people found out that you were innocent, everything went crazy. Twenty policemen have been killed in the last two days; scores of people have been killed... hundreds wounded—"

"And they want you to put an end to it," Marenga added.

"Yes," Randolph went on, either ignoring Marenga's sarcasm, or not acknowledging it, "we need your help."

When Roland looked away and said nothing, the Police Commissioner went on, "The National Guard has been called out. Martial Law has been instituted. Thousands of people have been left homeless by the fires."

Let it burn! Roland thought again.

"You have a right to be angry," Randolph was saying now. "It's natural..." But his words died off when Roland continued to stare into the distance. Randolph stood staring at the man for a while, then added: "I know something that might change your mind."

Roland looked up in annoyance as Randolph went to the door and whispered something to whoever was standing outside. The Mayor then returned to Roland, saying, "Like I said, you have a right to be angry—I was almost killed myself"—Marenga chuckled to himself—"but we need you—"

"You need me!" Roland screamed, his voice hoarse and horrible. He wanted to rant some more—to spring at all the men and claw their eyes out; but he was too weak. Moreover, just then, the door opened, and a police officer came in with a little girl that he didn't recognize at first.

Randolph started, "Cindy Phelps finally died of her injury. This little girl now has no one—she's been calling for you all these days."

Roland stared down at Mindy, and then looked at the men in the room with pure hatred. What the hell was this! What did they expect him to do about any of it! But the little girl...damn her, she was standing there looking wretched and unsure; then, seeming to recognize him, she ran up and jumped onto the bed, hugging him around the neck. Besides the sharp pain her grip caused (the doctor made her ease up a little bit after Roland gasped) her touch was disconcerting, setting off strange, contradictory feelings in him. A side of him wanted to wrench her from him and fling her away.... For her, he had almost been killed—maybe not even for her, but for the social construct that she was: a little tow-headed, blue-eyed white girl.... But then, something melted within him, and he lay there in a daze as she sobbed against his chest. It wasn't even that she was innocent, and innocent of all that he suddenly wanted to accuse her and her society of, but that even now, she still trusted him. It was not the loss of innocence that was the great evil, but the loss of trust. She was hardly innocent anymore, but she was still somehow trusting of the social contracts that seemed like so much shit to him now. The city was being torn apart because those social contracts had been thrown to the side. Without them, all that had been left was the same hate that he had fought against all his life. Hundreds of thousands of people were now either gripped by that madness or becoming victims of it: how could it possibly end, but with the end of the world...just as Kain had said. What was the use! he thought, just as the little girl disengaged from him a little to look at his face:

"You hurt bad, Uncle Roland?"

He stared at her a while, not knowing what to think; then, "I'll be fine"—he looked at the doctor—"...will make a full recovery."

"Maybe this might help," she said then, handing him her doll. It was the same repulsive abomination that could spit up, burp and shit its panties; but for some reason, he was on the verge of tears. A side of him still wanted to fling her away—to revert to the simple joy of bestiality. He suddenly wanted to be out there with the rest of them, tearing the world apart... But the little girl was there, still trusting him, despite the demon in his chest. How horrible the world was! he thought. He held her closely then—which was to say he moved his cast over her—wishing that the world would end quickly and brutally; but then, at the same time, he found himself hoping that a precious few, like the child in his arms, would be spared that sterilizing brutality: that they might be the seeds for a saner world...just as Kain had said. He felt so very tired now. Every time he thought it was over, it was only just beginning....

Randolph and the Police Commissioner were still staring down at him, hopefully. Watching them, Roland was again trapped between the urge to scream for the people to rip the world apart, and the impetus to stop them; but at last, reaching a conclusion that seemed just as futile as its opposite, he looked up at the Mayor and whispered, "What do you expect me to do?"

"Just a quick statement to the press," Randolph said eagerly. "Just a few words, so that people see that you're alive—and are willing to go on."

Roland sighed; the Police Commissioner quickly went on: "The media are already waiting. They heard that you were coming out of the coma, and began to gather downstairs. Just the sight of you might help bring this to an end."

They stood there, looking at him eagerly; Roland nodded, even though he didn't believe that he could do anything.

"Thank you!" the Mayor began—

"Can I have a few moments alone?" Roland cut him off....

All four men left the room solemnly, leaving Micheaux in the room with the little girl. When they had closed the door behind them, the Police Commissioner looked warily to the others and said:

"Do you think Micheaux will do it?"

"Will do *what?*" Marenga said in annoyance. "Look at what we're doing! The man is barely out of a coma and we're rushing him off to give a press conference! He can barely *move*"—Marenga looked at the doctor accusingly; the man looked away nervously—"and yet we're pushing him out there to fight our battles."

"We're desperate," Randolph said at last.

"But what the hell can we expect Micheaux to do?" Marenga returned. "Bring peace and order? No one man can do that when people are bent on killing one another and scavenging the world. If we're brutal enough, we may be able to keep them from killing one another; but in the long run, only *they* have the power to bring peace and order."

"Then we'll settle for the short term," Randolph replied. "One day at a time...start over if we can."

"Start over with the same old lies?" Marenga said in bewilderment. "And what was the meaning of bringing in that little girl? You've got to put a guilt trip on him to get him to act, and yet you want him to get people to start behaving with dignity and respect. Come on!" Marenga said, looking pointedly at the others. "This is bullshit and we all know it!"

"What are we supposed to do!" Randolph said in frustration. "The city's falling apart, Marenga! When someone's bleeding to death you don't stand there moralizing, you get in and do something. Yes, it's short term, but at least the bleeding will stop. I'll do whatever it takes!"

Marenga sighed and stood looking at the man. There was no true antagonism between them: they were only two desperate men trying to make sense of the world. At this pause in their exchange, the Police Commissioner nodded distractedly and walked off. Somehow, the man looked even more haggard than before—as if years had drained from his life in the last few minutes; the doctor, perhaps still smarting from Marenga's jibe about his ethics, bowed his head and walked off as well, leaving Marenga and Randolph standing there.

They were silent for a while, then: "I just hope this comes to an end," Randolph mused.

"It will never end," Marenga said, matter-of-factly.

544 D. V. BERNARD

"People will always find some excuse to hate one another—and to *kill* one another. Justifications and foes change, but the actions remain the same."

Randolph sighed thoughtfully. "Maybe you're right, Marenga ..."

"Being right doesn't matter anymore." Then, seeming to remember something he had meant to ask, Marenga ventured, "Did you find out why McPrice dropped out of the mayoral race at the last moment?"

"No—it doesn't make sense to me or to anyone. Some say her husband's death was too much for her: that she loved him so much..."—he sighed—"Only McPrice seems to know."

"So then, Mr. Mayor," Marenga said with a laugh, "I guess that congratulations are in order."

"No," Randolph said, smiling at his friend's baiting. "I'll only be Mayor until another election can be staged. I still feel the way I felt when I walked out on that last debate. I'll do my duty until then, but I'll never hold office again."

"What happened?" Marenga said with another laugh. "I thought you were willing to do 'whatever it takes'? Your generosity wear out?"

Randolph chuckled at Marenga's jibe at first, then sighed, shaking his head. "I don't know, Marenga," he said, pursing his lips, "—that's just the point. Something's changed in me. After the doctors bandaged me up and put my arm in a cast, there was this...*excitement* in me. I wanted the people to destroy one another: destroy everything...just like you said I did." He glanced at Marenga ashamedly. "I don't know anymore. For a while, I wanted to see it all scrapped—like a painting that didn't come out the way I'd wished. I guess that's human nature: destroying the things we can't fix...but if you are going to be people's leader, you should at least know what you think about them.... I look at them, and I cringe—but it's not fear, exactly: it's a reminder to be on my guard. It's *mistrust*."

"What do you expect?" Marenga began. "They almost *killed* you!"

"But it's more than a few bruises and broken bones, Marenga. I feel like some animal in the jungle. Is that what our society has come to? I want to *live*, Marenga—and live as a *man*, not as an animal." Laughing, he went on: "Maybe this would be a good chance for you to run for Mayor."

"No," Marenga said with chuckle, "...not me, my friend." And at that, he patted Randolph on the back and they walked down the corridor like two old men.

An hour later, Roland was wheeled into the cafeteria on his bed. The bed was on an incline—which is to say that his torso was elevated—so that he could see the hundreds of reporters and the three dozen or so camera crews that had gathered to hear his words. Before Roland arrived, there had been excitement in the air, with people talking like school children at an assembly;

but when Roland entered, a hush came over the room. The little girl, Mindy, held the cast over his right hand and walked by his side, while two orderlies wheeled him onto the dais. Roland didn't know why he had come—or what he would say. But what could possibly do it? What words could possibly put an end to the madness of thousands—of *millions*, in fact. With all that he had been through, he couldn't even be convinced of his own sanity, much less try to conjure sanity in others.

Randolph, Marenga and the Commissioner were all sitting in the front row. They, along with everyone else, were staring at him expectantly and silently. However, the silence was soon replaced by the cacophony of camera shutters; flash bulbs made him squint; camera crews and sound men were maneuvering to get the best vantage points... Before him, on the dais, were dozens of microphones, each with the logo of a network. All was in readiness for the elusive words that would save them all. The orderlies pushed him up to the edge of the podium; a technician came up and affixed a small microphone to his gown, then they all left the stage, leaving him lying there with Mindy standing by his side.

Yes, they've planned this well! he thought with a renewed feeling of revulsion. He glanced down at Mindy then: yes, they had seen her as their secret weapon against him; and having her there with him was perfect: a brutalized black man and an orphaned little white girl, loving one another...what could be more cinematic! He suddenly felt sick to his stomach! Even Maria Santos was here, waiting to question him and boost her ratings. People were dead, thousands were homeless...the very society was tearing itself apart, and yet all it was, was a feeding frenzy: another spectacle in a world of mindless spectacles! For the next few weeks, it would be the "hot" story around the world; and then, after the mandatory network specials asking how it had happened and why we weren't a peaceful nation, it would all fade away—until the next riot or whatever became "hot"; at which time, Americans would once again feel compelled to ask how it could possibly have happened, and why they didn't have a peaceful nation...*ad infinitum*! He had a sudden, violent impulse to curse them all: to leap up and yell, *Fuck you all!* But he knew that that wouldn't reach them—would only *add* to the spectacle. He sat there, trembling with rage and ineptitude, until, glancing at Maria Santos's expectant face, he saw something that made his breath get caught in his throat!

Right behind Maria Santos, there was a man whose existence was impossible! The man was in a suit and tie, looking up at Roland with his usual calmness. *It was Jasper Kain*! All Roland could do, was stare. *Kain was alive*! Roland couldn't even begin to conceptualize it. Had the man been wearing a bulletproof vest perhaps? Or maybe the man was a ghost, haunting Roland from hell—or a lingering delusion from his coma... All the possibilities flared up in his mind, so that he knew at once that he was no match for them. There was an inscrutable smile on Kain's face now—a look of triumph, almost *transcendence*. The man was clean-shaven now; and with his suit and tie, and his stylish, wire-rimmed glasses, his existence was potent proof that the world was mad. Just then, inexplicably, the man winked at Roland; and, as though his only reason for being there had been to show Roland that he was still alive, Kain began navigating his way through the media and toward the exit.

Roland stared at Kain's retreating back in shock, already believing he had imagined it all. And Kain looked so normal—so *sane*—especially in comparison to everyone else, that a side of Roland began to wonder if the entire thing hadn't been an act: all the supposed madness, all the rants... Like everything else, it seemed both possible and impossible.

Presently, Kain stopped in the crowded exit (which was crammed with people who had come to get a glimpse of Roland). At that moment, Kain turned back, and nodded his head—like a proud teacher. They stared at one another for a while, then Kain smiled—as if suddenly at peace. A second later, he was gone, and there was again a horrible void left by his absence.

It seemed as though minutes had passed. Now that Kain was gone, Roland was overcome by a feeling of loneliness and isolation. Looking around—perhaps for someone or something to take Kain's place—he remembered the people were still waiting to hear his words:

the elusive incantations that would make everything right. All those parasites and scavengers were still waiting for the meal that Roland was to provide, and the hatred began to grow in him again. However, that was when he remembered Kain's lesson—that madness was wanting the unattainable. Roland thought about it for a few seconds, then a faint glimmer of a smile came to his face when he saw how easy it would be to thwart them all. *Yes!* he thought to himself, either fully in the throes of Kain's madness or his *sanity*. It was all so simple! The only hope for them—the only thing that might stun them into consciousness—was his refusal to comply. Thousands of them were out on the streets now, deluded by thoughts of justice and right and wrong, when all that they were possessed by, was the chaos of the human will. The only thing that could save them was the brutal realization that there was in fact no justice—no right and wrong: that there were, in the final analysis, no pithy answers; no prefabricated solutions. They had wheeled him out there in order to add to the chaos and keep the farce going, but he refused to be a harlequin at his own funeral! Yes, he thought with an inner smile: let them sit there in the wake of his silence and take him in; and realize the brutal truths for themselves. By now, a few of the reporters were shuffling uncomfortably in their seats as they looked up at him in the uncomfortable silence. *Good*, Roland thought as the moment dragged on, *let them see for themselves that they have no power over me, and that I am still a man!*

ABOUT THE AUTHOR

David Valentine Bernard emigrated from the Caribbean nation of Grenada when he was nine years old, and settled in New York City. He recently spent a year and a half in Jamaica, completing a master's degree in the sociology of international development; and currently, he works as a database manager for an HIV/AIDS program in New York City. He is the author of five critically acclaimed novels—including *Intimate Relations With Strangers* and *God in the Image of Woman*. Visit www.dvbernard.com to find out more.